PARADISE

Madeline Baker
"Jessie's Girl"

"Madeline Baker is always a pleasure to read!"

—*Romantic Times*

Nina Bangs
"The Hunka Hunka and the Penny-Pincher"

"Funny characters, sizzling dialogue and plenty of HEAT! Ms. Bangs dishes up the perfect recipe for an incredible read!"

—Kimberly Raye, bestselling author of
Something Wild

Ann Lawrence
"Heaven-Sent"

"Ms. Lawrence is without a doubt one writer on the way to the top."

—*Bell, Book and Candle*

Kathleen Nance
"The Best-Laid Plans"

"Ms. Nance is a fresh and invigorating new talent!"

—*The Literary Times*

Other anthologies from *Leisure* and *Love Spell:*
SWEPT AWAY
CELEBRATIONS
INDULGENCE
MIDSUMMER NIGHT'S MAGIC
LOVESCAPE
LOVE'S LEGACY
ENCHANTED CROSSINGS

Paradise

MADELINE BAKER
NINA BANGS
ANN LAWRENCE
KATHLEEN NANCE

LEISURE BOOKS NEW YORK CITY

A LEISURE BOOK®

July 1999

Published by

Dorchester Publishing Co., Inc.
276 Fifth Avenue
New York, NY 10001

ISBN 0-8439-4552-4

MADELINE BAKER

JESSIE'S GIRL

To Elvis
You'll Always Be the King

And to Mitch
Thanks for sharing
your poetry with me

Darkness

If I walk, will I feel the pain?
As I run, will I taste the rain?

Cover me . . . dark night
surround me . . . wither my soul
for I ache for release
from this pitiful existence

Your laugh sends
the air piercing me with
blackness
throwing my soul into
currents of time

Lost . . .
If only I were lost
in a field of warm sunshine
lost . . .
against her embrace
smelling the scent
of flowers
watching as they
twirl in the morning light

Light . . .
I scream for its subtle flow
playing on my skin

Cover me
Drown me
Tell me?
If I walk
will I feel the pain?

—M. Dearmond

Chapter One

He called himself Jessie Garon Presley, and he was the most amazing Elvis look-alike Kathy Browne had ever seen. He had the same intense blue eyes, the same pouty lower lip, and he wore his thick black hair in the style Elvis had made famous back in the '50's—sideburns and a ducktail. But instead of wearing the flashy, sequined jumpsuits Elvis had favored in his later years, Jessie wore a pair of slick black pants and a black silk shirt open at the throat. A thick gold chain encircled his neck. A gold ring with a diamond the size of a golf ball winked on the middle finger of his right hand.

If she hadn't known better, she would have sworn he really was Elvis, but the King had died of a heart attack over twenty years ago. Of course, there were those who insisted Elvis was still alive, but even if that were true, he would be in his sixties, and the man on the stage couldn't be more than thirty-three,

9

about the same age Elvis had been when he did his comeback special in '68. It was her favorite concert video and she watched it over and over again. That, and *Aloha From Hawaii.*

Jessie Garon Presley did two shows a night at a new casino on the Strip. Kathy had wandered into the place her first night in town, seen his picture advertised in the lobby, and immediately bought a ticket for the first show. When it was over, she had hurried out and bought a ticket for the ten o'clock show, too. She had gone back every night for the last six days, staying for both shows.

She had always been an Elvis fan. She had scrapbooks full of pictures and newspaper articles, and every record and video he had ever made. She had framed posters of the King on her walls; Elvis watches and beach towels; an Elvis telephone; Elvis trading cards and playing cards; Elvisopoly, The Rock- 'n'-Roll Game of Fortune and Fame; Elvis collector plates; Elvis Barbie dolls; and even a pair of Elvis socks a friend had brought her from Graceland. She haunted antique stores and malls looking for old magazines and newspapers, anything re- lated to Elvis. If it had his name or his picture on it, she bought it. Her condo looked like a shrine. Her friends thought she was insane. But she wasn't. Just in love. With a man who was dead.

She leaned forward as Jessie began to sing "Kentucky Rain."

He walked slowly back and forth along the front of the stage, his voice filled with emotion as he sang of a man look- ing for his lost love.

The room was utterly still save for the sound of his voice, low and intimate as it caressed the crowd.

He sang all her favorite songs: "If I Can Dream," "Heart- break Hotel," "I Want You, I Need You, I Love You," "Lit- tle Sister," "(Marie's the Name) His Latest Flame," "In the Ghetto," "Crying in the Chapel," "The Wonder of You." It was as if he'd read her mind.

Mesmerized, she gazed up at him, totally lost in the fantasy that he was really Elvis, that he would look out over the crowd, that his gaze would meet hers, that he would walk down the stairs, sit down at her table, and sing to her and her alone.

And even as the thought crossed her mind, it was happening.

He paused in the center of the stage, his gaze sweeping the crowd, settling on her face. Her heart skipped a beat as his gaze met hers; her pulse began to beat wildly as he descended the stairs.

The music changed and she recognized the strains of "Can't Help Falling in Love" as he walked toward her. She could barely hear the music over the pounding of her heart.

No, she thought, *this can't be happening. Not to me.*

But it was. He had eyes only for her as he sat down in the empty chair at her table. Something hot and sweet flowed between them. It danced across her skin, arousing all her senses.

The spotlight focused on her table, bathing them in a pale pink glow. Her breath caught in her throat when he reached out and covered her hand with his.

Her mouth was dry, her heart beating a mile a minute as he sang to her, only to her. *Stay,* she thought frantically. *Stay with me forever.*

His hand squeezed hers. His eyes—those sleepy, sexy Elvis eyes—gazed deep into her own.

This can't be real, she thought. *I must be dreaming.*

His thumb made lazy circles on her palm while he sang to her. His gaze never left hers. They might have been alone in the room, in the world. She wished the song would never end, wished the moment would never end, but all too soon the song was over and the room filled with applause.

He lifted her hand and brushed his lips across her knuckles. Kathy gasped as the touch of his lips seemed to sear her skin, their heat traveling up her arm and curling around her heart. He smiled at her, a roguish smile, as if he knew exactly what

11

effect he was having on her, and then he rose smoothly to his feet and walked back up onto the stage.

"Memories" was his closing number. It was her favorite song, and hearing it always made her cry. Tonight was no exception. Tears welled in her eyes and trickled down her cheeks as she gazed up at him, hoping he knew somehow that she would never forget this night, never forget him.

He looked down at her from the stage as he sang, and she knew this night would be her most cherished memory of all.

She stood up, applauding wildly as he left the stage.

If only she could stay one more night, see one more show, but her flight left tomorrow afternoon at four, and Jessie never did matinees, not even on weekends.

With a sigh, Kathy followed the others out of the theater and into the casino.

The room was filled with noise—laughter, music, the sound of the roulette wheel, the rattle and whir of a thousand slot machines, the slap of cards at the blackjack table.

She wasn't much of a gambler, but it was her last night. What could it hurt to try her luck?

She stopped one of the people who made change and got twenty dollars' worth of quarters, then found an empty slot machine and sat down.

"Here goes," she muttered, and, after breaking open the first roll of quarters, she fed three coins into the machine.

There was a strange excitement in watching the wheels go round, a sense of anticipation as she waited for them to come to a stop and tell her if she had won.

Three bars!

"I won!" she exclaimed as the coin tray filled with quarters. "I won."

She heard a low, throaty chuckle behind her, felt a shiver of anticipation run down her spine.

She turned to find Jessie Garon Presley standing at her elbow.

A slow smile spread over his face as he drawled, "Honey, tonight you can't lose."

Chapter Two

Kathy couldn't speak. She could only stare up at him. He wore a deep blue jacket over his black shirt. The color made his blue eyes seem deeper, darker, more mysterious. She could dive into those eyes, she thought, and never come up.

A faint smile played over his lips, making her wonder if he had somehow divined her thoughts.

"You all right, darlin'?" he asked with a wry grin.

She nodded, thinking that he looked exactly the way Elvis had in *Blue Hawaii*. A lock of black hair fell across his forehead, making her fingers itch to reach up and brush it back.

He nodded at the slot machine. "Mind if I watch?"

She tried to speak, but she couldn't seem to get the words past her throat.

He laughed softly as he sat down on the stool beside hers.

Feeling shaky inside, she put another quarter in the machine and pulled the handle.

Three bars. A winner again.

"I seem to have brought you luck," Jessie remarked.

"Yes." Finally, she managed to get a word out.

He smiled. "You've been at every one of my shows this past week."

She nodded, suddenly self-conscious. He probably thought she was some sort of weirdo groupie incapable of speaking coherently.

"Why?"

She shrugged. "I like the show."

He laughed, soft and sexy. "Big Elvis fan, were you?"

"Oh, yes. He was so wonderful."

Sadness shadowed his eyes, then was gone. "Lots of people thought so."

"You sound just like him. Look just like him."

"You mean before he got old and fat and made a fool of himself?"

Kathy looked up at him, startled by the underlying bitterness in his voice. "I never thought of him as old and fat. He was always wonderful. And his voice . . ." She shook her head. "I loved to hear him sing. Even now, when I watch one of his videos, I find myself smiling. It was a rare gift he had, to make people feel good."

He grunted softly. "You gonna play again?"

"What? Oh, yes, I guess so."

She fed three quarters into the machine, listened to the whir of the wheels.

Seven.

Seven.

Seven.

She stared at the machine, unable to believe her eyes and ears as the one-armed bandit suddenly went wild, its lights flashing and its sirens screaming. Quarters poured out of the machine in a river of silver.

She'd hit the jackpot. Ten thousand dollars.

She looked at Jessie and laughed. Before tonight, the only thing she'd ever won was a stuffed rabbit at a school carnival when she was six.

The people standing nearby gathered around. A man toasted her good fortune; a woman rubbed her arm "for luck." A rather somber-faced man from the casino approached to tell her that the balance of her winnings would be waiting for her when she was ready to pick it up, along with some tax forms that had to be filled out.

A waitress came by with free drinks. Kathy accepted a glass of champagne, but Jesse declined.

"I guess you really did bring me luck," Kathy said when the excitement died down and everyone else had moved away.

"Glad to do it, darlin'."

His voice moved through her like thick honey, warm and sweet. No one had ever called her *darlin'* before.

She had once read a description of what Elvis's dream girl was supposed to look like: twenty years old, and about five feet, four inches tall, 34-24-34, brown hair, brown eyes. She fit that description to a tee. She wondered fleetingly what Jessie's ideal girl looked like.

He stood up, and despair clutched at her heart. The small fortune she had won suddenly didn't seem as important as the fact that he was leaving. The champagne suddenly tasted flat, and she put the glass down.

"I think I'll go stretch my legs," he said.

Kathy nodded, saddened that he was going so soon.

"Would you like to take a walk with me?"

"Oh! Oh, yes."

"Let's go cash in your winnings."

She quickly scooped her change into several of the big plastic containers stacked beside her slot machine. Jessie followed her to the cashier and waited while she exchanged six hundred dollars' worth of quarters for six crisp one-hundred-dollar bills.

She would pick up the rest of her winnings in the morning before she left for the airport.

She stared at the greenbacks in her hand, then slipped them into her handbag. She'd never had so much cash in her life.

She looked up at Jessie, suddenly nervous at the idea of being alone with him.

"Nothing to be afraid of, darlin'," he drawled softly and held out his hand. His fingers were warm and firm as they curled over hers. People turned to stare as they walked through the casino.

"Do you ever get tired of people gawking at you?" Kathy asked.

Jessie shrugged. "Not anymore. I'm used to it."

It was almost as bright as day outside. Lights from dozens of casinos lit the sidewalk. Crowds of people hurried up and down, laughing and talking. The street was clogged with traffic—cars and taxicabs and campers, all in a hurry, even late at night.

"This city never sleeps, does it?" Kathy remarked.

"Nope. Is this your first time in Vegas?"

"It's my first time anywhere," she admitted. "Well, not quite. I went to Graceland last week."

"Did you?" he asked, and she detected a note of wistfulness in his voice. "I haven't been there in years, but I suppose it looks the same. What did you think of it?"

"I loved it." Walking where Elvis had walked, seeing where he'd lived . . . it had been an awesome experience.

"What made you decide to come to Vegas?"

She felt her cheeks grow hot. "Because I knew it had the most Elvis impersonators."

"I see," he said, grinning. "Really stuck on him, aren't you?"

"Yes."

"You couldn't have been more than a baby when he died," Jessie remarked, and she heard a hint of sadness in his voice. "All that talk about his overdosing on drugs." He shook his head. "Damn reporters, always looking for dirt, always thinking the worst. They didn't know what the hell they were talking about."

He looked down at her, as if seeing her for the first time.

"Sorry," he muttered. "So tell me, how'd you get to be such a big fan?"

She laughed self-consciously. "I guess it's hereditary. My mother's a big fan. Instead of singing me lullabies, she sang me Elvis songs. I grew up listening to his music, watching his movies." She shrugged. "I think I fell in love with his voice the first time I heard him sing 'Heartbreak Hotel.' I'd never heard anything like it. I used to spend all my allowance money buying his videos. I have them all. His records, too." It was something she hadn't outgrown ... occasionally spending money that should be used for necessities on Elvis memorabilia. "My friends all think I'm insane."

"Well, I don't." He laughed softly. "I'm sure Elvis would be flattered. He loved his fans, you know. He needed them. That's why he went back to performing onstage. He missed the closeness." He hesitated a moment. "The applause."

"There's never been a performer like him," she said fervently. "Before or since."

"Yeah," Jessie said. "He was one of a kind, all right."

"Did you ever get to see him in person?"

"Oh, yeah. I guess you could say I was a big fan, too."

They had left the Strip and the lights behind. The darkness settled around them, warm and intimate. Kathy felt a little tremor of apprehension as she realized they were very much alone. She was suddenly aware that she had a great deal of money in her handbag. She clutched it tighter, her imagination running wild as she imagined him knocking her unconscious and robbing her. She was being ridiculous, and she knew it. On the other hand, she didn't know anything about Jessie except that he looked exactly like the man she had idolized her whole life.

Dropping her hand, he came to an abrupt halt. "Do you want me to take you back to your hotel?"

Kathy looked up at him, wondering if he had read her mind. In the dim glow of a single streetlight, his eyes seemed to burn with a dark blue flame.

"No."

"I mean you no harm, Kathy Browne."

She stared at him, wondering, in a distant part of her mind, how he knew her last name.

"You're quite beautiful, you know." His fingertips traced the curve of her cheek and slid down her neck. "Not bright and flashy, like most of the girls I meet. But soft and warm." He ran the tip of his finger over her lower lip. "Do you taste as sweet as you look?"

Kathy looked up at him, speechless.

"Do I dare find out?" His voice was low, filled with wry amusement. "Do I dare, Kathy?"

She leaned toward him, incapable of speech, her whole body quivering with anticipation.

Slowly he wrapped his arms around her and lowered his head, blocking everything from her sight but his face. His eyes, those deep, dark blue eyes, burned into her own, burned so hot that for a moment they seemed to glow red, but before she could separate the real from the imagined, he was kissing her.

Heat suffused her, engulfing her, burning away every thought, every desire save the need to be held in this man's arms, to feel his lips on hers.

He whispered her name, his mouth moving over her face, dropping kisses on her cheeks, her nose, drifting over her throat. She moaned softly, urgently, as his teeth grazed her neck, and she pressed herself against him, wanting to be closer, closer.

He drew back a little, staring deep into her eyes, and then he kissed her again, and she felt herself falling . . .

falling . . .

spinning down . . .

down . . .

into nothingness. . . .

Chapter Three

Kathy woke slowly, reluctant to return to the real world after the wonderful dream she'd had the night before. She had spent the night with Elvis, in his arms, in his room, in his bed. He had made love to her as gently and tenderly as ever a man had made love to a woman, and afterward he had held her in his arms. She had asked him to sing to her, and he had, his voice low and husky, as soft as a sigh, as intimate as a lover's caress. But it had been only a dream, nothing more. . . . True, she had been with Jessie, but they hadn't made love.

She took a deep breath, her nostrils filling with the scent of roses.

Suddenly wide-awake, she opened her eyes and sat up, the last vestiges of her dream fading into reality.

There were roses everywhere. Crystal vases filled with roses. On the floor. On the dresser. On the desk. Dozens and dozens of bloodred blooms. And on the pillow beside her was a single, perfect white rose. And beneath the bud was a sheet of paper, neatly folded in half.

Her hand trembled as she picked up the paper and opened it.

Kathy, please don't go home today. Jessie.

Seven words. She read them over and over again, her heart pounding.

Please don't go home today.

How had he known she was leaving today?

Please don't go home.

Oh, but she couldn't stay. She had to be at work tomorrow morning . . . didn't she?

She picked up the white rose, inhaled its fragrance, and brushed the velvet-soft petals across her lips. What would happen if she called Mr. Whitney and told him she was taking an extra day? She had some sick time accumulated. Surely he could spare her for just one more day.

She made a quick phone call, all her arguments lined up. As it turned out, they were unnecessary.

"Things are pretty slow right now, Kathy," Mr. Whitney said. "Take the rest of the week off, if you want. Myrna can cover for you."

She was grinning when she hung up the phone. Another week. And thanks to the money she had won the night before, she could afford to stay!

She called the airline and changed her ticket, took a long, hot shower, and washed her hair.

Even though Jessie had asked her not to go home, he hadn't mentioned anything about meeting her later, but surely, since he'd asked her to stay, he intended to see her tonight.

She dressed quickly, grabbed her handbag, and left the hotel. She had seen a darling little black cocktail dress in the window of an exclusive shop yesterday afternoon. At the time, four hundred dollars had been out of her price range. But not anymore.

There were more roses when she returned to her room later that day: pink ones, yellow ones, lavender ones. And another perfect white bloom stood in a delicate crystal vase. There was a red ribbon tied around the vase, and attached to the ribbon was a small white envelope. Inside she found a ticket for a front-row table at the eight o'clock show, and a short note that read, *Order anything you want tonight. It's on me. Jessie.*

Singing "I Want You, I Need You, I Love You," she went into the bathroom to shower and get dressed.

Kathy stood in front of the full-length mirror in the bedroom, hardly able to believe her eyes. The dress, of crushed black velvet, had a square neck and long sleeves. Just a simple black dress, but it fit as though it had been made for her, complementing her hair and eyes, flattering her figure.

She spritzed herself with Shalimar perfume, grabbed her handbag, and left her room.

Crossing the lobby, she was aware of several men looking her way. After hailing a cab, she slid into the backseat and told the driver her destination.

When she entered the theater, the maitre d' immediately came forward to seat her. Moments later a waiter appeared with a menu.

After a good deal of deliberation between lobster and filet mignon, Kathy ordered the lobster. She'd had it only once before. On her modest budget it had always been a luxury she couldn't afford.

Shortly after she ordered, the waiter returned with a bottle of chilled champagne.

Kathy gasped when she caught a glimpse of the fancy gold label. "I didn't order that," she said, shaking her head.

The waiter smiled at her. "Mr. Presley sent it, with his compliments."

"Oh." She felt a rush of heat flood her cheeks. "Thank you."

He inclined his head and left the table.

The waiter had no sooner left than a woman approached her table. "Miss Browne?"

"Yes."

"These are for you," the woman said, and handed Kathy a corsage of white orchids.

Kathy looked up. "But . . ."

"Compliments of Mr. Presley."

Kathy nodded, feeling the warmth in her cheeks grow hotter. "Thank you."

"He said to give you this, as well," the woman said, and handed her a small black box.

"Oh, my." Kathy stared at the box a moment and then opened it. Inside, nestled against a bed of deep red velvet, she found a small gold heart on a delicate gold chain, and a note that read, *I canceled the second show so I could spend more time with you. Can I walk you home? Jessie.*

She lifted the locket from the box. It was the most beautiful thing she had ever seen, real gold. She fastened the chain around her neck. The locket felt cool against her heated skin.

Her dinner arrived a short time later. There was a slender crystal vase on the tray, and in the vase, a single perfect white rose.

Her heart swelled with emotion, and she blinked rapidly to hold back her tears. No one had ever wooed her quite so sweetly, so romantically.

She had been shy and awkward in high school, had spent most of her time studying or working on the school newspaper. She had avoided dances, hadn't been invited to the cool parties. She'd had but few dates, and they had all been disasters. The boys who had asked her out had been just as shy and unsure of themselves as she was.

After high school, she had gone to secretarial college, and after she'd graduated, she'd gone to work for Mr. Whitney, owner of Whitney Accounting. She was a small-town girl with a small-town job, single and likely to stay that way.

She had worked and saved for this, her dream vacation. She had spent last week in Memphis, touring Graceland and the surrounding area. She had been surprised by the sense of awe and reverence she felt as she toured the house and the grounds where Elvis had lived. She had read in a magazine that he had bought the house for $100,000 in 1957. She had seen his cars and his airplane, and tried to imagine what it had been like to live there. The guide had told them that the den, known as the Jungle Room, had been Elvis's favorite. It was decorated with fake-animal-skin upholstery, a waterfall, and fur lampshades. It was said he ate breakfast in this room, watching a huge TV.

She had seen the billiard room, and learned that it had taken ten men six days to hang the 750 yards of paisley fabric that decorated the room. Another room had three televisions, an idea Elvis had supposedly borrowed from President Johnson so he could watch each network at the same time. The room also had a soda fountain, a record player, and Elvis's record collection, as well as Elvis's personal lightning-bolt logo, his symbol for "taking care of business."

She had wept as she entered Graceland's Meditation Gardens and placed a bouquet of flowers beside the hundreds of others on his grave. She had walked down Elvis Presley Boulevard, visited the souvenir shops and museums. And now she was here, in Las Vegas, because he had been here.

Kathy ran her fingertips over her forearm, delighting in the feel of the rich velvet beneath her hand. Her new dress gave her an air of confidence she had never known before. For the first time she could remember, she felt beautiful. Maybe it was time to break out of her mousy little shell and be the woman she had always wanted to be, a woman who would have brought even Elvis to his knees.

The meal was the best she'd ever had. Just moments after she finished eating, the lights dimmed, a pale blue spot lit the stage, and the strains of "The Wonder of You" filled the room.

The crowd burst into applause as Jessie appeared in the spotlight. He wore black again tonight: tight black leather pants, a short leather jacket over a black tee shirt, and soft black leather boots.

She would have closed her eyes and lost herself in the music, but she didn't want to take her eyes off Jessie for a moment. He swayed to the beat, his movements sensuous and a little suggestive, mesmerizing, tantalizing.

He moved to the center of the stage, his gaze searching for her, finding her. She looked up at him and smiled, and he winked at her.

He sang "Crying in the Chapel" and "She's Not You" and "Always on My Mind," and even though he moved from one end of the stage to the other, he had eyes only for her. He had wonderfully expressive eyes. They held her, caressing her, holding her, making her think of soft summer nights and smooth satin sheets.

And then he stood in the center of the stage, his gaze focused on her, and sang "Playing for Keeps."

Kathy could feel people staring at her, wondering who she was.

Most singers did the same show every night, but not Jessie. In the week she had been there, she had rarely heard him sing the same song twice.

But tonight, at the end of the show, he sang "Memories" again.

That was all she would be left with when this night was over, she thought regretfully.

Memories.

Chapter Four

When the show was over, she waited for the crowd to thin out before she stood up. She was wondering if she had misunderstood, or if Jessie had changed his mind, when a man dressed in an expensive dark blue suit approached her.

"Miss Browne?"

"Yes."

"I'm Walter Dodge. Mr. Presley asked me to escort you to his limo."

"Nice to meet you, Mr. Dodge."

"This way," he said, indicating a door to the left of the stage.

Kathy followed him through the doorway, down a narrow, dimly lit corridor, and out into a private parking lot at the rear of the casino. A white stretch limo waited outside the door.

The driver, who had been leaning against the front fender, quickly opened the back door for her. "Mr. Presley will be along in a few minutes," he said with a smile.

Kathy slid into the backseat, and the chauffeur shut the door.

She sat there, feeling like a movie star. She had never been inside a limo before, never seen a car so luxurious. There was a color TV, a VCR, a CD player, and a telephone. A small bar was stocked with rum, vodka, gin, and scotch in monogrammed crystal decanters. There were matching glasses, cloth napkins, and ice, if she wanted it.

She ran her hands over the leather upholstery. It was pale gray, smooth, and butter soft.

She looked up as the opposite door opened and Jessie slid in beside her.

"Hi, darlin'." His gaze moved over her. "Wow, you look fantastic in that dress. I couldn't keep my eyes off you while I was singing." He grinned at her. "Almost forgot the words a couple times tonight 'cause I was so busy looking at you."

She felt herself blushing. She started to look away, but that was what the old Kathy would have done. The new Kathy met his gaze with what she hoped was a seductive smile and purred, "Thank you."

He laughed softly, and the attraction between them hummed to life, hotter than the lights that illuminated the city.

Leaning forward, he rapped on the glass that separated the backseat from the front, and the car surged forward.

"Where are we going?" she asked.

"Anywhere you want, darlin'."

"I don't care, as long as I'm with you."

They went everywhere. He took her to see Siegfried and Roy and she sat on the edge of her seat, enthralled by their magical illusions, by the beautiful white tigers, the costumes, the music. They went to the MGM Grand and the Excalibur, and everywhere they went, people turned to stare at Jessie.

She laughed as she had not laughed in years, caught up in the magic that was Jessie, in the wonder of being with him, of seeing his eyes glow with admiration and desire when he looked at her.

Once, she caught a glimpse of the two of them in a mirror and she smiled, thinking what a handsome couple they made. And then she frowned as Jessie's reflection seemed to shimmer, almost as though it were a reflection of a reflection. A chill slid down her spine as his image seemed to vanish and then reappear. She blinked and then laughed softly, realizing it was probably just a trick of the lights.

It was near dawn when he took her back to her hotel. They held hands in the elevator, giggling like teenagers.

He unlocked her door for her and followed her inside, and there, in the dark of her room, alone at last, he took her in his arms and kissed her.

His arms were strong around her, his tongue like a flame as he deepened the kiss.

"Oh, baby," he groaned, "do you know what you do to me?"

She looked up at him, his face barely visible in the glow of the lights that filtered into the room from the window behind him.

She shook her head. "Tell me."

"I've never felt this way before," he mused, his voice edged with wonder. "Not even—" He paused. "Never." He gazed deep into her eyes, his expression somber, intense. "You won't leave me, will you?"

"I don't want to, Jessie, but I have to go back to work next week."

"No!"

"I have to. My job . . ."

"Kathy." His voice moved over her, low, enthralling, and she swayed toward him.

"Quit your job, Kathy," he went on in the same hypnotic tone. "Stay here with me."

"I can't. . . ." she said, but it was what she wanted, to stay there with him forever.

"It's what you want."

"Yes," she replied. "Yes . . ."

27

"No!" He looked away from her. "I won't make you."

She blinked, then blinked again, feeling as though she had been released from some sort of spell. "I want to, Jessie, really I do. But I have to work."

"I'll find you something to do here; how's that?"

"I don't know. It's all so sudden."

"That's how love is, darlin'. Sudden."

"You really want me to stay?"

"With all my heart."

"All right," the new Kathy said. "I will."

A slow smile spread over his face as he drew her close against him. "You've just made me the happiest man in the world."

He glanced out the window. The sky was rapidly growing light. She heard him swear under his breath, and then he kissed her again, hard and quick. "I've got to go."

She felt a twinge of regret that he didn't want to stay the night, along with a surge of relief that he hadn't asked. Even the new Kathy wasn't quite ready to hop into bed with a man, any man, after only two dates.

"I never thanked you for all the flowers," she said.

"No need, darlin'. You put them to shame." He hugged her. "I'll see you tomorrow night, front-row center."

She nodded as he left the room. "I'll be there."

Chapter Five

The next week was the most incredible of her life. She called Mr. Whitney and told him she was sorry, but she was quitting her job. She went shopping and bought herself a whole new wardrobe—underwear, shoes, dresses, the works, then called her sister, Keri, and asked her to pack up all her old clothes and give them to the Salvation Army, put the rest of her stuff in storage, and then put her condo up for rent on a month-to-month basis.

Of course, Keri wouldn't let her off the phone until she had heard the whole story, and when Kathy finished, Keri told her she was crazy and wished her well.

That quickly, Kathy's whole world turned upside down. Mesmerized by the wonder and the magic that was Jessie, she found herself caught up in the nightlife of Las Vegas. She went to Jessie's show every night, never tiring of watching him, hearing him.

On his nights off they went to other shows, and he introduced her to stars like Wayne Newton and Rod Stewart and

Billy Ray Cyrus. They were invited to lavish parties, went dancing at the Sahara, and took moonlit walks.

He moved her into a suite at his hotel. When she protested that she couldn't afford such lavish accommodations, he told her not to worry about it, that it was all taken care of. *Don't worry, darlin',* he'd said. *I don't expect anything in return. I just want you to be comfortable while you're here.* He installed a big-screen TV, and had access to movies that weren't available to the general public yet. The best times were the nights they spent in her room, alone, watching TV.

She had only to mention she wanted something, liked something, needed something, and it appeared in her room the next day as if by magic.

She was Cinderella, and Jessie was her Prince Charming, and she hoped the fairy tale would never end.

They were at a birthday party for one of the members of Jessie's band when Kathy realized that she had never seen Jessie eat anything. Occasionally he shared a sip of her wine, but that was all.

She asked him about it that night on the way home.

Jessie shrugged. "I'm on a strict diet," he replied with a grin. "Never eat a thing after three o'clock." He patted his stomach. "Gotta watch my weight."

"Of course," she said, and laughed. She knew a lot of people who didn't eat after a certain time of day. "Do you think we could drive out to Hoover Dam tomorrow? I'd love to see it in the daylight."

"I'd love to, darlin', but I'm gonna be tied up in a meeting all day. Why don't you have Walter take you?"

"No, that's all right. I'll wait until you can go."

He patted her hand, a hint of sadness in his eyes. "All right, darlin', if that's what you want."

Twenty minutes later, Jessie kissed Kathy good night at her door. He couldn't believe his good fortune in meeting her. She was everything he had ever wanted in a woman: warm, caring, fun to be with, completely unaware of how beautiful she was. He loved the way she looked at him, her dark brown eyes filled with adoration. *Kathy* . . .

He slid into the backseat of the limo and rapped on the glass, and the car pulled away from the curb.

He settled back in the seat, his hands curling into tight fists as hunger gnawed at his belly. His new lifestyle pleased him greatly, though he did occasionally miss eating solid food. Once he'd loved nothing more than a big meal; now, even the thought of a peanut butter–and–banana sandwich turned his stomach.

But it was a small price to pay to be young again, thin again, to hear the cheers and applause of the crowd, to see his name in lights. His fans. They had loved him to the end. He had seen the crowds that thronged Graceland when Elvis was laid to rest. It had grieved him to see their tears. He had wanted to go to them, all of them, and tell them he wasn't dead at all, but of course that had been impossible.

Lost in the past, it took him a moment to realize the car had stopped.

He looked up to find his driver peering at him through the glass. Jessie nodded, and Frank got out of the car and opened the rear door.

Jessie looked at the small white house as he stepped out of the car. It was an innocuous place, with its weedy yard and crooked front porch. No one would guess that the little old woman who lived there sold drugs from time to time, among other things.

He felt the familiar ache in his jaw as he walked up the creaky steps and knocked on the door.

It was opened almost immediately and Hester Greene stood in the doorway. She was short and round, with rosy cheeks, sharp black eyes, and long gray hair.

"Mr. Singer." The old woman smiled, revealing a dimple in her left cheek. "I've been expecting you."

Jessie nodded and stepped inside.

The woman closed and locked the door behind him.

"You ready?" he asked.

She held out a gnarled hand. "If you have the money."

Reaching into his pocket, he withdrew ten crisp one-hundred-dollar bills and slapped them into her outstretched palm. There had been a time when she would have counted them, but no more. She trusted him now, as he trusted her.

She folded the bills in half and shoved them into her skirt pocket, then moved into the parlor and sat down on the sofa.

Jessie followed her, his gaze moving over the room, his senses exploring to make sure they were alone. It was a small house, surprisingly neat—the kind of house one would expect to shelter a kindly grandmother. It was rumored by some that she was a powerful witch—and he knew the truth of that.

Jessie sat down beside her, and she tilted her head to the side, granting him access to her throat. Her big black cat stared at them from the back of a chair.

He closed his eyes as his teeth grazed the woman's neck, pretending it was Kathy sitting there beside him, willingly offering him her life's blood.

Chapter Six

TWENTY-SECOND ANNIVERSARY OF THE KING'S DEATH.

The headline screamed across the front page of a national news magazine. Even after all these years, his death made the front page, along with the usual side articles: WHO KILLED ELVIS? REMEMBERING ELVIS. ELVIS—MORE POPULAR DEAD THAN ALIVE. THE WOMEN ELVIS LOVED. A SPECIAL 10-PAGE TRIBUTE TO THE KING.

Kathy put fifty cents in the slot and took out one of the papers, wondering what Elvis would think if he were alive today.

Tucking the paper under her arm, she checked her watch as she continued down the street. Ten after six.

Hailing a cab, she gave the driver directions, then sat back and opened the magazine. Inside were the usual pictures—Elvis as a little boy standing between his parents, Elvis as a young man, Elvis in uniform, Elvis with Priscilla, Elvis and Priscilla holding a newborn Lisa Marie. Elvis in black leather. Elvis onstage in a white jumpsuit, a silk scarf draped around his neck, a wide belt circling his waist. And on the next page, an aging Elvis, a bloated Elvis . . .

It made her sad to see him that way.

She glanced out the window. It amazed her how quickly she had come to think of Vegas as home. Looking at it now, filled with tourists, it was hard to believe that only seventy years ago it had been little more than a dusty watering hole. She'd read somewhere that more than thirty million visitors came here each year, spending more than five billion dollars. She'd also read that four thousand people a month moved to Vegas. She was glad she was one of them.

The cab made a screeching halt in front of her hotel. She paid the fare, gave the driver a generous tip, and hurried inside, sighing as she left the heat of the day behind.

She smiled at the clerk at the desk. Everyone in the hotel knew who she was, knew she was Jessie's girl.

The thought reminded her of the old Rick Springfield song and made her smile.

Inside her room she tossed her packages on the bed. She had become quite the shopper in the last few days. No more pawing through rack after rack looking for bargains, no more worrying about whether she could afford things. If she was frugal in other areas, the money she had won, plus the small savings she had in the bank back home, would last her a good long while, especially since Jessie insisted on paying her rent. She had argued that it wasn't seemly for him to do so, that she could afford it, but he refused to listen to her arguments.

You're staying here because I asked you to, he had insisted. *Besides, I can afford it more than you can.*

She couldn't argue with that.

She took a quick shower, washed and blow-dried her hair, and pulled on the lacy new underwear she had bought. It was pale blue silk, almost transparent. She slid a matching slip over her head and smoothed it over her hips, loving the feel of the cool silk beneath her hands. A blue jersey dress followed. It was soft and clingy and outlined every curve—curves she had never given any thought to, until Jessie had noticed them.

There was something wonderfully exciting about dressing for a man.

Sitting on the edge of the bed, she put on her nylons and stepped into a pair of spiked heels that matched her dress. One last look in the mirror, and she was ready.

When she opened her door, Walter Dodge was waiting.

"Evening, Miss Browne."

"Hi, Walter."

"You ready to go?"

She nodded, the mere thought of seeing Jessie making her glow with pleasure.

She stepped into the limousine as if she'd been doing it all her life.

A short time later, she was seated at the front-row table that was now hers. As always, there was a single perfect white rose in a crystal vase in the center of the table, and a brightly wrapped present. He gave her a gift every night. A diamond watch. A ruby brooch in the shape of a guitar. A fine gold chain. A pair of ivory combs for her hair.

She had begged him to stop. She didn't want him to think she liked him only because he was a celebrity, because he paid her rent, bought her expensive gifts, but he insisted it gave him pleasure to buy her things. *You give me a gift every night just by being at the show*, he had said. *Knowing you care is worth far more than the handful of trinkets I've given you.*

Trinkets, indeed, she mused as she opened the box. Inside she found a diamond tennis bracelet.

She slipped it on her wrist, then ate a leisurely dinner. It was a heady experience, being "somebody." And she was really nobody. No wonder movie stars and heads of state behaved the way they did. After being fawned on and waited on hand and foot, who could blame them if they started to take it for granted, if they began to believe they really were better than everyone else?

She sat back in her seat, sipping a glass of champagne as the lights dimmed. And then he was there, onstage. His presence filled the room, bigger than life. He looked at her and winked. The orchestra began to play, and he broke into "I Got a Woman."

She winked back at him, lifted her glass in a silent toast, felt a thrill of excitement rush through her as his voice began to weave its magic spell. As always, she felt herself smiling, tapping her foot to the music, caught up in the excitement of being Jessie's girl.

The limo was waiting for them after the show, but Kathy felt like walking, so Jessie told the driver to go home.

Hand in hand, they walked down the street, stopping now and then to drop a quarter or a dollar into one of the slot machines they passed. To Kathy's amazement, she won a small jackpot every time.

"If I'd known I was this lucky, I'd have come to Vegas long ago," she remarked as she cashed in a hundred dollars' worth of quarters.

"I'm feeling pretty lucky myself," Jessie remarked.

"Really?" she asked. "Why? I'm the one who's winning."

"Because I found you, of course," he replied quietly, and his voice washed over her, warm and rich and filled with a need so primal it made her heart skip a beat.

They had never done more than kiss and hold each other close, but her mind suddenly filled with an image of black satin sheets and iced champagne, of a tub swirling with frothy bubbles surrounded by candlelight.

"Jessie . . ."

His eyes burned with a dark blue flame. "Do you know how much I want you? How much I need you?"

She shook her head, certain she was going to drown in the fathomless depths of his eyes. He wanted her. And she wanted him, desperately, with every fiber of her being, every beat of her heart. But she'd known him such a short time. What would he think of her if they made love so soon? What would she think of herself? She grinned inwardly. What would her mother think?

"Jessie . . ."

"It's all right, darlin'." He cupped her chin in his palm. "I know you're a nice girl."

A nice girl. She hadn't heard that expression in years. But it was true. She was a nice girl from a nice family. Her friends not only thought she was insane because she collected Elvis memorabilia, but because she was still a virgin. But she was proud of that fact. Not that she hadn't come close . . . She had been tempted on several occasions, but she'd always found the courage to say no before it was too late. But looking into Jessie's eyes, she doubted she would be able to resist him for very long. Impossible as it seemed, she knew she was falling in love with him, and not just because he looked like her idol. He was sweet and fun and kind and generous. . . .

"What are you thinkin', darlin'?" he asked.

"Nothing."

He lifted one dark brow in disbelief. "Nothing? You wouldn't lie to me, would you, now?"

He knew, she thought; he knew exactly what she was thinking.

"You can tell me," he said. "Don't you know you can tell me anything?"

"I was just thinking about you . . . about us . . . about . . ."

He smiled at her, that slow, lazy smile that made her insides turn to mush. "I spend a lot of time thinking about us, too."

"Do you?"

He drew her into a dark alley between two buildings, his arms sliding around her waist. "Oh, yeah."

"I'm glad." She looked up at him, trying to see his face in the dark, but all she could see was a strange red reflection in his eyes. She felt a sudden dizziness, felt herself swaying toward him, lifting her head, brushing the hair away from her neck.

"Kathy . . ." He groaned softly as his teeth grazed her throat. His arms trembled as they tightened around her. "Kathy, I need . . ." He pushed her away abruptly. "I've got to go."

"What?" She shook her head, trying to clear it. "Where are you going?"

"I'll see you tomorrow night," he said, and left her standing there, alone in the dark, feeling lost and confused.

Chapter Seven

"But you must get a day off sometime," Kathy said. "I mean, I've been here almost a month and we've never spent the day together."

"What are you talkin' about, darlin'? We're together every night."

"Nights, yes. But not during the day. Can't we take a drive tomorrow morning? I'd like to go sight-seeing, maybe pack a picnic lunch and drive out to Hoover Dam, or Lake Mead."

Jessie blew out a sigh. He should have known this would happen, but he hadn't had a steady girl in years. The groupies who flocked around him never expected to see him during the day. They were content to hang out with him in the casinos at night, pleased to be seen on his arm, in his company, to share a night of passion and then move on. He had always made it clear that he wasn't looking for anything permanent. But Kathy was different. She wasn't an easy lay, a quick conquest. She was a forever girl. . . . He grinned. He could give her forever. He just couldn't give her a day at Hoover Dam.

"Please, Jessie," she said, smiling at him. "Just one day."

"I can't, darlin'. I wish I could, but I can't." And for the first time, he regretted what he was, regretted that he couldn't spend just one day in Kathy's company, that he couldn't walk along the shore with her, see the sun reflected in her eyes.

The smile faded from her face and sadness etched her features. "All right, Jessie. I won't ask you again."

"Kathy. Darlin' . . ."

"It's all right." She stood up and moved across the room. Drawing back the drapes, she looked down on the street below, at the flashing lights, the people hurrying across the street. She stared at her reflection, thinking how much she had changed since coming here. She hardly looked like the same girl.

She frowned as she realized she could see the room behind her reflected in the glass as well—the fireplace, the lights, the sofa where Jessie was sitting. . . .

A chill ran down her spine as she stared at the sofa's reflection. She could see it clearly, but not Jessie. She glanced over her shoulder, thinking he must have left the room, but he was sitting as before, one arm flung across the back of the couch.

Heart pounding, she looked at the glass again. The sofa looked empty.

"Jessie . . ."

"What's wrong, darlin'?"

"I can't see you."

"What do you mean? I'm right—" He swore under his breath. He'd been so worried about coming up with a good excuse as to why he couldn't see her during the day that he'd forgotten to plant his image in her mind.

Slowly, she turned around to face him, her face as pale as the long white gown she wore. "Why can't I see you in the glass?"

"I don't know. I can see myself."

"You can?" She spun around and sure enough, she could see his reflection in the glass.

She laughed softly, relief evident in her voice, her expression. "Must have been a trick of the light."

"Yes." He stood up and moved across the room to take her in his arms. "It's getting late. I'd best be going."

She wrapped her arms around his waist and held him tight. It was getting more and more difficult to say good-bye each night. Sometimes it took hours. She had never spent much time petting when she was growing up, but she was making up for it now. Time seemed to lose all meaning when she was in his arms. His kisses were more addictive than drugs. The sound of his voice, whispering that he adored her, loved her, needed her, was like music to her ears. He wooed her with flowers and candy, with soft, sensual kisses, with words that painted erotic pictures in her mind. And yet he never crossed the line she had set, never demanded more than she was willing to give, and that in itself was a powerful lure.

She wanted him, wanted to wrap herself in his kisses, drown herself in the depths of his eyes, inhale his every breath, spend the rest of her life in his arms.

"Kathy, darlin'!"

He held her tight, tighter, his eyes glowing with love and desire as he gazed into her face, and she had the feeling, as she so often did, that he had read her thoughts, knew her mind, her heart.

"I love you," she said.

"Ah, darlin'."

His hands stroked her back lightly, intimately, sending shivers down her spine. His voice, low and sweet, whispered in her ear.

"While you sleep, my love . . . feel me close . . . whispering memories. While you sleep . . . my softness . . . taste me . . . as our lips touch lightly . . . breathe the love I have for you deep inside . . . hold it for eternity. While you sleep . . . my mind hears your laugh . . . moving my blood . . . as my heart flies to

41

touch a dream. While you sleep . . . I am a dream . . . I do not exist . . . real . . . my heart beats . . . yet I feel no heat. While you sleep . . . turn with time . . . your lips moist as I kiss your face next to mine. While you sleep . . . watching the night's light swirl into warmth flowing across your skin . . . I rise . . . and leave . . . to save a heart. So close your eyes . . . dream . . . a dream . . . while you sleep. . . .''

"Oh, Jesse, that was beautiful."

He smiled down at her. "You think so?"

"Yes. Where did you find it?"

"I wrote it last night, for you."

"Oh."

"You really like it?"

"I love it."

"Good. It's called 'While You Sleep.' Vince is putting it to music for me. I'll sing it for you tomorrow night."

"I don't know what to say. No one ever wrote me a song before."

He kissed the top of her head, pleased beyond words by the sincerity of her gratitude, by the joy in her eyes. And then he felt it, the subtle hint of dawn's first light.

He held her close a moment longer, then kissed her, hard and deep. "I've got to go get some sleep, darlin'."

"All right. Sweet dreams, Jessie. I love you."

"Sweet dreams, darlin'."

He kissed her again, and then he was gone.

Alone, Kathy looked at the window again, a shiver of unease moving down her spine. She shook it off, telling herself that she was being silly, that there was a perfectly logical reason why she hadn't seen his reflection in the glass.

Why she never saw him during the day.

Why she never saw him eat . . .

"Oh, good grief," she exclaimed. "That's the last time you watch a vampire movie before you go to sleep."

Laughing softly, she went into the bedroom to get ready for bed.

Chapter Eight

She loved him.

The words repeated themselves in Jessie's mind as he waited for the deathlike sleep that came to him each night.

She loved him.

His hand stroked the black silk sheet beneath him. The silk was soft and cool, like her skin.

Staring up at the ceiling, he thought of the song he had written for her. He had never been given much to writing poetry before, but something about Kathy awakened the romantic in him, made him want to write sonnets to her beauty.

Rising, he padded into the living room and sat down at the desk in the corner. Withdrawing a sheet of paper from the desk, he began to pour out his thoughts.

feel the air and know . . .
it's my soul that wraps your sighs
taste the rain and feel . . .

my kiss so deep inside
run with the sun
its light is my skin
warm against yours....

smile...when you walk
I am the path that
will carry you safely....

tears that burn an empty
heart
I will sweeten with
one word
watch as it flows down your cheeks
and tastes your lips

move with time
I am the sound of the air
swirling around your thoughts
fear runs from my glance

rest on the softest bed of
flowers
I am the fragrance
that filters into your soul....

feel the air and know...
my heart's beat
resounds with your smile....

He grunted with wry amusement as he put the pen aside, wondering what his fans would think if they knew the truth, wondering what Kathy would think.

Would people rise up against him, hunt him down, drive a stake into his heart and fill his mouth with garlic, as vampire hunters had done in days of old? Or would they merely shake their heads in disbelief and proclaim him mad?

Leaning back in his chair, he closed his eyes, remembering how it had all come about. . . .

His body had failed him. Only his voice stayed the same. Even though his fans might look at him with pity, he could still mesmerize them with his voice. His voice . . . it had made him rich, famous beyond his wildest dreams.

He was drowning in despair the night he left Graceland. Carefully disguised, he sought escape from the house, from the bodyguards, from the constant attention.

He slipped into a small bar, took a seat in a booth in the back, ordered a beer.

He needed a change in his life.

No sooner had the thought crossed his mind than a woman slipped into the booth across from him. She was beautiful, more beautiful than any woman he had ever seen. Her skin was flawless, translucent. Her blond hair fell over her shoulders in thick waves. And her eyes . . . they were the greenest green he had ever seen.

"What can I do for ya, honey?" Assuming she had recognized him, he expected her to ask for his autograph.

"I'm here to do something for you." Her voice was soft and low, with an accent he didn't recognize.

He laughed softly. "What can you do for me?"

"I can change your life."

In spite of the heat of the evening, he shivered at her words. "What do you mean?"

"You want a change. You're tired of your life, the way you look. You're afraid of getting old, of dying."

"You don't know what the hell you're talking about," he said curtly, but, deep inside, he felt the cold hand of fear. "What are you?" he said, forcing a laugh, "a mind reader?"

"In a way." She leaned toward him and smiled. Her teeth

45

were perfect and very white. "I can give you everything you desire."

He laughed again. She was nothing but a hooker.

"No," she said, sounding annoyed. "I am not a hooker. Or a gypsy. Or a mind reader." She stood up and offered him her hand. "Come with me, and I'll show you what I am."

Like a robot he stood up and put his hand in hers, and she led him out of the bar, down the street, and into a small motel.

Inside, she closed and locked the door.

He took a deep breath, fighting the fear that threatened to swamp him. Why had he come here?

She sat on the edge of the bed and patted the mattress beside her. "Come, join me," she invited, and laughed softly.

Again, without knowing why, he did as she asked.

"I've always been a fan of yours," she said quietly. "I was there when you first began, and I knew that you would stun the world with your talent."

"How could you have been there when I began?" he asked. "You can't be more than twenty-five."

She threw back her head and laughed, the sound soft and sexy. "Oh, I'm much older than that," she said, "but we were talking about you. I saw how the women reacted to you. You drove them wild. I watched the way you played with the audience, teasing them with a look, a smile, a twitch of your hips, and I knew there would be no stopping you. And I was right."

"Who are you?" he demanded.

"Just a fan." Lifting one hand, she brushed a lock of unruly hair from his brow. "I've always wanted to do that."

He started to stand up, fear twisting through him. She put her hand on his shoulder and held him in place with just one hand.

"I'm here to help you, not hurt you," she said. "I'm going to give you a chance to start over."

He looked down at his bloated body and laughed bitterly. "That's impossible."

"For me nothing is impossible. Only tell me it's what you want."

"To be young again?" he asked. "Who wouldn't want it?"

"Then look into my eyes." Her voice was lower now, almost a growl.

And he had looked into her eyes and seen the abyss of eternity there. . . .

He felt a familiar tingle slide down his spine and knew the rising of the sun was only a few minutes away.

Going into his bedroom, he closed and double-locked the door; then he settled into the big king-size bed. No one was allowed in this room; he had never shared this bed with anyone, but as his eyelids closed, he imagined Kathy there beside him, her head pillowed on his shoulder, imagined that he heard her voice whispering that she loved him as the sky turned light and the darkness that was inside him dragged him down, down, into eternity. . . .

Chapter Nine

It was a sold-out crowd again. He stood in the wings, listening to the orchestra play his introduction, remembering the early years, remembering the day he'd cut his first record. He recalled Sam Phillips saying, *If you aren't doing something different, you aren't doing anything.* They'd been working on recording "I Love You Because," and during a break he'd grabbed his guitar and starting singing "That's All Right (Mama)." Scotty Moore and Bill Black had joined in and that, as they say, was that. He remembered cutting records for RCA, coming in late so they could have some privacy, sending out for Krystal burgers at midnight. Those had been good times, fun times. In the beginning it had all seemed like a dream come true—making records—he'd had four number one hits in '56. Perhaps the biggest coup of all was appearing on the Ed Sullivan show. Sullivan had once said that Elvis was unfit for family viewing, but somewhere along the way he'd changed his mind. It had been a hell of a night, performing on television before fifty-four million viewers, with girls in the audience screaming and swooning.

His performance had caused a public outcry. He'd been hanged in effigy in Nashville and burned in absentia in St. Louis. The Reverend Billy Graham had said he wouldn't want his children watching such a display. He'd been banned in Florida.

But he'd had the last laugh. By the end of 1956, there were seventy-eight Elvis Presley products on the market; he grossed close to two million dollars in his first two years. He'd had a Jeep, a dune buggy, three motorcycles, three jets, two Cadillacs, including a limo, a Rolls Royce, a Lincoln Continental, and two station wagons. He had loved cars, and he had loved giving them away to his friends.

Of course, being famous had had its downside, too. By the end of the year he was too well known to go out in public, so he'd rented skating rinks and movie theaters and amusement parks and filled them with his friends.

Those had been the good times. Pulling down over five million dollars a year. *Damn.* During the '60s, he'd been the highest-paid entertainer in the world. They'd paid him a $125,000 for a single guest appearance on a Frank Sinatra special. He'd sold more than 500 million records and made thirty-three films, though *King Creole* had always been his favorite.

And then things had started to go bad. Somewhere along the way, the magic died. The hits stopped coming. Priscilla divorced him. He started gaining weight. Surrounded by people, he had never felt more alone.

Sometimes, looking at old pictures, it was hard to believe any of it had been real.

It had been worse after his "death." People claimed to see him everywhere. He had laughed at some of the headlines he'd read in papers like the *Enquirer*.

THE GHOST OF ELVIS IS HAUNTING MY HOUSE, SAYS EX-GIRLFRIEND.

Madeline Baker

FIVE-HUNDRED-YEAR-OLD STATUE OF THE KING FOUND IN PERU—PROOF HE LIVED IN PERU, ANCIENT EGYPT.

I BROUGHT ELVIS BACK TO LIFE.

ELVIS BODY SNATCH PLOT.

That would have been some trick, he mused, when there was no body. . . . Taking a deep breath, he stepped out on-stage. It felt good to perform before a live audience again, to hear the applause of the crowd, to feel the adoration of the women, the envy of the men, to be able to sing at his best, look his best. He had never felt better, looked better. And yet, in spite of everything, he had been more lonely than ever these past twenty-two years. He had known the price for eternal life would be eternal darkness, and he had been prepared for that. What he had not expected was the loneliness, the awful sense of being separate from the rest of humanity.

It should have been an easy price to pay. His celebrity had always set him apart from the rest of the world. Even in life, he'd been unable to take a walk on a busy street, go to a movie, walk into a store, without being mobbed by fans. He should have been used to it, but he wasn't, and somehow this was far worse.

His gaze darted toward the front table. Ah, she was there. Pure and perfect, her brown eyes shining as she smiled up at him. He could smell her perfume, hear the blood flowing warm and sweet in her veins, the way her heartbeat increased when their gazes met. Desire stirred deep within him, and with it the desire to taste her sweetness. She was the first truly honest woman he had ever known, perhaps the only one he had ever met who loved him for himself. He had showered her with gifts, pleased to find she was as happy with a single rose bought on a street corner as she was with diamonds. Kathy. He had been lonely all his life until he met her.

Soon, he thought, soon she would be his.

*   *   *

Kathy felt a warm glow as Jessie's gaze rested on her. She hadn't thought it possible to fall in love so hard, so quickly, but she had. At first she had been hesitant to trust her feelings, afraid that what she felt wasn't love at all but a bad case of idol worship because Jessie looked so much like Elvis. But as the days and weeks went by, as she grew to know him as he really was, she stopped seeing him as an Elvis look-alike and saw him for the man he was—warm and generous, kind and caring, unfailingly romantic.

Tomorrow, she thought. Tomorrow she would surprise him.

Chapter Ten

Kathy knocked on Jessie's door, waited, and knocked again. It was still early. Surely he hadn't gone out already? She pressed her ear to the door, but couldn't hear anything. With a sigh, she knocked again. He had told her he slept late, that he rarely went out during the day, but she was determined that they would spend one afternoon together. She had asked the hotel to pack them a picnic lunch. She expected a couple of sandwiches and some potato chips. When she peeked inside the basket, she saw two enormous ham-and-cheese sandwiches with all the trimmings, a roast chicken, potato salad, pickles, and a bottle of champagne. And two huge slices of dark-chocolate fudge cake for dessert.

Knowing it was useless, she knocked on the door one more time; then, feeling utterly depressed, she left the hotel. She wanted to see Hoover Dam and she was going to see it. She might not have any company, but she was going to have a terrific lunch.

* * *

Jessie slid a glance at Kathy. She was sitting on the sofa, her feet curled beneath her, a pensive look on her face. She had been strangely quiet this evening.

"What is it, darlin'?" he asked. "What's troubling you?"

She shrugged. "It's not important."

"Of course it is." He slid his arm around her shoulders and smiled down at her. "Whatever it is, you can tell me."

"I came by your room this morning."

He went suddenly still. "You did?"

She nodded. "I wanted to surprise you. I had the hotel pack us a lunch. I was going to kidnap you and take you on a picnic."

"To Hoover Dam," he murmured.

"Yes. But you weren't in your room." She looked up at him, her eyes wide. "Where were you?"

A dozen lies chased through his mind, but he discarded them all. He couldn't lie to her, not to Kathy, not when she was looking at him like that, as if she were just waiting for him to break her heart. "I was asleep."

"Didn't you hear me knocking?"

He had sensed her presence, had known she was outside his room, but the deathlike sleep that engulfed him when the sun was high in the sky had held him immobile.

He brushed his knuckles over her cheek. "I'm a very sound sleeper." He smiled at her. "We had a late night last night, remember? And I did two shows, plus that benefit with Wayne Newton." He shrugged. "I was really wrung out when I went to bed."

She let out a tremendous sigh. "I'm sorry. I just wanted to surprise you with something fun."

"I'm sorry, darlin'."

"Maybe another time?"

He nodded. "Maybe." He drew her into his arms and held her close, wondering if he should send her away. She was a creature of light and life. Would she wither and die in the darkness of his life? Could his love be payment enough for the world she would have to leave behind? Would she grow to hate him for what he was? Or would she embrace his new lifestyle and all that it entailed?

If he told her the truth, would she run screaming from the room?

"Kathy . . ."

She looked up at him, her eyes shining with love and trust.

"Kathy, I . . . Damn."

Her brow furrowed with alarm. "What is it?"

"Nothing, darlin'. Nothing at all."

"Oh, I hate it when people do that!" she exclaimed. "Tell me."

Jessie shook his head. "It's not important."

"Jessie . . ."

He silenced her the only way he knew how. Planting his hands on her shoulders, he drew her up against him and kissed her. Her surrender was immediate and complete. Her eyelids fluttered down and she melted against him, a soft purr of contentment rising in her throat.

Desire burst to life within him, hotter than the flames that entertained visitors to the Mirage.

"Kathy, darlin' . . ." He groaned softly, his need for her like a physical pain. Damn, he thought, he couldn't go on like this much longer. There had been no other women in his life since the first night he'd met Kathy. He'd never been a monk, certainly not in his old life, and not in this one, but he'd never wanted a woman the way he wanted the woman in his arms. Her innocence, her sweetness, the passion he sensed within her, all called to everything male within him, begging him to take her, to make her his own in the most primal way of all.

"Jessie, oh, Jessie . . ." She pressed herself against him, wanting to be closer.

He blew out a sigh that came from the very depths of his being. "Dammit, darlin'," he muttered, "I'm not made of stone."

She laughed softly as she felt the very real evidence of his desire. "You could have fooled me."

He grinned down at her. "I think I'd better go before one of us gets in trouble."

"Don't go."

"I don't want to, but . . ." Slowly, he sat back and put some distance between them. "You're far too tempting, darlin', and I'm far too weak."

"Are you?" She smiled at him, her eyes glowing with the same expression Eve's must have had the first time she tempted Adam.

Jesse stood up, knowing if he didn't get out of there right then, he'd take her, willing or not.

"See you tomorrow night, darlin'." Bending, he placed a quick kiss on the top of her head and fled the room as if the sun itself were chasing him.

He prowled the dark streets beyond the Strip the rest of the night, his thirst and his desire warring with what he knew to be right.

Kathy . . . she was like the sun, chasing away the shadows in his dark world. How could he defile her with his presence? How could he let her go? She was a forever kind of girl, he mused, a wry grin twisting his lips. And he could give her forever. If he offered it, would she accept?

He held the thought close, letting his imagination consider the possibilities . . . marriage, a companion to share his life, someone he could confide in, someone he could trust with the truth. Kathy . . . it would be heaven to meet the dark sleep in her arms, awaken with her beside him.

Ah, but it could never be. What woman would settle for a man who could never share her whole life? She would soon tire of him, tire of his excuses and half-truths, grow weary of being with a man who could never share the daylight hours with her, who couldn't even share a picnic with her, except by the pale light of the moon ... although, he thought as an idea occurred to him, that might not be a bad idea. ...

"Where are we going?" Kathy asked. It was Monday night. There was no late show on Monday nights, and they usually spent the evening seeing a show at one of the other casinos, or just wandering down the Strip, stopping now and then to look in a window, touring the gift shops at the other hotels. She loved the Excalibur with its moat and its fire-breathing dragon. They often went to the Circus Circus. Jessie loved playing the carnival games upstairs. He was good at them, too, and she had dozens of stuffed animals to prove it. Sometimes they tried their luck at the gaming tables, and sometimes they spent the evening in her room, watching a movie. Jessie loved movies.

"It's a surprise."

Kathy sat back in the seat, enjoying the feel of the wind in her hair. They'd left the limo behind tonight and were driving in Jessie's baby blue Corvette convertible.

For a time she watched the countryside go by. The world looked different at night. A full moon bathed the landscape with silver shadows.

It was peaceful, quiet save for the low purr of the Corvette's motor and the sound of the tires on the road.

Tiring of the scenery, she focused her attention on Jessie's profile. It was sharp and clean and handsome, so handsome. She never tired of looking at him, of touching him. Even now her hand strayed onto his thigh, and he covered it with his own. He gave her a quick glance, his smile warm with promise, his eyes glowing with love and desire.

Her stomach seemed to do a flip-flop as his gaze rested on her face. Mesmerized by his eyes as she was, time and place lost all meaning to her.

She blinked when the car stopped, surprised to find that they were at a deserted spot on Lake Mead.

Jessie vaulted over the door, then came around to open hers.

Taking her hand, he bowed her out of the car, then reached into the backseat and pulled out a picnic basket and a blanket.

Kathy grinned at him. "A midnight picnic! How romantic."

"I thought you'd like it, darlin'."

"I like you."

"Why, thank you, ma'am," he drawled. "You may have guessed that I'm rather fond of you, too."

"Fond of me?" she replied, pouting. "That's all?"

"Very fond?" he said, grinning as he squeezed her hand. "Come on."

They found a flat spot near the lake. Jessie spread a blanket on the ground, then opened the basket, withdrawing a loaf of bread, a book, and a bottle of wine.

Kathy looked at him and grinned. "A loaf of bread, a jug of wine?"

"And thou beside me."

She picked up the book. It was a small volume bound in maroon leather. The title, *Poetry, Prayers, and Promises*, was lettered in gold. "Love poems?"

Jessie nodded.

"I've never heard of the poet. Where did you find it?"

He shrugged. "In a used-book store."

Kathy opened the book to the middle and began to read:

> *The warmth of her touch*
> *moved through my being*
> *searing my soul*
> *forever yearning*
> *never to be quenched.*
> *My heart dissolved*
> *falling away*
> *leaving me naked.*
> *Flesh consumed with desire*
> *to be moistened by her lips*
> *caressed by her breath*
> *moving like light*

dancing on the wind.
I run
burning from the fire of her touch
overwhelmed with surges of pulsing passion.
Escape
before I never want to leave
the warmth of her touch.

"Wow," she exclaimed softly. "That's what I call hot!"

Jessie grinned at her as he took the book from her hand and turned a couple of pages. "I think this one is my favorite."

"Read it to me," Kathy said.

He looked at her a moment, and then began to read.

" 'If I say with mere words that I want you, will you move to my side? If I move with simple strokes, will you comfort my eyes? To taste the lips that speak of love . . . to inhale the breath that whispers my name . . . will you hold my soul for a moment . . . let me empty my heart . . . and fill it with your taste. I lie alone . . . with only your voice filling my being; I breathe, knowing my air will find your soul. If I walk through time of need, will you be at my side, holding what's left of me? I move . . . wanting. I taste . . . needing. I will always ache for just one glance. Walking, I feel the sun kiss my skin. Your lips touch mine. Sitting, I gaze upon the light. Your eyes cover me. Oh, so sweet, your embrace. My mind, lost in a deep pool . . . warmth flowing through my blood. If I say with mere words that I love you, will you fly with my soul . . . through eternity?' "

"I think he just became my favorite poet," Kathy murmured. "That was beautiful."

Jessie tilted her face up. "So are you," he said softly, and kissed her. "Oh, darlin'," he murmured. "Do you know what you do to me?"

"Hopefully the same thing you do to me."

He laughed softly. "I didn't bring you out here to seduce

you, but . . ." His lips slid over her throat. "It's a mighty tempting thought."

It was tempting, Kathy thought. Too tempting.

She gazed up into Jessie's eyes and wondered what she would do if he tried to make love to her. Would she resist? Did she want to resist?

Time lost all meaning. The bread and wine were forgotten as he kissed her again, his hands lightly skimming her body until she burned for him, yearned for him.

Jessie drew back, his breathing ragged with the need to possess her, to taste her. But not here, he thought, not now.

"Come," he said. Taking her by the hand, he helped her to her feet.

Kathy blew out a sigh, grateful for his restraint. Another few minutes, she mused, and she might have done something she would regret.

She snuggled against him on the ride back to the hotel.

"Sleepy?" he asked.

"A little." With Jessie's arm around her and the desert wind caressing her face, she closed her eyes, drifting in the netherworld between sleep and wakefulness. His voice found her there, low, seductive, touched with magic.

Tomorrow night I will come to your room. Don't breathe too deeply, or you will pull me inside. I will lift you into my world. Yours will no longer exist. Eternity with me, tasting you, devouring your smile, surrounding your life with my kiss . . .

She woke with a start. "Did you say something?"

Jessie shook his head. "No, why?"

"I guess I was dreaming."

He looked down at her and smiled. "I hope I was in it."

Chapter Eleven

With a sigh, Kathy hung up the receiver. Every time she called that man before dark, she got his answering machine. It annoyed her that he was always so busy during the day that he never had time for her. How many meetings could one man have? She knew if she asked him about it, she'd get the same old answer.

I work late, and I sleep late, darlin', and then I take care of business so I can spend my nights with you.

She couldn't argue with that. She stayed up late to be with him, rarely getting into bed before four or five in the morning. She slept late, usually until one or two in the afternoon.

She looked at the clock. It was a little after four. Jessie usually showed up around six.

She took a leisurely bubble bath, combed her hair, and slid into a dark green dress that managed to be modest and sexy at the same time.

When she stepped into the living room, Jessie was there waiting for her.

Her heart skipped a beat. "You're early," she exclaimed softly.

"Want me to leave, darlin'?"

"Don't be silly."

He moved toward her. Dressed in a bulky black sweater and tight black jeans, he looked like a sleek black panther stalking its prey.

I will lift you into my world. Yours will no longer exist. Eternity with me, tasting you, devouring your smile, surrounding your life with my kiss . . .

She shivered as those words, the same words she had heard last night, tiptoed down the corridors of her mind.

"Something wrong, darlin'?"

He was standing in front of her, his deep blue eyes intent upon her face.

Don't breathe too deeply, or you will pull me inside. "No."

His arms slid around her waist, drawing her body against his. His lips nuzzled her throat. "You look good enough to eat," he murmured, and felt his fangs lengthen at the thought.

"Jessie . . ." She couldn't think when she was in his arms. His tongue laved her throat, and she closed her eyes as shivers of pleasure slid down her spine. Magic, she thought. He was magic.

"I love you, Kathy, darlin'." He whispered the words in her ear, soft words that buried themselves in her soul.

"Jessie! Oh, Jessie, I love you, too."

He kissed her again. Heat shot through her, blinding white heat that burned away every thought, every doubt, everything except her need for this man above all others, and she knew she had waited for this man, this moment, all her life. Though they had known each other only a few weeks, she felt as though she had known him forever. Seeing him, being with him, made her feel warm, secure, complete. Excitement threaded through her veins, making her heart beat fast, filling her with a delicious heat.

He lifted her effortlessly into his arms and carried her into

61

the bedroom. Holding her with one arm, he pulled back the blankets and eased her down on the bed, then slid in beside her and drew her into his embrace.

She knew she should push him away, tell him no, but even as the thought crossed her mind, it was burned away by the heat of his eyes.

"Jessie . . . Jessie . . ."

"I'm here, darlin'."

She snuggled deeper into his arms, her body fitting to his as if she had been made for him. His hands slid over her back in lazy circles, sending shivers of delight down her spine. She murmured his name as she lifted her face for his kiss. Desire arced between them, sizzling like the summer lightning that flashed across the sky.

She slid her hands under his sweater, lifted it over his head, and tossed it aside. His skin was cool and smooth beneath her fingertips. With hands that trembled, she divested him of his jeans and boots, until he wore nothing but a pair of navy blue jockey shorts that she found sexy and provocative.

"No fair," he whispered, and caressed her out of her clothing until she wore nothing but a smile and a promise.

She looked into his eyes and knew he found her beautiful, desirable. "Jessie . . ." Just his name, soft as a sigh, fervent as a prayer.

His gaze moved over her, warmer than sunshine, sweeter than summer wine, and then he was kissing her again, his hands gentle as he explored the hills and valleys of her body, learning what made her gasp with pleasure, what made her purr with delight.

And then she turned the tables on him, her hands boldly roaming over his broad shoulders, across his hard-muscled chest, glorying in the strength that lay quiescent beneath her questing fingertips.

A smile of purely feminine pleasure lit her face as the rigid evidence of his desire swelled against her belly.

They tasted and touched with gentle urgency, their tongues

dueling in a mating dance as old as time. She stirred restlessly in his arms, wanting to savor every moment, every sensation, wanting to know his mind and heart as well as the enticing contours of his body. Her fingers memorized the width of his shoulders, the flat planes of his chest and belly.

He drew in a deep breath as her fingers slid lower, lower, shuddered with pleasure as she found the growing evidence of his desire.

"Bet I know what you're thinking," she teased.

He laughed softly, but it was a shaky kind of laugh. "Can't fool you, can I, darlin'?" he growled with mock ferocity.

"No." She nibbled on his earlobe, then kissed her way back to his lips. When their bodies came together at last, she was ready, more than ready. She rose up to meet him, her arms drawing him closer, tighter, as his body merged with hers. The romance novels she loved to read had often spoke of a man and woman coming together as two halves of a whole. . . . She had never known what that meant until now.

She gasped as he breached her maidenhead, but the pain was brief and quickly forgotten in the pleasure that followed. Her hands curled over his shoulders; her legs wrapped around his waist, drawing him closer, deeper. Instinct older than time taught her what to do.

She held on to him as if she would never let him go, clung to him as the only solid object in a world that was spinning out of control as wave after wave of sensual pleasure washed over her and through her, filling her with a delicious heat. His hands played over her, a master musician drawing out each note of delight, each finger like a flame, igniting tiny fires everywhere he touched. She had never known such pleasure, such a sense of urgency, of desperate need. He moved deep inside her and she gave herself up to the flames, felt the heat engulf her, until there was no more time for thought.

Eternity with me, tasting you, devouring your smile, surrounding your life with my kiss . . .

*   *   *

Jessie rained kisses over her face, lingering on her lips, drinking in their sweetness. No other woman had ever made him feel like this . . . strong yet tender, masterful yet vulnerable. He had made love to other women, but never like this. Her very innocence intoxicated him, and he found that she had given him the best gift of all, had reminded him of the unspeakable joy, the incredible wonder of the first time he had held a woman in his arms and discovered what it meant to be a man.

"Kathy . . ."

She moaned softly.

"Kathy, darlin'."

She shuddered beneath him, and he convulsed a moment later, a deep groan rising in his throat as he clung to her, and she to him, her nails raking his back as he felt her find fulfillment in a man's arms for the first time.

She was drifting, floating on a cloud of sweet contentment, and she never wanted to come down. She felt him move, knew he was going to leave her, and she wrapped her arms around him and held on tight.

"Don't go."

A soft chuckle as he shifted his weight a little to the side so she could breathe.

"Don't ever go."

"Never?"

"Never. Oh, Jessie, I wish I could spend eternity in your arms."

He lifted himself up on his elbows and gazed down at her, his eyes burning with a fierce inner glow. "Ah, darlin'," he murmured as he lightly bit her neck, "I might be able to arrange that."

Chapter Twelve

It was near dawn when he left the hotel. Feeling the need to walk, he sent the limo away. Alone in the dark, he felt his euphoria fade in the face of reality. It was time to end it, now, before it went any farther, before he hurt her, before he did something they would both regret. Oh, but it would be so easy to enslave her, to cloud her mind and put her under his spell.

Not that he had ever needed to use his vampire powers to get a woman. Women had always come easily to him, drawn by his celebrity, excited to be seen in his company. That hadn't changed. Women flocked to the stage door hoping to meet him, get his autograph, pose for a picture. They slipped their phone numbers into his hand, and sometimes their room keys.

He walked down the street, his feet skimming the concrete, moving so fast he was no more than a breath of cool air to those he passed by. He had to let her go, but how? She was everything he had ever dreamed of, everything he had ever wanted, ever needed. For the first time he regretted what he had become, but there was no way back, no way to undo what he had done.

Anger and frustration warred within him, arousing his hunger. He wasn't surprised when he found himself at the old woman's house. Putting thoughts of Kathy from his mind, he knocked on the door.

Hester Greene peered at him though the peephole. "Mr. Singer!" she exclaimed. "I wasn't expecting you tonight."

"Let me in."

She stared at him a moment, then unlocked and opened the door.

He brushed past her and went into the parlor, pacing back and forth while she locked the door.

"Is something wrong?" she asked.

He whirled around to face her, and knew his eyes must be glowing red by the expression on her face. "I need to feed."

"It will cost you extra."

"How much?"

"Double the usual."

Reaching into his pocket, he pulled out a fistful of hundred-dollar bills and thrust them at her. "Take it. Take it all."

She didn't argue, and she didn't count it. Shoving it into her pocket, she took her usual place on the sofa.

He watched her brush her long gray hair aside, watched her tilt her head to the side, close her eyes, and he hated her. Hated her because she was willing, because she wasn't Kathy. Kathy . . . her blood would be sweet, so sweet . . . and she would hate him if she knew what he was.

He finally pushed the woman away, wiped her blood from his mouth with the back of his hand. For the first time since he had accepted the Dark Gift, he felt like a monster. How could he hold Kathy, kiss her, make love to her, when he was nothing more than a fiend who preyed on the blood of others?

He stalked out of the house, seeking the dark shadows of the night.

He had made love to her. Taken her innocence. Defiled her!

How could he have done such a thing? How could he have forgotten what he was? Oh, but it was easy to forget when he was in her arms. With Kathy, he forgot everything but her sweetness, her innocence. Her goodness beckoned him like sunlight, tempting him away from the darkness.

Hiding in the shadows, he wondered if, like the sunlight, she would destroy him.

Chapter Thirteen

Kathy woke slowly, disappointed to find herself alone in bed. The clock showed it was almost three.

"Jessie?" She called his name, hoping he was in the kitchen or the living room. "Jessie?"

Nothing. How could he have left without so much as a word after the night they had shared?

She looked up at the ceiling and sighed, not certain how she felt about what had happened between them.

It had been wonderful.

Magical.

She had been nervous, afraid, excited.

He had been wonderful.

She frowned as an image of burning eyes flashed across her mind: deep blue eyes tinged with red. A trick of the light, she thought. That was all.

Without knowing why, she lifted a hand to her neck, her fingers exploring, pausing over what felt like two small insect bites.

She felt a sudden, unexplained twinge of fear as she slipped out of bed and padded barefooted into the bathroom.

Switching on the light, she turned her head to the side and peered into the lighted mirror. There. Just under her left ear. Two tiny red marks, identical in size and shape. And even as she watched, they faded.

She blinked, then blinked again, and they were gone.

She stared in the mirror, a mind-numbing coldness creeping over her.

She closed her eyes. Her heart was pounding loudly in her ears; she could feel the pulse beating fast in her throat.

And then there was darkness. She was surrounded by soft, velvet darkness. And in that darkness echoed a slow, steady beat. It was low and reassuring, comforting somehow. Her own heart ceased its frantic rhythm until it was beating in time with that slow, steady beat. Her panic subsided, disappeared, to be replaced by a sense of well-being.

She frowned at her reflection in the mirror. Why had she come in here? With a shrug, she left the room and went into the kitchen to fix something to eat.

She dressed with care that night, hands a little shaky at the thought of seeing him again. She found herself smiling for no reason, humming Elvis songs, wondering if they would make love again later that night.

Jessie . . . how had she ever lived without him?

Too nervous to sit still, she wandered through the suite. If she'd been in her condo, she would be dusting, sweeping, vacuuming, anything to pass the time, to work off the nervous energy that hummed through her.

She had expected him to arrive early, felt a twinge of unease when six-thirty came and went.

He could have been delayed. Business. A late appointment.

She was still making excuses at seven. At seven-thirty, she picked up the phone and started to dial his number, only to hang up before the call went through.

She would not call him.

Why hadn't he called her? Where was he?

Doubts filled her mind, her heart. *You gave him what he wanted*, her conscience whispered. *Now he's gone.*

No, that couldn't be true. She wouldn't believe it, but the thought lingered in her mind.

At eight o'clock, she took off her shoes and stockings.

At eight-thirty, she took off her dress and put on a robe.

At nine, she cried herself to sleep.

Jessie paused in the middle of a song as a sharp pain pierced his heart. She was crying, each tear burning him like a drop of liquid sunshine.

He looked out over the crowd. They were staring at him, wondering what was wrong, why he had stopped singing.

The orchestra continued playing, waiting for him to go on with the song.

"Sorry, folks," he said. He glanced at the conductor. "Let's do 'It's Over.' "

He sang it for her, for Kathy, knowing she would hear, hoping she would forgive.

She woke with the sound of his voice echoing in her mind, so real, so close, she sat up, expecting him to be there in the room, beside her.

"Jessie?"

Throwing back the covers, she slid out of bed and went into the living room, turning on the hall light as she passed by. "Jessie?"

She looked at the clock on the VCR. Two A.M.

She felt a sudden tingling down her spine, a coolness, like a draft blowing over her skin. "Jessie?"

She whispered his name, then laughed, wondering what made her think he was there.

"I'm here, Kathy."

She whirled around, her gaze searching the darkness. "Where are you?"

"Here."

He stepped out of the shadows in the corner of the room. Dressed all in black, he looked as though he were a part of the night, a part of the darkness that surrounded him.

He took a step toward her and she retreated, afraid without knowing why.

"Kathy . . ."

"Where were you tonight? Why didn't you come for me?"

"I wanted to."

"But you didn't. Why?"

He heard the anguish in her voice, the doubts, knew her thoughts better than she did. He had come here tonight to wipe the memory of all they had shared from her mind, to make her forget all that had happened between them. He was going to send her back home to her uncomplicated life, where she would look back and remember nothing except that she had enjoyed her vacation at Graceland and won a jackpot in Vegas.

But she had awakened the moment he entered her suite, had known, on some subconscious level, that he was there.

Perhaps it was the blood bond they now shared; perhaps it was simply that she loved him. He could feel it even now, beckoning him, brighter than the sun, more compelling than the quiet rush of blood in her veins.

"Kathy." He held out his hand, palm up. "Don't be afraid."

She blinked at him, wondering how he knew she was scared, wondering why she was. She had never been afraid of him before. But tonight . . . she wrapped her arms around her body. She could feel something moving in the room, something that slid over her skin, something that was hot and cold at the same time.

"What is it?" she asked. "What's wrong?"

He laughed softly. "Nothing. Everything."

"Jessie, I'm afraid."

"I know." He turned away from her for a moment.

Kathy looked around the room, shivering. The air seemed thick, cool. She reached for the cotton throw on the sofa, felt her heart skip a beat as she caught a glimpse of herself in the big mirror on the far side of the room.

Jessie's reflection should have been there, too.

But it wasn't.

She closed her eyes. Opened them. Looked again, more closely. She saw a faint shimmer, like the ripples of a pond ruffled by the wind.

Her breath caught in her throat. Feeling suddenly weak and light-headed, she sat down on the sofa.

"Kathy, are you all right?"

She looked up at him, her eyes wide, her heart pounding.

"Kathy?"

She pointed at the mirror.

He looked at the mirror, a soft oath escaping his lips. "I can explain."

She shook her head. "Who are you? *What* are you?"

"Do you really want to know?"

She nodded, her curiosity stronger than her fear.

"You won't believe me." He began to pace the floor, his agitation growing. "I've never told anyone. I probably shouldn't tell you, either."

He stopped in front of her, wondering if he was making a mistake, wondering if he shouldn't wipe his memory from her mind, but the very idea was repugnant. To do so would be like dying all over again.

He held out his hand. If she took it, he would tell her the truth. If not, he would erase his memory from her mind.

She gazed into his eyes for a moment, and then she placed her hand in his. And she knew, in that instant, that her life was about to be changed forever.

She listened as he told her of his life, his death, his new life. Listened, not wanting to believe, yet knowing deep inside that every word was true. That the man kneeling before her, holding her hand as though he would never let go, was a vampire.

He told her how it had happened, and it explained everything—the reason he looked like Elvis, sounded like Elvis, why she had never seen him eat, why she never saw him in daylight, why he cast no reflection in a mirror, why he had left her after they made love.

It made perfect sense. But she refused to believe it. It was outside the realm of possibility. She knew there were people who claimed to be vampires, people who actually drank blood, but they weren't paranormal creatures. They were just mortals living a peculiar lifestyle. "There's no such thing as vampires."

"That's what I always thought."

"Fine, if you're a vampire, turn into a bat."

"I'm afraid that's a Hollywood invention."

"Then show me your coffin."

"I sleep in a bed. A big one," he added with a wry grin.

"Then show me your fangs."

He took a deep breath, and then opened his mouth.

A slow feeling of horror engulfed her. He did, indeed, have fangs. She might have thought they were fake, but as she watched, they slowly receded. It was true.

"The first night we met. Did you . . . did you drink from me?"

"No. But I wanted to."

"It was all a dream then?"

He smiled faintly. "My dream."

She lifted a hand to her throat. "But you took my blood when we made love, didn't you?"

He nodded. "Only a little, darlin'. I'm sorry."

"Am I going to become a vampire now?"

He laughed softly. "No, darlin'."

"Why are you telling me this?"

He heard the fear in her voice. "After last night, I felt you had a right to know."

"Don't you think you should have told me *before* we made love?"

"I should have," he allowed, "but I wanted you, needed you so damn bad. And I was afraid you'd refuse if you knew."

She had made love to a vampire. She waited, expecting to feel revulsion, remorse, horror. But she felt none of those things, only a desire to be in his arms again, to experience the wonder and the magic she had found the night before.

"So," she said, "where do we go from here?"

He smiled at her, that wonderfully sexy smile that made her heart skip a beat. "That's up to you, darlin'." He lifted her hand to his lips and kissed her palm. "Does it bother you, what I am?"

She thought about it, trying to sort out her feelings. She thought about her life, the way it had been before she met him, the way it was now, and knew she'd rather live with him than without him.

"I love you, Jessie, just the way you are."

"Kathy!" He drew her into his arms and held her tight. "I was afraid to tell you, afraid you'd hate me, fear me." He took a deep breath. "I was afraid you'd leave me."

She snuggled into his arms. "I'd rather have you as a vampire than not at all."

He drew back a little so he could see her face. "You can't tell anyone. You know that?"

"I won't." She laughed softly. "Who would believe me?"

"You believe me."

"Do you like being a vampire?"

"Most of the time." There were a few drawbacks. He couldn't see any of the people he had once cared for. Being a vampire had given him a new life, but effectively cut him off from his old one.

"But the blood . . . how can you drink it? You don't go around killing people, do you?"

"No." He stroked her hair. "I need only a little to survive." But lately he had been tormented by the need for more. The vampire who had made him had warned him that the craving for blood would grow stronger as he grew older. He would not need more, she had said, but he would want more.

"Don't you miss eating?" Kathy asked, wondering if she would be willing to give up bread and pasta and chocolate for eternity. "And sunshine?"

"I sure do miss eating solid food," he admitted. "As for sunshine . . ." He shrugged. "You're my sunshine, darlin'. I can smell it in your hair, taste it on your skin."

"Oh, Jessie . . ."

"Will you marry me, Kathy?"

"Yes, oh, yes, just name the day."

He laughed, and it was a deep, rich sound filled with love and amusement. "The day?"

She looked at him and frowned, then giggled. "The night, then."

"Tomorrow night is good for me," Jessie said. "How about you?"

"So soon?"

"Didn't you just tell me to name the day?"

"The night, you mean, and yes, I did, but . . ."

"Change your mind already?"

She started to say no, then hesitated. "Jessie, what about children?"

He thought briefly of his daughter, the grandchildren he had never seen. "What about them?"

"Can you . . . can we have children?"

"No." He let go of her hand and stood up. "Maybe you'd better think this over for a few days."

"Jessie . . ."

"Think about it, Kathy. I want you to be sure." He gazed deep into her eyes. "If you say yes, I'll hold you to it for as long as you live."

*   *   *

As long as you live. Those words went through her mind over and over again as the dark of night gave way to the cool gray of morning. As long as she lived. But would he want her that long? Would he still love her when she was old and gray and wrinkled and he was still young? Would she want to be seen with him—would he want to be seen with her—when people mistook her for his mother? And how would they explain the fact that she aged and he did not?

And children, what about children? She wanted a child. Was she willing to give up being a mother to be his wife? Was she willing to spend the rest of her life with a man who could share only half her life? Would she start to hate him when she aged and he did not?

Perhaps he could make her a vampire . . . her mind shied away from the thought before it was fully formed. Not even for Jessie could she become what he was. She didn't want to give up food and sunlight for blood and darkness, didn't want to sacrifice the joy of motherhood. She loved children, hoped to have a dozen of her own. She had been with Keri when her first child was born, had watched in awe as her sister's baby entered the world, a tiny, perfect being born out of the love Keri shared with Todd.

Feeling as though her heart would break, she curled up in a corner of the sofa and watched the sun come up. Where was Jessie? What was it like for him during the day? Did he dream? How did he endure not being able to see his daughter? And what about the people he knew now? He had been in Vegas for five years. How much longer could he stay here before people began to notice that he never changed, never grew any older?

Despair perched on her shoulders. She loved him so much, but did she love him enough to overcome the obstacles between them?

"Jessie, oh, Jessie . . . what am I going to do?"

Chapter Fourteen

Lying in bed, trapped in the netherworld between life and death before the dark sleep claimed him, he heard her tears, felt her pain and confusion. Whether she stayed with him or left, she would always be a part of him, bound to him by the blood he had taken from her. Such a small amount. She would never miss it. But it flowed through his veins, warm and sweet, binding them together.

He wondered, in a distant part of his mind, why he felt no such bond to Hester Greene. He had been taking her blood for years, yet he felt no link to her, no sense of connection. She meant nothing to him save as a source of nourishment. He knew what she was, as she knew what he was. He recalled the night they had met. He had been wandering the streets, searching for prey, when she'd called to him.

"I know what you seek," she said. "For the right price, I can give it to you."

"I don't know what you're talking about," he replied. "Go away, old woman."

"My blood is strong. It will nourish you well."

He stared at her, speechless.

She laughed softly. More like a cackle, he thought at the time.

"You are vampyre, are you not?"

He started to deny it, but she held up her hand. "Come with me," she said. "Let us talk."

"Aren't you afraid to be alone with me? Aren't you afraid I might rip out your throat and drink you dry?"

"My blood, taken by force, would poison you. Freely given, it will be sweet to the taste."

He had followed her home that night, and her blood had been sweet indeed, though not as sweet as the nectar that flowed through Kathy's veins. They had formed a friendship of sorts, the witch and the vampire. He had watched her work her magic, seen her cast spells. She sold love potions and charms, tonics to boost fertility and sexual potency. He had never believed in witchcraft, but he believed in Hester's magic.

Magic, he thought. Maybe that was the answer.

Hester frowned at the man sitting across the table. "Why do you wish to know? Has immortality lost its appeal?"

"You could say that."

She looked at him through shrewd black eyes. "You've fallen in love."

Jessie nodded. "I don't want to live without her."

"Make her as you are."

He considered that a moment, then shook his head. Even if Kathy would accept the Dark Gift, he would not wish it upon her. Not his Kathy. She was a child of the sun; she would wither and die in his dark world. Once, he had thought he wanted to live forever as he was, but no more. What good was immortality if he had to live without the woman he loved?

78

"Does she know what you are?"

Jessie nodded.

"Then why not go on as you are?"

"I can't. You understand?"

"As your feelings for the woman grow deeper, the hunger grows stronger within you. You are afraid of what you might do in a moment of passion, of weakness?"

"Yes. Can you help me?"

"It will be costly," Hester replied, "but there is a way. . . ."

Kathy didn't see Jessie for the next four nights. She wasn't surprised, but she couldn't help feeling hurt. And lonely. He had been such a part of her life for the past few weeks. Even when they weren't together, he was constantly in her thoughts. She knew he was giving her time to think, but it hurt nonetheless.

Think. That was all she did. She hardly left her room except for meals. Shopping had lost its appeal. The bright lights seemed dull and ordinary, the whir of the roulette wheel, the click of dice, all seemed to mock her loneliness. Everywhere she looked, there were people laughing, having fun. She had never felt so alone in her whole life.

On the fifth night without him, she went to the late show at the casino. Needing to see him, hear his voice, but not wanting to be seen, she took a table in a back corner.

Her heartbeat increased the moment he stepped onstage. Hungry for the sight of him, her eyes devoured him. *Jessie . . . oh, Jessie, how I've missed you.*

She sat in the shadows, never taking her gaze from his face. She would leave as soon as the show was over, and he would never know she had been there. Or so she thought.

He was halfway into his first song when his gaze swept the crowd and settled on her face.

He went on singing, never missing a beat, but it wasn't the words of the song she heard. It was his voice in her mind.

I've missed you, darlin'. Will you meet me after the show?

She nodded, and a flood of warmth flowed through her at the mere thought of being with him again. Four days without him was time enough to know she didn't want to live without him. It didn't matter that he was a vampire, didn't matter that he couldn't share her days, give her children. All that mattered was that she loved him more than anything in the world. She would share his nights, and if he agreed, they could adopt a child.

I love you, darlin'.

And I love you!

His eyes burned into hers, flooding her with heat. And then, incredible as it seemed, she felt his mouth on hers, his hands moving in her hair. She stared at him, wondering how it was possible for him to be onstage, singing, when she could feel his lips on hers.

Jessie . . . oh, Jessie!

She was breathing heavily when he broke the bond between them.

Later, darlin'.

Yes. Oh, yes.

She glanced at her watch, willing the hands to move faster.

It had been four nights since she had watched him perform. Only four nights, yet he seemed more vibrant than she remembered. More alive, she thought, and laughed out loud. Alive. That was funny. More undead? No, that didn't work either. But something had changed. And she knew, somehow, that it was because he had taken her blood.

No, darlin'. His voice again, whispering in her mind. *It's knowing you love me.*

That night, every song he sang seemed to have a message that was just for her. "Playing for Keeps." "Pocketful of Rainbows." "Today, Tomorrow and Forever." "Any Way You Want Me (That's How I Will Be)." "Tonight Is So Right for Love." "Always on My Mind." "Burning Love."

He closed with "I Want You, I Need You, I Love You."

By then, her heart was pounding with anticipation.

The crowd was on its feet, applauding wildly, as he took a bow.

As though drawn by a string, Kathy stood up and hurried toward the side door that led backstage. Walter was waiting for her, a huge grin on his face.

"It's good to see you again, Miss Browne."

"Thank you, Walter."

"He's missed you."

"Oh, and I've missed him."

And then he was there, sweeping her into his arms. The crowd was still applauding, and she knew he had cut his curtain call short, knew that tonight he wouldn't go back and sing just one more song.

"The car's waiting," Walter said.

Jessie nodded. "Good, let's get out of here."

As soon as they were in the car, Jessie drew her into his arms again. "Four nights without you was four too many, darlin'."

"I know."

He kissed her then, the heat of his lips burning away the last vestiges of doubt.

"Miss me?" He murmured the question between hungry kisses.

"You know I did."

"I'm glad you came tonight."

"You weren't supposed to know I was here."

He laughed softly. "Ah, darlin', I will always know when you're near."

"Jessie, let's get married. Now. Tonight."

He laughed again. "I guess you really did miss me."

"More than you can imagine."

"Oh, I don't know. I can imagine quite a bit."

She went suddenly still as his lips nibbled the tender skin behind her ear. She felt his teeth graze her neck.

"Relax, darlin'. It's just a kiss." But he could smell her

81

blood flowing warm and sweet, calling to him. He felt the prick of his fangs against his tongue, and he drew back. "I'm sorry."

She took a deep breath. "Do you want to . . . need to . . . ?"

Did he want to? Foolish question.

"It's all right, if you do."

"Kathy . . ."

"Really, it's all right."

He cupped her face in his hands, loving her more in that moment than ever before. "Kathy . . ."

She looked deep into his eyes, her expression earnest. "What do you do when you . . . you know?"

"A little old lady takes care of it."

Kathy frowned as images from old Dracula movies flashed through her mind. In the movies, the vampires always ravished innocent young women, stealing their blood and their virtue.

"It's not like in the movies, darlin'. This little old lady is a witch."

"A witch!"

Jessie nodded, suddenly serious. "Kathy, she thinks she can make me mortal again."

"Really? Oh, Jessie, that would be wonderful!" Excitement raced through her as she imagined a life with Jessie, a real life, a whole life. And then, seeing his expression, she frowned. "Is it what you want?"

"Yes."

"What aren't you telling me?"

"It carries an element of risk."

"What kind of risk?"

Jessie lowered the window that divided the front seat from the back. "Walter, take us to Hester's."

"Yes, sir, boss."

Kathy waited until the window was up again before she asked, "Is she the witch?"

"Yeah. I think she'd better explain it to you."

* * *

Hester Greene didn't look like a witch, Kathy thought, more like an old-fashioned grandmother.

"So," Hester said as she led them into the parlor. "This is the one."

Jessie nodded.

"Have you told her?"

"I thought I'd let you do it."

Hester smiled as she sat down in a wooden rocking chair. A large black cat jumped into her lap. She stroked it absently. "Mr. Singer has asked me about the possibility of becoming human again," she began. "I have told him there is a way."

"But it's dangerous, is that right?"

"Yes, there is a risk."

"What kind of risk?"

"It is an ancient cure, based on love."

"I don't understand."

"To restore his humanity, he will need the blood of one who has nourished life. . . ." She inclined her head. "My blood. And the blood of love. Your blood. We will add a few ingredients. . . ." She laughed, though Kathy thought it was more of a cackle. "Not eye of newt or the tail of a lizard, I assure you. Merely some rare herbs."

"And then what?"

"He must drink it."

"At midnight during a full moon?" Kathy asked sarcastically, and instantly regretted her words. But it all seemed so bizarre. Vampires and witches and magic spells.

"I understand your hesitation, your skepticism," Hester said. "Your fear."

"What will happen if it doesn't work?"

"I'm afraid Mr. Singer will die."

Kathy shuddered. "Isn't he already . . . ?" She couldn't say the word.

"In a manner of speaking."

Kathy took Jessie's hand in hers and stood up. "Let's go."

"No, Kathy. I want to do this."

"Now?"

He nodded.

"No. I'm not willing to risk your life."

Hester stood up, cradling the cat against her shoulder. "I think you two need to discuss this in private," she said, and left the room.

"Kathy, I've thought it over. I can't ask you to give up everything you want out of life to be with me. It isn't fair."

"You're everything I want. I won't let you do this."

"I thought you loved me."

"I do! You know I do!"

"Then it will work. If our love is as strong, as true, as we think it is, everything will be all right."

Kathy shook her head. "No, please, Jessie, I'm afraid."

"Kathy, I want to share all your life. Not just the nights, but the mornings and afternoons. I want to give you children. Lots of children. I want to show you the world."

"Can't we wait awhile? There's no rush, is there?"

"With every day that passes, I lose a little more of myself. Do you understand?"

"No."

He drew her back down on the sofa. "I don't need much blood to survive, but I find myself wanting it, craving it. I don't want to lose what's left of my humanity, Kathy. I'm afraid I might hurt you." He took a deep breath. Even now, the beast within him was stirring, making itself known.

"I'm not afraid."

"But I am."

"Let's go, Jessie. I don't want to decide tonight." She looked up at him. "Please."

"All right, darlin'."

Hester materialized in the room as if she'd been conjured there, and walked them to the door. "Let me know when you're ready."

* * *

When they reached the hotel, Jessie sent the car away. Hand in hand, they crossed the lobby toward the elevators.

Kathy's heart was pounding in her ears when they entered her room.

As soon as Jessie closed the door, she moved into his arms, her mouth seeking his.

There was no need for words, not now.

Jessie carried her into the bedroom, gently removed her clothes, then quickly shed his own. She drew him against her when he slipped into bed beside her, buried her head in the hollow of his shoulder.

"I've got to do it, Kathy," he said quietly. "Please try to understand."

"I am."

"I believe in you," he said, stroking her hair. "In us. I'm not afraid."

He made love to her ever so gently, as if they had all the time in the world, as if it didn't matter that dawn was only a few short hours away. He held her and caressed her, and all the while he whispered that he loved her, would always love her.

She wept bittersweet tears, knowing that if her love wasn't true enough, if Hester's power wasn't strong enough, this would be the last night they spent together.

With a cry, she drew him closer. The spark between them ignited again, burning hotter and brighter than the sun he had not seen for over two decades, burned and burned again, until she felt him go suddenly still.

"What is it?" she asked.

"Dawn . . ."

She glanced at the window, saw that the sky was growing bright.

"Kathy, go."

"What?"

"Leave me. Now."

"But why?"

"I don't . . ." He took a deep breath, as if it was an effort to speak. "Don't want you to . . . see me."

She started to scoot out of bed and then stopped, hypnotized by what was happening to him. His eyes closed and he went still all over. She placed her hand on his chest. She could detect no heartbeat, no sign of life at all. His skin was cold.

"Jessie? Jessie!"

She scrambled off the bed, shaken to the very core of her being by the sight of him lying there as still as death.

Time and again, as the day wore on, she went into the bedroom to look at him. He never moved. What if he really was dead? In the movies, the vampire always had to return to his coffin before dawn. What if Jessie had to sleep in his own bed?

It was the longest day of her life. She tried to read, tried to watch TV, but she couldn't concentrate on anything, think of anything, except the man sleeping the sleep of the dead, or the undead, in the next room.

She had thought that maybe, just maybe, she would ask Jessie to make her a vampire, but after today, she knew the vampire life—or, death, or whatever it was—was definitely not for her.

Slowly, oh, so slowly, the hours slid by. She was standing at the window, watching the sun set, when she felt his presence behind her.

"Kathy. Kathy?"

"What?"

Jessie took a deep breath. Since he'd been made a vampire, no one had seen him while he was caught in the dark sleep of the undead. He could only imagine what it had been like for her to have him there. What had she thought when she looked at him?

"Are you ready to go see Hester now?" he asked.

Chapter Fifteen

Kathy felt a sharp stab of trepidation as she crossed the threshold into Hester Greene's house. *Come into my parlor, said the spider to the fly. . . .*

She reached for Jessie's hand as she sat down on the sofa beside him, her heart pounding wildly as she watched Hester move about the room. Tonight the old woman looked like a witch. She wore a flowing black dress. The skirt was embroidered with yellow moons and silver stars. A heavy gold pendant in the shape of an *X* hung from her neck. Silver bracelets adorned her wrists. A large black cat followed at her heels like a puppy.

Dozens of white candles lit the room.

She swallowed hard as Hester placed a small silver goblet on the table in front of them. She left the room for a moment, returning with two hypodermic needles.

"The omens are favorable," Hester said as she pulled a small bottle of alcohol and two cotton balls from one of her voluminous pockets.

"Favorable?" Jessie asked.

"Yes, I have consulted the stars. Mars and Jupiter are in close conjunction. It is a good omen for change." Hester looked at Kathy. "Your arm, please."

Kathy held her breath as Hester swabbed her arm with alcohol. She winced at the prick of the needle, looked away as the syringe began to fill with blood. Her blood.

Feeling the blood leave her body made her sick to her stomach. How did Jessie drink it?

"Done," Hester said. She slapped a bandage on Kathy's arm, withdrew blood from her own arm, and mingled it with Kathy's blood, which she had emptied from the syringe into the goblet.

Opening several small vials, she sprinkled the contents into the goblet. She stirred the mixture with a silver spoon, chanting all the while. She opened another vial and poured in a liquid that was thick and yellow. A thin column of black smoke rose from the goblet as Hester picked it up and turned it back and forth in her hands.

She stopped chanting and looked at Kathy, her black eyes sharp. "Do you love this man here beside you and no other?"

"Yes."

"Do you swear your love is true?"

"Yes."

Hester looked at Jessie. "And you? Do you love this woman here beside you and no other?"

"Yes," Jessie replied quietly.

"Do you swear your love is true?"

He nodded. "Yes."

Hester passed one hand over the goblet. "From dark to light, from death to life, true love will prevail." She handed Jessie the goblet. "Drink it. Quickly! Before the blood cools."

Jessie gazed deeply into Kathy's eyes as he lifted the cup. "I love you, darlin'. Whatever happens, remember that," he said, and, lifting the goblet, he downed the contents in one long swallow.

"Kathy." He gasped her name as the goblet fell from his hand. "Kathy . . ."

The cup rolled to a stop. A single drop of dark red blood spilled out onto the floor.

"Jessie!" She screamed his name as he fell back on the sofa. She screamed his name again, felt the world spin around her, and then everything went black.

Chapter Sixteen

She woke in her room, in her bed, alone. For a moment her mind was mercifully blank, and then it all came back to her—Hester, the blood . . . and Jessie.

He was dead, she thought, really dead this time. Her love hadn't been strong enough, true enough, and her blood had destroyed him.

Tears burned her eyes. Jessie . . . Jessie . . . how was she going to go on without him? She should have insisted he make her what he was. At least then they would still be together.

She rolled onto her side and buried her face in the pillow he had slept on. She took a deep breath, inhaling his scent. *Jessie* . . . She felt numb inside, and empty, so empty. She tried to think of what she would do now. She didn't want to stay here without him.

Rising, she went to the window and opened the drapes. The rising sun was streaking the sky with long fingers of crimson. It reminded her of blood, and she turned away.

This afternoon she would call Keri and tell her she was

coming home and ask her to get in touch with the couple renting her condo and give them thirty days' notice.

She climbed back into bed and pulled the covers over her. She was reaching for Jessie's pillow when she heard a knock at the door.

Frowning, she slid out of bed, grabbed her robe, and went to the door, wondering who on earth it could be.

"Who is it?"

A muffled voice answered. "Room service."

Kathy frowned as she opened the door. "I didn't order any . . ."

The words died in her throat. She took a step backward, one hand pressed to her heart. "Jessie!"

His grin was as wide as the Grand Canyon. "Mornin', darlin'," he said. "I brought breakfast." He lifted the lid on a large tray. "I didn't know what you liked, and I haven't eaten in a while, so I brought everything I could think of. Ham and eggs, bacon, sausage, pancakes, waffles, biscuits and honey, French toast, bagels, chocolate-chip muffins."

She stared at him, at the mountain of food on the tray, then turned to look out the window. The sun was shining brightly. "I must be dreaming," she murmured.

"You gonna invite me in?" Jessie asked, "or make me eat my first breakfast in over twenty years standing out here in the hallway?"

Speechless, she moved out of the doorway. Jessie entered the room, then nudged the door shut with his heel.

"It's daytime," Kathy said. "You're here. How?" She shook her head. "Last time I saw you, you were . . . you . . . I thought I'd killed you."

Jessie put the tray on the coffee table, then folded Kathy in his arms. "It worked, darlin'. I'm human again."

"But last night—"

"I died. That is, the vampire died."

She didn't know what to say, what to think. She could only stare up at him, breathless, speechless.

"Kathy?" He grinned at her. "You might say you're glad to see me."

"Oh, Jessie," she exclaimed softly. "Oh, Jessie, you're alive!"

He laughed then, a deep, full-throated laugh that filled her heart and soul.

"Jessie! Jessie!" She threw her arms around his neck and kissed him. She kissed him and kissed him again as happiness welled up inside her, bubbling like sparkling champagne.

She leaned back a little so she could see his face. "Should I call you Elvis now?"

"No, darlin'. I'm Jessie now. Your Jessie, if you'll have me."

"I've always been Jessie's girl," she replied with a saucy grin. "And I intend to have you in every way possible."

"Here I am, darlin'," he said. "Do your worst."

"Quite the contrary," she replied, taking him by the hand. "I intend to do my best."

Breakfast was a long time cold before they got back to it.

Epilogue

"Oh, Jessie, it's so beautiful here."

"It is that," he agreed. "But not as beautiful as my bride. Happy, darlin'?"

"Yes, oh, yes." She held up her hand, admiring her wedding ring. It was simple, yet elegant, a flawless diamond big enough to ice-skate on.

With a sigh, she leaned back against him. They had been married in Las Vegas the day before, then flown to Maui for their honeymoon. She had always wanted to see the islands, ever since she saw the movie *Blue Hawaii*. It was like paradise, she mused, the vast blue ocean, the white sand, the palm trees.

They had toured the islands—Kauai and Oahu and the big island of Hawaii. They had been to a luau, taken hula-dancing lessons, gone scuba diving, seen volcanoes and waterfalls. But the best times had been the early mornings and late nights in their room, in Jessie's arms.

She watched the waves dancing on the shore, watched the

sun rise on a new day, its light shining on them like a benediction. Their lives spread out before them. Like the ocean, they would have highs and lows, but the love they shared would see them through.

She sighed with pleasure as Jessie hugged her close, felt her heart skip a beat as he swung her up into his arms and carried her inside, happy beyond measure to be Jessie's girl.

Good Morning

For the rest of my life
hold me now as I feel the sun
hot on my flesh
warming my soul

Good morning . . .
Sweetest words from my heart
My eyes behold the light
moving across time's caress
now holding me once again

Good morning . . .
Kiss these lips of fresh life
Let me devour
these simple rays of sunlight
now dancing upon my skin
floating inside my soul
I have lifted to Heaven

Good morning . . .
For the rest of my life
resting in your arms
Kathy
Good mornin', darlin'

94

Dear Reader:

Aloha! I hope you enjoyed my story. I can't begin to tell you how much fun it was to write. I have always been a HUGE Elvis fan. I don't have quite as much Elvis stuff as Kathy, but I do have plates, socks, records, CDs, dolls, movies, etc.

I especially want to thank Mitch Dearmond for allowing me to use his poetry, and for reading my story. Thanks, Mitch, for your encouragement and enthusiasm. You're the best!

If you have access to the web, you can get a sneak peek at some of the stories I'm currently working on, as well as a link to Mitch's page, if you'd like to read more of his poetry.

http://www.angelfire.com/ga/apachefire/index.html

Hope you're all having a wonderful summer.

Madeline
DarkWritr@aol.com

NINA BANGS

THE HUNKA HUNKA AND THE PENNY-PINCHER

Prologue

"Elvis will set you free!"

"Oh, brother," Candy muttered. She stretched to get a better view of the hypnotist and her stepdaughter over the heads of Hawaiian-shirted tourists crowding the small club.

"You will fall into glorious lust with the hunka hunka burning love nearest you when the King sings. Ah, *amour*." The small man kissed the tips of his fingers in ecstatic enthusiasm.

Candy couldn't keep quiet. "What if there's only a hunka hunka burning jerk near her when the King sings?" She grunted as a waiter complete with sideburns, pompadour, and a tray of Hawaiian Hound Dawgs elbowed her on his way to the bar.

"Sorry, li'l darlin'," he apologized.

The hypnotist cast her a quelling glance. "What is passion without danger? But do not worry. I am an artiste." He pressed a hand to his heart. "If necessary, *I* will stand beside her when Elvis sings."

Candy frowned. "That's what I was afraid of." The hypnotist glared. "Silence." He returned his attention to his victims. "When I snap my fingers, you will awaken."

He snapped his fingers, then turned to his audience. "These ladies"—he gestured at the row of women taking part in the group-hypnosis session—"are now under my suggestion."

While husbands filed up to stand beside their wives, Candy cast a frantic glance into the audience. There must be *someone* besides the "artiste" who could stand beside Julia.

She'd settle for a big green frog. At least if Julia kissed the frog, she'd have a shot at a prince.

Nope, no frogs. Only a few lounge lizards.

A gurgled groan brought her attention back to the hypnotist. "*Excuse-moi.* An urgent message. I must leave for a few moments only. When I return, I will complete my demonstration, then erase the suggestion." He rushed from the stage.

Twenty minutes later, Candy glanced impatiently at her watch. Blue Hawaii would close in ten minutes. The other women had left with comments about it being only entertainment. *Huh.* She wondered how entertained they'd be when their husbands caught them kissing the butcher to the tune of "Love Me Tender."

"Tell me what the suggestion was, Candy." Julia sipped her drink. "I didn't hear because I was thinking about Wonder World. How about rubber fish? They don't go belly-up like the real thing, so there's no replacement cost."

Candy scanned the room. Even Half-wit the Hypnotist was better than listening to more of Julia's money-saving ideas. She gave up with a sigh. "What do rubber fish do?"

Julia shrugged. "You're right, Connally wouldn't go for it. I could tell from his picture he's the inflexible type."

"Really? Wasn't that the picture of him in the gorilla suit?" One more minute; then she'd go hypnotist hunting.

"Okay, so I couldn't see him, but if I could he'd have *stubborn* written right across his forehead. And what kind of man dresses up in a gorilla outfit? Anyway, I didn't hear the suggestion because I was concentrating on the park. So tell me.''

"In . . .'' Candy paused as a man walked to the microphone.

"Monsieur Dupre had to leave. An emergency. He'll be unable to return tonight.''

"He's got the runs,'' a loud whisper explained. "Locked himself in the john. Says he won't be out till next year.''

"He hopes you all had a wonderful time and will return to Blue Hawaii soon.'' The speaker disappeared into the crowd.

Julia stood. "Guess we can leave now. Whatever suggestion he made didn't work because I don't feel any different. Why'd I let you talk me into coming here? I could've been back at the motel looking at discount catalogs.'' She made her way to the exit. "By the way, you still haven't told me what the suggestion was.'' Julia didn't turn around.

Possibilities. "Nothing, dear. Just something about kissing a frog.'' *Or a gorilla.* Candy smiled.

Chapter One

"Okay, you're the King. Give with some kingly advice. What should I do about Julia Raine?" Dylan Connally tugged at his gaping shirt. Pirates needed more buttons.

"Hard Headed Woman, uh-huh," the Elvis figure agreed.

"Yeah. Tell me something I don't know." He adjusted his eye patch, then cocked his head so he could see better. "Even as we speak, the Wicked Witch of Weird Ideas is climbing on her broomstick. Wants to nix all my virtual-reality ideas. Can you believe it? So what should I *do* about her?"

"Return to Sender." His companion swiveled his hips to emphasize the advice.

"Great. I'll UPS her right back to the mainland." He turned to glance at other figures frozen on ministages around the cavernous room that was his Rock 'n' roll Legends theme building. No use asking them. If the King couldn't help him . . .

Funny, he'd put the same sweat into programming all his figures, but he'd always felt a little something extra for the King. As if there were a kind of connection. *Dumb.*

"God, I love this place." He breathed deeply, absorbing the smell, the special excitement he always felt here. "Maybe I'll give a listen to her ideas about the rest of the park, but if she tries messing with you and the rest of the legends, it's war, baby." He pulled at the waist of his pants. No way could pirates make it with fair maidens in this outfit. Too tight. No expansion room. "Hmm. Maybe her broomstick will run into a headwind. Slow her down a little."

He turned at the sound of an opening door. *Damn.* No one should be here this early. This was his time alone with his friends. Sure, their vocabulary was a little limited, but he did his best thinking around them. He'd just kick out the intruder.

Maybe not. The woman walking toward him was ... incredible. He liked tall women with curves that were curves and not acute angles. He liked long golden hair touched with the red of a Hawaiian sinrise, uh, sunrise.

She stopped in front of him, and he shifted his gaze to her face. *Wow. Killer eyes.* Blue eyes that reminded him of—

Without warning, Elvis shattered the silence with "Mean Woman Blues." *What the ...* He could have sworn that song wasn't in the King's programming. He'd talk to Carlos.

Forget talk. As he stared into the woman's eyes, something so strong it made him catch his breath flowed between them. Her eyes widened and her full lips parted.

He had only a moment to realize that she felt the current, too, before she stepped back and stumbled over an exposed cable.

Too stunned to move, he watched her teeter, then totter. *Do something.* Any second she'd go bump on her beautiful behind. In the end, instinct took over as he flung himself to his knees and caught her just before she bounced off the red carpet.

Fragmented thoughts fought for dominance. Sex. This must be the software saleswoman he'd expected. Sex. Why was she here so early? Sex.

He shook his head to clear it.

So close. She gazed up at him, and he could see his own confusion mixed with the heat of instant flame reflected in her eyes. She skimmed the side of his face with shaking fingers, then touched the medallion that lay against his chest.

Sexy software saleswoman. He'd never appreciated the beauty of *S* words before. Enough. He had to get up off the floor. Kneeling was not a great position from which to begin a business relationship. *If* he could get up. No wonder pirates always looked mad. Tight pants didn't make for happy faces.

But even shrink-wrap pants couldn't keep his attention from her. She sure had a winning sales approach. He'd buy—

She kissed him.

Kissed him long, hard, and with her mouth still open to tell him whatever she'd been about to tell him.

Vaguely, he noted that the King had switched to "All Shook Up." Things were out of sync. He'd have to check . . .

Then her mouth moved against his, and he forgot everything.

He slanted his lips across hers, absorbing the scent of vanilla and the taste of desire. Hers or his? Who cared? Deepening the kiss, he savored the hot sweetness of her mouth, closed his eyes to the spiraling excitement that her small moan of pleasure loosed, felt her deep shudder of regret, withdrawal.

Too soon. He wasn't ready for it to end. His hard-and-ready-to-party engine was just revving up.

The last notes of "All Shook Up" ended. *Uh-oh, Sexual-harrassment suit.* He'd kissed her. No, *she'd* kissed him. He brightened. It was all *her* fault.

Turning her head from him, she scrambled to her feet. He followed—more slowly, more carefully—listening for the telltale sound of ripping seams.

When she finally looked at him, he saw the memory of their kiss warm and alive in her gaze. *Good.*

"That shouldn't have happened. I'm sorry. I don't know why I . . ." Distractedly, she brushed at a nonexistent spot on her suit skirt. "I'm Julia Raine, and I'm looking for Mr. Connally. The man at the gate told me he was in here.'' She glanced around. ''He said today was Mr. Connally's gorilla day.''

Dylan narrowed his gaze. Betrayed. Sure she had killer eyes, eyes that reminded him of Malia's Siamese cat, Regret, just before it pounced on an unsuspecting lizard. ''Ah, the Queen of Cheap has arrived. Wanted to get an early start on your reign of terror, right?'' He smiled his deadliest smile. ''Oh, and today is Mr. Connally's *pirate* day.''

She blinked. ''You can't be.''

Her gaze slid the length of his body, and his body responded with interest. No, not interest, anger. Definitely anger.

She sighed, and his gaze followed the lift of her breasts beneath the silky blouse she wore, remembered their softness pressed against him. He forced his attention back to her face.

Classic. Okay, so maybe her nose looked a little bent out of shape right now. Maybe her lips were a little tight. He guessed having someone call her the Queen of Cheap could do that.

''Look, I don't want to be here either.'' She opened her eyes wide as though she could see more of him that way.

He sucked in his breath at the mule-kick affect those eyes had on him. ''Great. We agree. You can leave now.''

She shook her head, and he was momentarily diverted by the golden swirl of her hair as it fell across one shoulder.

''Sorry. It's not that easy. Dad's your major investor. He wants costs down and profits up. I'm here to make it happen.'' She glanced around. ''For starters, I'd update this place. Limited appeal. Bring in figures to attract young kids.'' Her eyes glowed. He could almost see dollar signs reflected in them. ''I have it. Cartoon characters. And we could sell T-shirts by the door. Maybe you could program the figures to remind people to buy a shirt before they left. What do you think?''

''It stinks.'' He gazed around him, seeing it through her eyes. The ministages, the plush seats and red carpeting.

He closed his eyes, remembering his first rock concert. The

Stones. His father had yelled that he'd raised his son to appreciate *good* music, classical music. Dylan had responded that he was old enough to make his own decisions. After that, he'd moved away from his parents' influence and never looked back.

He opened his eyes. She wanted to get rid of the legends! His anger gathered force and violence, like one of those monster hurricanes surging in from the Pacific. No Beatles? No Van Halen? Julia Raine intended to turn his vision into a sale at Buddy's Bargain Barn. *No way!* She'd cut him where it hurt.

"You're letting your emotions get in the way." She tilted her head. Probably so all her blood could flow to the left side of her brain. She didn't need any right-brained warmth and creativity creeping into her cold logic.

"I could've sworn Elvis just winked at me." She leaned forward to get a better look.

"Lady, you're crazy if you think I'll get rid of my Rock 'n' Roll Legends." The rest of his theme park was for the public, but this . . . this was for him. His passion.

She frowned. "There. He did it again."

"You're seeing things. Elvis isn't programmed to—"

She offered him a tentative smile. "Well, if he were programmed to wink it'd be a cute touch."

He heaved a sigh of resignation. "Right."

Dylan glanced away from her mouth, still swollen from his kiss. *Ignore her mouth. Remember the cartoon characters.* He'd think ugly thoughts of Bugs Bunny, and that should take care of his body's renewed clamor of interest.

"Guess I'm suffering from jet lag. My stepmother and I had a long flight from New Jersey. Got in last night; then Candy dragged me to that club and—" Her smile faded. "Look, we don't have to be enemies. I know you're not receptive right now, but give my ideas a chance."

"What ideas? If they're all like the cartoon character one, forget it." He didn't trust her. Wouldn't trust anyone who suggested he get rid of his Rock 'n' Roll Legends.

She shrugged. "We can discuss them tomorrow. I'm still tired, so now that I've met you, I think I'll head back to my motel." The champion of careful spending turned to leave.

"Wait." Why had he stopped her? His best sight all day would be the view of her rounded bottom swaying out the door. "This park means a lot to me." *The fun I never had, the reality I was never part of.* "I won't stand by and let anyone trash it."

She lifted the weight of her hair from her neck, then let it slide through her fingers. The dim light lent each strand a golden sheen. Sighing, Julia looked back over one shoulder. "No one's going to *trash* your park. Believe it or not, Connally, I do know when to buy the best and say to heck with the cost."

"Like when?" He wondered how much their kiss would cost. She might be a cost-cutting dynamo with his park, but with her kissing? Her kissing was pure spend-it-all-then-borrow-more.

"I like rich, smooth ice cream. Strawberry." She offered him a teasing smile. "I like fine wine. Red." She strolled toward the door. With each step, her hair swung like a pendulum of temptation. "And I like—" Janis Joplin interrupted to beg her lover to "take another little piece of my heart." When the volume lowered a moment later, he caught "—big and bold."

What? What did she like big and bold? Dylan had to know. "Wait. You didn't see the rest of the legends."

She glanced one last time over her shoulder, and she'd stopped smiling. "I've seen all I need to see. I'll admit it's . . . extraordinary."

Ask her. "What do you like big and bold?"

Her lips curved up slightly, a coming-attraction smile. "Horses, of course. I love horses." She pulled open the door.

"Wait. I'll walk you back to the motel." *Shut up, Connally. You don't need to walk her anywhere except to the airport.*

She's dangerous. Got it? D-A-N-G-E-R-O-U-S.

But hey, he couldn't waste a chance to force her to listen to his side of the story, make her see the logic of spending more on new technology, to quote a few statistics. It wasn't as though he *wanted* to walk her anywhere. Nope, this was battle strategy.

"Uh, thank you." She didn't look thankful. "I'll wait outside." She slipped out the door and slammed it behind her.

"Shoot." Dylan stared at the closed door. "Horses."

Who would've thought? He'd expected her to be thin lipped, beady eyed, a woman of few words and no laughter. So much for preconceptions.

He glanced up at the King. "I don't know who's been messing with your programming, but Carlos'd better fix it."

"Uh-huh," the King agreed.

Julia leaned against the closed door of the Rock 'n' Roll Legends building. If Dylan opened it now, he'd knock her flat on her face. *Okay, be honest.* He'd already done that.

Dad had said Dylan was brilliant and financially impulsive, but he hadn't mentioned physically spectacular.

The eye patch was a stroke of luck. One hazel eye framed by a thick, dark fringe of lashes was all she could take at first shot. She'd work up to both eyes later. High cheekbones, a determined mouth that refused to look harsh with its sensual slant. Sensual slant? *Yep.* She had tactile proof of that. And his hair—dark, long. With that white shirt practically open to Texas, and those tight black pants . . .

Then he'd smiled. The power of that smile had almost blown her back to her reasonably priced apartment in the reasonably priced section of Haddonfield, New Jersey.

She wondered how much pirates were going for on the open market. Heck, she'd pay full price for *him*.

But why had she kissed him? She wasn't impulsive. Sure, those incredible lips just inches away had tempted her, but she'd spent a lifetime resisting temptation. *Not like Dylan*

Connally. Never like Dylan Connally. It had to be jet lag. She was too tired to think straight.

Recovering enough to push away from the door, she waited. When he finally emerged, he'd removed the eye patch. He smiled at her.

She started walking. *Not now.* She didn't have the strength to deal with two eyes and the smile at the same time. Instead, she stared at the scenery. "It's almost too much, isn't it?"

"What?" He sounded distracted.

"The sky, the water, the plants. Colors so intense they hurt your eyes. Too lush. Too rich." She turned to him and found him staring at her. She looked away again. "You know, when you eat something so sweet it makes your teeth ache? You love it, but you can't take too much."

His deep chuckle moved across her skin and she shivered.

"That's why I had to walk you back to your motel. Kauai is dangerous country."

Julia couldn't let that go. She turned to cast him a skeptical glance. "Right. A kukui tree tried to mug me on the way in this morning."

He grinned.

Good, she thought. She hadn't even twitched.

"There're dangers everywhere. You can't be cheap with your emotions here. The island won't let you." He ran the tip of his finger the length of her jaw, then traced the curve of her neck—a searing line of heat. "How much are you willing to spend, Julia?" Her name on his lips was a husky whisper.

Uh-oh. Time for a conversational detour. "That hotel over there." She pointed. "I'd love to stay there, but I guess it costs a bundle."

She frowned. Did she sound wistful? Wistful was bad. She should sound contemptuous of any place that cost more than $39.99 plus tax per night. She called up Dad's mantra—*A bathroom, a bed, that's all anyone needs.*

Her frown deepened. Dad. This was all his fault. He was the one who'd insisted she could make Dylan Connally toe the mark. *Huh. Not likely.* She knew zip about theme parks, had never even been to one. Theme parks came under the heading of extravagant spending for Dad. And after she had gotten old enough to pay her own way . . . Well, theme parks were for kids, weren't they?

Cost cutting? Sure, she knew about that. Dad had taught her the power of saving a buck. He had the first penny he'd ever made. He had a lot of people's first pennies. She banished that cynical thought.

"This must be your motel. It's the cheapest one around."

"Huh?" She blinked. "Oh, yes." She cast one last glance at the shining hotel in the distance. Room service, satin sheets. Plush carpet, satin sheets. Panoramic views, satin sheets. *Hmm.* There seemed to be a pattern forming here.

Looking away from the hotel, she gazed up at Dylan, a living, breathing pirate who'd already managed to steal a big chunk of her peace of mind. She cherished the little that was left.

He plucked a feathery red blossom, then carefully tucked it behind her ear. He skimmed the length of her hair, running his fingers through the strands, and like a serious attack of static electricity, she felt the tingle in every nerve ending.

"It's ohia-lehua. In early Hawaii, the blossoms were considered sacred. Chiefs made leis of them for Pele, the volcano goddess." He grinned. "Suits you." He walked away.

Kauai was beautiful. She couldn't deny the undeniable as she touched the flower.

Watching him stride away, she admitted another truth. She'd wanted to go on a spending spree all her life. And like a lifetime dieter, she had to beat back the temptation daily. Her fear? Dylan Connally had *outrageously expensive* stamped on every delicious inch of his body.

The next morning Julia shuffled out of the bathroom feeling only marginally less tired than the day before. She should've been too exhausted even to turn over during the night, but her dreams of a broad, tanned chest exposed by an open pirate shirt refused to leave her.

Flop. On her back, staring at the ceiling. The smile transfixed her.

Flop. On her side, staring at the bureau mirror. Those hazel eyes taunted her.

Flop. On her stomach. *Hah!* She wouldn't see anything now. Wrong. Dylan Connally's total amazing package stared at her from the white surface of the pillow. *Give it up.* She needed a cup of coffee.

Candy stood in the middle of the motel room, her petite form rigid, arms outstretched, eyes closed.

Julia walked around her stepmother, then poured herself a cup of coffee. Caffeine. She'd need all the stimulation she could get today. *Hmm, stimulation.* No, she wouldn't go there.

She sat down on the bed and asked the question she knew her stepmother had been waiting for her to ask. "What're you doing?"

Candy took a deep breath, opened her eyes, then relaxed. She reached for her cup of herbal tea. "Visualizing you."

"Good." No harm in visualizing.

"With a man." Candy smoothed her gauzy purple nightgown. The shiny gold moons and stars scattered across its surface made Julia blink.

Nothing new. Candy was always visualizing her with a man.

"He's tall, dark, with long hair, and he'll fulfill your sensual destiny."

Julia carefully set her cup on the nightstand. "I think I see where you're headed, and that road's closed for lack of interest." Would her nose start growing now?

Candy fluffed up her bright red hair, then cast Julia a sly glance. "I've placed you both within a protective white light. Together."

Oh, no. Trapped in a white light with Mr. Spare-no-expense Connally. "It won't work, you know."

Candy took a sip of tea. "He's very big."

109

"Right. Broad shoulders, yadda, yadda." She sounded indifferent. Too bad she didn't feel the same way.

Candy cast her an impatient glance. "No. I mean he's very *big*." She made the appropriate shape with her hands.

Great. She could look forward to another restful night. Flop. She'd land on her belly and come face-to-whatever with Mr. Big. She could already feel the heat level rising. "Give me a break, Candy. You have no way of knowing that."

Candy moved deliberately toward the bathroom, but before she closed the door she flung an unarguable dart at her stepdaughter. "Gifted psychics know these things."

It was going to be a long day.

Julia dressed carefully while Candy hummed what sounded like a Gregorian chant in the shower.

Jeans. No shorts for her. Too exposed. Plain white blouse. One button undone to indicate casual indifference. No more than one. Two buttons might give him the impression she was interested, which she wasn't. Sturdy walking shoes to show him she was ready to get down to the business of cutting the fat from *his* business. She liked that image. Of course, he personally had no fat to cut. She'd noticed that.

By the time Julia had dressed, Candy emerged from the steamy bathroom. Her stepmother cast Julia a long-suffering look. "I suppose your clothes are meant to proclaim your complete obliviousness to the male animal?"

Julia sighed. "They're just comfortable clothes. No statement." *Liar.*

"Hmm." Candy picked up her tarot cards, which were wrapped in silk. "Perhaps a reading might get to the bottom of this."

"No!" Thank heavens Candy had to do her yoga and wouldn't be tagging along with her this morning.

"You're resistent to the spirit guides trying to help you fulfill your destiny, dear."

"Guides? What guides?" Julia cast a quick glance to either side of her. Sometimes Candy was downright scary.

Candy closed her eyes. "I see one now. He has sideburns, a pompadour, and is so bright I can hardly watch him."

"Sequins."

"Sequins?" Candy's eyes popped open.

"You're seeing Elvis. Probably one of the waiters at the club you dragged me to the other night. Blue Hawaii, wasn't it? I can't believe you talked me into that group-hypnotism session."

Candy brightened. "Wonderful. Imagine. Elvis is your spirit guide."

"Sheesh. Elvis is *not* my spirit guide." And Elvis had not *winked* at her over Dylan's shoulder. Dylan had said that Elvis wasn't programmed to wink, and she believed him on that. *Only* that. Not other things. *Definitely* not other things.

Candy's gaze turned thoughtful. "Are you sure you don't remember the suggestion?"

Julia edged toward the door. "Nope. Everything's sort of vague and blurry." *Vague and blurry, hah.* The truth? She'd been so tired from the plane ride she'd fallen asleep the minute the lights had dimmed and hadn't wakened until the hypnotist snapped his fingers. She'd never admit it to Candy, the Energizer Bunny of the baby boomer set, because Candy would just brew up some noxious potion for her. Julia had experience with Candy's potions.

"Vague and blurry?" Candy grinned. "Good. Oh, I have a few errands for you to run before you see Mr. Connally." She pulled out a list that in Julia's mind almost reached the floor.

"Fine." Julia grabbed the list. Talk about opposites attracting. Candy spent money as though it were her sole duty to keep the world's economy afloat, and Dad never said a word. *Go figure.* At least Candy's errands would give her time to ready her ammunition for Wonder World's free-spending owner.

"I don't know about the vampire outfit, Malia." Dylan studied his secretary. "Undead isn't you. Too tanned, too—"

Malia glared at him. "I'm a big woman. You have something against big vampires?"

"Hey, I love big vampires, but most vampires I've seen look sorta . . . unhealthy. Guess it's their basic blood diet. You look way too healthy, Malia." *Whew.*

"Like I had another choice, boss?" Malia's gaze narrowed. "Werewolves have fuzzy faces. No way I do the tweezer thing at home, then come to work and glue hair back on my face. And ghosts wear white. White's fattening. And I don't do mummies. Daddies, maybe, but not mummies." She grinned.

Dylan breathed out on a gust of impatience. Bad jokes were the price he paid for having his office in the Haunted Castle.

Okay, so he insisted everyone in the park dress in costume. He watched Malia study one of her perfectly manicured, inch-long nails. Okay, so the nails matched the outfit.

"I'll be out for most of the day, Malia. Have to make sure Julia Raine doesn't turn my Rock 'n' Roll Legends into Toon Town. Oh, and if Raddock calls, tell him to go to hell."

Malia's attention never wavered from her nail. "Should I schedule that for A.M. or P.M.?"

Dylan raked his fingers through his hair. "I don't give a damn." He turned toward the door, which was disguised as an iron maiden.

"One more thing, boss."

He almost groaned. He couldn't take one more thing.

"There's someone waiting in your office." She shuffled some papers on her desk, which was disguised as a coffin.

"Who? Why didn't you stop them? That's in your job description. It's even on your desk." He pointed to the small nameplate. "Malia. Keeper of the Gate to Hell."

Malia avoided his gaze. "Couldn't stop her. Threatened to break all my nails if I got in her way." She made a moue of apology. "A girl's gotta protect her best assets. Can't let loyalty get in the way."

"Right. No loyalty. Remind me of this when it's time to negotiate your next raise."

Dylan flung open his office door, stepped inside, then slammed the door shut behind him.

The overpowering scent of vanilla pushed him back against the door, and he glared at the lit candle glowing happily on his desk. Then he glared at the woman sitting next to his desk.

Must be a full moon tonight. The stars dangled from her ears. Every stone known to man and some he suspected had originated on alien planets hung from her neck. She was petite, with purple shorts and red hair. *Hmm. Trouble.*

He opened his office door and pointed. "Out. Whatever you're selling, I don't want any."

Her smile said she was serenely unimpressed. "I don't think you want me leaving right now. Julia just came in toting a whole list of major changes for your park. You need my help." Her smile widened. "Oh, and I'm Candy, Julia's stepmother."

He peered out the door, then slammed it shut again. *Rats.*

"I admire *big* men secure in their masculinity." Her gaze drifted down his body, then stopped.

Uh-oh.

From outside, Julia's voice drifted through the door. "Why can't I see him? I told him— Ohmigod! Those spiders are a foot wide."

Candy sighed. "But that's not why I'm here. There's something you need to know. Julia will disturb your cosmic balance, but she has the potential—under the right guidance—to release her inner passion and become one with the universe. She needs you to channel her inner sensuality in a way that will create a calm, fulfilled aura. I hope you're a Scorpio."

"Huh?" Dylan scowled. How could he concentrate with Julia making all that noise?

"I demand to see him right— Did you know there's a severed head in the file drawer you just opened?"

Dylan massaged the bridge of his nose. "Get to the point."

Candy blinked at him. "Let me guess, a Taurus." Her smile

returned. "Anyway, I love Julia like she was my own, and I want her to be happy. At her age I was a slave to passion, but she's just a slave to her store, Cheap Chic. Every woman should experience some lust in her life. What do you think?"

"Right. Lust is good."

Julia's voice grabbed his attention once again. "I think I need to use your rest room."

He drew in a deep breath of inevitability.

"We're going to do each other a favor." Candy rooted through her purple beaded purse, then pulled out a tape of Elvis's greatest hits. "Elvis is the answer."

And here he hadn't even heard the question. *Oh, boy.* Where was his faithful secretary, she of the inch-long nails able to rip out Godzilla's heart at a single swipe?

He forgot about Malia, though, as Julia's shriek shattered the semisilence. "The ghost of Alfred Hitchcock is sitting on your toilet! Ghosts don't need to go. I do."

Candy looked unconcerned. "She's screaming, so she's alive. Anyway, Julia has a small cosmic blip in her personality. She becomes passionate when she hears Elvis sing." She thrust a purple-nailed finger at his chest. "Passionate with the nearest man when the music begins. That's going to be you, handsome."

Crazy. The woman was crazy. But a part of his body that shouldn't be listening was starting to pay attention.

Julia's voice sounded faintly through the door. "I think I'll sit on your couch for a moment . . . as soon as I pry this body part from between the cushions. Where should I put it?"

Candy droned on. "It's a win-win situation. You distract Julia from cutting all your expensive upgrades, and Julia experiences a fun time with a good-looking man."

She gave him no chance to respond as she put down the tape and hurried from his office. He heard Julia's surprised exclamation before he quietly closed the door behind Candy.

What a crock of . . . Then he remembered. The kiss. The

heat of her body pressed to his. The sweetness of her mouth. *She'd* kissed *him*.

When? He closed his eyes. Elvis. "Mean Woman Blues." His eyes popped open. *Impossible.* Then a surprising stab of disappointment. If what Candy said was true, then Julia's . . . enthusiasm had been Elvis-induced, not for him at all.

Dylan glanced at the Elvis tape. Tempting, but he still had some ethics. He slipped the tape into a drawer, then blew out the candle with more enthusiasm than the act warranted.

Maybe he had a few cosmic blips in his own personality. He liked vanilla; he just didn't like it rammed down his throat—or up his nose, in this case.

He'd spent a lifetime battling to build his park, to be himself. He'd thought the battle was over, but he was wrong. First Julia's father, now Julia. And if that wasn't enough, Phil Raddock, like a damned hyena, was still sneaking around in hopes of being in on the kill. The slimeball thought that if Dylan went belly-up, he could move in and buy the park cheap.

Not in this lifetime. He yanked open the desk drawer and pulled out the tape. Slipping it into his jeans pocket, he turned toward the door . . . and found Julia watching him.

Chapter Two

"Why is a ghost sitting on your toilet?" Impatiently, Julia shoved aside the feathery cobweb from the doorway.

"For fun. When was the last time you had fun, Julia?"

She ignored his question. "He won't get off the seat, and I have to go. Get rid of him."

Without comment, Dylan walked over to a bank of switches and flipped one off.

"Thank you." She headed back to the rest room, but paused midway. "Any other surprises in there?"

"Depends on what surprises you." He grinned.

As soon as she disappeared, he went to Malia, who was carefully buffing her nails. Pulling out the tape, he handed it to his secretary. "Don't ask questions. As soon as we leave, run this over to Lynn in Jungle Land. Tell her when I rake my fingers through my hair, she plays that baby."

Malia stopped buffing. "Elvis? What's going on?"

"The less you know, the better. That way you won't give any information away under torture." He smiled at her.

Malia tucked the tape into her black cape. She tried on her hurt-feelings look. "Suit yourself. *I* don't care if you don't want to confide in your dedicated secretary, your devoted workhorse." The workhorse went back to buffing her nails.

"Come off it, Malia. I—" He was saved the job of soothing Malia as Julia emerged from the rest room.

"You forgot to turn off a few other things in there, Connally. Like the demon living in the toilet paper roll. Oh, and the witch who thinks flushing is a real cackle." She reached him and stood, hands on hips, glaring. "You are a certifiable—"

"Genius," Malia supplied.

Startled, Julia looked at her.

"Yep. The boss did every hologram, every special effect in the park. He can do anything."

Dylan was touched.

Julia looked skeptical.

"He has an IQ that's off the charts. His dad told me he graduated from college when he was seventeen. His dad said—"

"Enough, Malia."

She subsided into grumbling complaint. "I just wanted her to know you're no weirdo, boss."

He could almost see the curiosity bubbling in Julia's gaze.

"Let's get out of here." Without giving Julia a chance to question, he guided her toward the door. "Malia, we're taking a short walk, then heading over to Jungle Land." He didn't wait for Malia's reply before closing the door behind him.

Julia blinked in the bright morning light. Geniuses weren't supposed to look like Dylan Connally, were they? With all that power going to their brains, shouldn't the rest of them be withered and uninteresting?

She allowed herself to fall a few steps behind, then studied the situation. Hmm, shorts this morning, not baggy. Strong legs and amazing buns . . .

"So, no costume today?" *No* tight tush could generate this

117

much heart-pounding, mouthwatering excitement. Even Louis-the-liar Kinsey, the prenup and divorce lawyer she'd thought herself in love with, couldn't mobilize her take-it-or-leave-it sexual urges into an organized fighting unit.

He glanced over his shoulder. "Nope. Today I'm me."

"And who is *me?*" Buns of steel? No. They'd be firm, smooth, but she'd be able to sink her fingers into them, feel—

"*Me* is whoever I want to be. You should try it sometime." He kept walking. "Want to tell me about some of your ideas?"

Amazing buns. "Hot buns."

"What?" He swung to face her, cutting off her view, and re-engaging her brain.

Lordy, give me inspiration. "I . . . was thinking that the park needs a hot-bun stand."

"Hot buns?" For the first time he truly looked puzzled.

"Yes." She warmed to her subject. "People go crazy over cinnamon buns with lots of icing and nuts. I love to lick off the icing." The mental picture was too much. She popped open the second button on her blouse. Who cared what he thought.

"Gotcha. Licking is good." He moved closer.

His old T-shirt with the sleeves and bottom cut off shouldn't be sexy, but the close-up of muscled biceps and peekaboo view of flat stomach had her reaching for her third button, and damn the consequences.

He touched her bottom lip with the tip of one finger. "The repetitive motion of licking calms, relieves stress." He traced the shape of her lip, then dropped his hand and turned away.

Calming? Julia didn't think so. She was left standing there with her mouth open and her lips alive with possibilities.

He turned and grinned at her. She'd forgotten the power of his smile. "You said you liked ice cream. I'm in the mood."

Following him toward a battered old ice-cream truck, she tried to dredge up her ideas for the park. It didn't take a genius to realize she needed a change of topic. *Remember why you're here.* She *had* to make him see reason.

"I have a few ideas to make the park more cost-effective. I noticed that the monkeys—"

"What flavor do you want?"

Glancing up at the sound of Dylan's impatient question, she shrugged. "Doesn't matter. Now about those monkeys—"

"Why not try a cone of my Sensuous Strawberry ice cream? It'll set you on the right path for a glorious day."

The ice-cream man's voice broke her concentration. Darn, she'd have to discuss the monkeys later. Dylan had done this on purpose. Well, no ice-cream cone would get in her way. "I'll pass on the cone, thank you. Okay, Dylan, let's get down to monkey talk."

Dylan raised one brow, then turned back to the ice-cream man. "I'll have a strawberry cone. Double dip."

Frustrated, Julia finally looked at the ice-cream man, willing him to disappear so she could get on with her agenda.

Fuzzy dark hair framed a face with eyes . . . What color *were* his eyes? He smiled. "I'd say you need something to cool what's hot and bothered in your heart."

He looked away to hand Dylan his cone. Something about him disturbed Julia. Almost as if he knew . . .

"You're missing a real treat. My strawberry ice cream is just short of paradise." He winked at her. "And I'm an expert on paradise."

The man reached into his truck. "Met a cat a while back who didn't like my music. Got real upset and did a job on my recorder. It goes out on me every once in a while. Think I have it fixed now. Can't have an ice-cream truck without music." He chuckled, then pressed a button. Elvis's voice drifted from the loudspeaker bemoaning the tragedy of "Suspicious Minds."

Let's hear it for the cat. "Why the heck is everyone so fixated on Elvis around here?" Julia asked no one in particular.

119

The ice-cream man climbed into his truck. "Guess it's natural. *Blue Hawaii* was filmed close by." He pointed in the general direction of the hotel with the satin sheets she'd fantasized about the day before. "Good luck and enjoy the ice cream." He leaned out of his truck to take another order.

"That wasn't the usual vendor."

The sound of Dylan's voice so close behind her startled Julia. She turned and came face-to-face with Dylan's cone. As Elvis's voice wrapped around her, she watched a drop of ice cream melt and start to slide down the cone. Instinctively she leaned forward and licked the drop before it could reach Dylan's fingers. *Umm. Delicious.* She'd never tasted . . .

Glancing up, she met Dylan's gaze across the width of the cone. Breathing room. She needed breathing room. Something hot and searching moved in his eyes. Surprised, she noticed the cone hadn't dissolved into a creamy puddle.

"There's a strawberry on this side, Julia." His husky voice tempted. His smile invited, promised.

Okay, the Garden of Eden had its apple, and Wonder World had its strawberry. Who was she to resist? Moving closer so she could reach his side of the cone, she drew the ripe fruit into her mouth, then chewed slowly, savoring every trickle of flavor.

Juice covered her lips, and she drew her tongue across them. Nothing could taste this . . .

Glancing up, she realized Dylan had moved the cone from between them. His gaze riveted on her lips, he was heedless of a small smear of ice cream on his own.

Fine, so maybe something could taste as . . . She didn't think. This wasn't a thinking situation. She leaned forward and slid her tongue across his lower lip. He tasted of cool strawberry and hot male.

"You started it." He dropped the remainder of his melting cone and wrapped his arms around her.

Elvis asked, "Are You Sincere?" Who cared about sincere? This was pure, raw *want. Make that a double dip.*

Expensive lips. Definitely out of her price range. There was nothing tentative about them. Strong, they demanded a response from her. Soft and smooth as silk, they seduced her senses. The taste of strawberry would always trigger this memory; she knew it with every despairing inch of her soul.

She couldn't help herself. When he opened his mouth to deepen the kiss, she took the invitation and entered, exploring the soft lining of his mouth, tasting the sweetness, the heat, feeling his small start of surprise.

Drawing in a deep breath, she broke contact. Was she crazy? Two days and she'd kissed him twice. *She'd* kissed *him*. Even in her hormone-driven teen years, she'd never been this involved in a kiss. Kisses had been wet, dry, or yawn. But never like this.

Moving away from his magnetic field, she noted that Elvis's voice had faded and the ice-cream truck had finally left.

Without speaking, Dylan guided her down a quiet path, avoiding the milling crowds filling the park.

Casting Dylan a quick glance, she strove for normalcy. "So, about those monkeys."

"Right. Monkeys." If he'd had doubts before, they were gone. Elvis had worked. Okay, so he'd been a willing participant, but she'd started it. Well, maybe he'd encouraged her a little. Very little.

Candy had been right. Guilt poked at him, and, okay, disappointment. She hadn't reacted to *him*. Maybe he should just toss the tape. After all, once she listened to his side of the story, she'd give up on this—"

"Fake monkeys."

"What?" Startled, he looked across at her.

"You have *real* monkeys in Jungle Land. Think of the cost in food, vet bills. Besides, monkeys are dirty. The cost of cleanup must be substantial."

He could almost see her mental debit column with the heading *Miscellaneous: Monkey Business.*

121

How could she do that? Go from a spectacular kiss to . . . monkeys?

"You need fake monkeys. They'd keep the ambiance with none of the expense of real ones. You could find someone who'd make them with waterproof material. All you'd need to do is play some recorded monkey cries over the sound system." Her gaze turned thoughtful. "If you buy in bulk it'll be more cost-effective."

"Fake monkeys." His guilt evaporated in a surge of anger.

"Oh, and you have *real* plants. I bet you spend a fortune on groundskeeping fees." She tilted her head to glance up at the towering palms above her. "The trees can stay."

"Thanks." She had no idea death walked beside her.

"Hmm. Silk plants are pretty, but don't last outside." She rubbed the back of her neck.

Her neck. He should be thinking about his fingers tightening around it, but for some reason he could only imagine his lips touching the warm skin behind her ear.

"Got it." She radiated triumph. "Plastic. They do wonderful things with plastic nowadays. Realistic, and all you have to do is hose it down to get rid of dust and grime. You'd have the first theme park with a plastic forest."

"Right. Customers would flock to the park by the thousands." *Now* he was thinking about his fingers tightening.

He pulled her to a halt in the middle of the flagstone walkway wending through thick tree ferns and colorful exotic flowers. The sounds of laughing people on nearby paths faded. "Stop to smell the frangipani, Julia." Reaching up, he plucked a delicate pink bloom and held it to her nose. "Sniff. Will your plastic have the scent of the tropics—ripe, erotic?"

"Oh." Those killer eyes widened as she took the flower from him and nestled it in her hands.

His brain processed the picture, then ordered the appropriate body part on hard-alert. No amount of counterorders could stop the inevitable tightening at the thought of her holding him

in her cupped palms, looking at him with the same soft wonder.

She lifted the bloom to her nose, her lips, then closed her
eyes on a low moan of appreciation. And for one unbelievable
moment, he considered buying fake monkeys by the truckload
if he could cover her body with his and hear that moan for
him—not Elvis, for *him*.

Wake-up call. This wasn't about hard or soft body parts.
This was about a battle plan to save his park. *Remember that.*

She lowered the bloom, then sighed. "It's magical." Smiling, she tucked the flower behind her ear, the way he'd done
yesterday. "When I was a kid, lilacs grew near our apartment.
The scent was so beautiful it would almost make me cry."
She slanted him a searching glance. "Stupid, huh?"

He shook his head. "Nothing that makes you happy is stupid."

She gave him her full attention. "What makes *you* happy?"

"This park." *Watching you.*

A frown drew a fine line down the center of her forehead.
He resisted the urge to trace its path with his fingertip.

"But Malia said you were a genius, that you could be anything—a doctor, a scientist."

Now it was his turn to frown. "Malia says too much." He
exhaled sharply. "What's your definition of success, Julia?"

She shrugged. "Doing what I want and doing it well."

"Good." He adjusted her flower to a more secure position,
then made sure the back of his hand slid across the soft planes
of her cheek. This need to touch her was getting kind of scary.

No. Not a need. Touching her was just part of his plan. He
could stop touching her anytime he wanted. He mentally
snapped his fingers. "Dad is a CEO, has ulcers, and wants to
retire to Hawaii in a few years so he can have some fun. Mom
is a stockbroker. Had a nervous breakdown about ten years
ago. Sis is a neurosurgeon with stress-induced migraines.
She'd like to retire to Hawaii in about twenty years."

He grinned. "I always wanted to have a theme park, live

on Kauai, and have fun." He turned and started walking away from her. "Who's the success, Julia?"

She ran to catch up. "Okay, I get the point. But I think there's more to your story."

"There's always more to everyone's story." *Damn.* Why had he told her all that crap? She was the enemy. He'd better not let his body dictate terms or he might find himself negotiating a surrender. "Let's go. I have to be in Jungle Land by ten. You can tell the monkeys your plans."

She puffed to keep up. "I was wrong about the plants."

He stopped so suddenly that she plowed into him. Instinctively she put her hands on his waist to steady herself. His bare waist. The suppleness of firm flesh and warm skin beneath her fingers derailed her train of thought.

Appreciatively, she slid her fingers around the curve of his waist to the indentation of his spine, then dropped her hand. But not before she felt his sharp intake of breath.

Yes! Why did that make her so happy? Sheesh, he'd just taken a deep breath. He hadn't proclaimed undying love for her. Love? No, love and Dylan Connally didn't belong in the same sentence, the same paragraph, the same darn *book.*

He'd taken a deep breath because . . . he was allergic to spores. He didn't need *her*; he needed his inhaler.

Turning, he stared at her. "You changed your mind?"

Looking away, she carefully studied the play of shadows on a nearby rock. *His back. Rock hard, yet smooth, yielding.* "The way plants grow here, you won't need fakes or extra groundskeepers if—"

She felt his frustration. It hit her in waves of impatience. "Somehow I knew there'd be an *if.*"

Julia glanced at him, met his gaze. "Just listen. You have all this vegetation in neat groups, all arranged like some garden. This place needs to be wild, untamed. Its beauty needs to be *free.*" She didn't like the way he watched her, like some large jungle cat stalking its prey.

She rushed into speech. "Let it grow wild. Clear paths, but let the rest go. Give visitors the true feel of a jungle."

"Do you need to be wild, untamed?" His husky question scattered her thoughts.

"Of course not." She reached for her fourth button.

Suddenly he laughed. "I like your idea. I can't believe I just said that."

Her feeling of triumph was all out of proportion to his admission, but she sensed any win was a big win where Dylan Connally was concerned.

"Hi, folks. Hope I'm not intruding." One of the flowers stepped into their path.

Julia blinked. No, not a flower, a man. A tall stick of a man. Ichabod Crane in a Hawaiian shirt and neon green shorts.

"How did you find us, Raddock?"

Had Julia thought Dylan hot a second ago? Hot enough to force her to reach for a fourth button? He'd turned downright glacial at the sight of the walking flower-man.

"Now don't get cranky, Connally. Malia let it drop you were out on this trail." His smile was a mile wide and as insincere as the Mattress Monster's annual going-out-of-business sale.

"Malia did that?" Dylan's tone spoke of betrayal.

"Guess she was a mite distracted at the time." The flower-man studied Julia with bright-eyed interest. "She was trying on that new designer shade of nail polish I brought her."

"Right. Nail polish. You're low, Raddock."

Raddock nodded happily and continued to stare at Julia. "You must be Ms. Raine. Heard you were coming. We have a lot in common, little lady."

Little lady? Julia ground her teeth on the urge to kick him in one of his very knobby knees.

The flower continued on, blissfully ignoring her glare. "I like things run cheap. You like things run cheap. Convince your daddy to pull his investment money and this place'll fold. Then I can buy it cheap. With his investment money, and me

125

spending it careful-like, we'll make a real killing.''

With all those *cheap*s in his little speech, Raddock sounded like a bird. A stork? Not a flower, a stork.

Julia was still considering the merits of flower or bird when Raddock hit the ground.

"You hit me, Connally. I'll have your butt in court for this. Watch me.'' He glared up at Dylan.

"No one hit you, Raddock. You just slipped on your own slime. Now get out of my park.''

"You saw him hit me, didn't you, little lady?'' The flower-stork tried to look pitiful.

Julia widened her eyes. "I'm sorry, but I didn't see what happened. I was thinking. About birds and flowers and . . .''

Now she had Dylan's attention.

"Anyway, I didn't catch the action, *little man*.'' She smiled at Raddock.

Raddock scrambled to his feet. "Maybe I'll just go straight to the money. Your daddy'll listen to me. He'll know a good deal when he hears it.'' With that threat hanging in the air, he disappeared into the undergrowth.

Dylan drew in a deep breath, then smiled at Julia. "Sorry about that. Ever since the park started turning a profit, he's been sniffing around, making offers. Not the type to take no for an answer.'' His expression grew thoughtful. "I'm surprised, though. I thought you'd jump at the chance to work with someone who had the same vision as you.''

"The same vision?'' She swallowed her distaste at being compared to Raddock.

"Yeah. Both of you want to cut the park to bare bones. Make a bigger profit.'' He continued walking down the path, and she fell into step beside him.

More people hurried by, forcing Julia to press against Dylan's side to let them pass. She felt the tension, the frisson of excitement each time they touched. Mentally shoring up her resolve, she refused to wimp out and move away from him.

"That's not fair. I don't want to cut anything to 'bare

bones.' I just want to make the park cost-effective." *But isn't that what Dad wants? What he sent me to do?*

"Don't you ever have the urge to spend, Julia? To buy things you don't really need just because they'll make you feel good?" He didn't glance at her, didn't stop walking.

Yes! I want to check in to that hotel I saw. I want to get the most expensive suite. I want to lie on the king-size bed surrounded by soft pillows and black satin sheets. I want you naked on that bed with me. "Nope. Never."

She felt his disappointment. "Too bad." He pointed to a clearing ahead. "We're almost there."

Julia gasped when they finally emerged into the open area. *Perfect.* Lush green vegetation and brilliant flowers surrounded a small lake so blue it hurt her eyes. Monkeys chattered from surrounding trees, and colorful birds flitted in and out of the shadows.

Hmm, birds. Maybe she wouldn't tell him about her idea. Okay, so artificial birds that flapped their wings and squawked when the wind blew didn't have quite the . . . ambiance of the real thing. But she still liked her monkey idea. The real monkeys did look sorta cute, though.

Glancing around, she realized that while she'd been lost in thought, Dylan had disappeared, and a noisy, jostling crowd of people had collected along the edge of the lake.

"Great show. Tarzan dives from that cliff up there into the lake with all those crocodiles."

Julia turned at the sound of the woman's voice. "Tarzan? Crocodiles? Where?" She looked up at a waterfall that tumbled into the lake from a towering cliff. A small ledge stuck out at the top of the cliff.

She had no time to process the information, because without warning Dylan appeared on the ledge to the cheers of the still-growing crowd. A loincloth. All he wore was a loincloth.

Poised on the edge of the cliff, his muscular body was the focus of everyone's attention in the suddenly quiet crowd. Dread settled in Julia's stomach. He'd have to be crazy to try . . .

She wanted to close her eyes, but they seemed superglued open, because above and beyond the horror, she was fascinated.

Dylan dared all, grabbed for his dream. He didn't spend his life in little dribs and drabs. He was one of life's high rollers when it came to what he wanted.

A scary concept, but one that held the temptation of forbidden fruit. And because she was tempted, Julia fell back on her anger for protection. *How dare he endanger himself—*

He dove from the ledge, his body arcing gracefully above the lake, then cutting into the water with barely a ripple. She waited breathlessly for his head to appear, and when it did she felt weak with relief.

This diving thing had to stop. She made a conscious effort to still her shaking hands. They'd hire a stuntman to do the dive. To hell with the cost. *She'd* pay for the stuntman.

Her relief was short-lived. Blunt snouts broke the surface, moving toward Dylan.

"Maybe they'll get him this time," a bloodthirsty bystander whispered wistfully. "See that big croc over there? It almost took a piece outa his tasty tush last time I was here."

No! That tasty tush was hers. Hers? No time for deep thoughts on possessive pronouns. Taking a deep breath, Julia grabbed a short stick and waded into the lake.

"Swim, Dylan! I'll save you." The water had reached waist-high, and in the background she heard the crowd cheer. "And we're buying fake crocodiles. Damn it! Do you hear me? *Fake* crocodiles." The water took her feet from under her and she had to swim, leaving no breath to explain that she could get the crocodiles wholesale at Ephram's Exotics. Realistic. Waterproof. *Safe.*

Suddenly he was beside her, lifting her from the water and carrying her ashore to the hoots and whistles of the audience.

She leaned her head against his tanned chest and shuddered at how close he'd come to . . . "Don't you ever do that again, Dylan Connally. We're getting fake crocodiles and a stuntman. This is *not* negotiable." For absolutely no reason she could think of, tears trickled down her cheeks.

For a moment she didn't recognize the deep rumble for what it was. An eruption in Volcano Land? No. She glanced up at, then away from Dylan's face. The lowlife was *laughing* at her.

"They *are* fake, Julia." He lowered his head and kissed her forehead.

Startled, she looked at him. "You were very brave. Thank you." He set her on her feet, then moved away from her.

Not far enough. The crowd had drifted away, leaving them isolated in their small pocket of jungle with only the silence.

Julia's heart slowed; her breathing calmed. Then she looked at Dylan.

His loincloth. She fixed her gaze on this one safe island in a sea of woman-eating bare male. He took a step toward her, and she watched the movement beneath the small piece of cloth. Maybe not so safe. *Hmm.* It looked like Candy's size estimate was pretty close.

"Hey, you wanted cheap."

She lifted her gaze to the amused glitter in his eyes.

"You can't get cheaper than this unless—"

She was way ahead of him. "Take that off and you're dead." *Take it off. Please, please, please take it off.* "Besides, we have to talk about serious stuff like . . . monkeys."

She watched his gaze harden. "So we're back to cutting costs." He moved closer and, as in a ritualistic dance, she took the appropriate step back. "Look around you and tell me all this should be fake."

She couldn't have looked away from him if her life depended on it, and she had the stomach-churning feeling that it just might.

Chapter Three

Slick and beautiful, Dylan watched her with an intensity that had her expecting to see steam rising from her soaked and clinging blouse. She glanced down. Ohmigod, she looked like two Hershey's Kisses wrapped in a plastic baggy. She crossed her arms over her chest, then returned her attention to him.

His skin glistened as moisture beaded and wound in interesting paths down his broad chest. One diamond-bright drop lingered on his nipple, and she swallowed hard as it slid off and moved in slow motion over the flat planes of his stomach, only to disappear into the top of his loincloth.

She forced her gaze from the loincloth. *Talk.* She had to say something to drown out the staccato beat of her heart.

"This is really amazing." She looked around at the palms, the riot of colors, the vibrant green everywhere, but her gaze was a homing pigeon returning to roost as it settled once again on his loincloth, which continued to take on size and shape.

Babbling would be a good thing now. "This place reminds me of a lake I went to when I was a teen. I'd swim all day,

130

then scare myself silly walking in the woods at night searching for the Jersey Devil. I never found him," she finished lamely.

"Maybe you looked in the wrong place." He moved closer, so close she could smell the warm, musky scent of his skin, feel his damp heat touching her. Illogically, she shivered.

"Were you really hunting the Jersey Devil, or were you hunting men?" His question was a husky murmur.

He almost touched her now, but her brain remained out to lunch, ignoring her frantic orders to move away. "That's ridiculous." Then why could she feel warmth flooding her cheeks?

He smiled. "All women hunt. Like tigresses. A tigress stalks her prey without thought. She knows only hunger."

"I've never heard such sexist drivel. The only things I hunt are bargains." *Take that.*

She could almost feel the shimmer of sexual tension dissolve as he drew in a deep breath. "Right. Bargains. I forgot." He raked his fingers through his hair. "Woman, you drive me crazy."

Before she could investigate that intriguing thought, a noise from the lake swung her around.

No! He hadn't meant to do that. Hadn't meant to signal. She'd been so close. He'd seen the flare in her eyes, the attraction, the *want.* He needed her to come to *him,* not—

Too late. He watched with resignation as Herby the Hippo rose dramatically from the lake, opened his oversize mouth, and in Elvis's voice belted out "Devil in Disguise."

The thought of a devil in disguise must've triggered Julia's fight-or-flight response, because her feet were moving before she even turned and plowed into Dylan.

She wrapped her arms around him and held on, her breath coming in frantic gasps. His own breathing grew labored as the pressure of her body seared him from shoulder to hip. Her nipples were points of pleasure-agony against his chest.

Not again. The King wouldn't win this round. Dylan frowned. *Wait a minute.* When had this become about Elvis and him? It was supposed to be about Julia and his park.

His park. He still had to keep her from undercutting all his years of struggle. But not this way. No more Elvis.

Without the support of his arms, Julia slid down his body, leaving a heated path of regret in his heart.

Coming to rest seated at his feet, she glared up at him. "Thanks for lending a helping hand, Connally. King Arthur wouldn't even let you sit at his square table."

Without answering, Dylan walked around her to the edge of the lake. "Stop the damn music!" he thundered. Silence descended, except for chattering monkeys and the calls of birds.

Returning to Julia, he sat down beside her. But not touching. Never again touching. The thought saddened him.

"You need to understand something about me, Julia." He started to rake his fingers through his hair, but thought better of it. "Because of my IQ, my parents wanted what was best for me. For them, the best was school up the wazoo and exposure to what they thought would make me smarter. No riding my bike and hanging out with other kids when I could be inside exercising my mind. I never fit in anywhere. The kids I went to school with were always a lot older."

He glanced away from the sympathy he knew he'd see in her gaze. He didn't want her damn sympathy, only her understanding. "You know what I missed most? Music. My parents only let me listen to classical music. I never went to a rock concert, never got to hear all the legends I have in my exhibit."

He felt the touch of her hand on his shoulder, and he pulled away. Physical contact with her now could derail his determination to tell her the truth. "Anyway, when I got old enough to make my own decisions, I worked as a software designer just long enough to save some money to start this park."

He finally met her gaze, and the softness he saw there almost kept him from telling her what needed to be told. "*This* is my childhood. Not my second, my first.'' He stood then swept the park with an all-encompassing gesture. ''My favorite? The Rock 'n' Roll Legends. I can go in there at night after everyone's left, sit in those plush seats, and capture part of what I missed.'' Damn, this whole spiel sounded stupid. ''That's why I did what I did.''

''Did what?'' Puzzled, she pursed her lips, and it took every ounce of his self-control to keep from leaning down and . . .

He drew in a deep breath of courage. ''Took advantage of your weakness.''

She still looked puzzled. What if she never remembered what happened when Elvis sang? She'd be a helpless puppet in the hands of someone unscrupulous. Like him.

''You could go to a clinic, talk to a shrink, get rid of this compulsion.'' Lord, he was making a mess of things.

''What . . . compulsion?'' She sounded as if her patience had reached zero gravity.

''You really don't know, do you?'' Somehow that made it all the worse. ''Here it is straight. When you hear Elvis sing, you crawl all over any man who's near you. That's why Candy—''

''Candy?'' she whispered in a do-you-have-any-last-words tone.

He felt sweat beading on his forehead. ''Candy explained about your obsession. She said if I played Elvis, that would distract you from your plans and—''

Julia stood, scraped the grass and dirt from her still-damp clothes, then belted him in the stomach with a right that drove the air from his lungs. ''You thought you could use sex to make me forget why I was here? Of all the cheap, conniving . . .'' Words must have deserted her, because she looked down as she methodically buttoned each of the three top buttons on her blouse. Then without another word, she turned and strode away.

''Oh, hell.'' Dylan raked his fingers through his hair, and behind him he could hear Herby rising once again, winced as

Elvis launched into "Are You Lonesome Tonight?" Why hadn't he played the Elvis game to its finish, saved his park? Now Julia would be out for blood. *His* blood. He'd blown everything because he couldn't stand the thought of her responding to Elvis, not him. Just an ego attack? Maybe. Maybe not. The *not* bothered him.

Wearily, he retrieved his clothes and headed for home. He'd have to think up a new battle plan, and this time he wouldn't let emotion sidetrack him. He'd keep front and center why Julia was here, and what she intended for his park.

Fury carried Julia back to the motel. Fury and . . . *Okay, admit it, hurt.* She'd fallen for his tale of a childhood that wasn't a childhood at all. She'd fallen for his touch, his lips, his body. *Stupid, stupid, stupid.*

First she'd take care of Candy and her meddling; then she'd take care of Dylan Connally. His Rock 'n' Roll Legends would be rock 'n' debris by the time she finished. She might even send Elvis's head to him as a parting gift. She liked that. Shades of ancient wrath and punishment.

She was flame-driven as she flung open the motel door. "Where do you get off sticking your nose in my life, Candy? Tell me, just tell me."

"I can't tell you anything, dear, if you don't give me a chance to speak." Candy calmly continued studying the cards spread in front of her on the bed.

"You told Dylan Connally I lusted after any man I was near when Elvis started singing. Where did you get such a crock of—"

"You *did,* didn't you?" Candy turned over a card and made a moue of disappointment.

Startled, Julia blinked at her stepmother. "Did what?"

"Lusted after Dylan when Elvis sang." Candy continued studying the cards.

Julia moved over beside Candy, willing her stepmother to meet her angry glare. "I did *not* lust after him. Not once."

Candy finally glanced up. "Tsk, tsk, dear. Lying puts wrinkles in your forehead. Really unattractive."

"Do you know what the jerk did? He played Elvis just so he could distract me from cutting costs in his park. That's low."

Candy turned over another card. "That's what's *really* steaming you, isn't it? That it was Wonder World, not you."

Julia refused to go there. "Where'd you get this crazy idea about Elvis and me?"

"The hypnotist." Candy turned over the last card. "Good, good," she murmured.

"Hypnotist?" Julia frowned. "You mean the one at Blue Hawaii, the one with the phony French accent and the runs?"

Candy finally gave Julia her full attention. "Yep. He said you'd feel passionate whenever you heard Elvis sing. He was going to remove the suggestion, but . . ." She shrugged. "Nature called."

"How could you do this to me? I could've been with *anyone* when I heard Elvis. A serial killer, a kidnapper, a *lawyer*." Okay, so she was letting her bad experience with Louis-the-louse color her attitude toward all lawyers.

"But you weren't, dear. You were with one of the sexiest men I've seen in a long time. Don't tell your father I said that." She rose to slip on her purple silk blouse. "You're pale. You need a sexy man in your life to give you some color."

Candy didn't feel a smidgen of guilt. "I wasn't hypnotized. I was so tired after our trip I fell asleep as soon as the hypnotist began and didn't wake up till the end."

Candy beamed. "Wonderful. Monsieur Dupre said you wouldn't remember a thing. Go ahead, enjoy. Let Dylan put some passion in your life. Oh, and if you wear out the first tape, I have two more in the top drawer of the bureau."

"Dylan did not make me passionate." *Truth? He made me pant, drool, and sit up and beg.* "And I can't believe the lowlife would try to take advantage of me when he thought I was hypnotized."

"He didn't know about the hypnotist. I just told him you had a cosmic quirk in your personality."

"Fine. Now he thinks I'm crazy." Which was worse?

"Don't you think it's strange, dear, that Dylan chose to tell you the truth? I wonder why he did that?" Candy's small smile told Julia her stepmother had her own opinion.

"I don't know or care." She did care, more than she wanted to admit. "But I'm glad there's a logical explanation—"

"For the way you felt?" Candy busily stuffed lipstick and a compact into her purse.

"I felt *nothing*. Nope, not me. Sure, I tried to be nice to him for Dad's sake. And look where it got me! Dylan thinks I'm a love machine and Elvis is my button." How would she ever get Dylan to see reason when he thought she was a wacko?

"Hmm." Candy continued stuffing things into her purse. "Whatever you say, dear. If you need me, I'll be getting a massage and having my nails done."

Julia watched her stepmother drive off. "I am *not* hypnotized," she whispered after the departing car. She couldn't be hypnotized. She'd know, wouldn't she?

Suddenly she recognized her feeling. Disappointment. She wanted what she'd felt for Dylan to be real. *Go figure.* Even though she was mad as hell at him, she wanted her pounding heart, her aching excitement, her desire, to be real.

Julia Raine wasn't hypnotized. She'd prove it right now. Pulling an Elvis tape from the drawer, she slipped it into Candy's portable player, then called the motel office and asked them to send over more clean towels. She crossed her fingers they'd send a male. The chances were good, since the maids were off duty. Finally, finger on the play button, she waited.

When the knock came, she drew in a deep breath. Okay, she could do this. "Come in." Her shaky voice embarrassed her.

The door opened. "Gotcha some towels here, lady."

Her finger froze on the play button. *Ugh, yuk, gross.* He

looked like something Buffy the Vampire Slayer cheerfully staked each Tuesday night. She couldn't do it. End of experiment. "Thanks." Grabbing the towels, she closed the door in his face.

When she'd calmed down, she admitted he really hadn't been that bad. Young, pimply . . . The bottom line: he wasn't Dylan Connally. *Julia Raine, you are a weak woman.*

Sighing, she lay back on the bed to wait for Candy. By the time her stepmother returned, maybe she would've figured out how to work with Dylan Connally.

A week. One solid week of following Dylan Connally's incredible butt around Wonder World, trying to make him listen to her ideas. *Fat chance.* He'd been cool, polite, and totally unreceptive. She, on the other hand, had been hot, impolite—okay, bitchy—and would, under the right circumstances, have been totally receptive. She hated to admit that. Men didn't get to her. Total-control Raine. That was her.

The week did have its positive side, though. Not once in the entire week had she heard Elvis. This was good, right? If she were really hypnotized, she wouldn't have even thought once about Dylan's wonderful buns or . . . other things.

So here she stood at the door of Dylan's office feeling like hell. And it was all *his* fault. She should've dreamed of cheap and innovative ways to improve Wonder World without spending oodles of Dad's hard-earned money.

Instead, she'd dreamed she was back in those New Jersey pine forests. Hunting. With the heart and hunger of a tigress, she'd stalked her prey through the tree-shadowed night. She'd finally found him in a moonlit clearing. Waiting. He'd slowly licked his lower lip. In anticipation or fear?

He was nude, and she growled her pleasure as she closed in for the kill. Pulling her quarry to the ground, she devoured him with her tongue, her lips. His cries for mercy went unheeded as she licked a lingering path over those deliciously tight buns. Then . . . then she woke up. *Damn it!*

She'd better get rid of those dreams—easier said than done—because Dylan Connally could prove a lot more expensive to her peace of mind than his blasted park.

And she'd grown up respecting her father's belief that expensive was rarely better, that you could always get the same quality cheaper if you looked long enough. Admittedly, she hadn't seen anything that came even remotely close to Mr. Connally's high-priced equipment, but she hadn't really looked too hard. There was the lawyer, and the accountant from Philly— The door swung open, interrupting her listing of previous bargain-basement lovers.

The "high-priced equipment" towered over her, and she sighed for last night's dream. So wonderful, so futile.

"What the hell do you want?" His silky genie shirt gaped open, allowing her an enticing glimpse of one shadowed nipple.

His growl reminded her of last night, and her mind happily skipped off in that direction. "High-priced equipment." *Oops.*

He kept scowling. "Sit on the witch's cauldron over there and be quiet. I'm discussing business with my *secretary.*"

If his emphasis on *secretary* was meant to intimidate Malia, it didn't work. She continued to admire her green nail polish. "So, boss, I still don't see why you're all bent out of shape."

"*Twice* you've told Raddock where to find me." Dylan spoke through gritted teeth.

Malia shrugged, but she didn't look at him. *Wise move.* Julia knew the power of those eyes. Direct contact was deadly.

"Hey, it was an accident. I'd put on this great polish he gave me, and I just stuck out my arm to admire the color from a distance. Can I help it if he thought I was pointing in a certain direction?" She pushed the gargoyle phone to the left.

"You sold me out for green nail polish."

Sighing, Malia finally looked at him. "Boss, everyone has their price. In everyone's life, something comes along you know you have to have, no matter how much it costs. For me, it's nail polish. What can I say? Are you gonna fire me?'' For the first time, Malia seemed anxious.

No matter how much it costs. Julia cast a furtive glance at Dylan's ''high-priced equipment,'' thought about the tug she'd felt when he told her about his childhood, thought about her growing admiration for what he'd done with Wonder World.

No. She couldn't let him tap into her *real* weakness, her urge to spend recklessly on something she'd enjoy now, but pay on for a lifetime.

Exhaling sharply, Dylan shook his head. ''I guess we all have our weaknesses, Malia.''

Julia smiled, a smile that didn't reach her heart. ''And yours are expensive toys. Right, Dylan?'' Cold. When had she grown so cold? *When I realized the safest way to keep Dylan away from me was to attack his park.*

''Yeah.'' His glance was glacial. ''Since I guess you're here for your search-and-destroy mission, you may as well come with me. Something's wrong with Elvis.''

It always came back to Elvis. ''You need to get over your fixation with him. Why not replace him with the Spice Girls?'' She knew better than to suggest getting rid of the whole exhibit.

The woman had no heart. ''Replace the King? Never. Maybe we need to replace you with a living, breathing person.''

She looked as though he'd hit her, and he couldn't stop his twinge of guilt. Only a twinge.

''I never got too involved with music. When I was growing up, Dad had enough money to buy only essentials. Music wasn't an essential.'' She shrugged. ''I never went crazy over a singer, because then I'd want to buy tapes, and I couldn't.''

''So that's your philosophy? No involvement, no want?''

She looked uneasy. ''I guess.''

Maybe they had something in common. Her childhood didn't sound like a ton of fun either. But there the similarity ended. As soon as he'd escaped, he'd indulged his inner child.

Julia? He'd bet she had a lot of indulging to catch up on.

Thankfully, they reached the Rock 'n' Roll Legends. His chief mechanic and resident genius, Carlos, was standing beside Elvis.

As they approached, Carlos threw his hands into the air. "I have checked him out completely. Everything is working perfectly, but he still does not move. *Nada.*"

A noncommittal comment was called for here, just so Julia wouldn't get the bright idea that since Elvis was broken already, they might as well heave him in the junk heap. "Hmm." *Good.* He sounded hopeful yet cautious, wise yet discreet.

"I guess that means you haven't a clue. Right, Connally?" She grinned at him, and the sudden sparkle of fun in her eyes made him want to kiss her smart mouth until she collapsed at his feet. He drew in a deep breath on that image.

Cocking her head, she slowly circled Elvis. Fascinated, he followed the sway of her hips. *Great hips. Perfect for childbearing. Uh-oh. Dangerous thought zone. Leave area immediately.* He shifted his gaze to her red blouse, buttoned all the way to her neck. He almost smiled. *Obvious, Julia.*

"You might be a super technician, but you really need a lesson in style." She reached out and ran her fingers over Elvis's sequined gold jacket, then continued on to his wide belt with the huge buckle. "You know, I bet the King would love a pair of faded jeans and an old T-shirt. After all these years, he deserves to feel young again, comfortable."

"And the fact that jeans and a T-shirt would be cheap never occurred to you."

She looked startled. "No, it didn't."

He believed her, and his spurt of joy surprised him. She'd said something caring about Elvis, something not attached to cost management. It made him feel damn good. Too good.

Stepping between Elvis and him, she turned to face Dylan. "It doesn't matter, though. I still think the Spice Girls would be a better bet than old Swivel-hips."

The Hunka Hunka and the Penny-Pincher

Without warning, Elvis cranked into action. He swung his guitar into position, and in the process whacked Julia across her rounded bottom. Not a bunt, but a no-doubt-about-it home run. With a yelp of surprise, she shot into Dylan's waiting arms.

No one could ever say he wasn't open to opportunity. Closing his arms around her, he stared into blue eyes that promised lethal reprisal, and . . . other things. It was the *other things* that interested him. He almost didn't notice Elvis launching into "Don't Be Cruel."

"Elvis did that on purpose." Her breathy accusation fanned his face, but it did nothing to cool lower regions that were heating up fast.

"He's only one of my *toys*. Remember?" *Remember the feel of your mouth on mine, your hands skimming my body.* He was so close he could see a light sprinkling of freckles across the bridge of her nose. Ecstasy would be kissing each one of them. Lingeringly. In a moonlit room with her naked beside him so he could search out other freckles, on other, less-exposed body parts. "You were just in the wrong place at the wrong time."

Her mouth was inches from his. He waited. Elvis sang on. *Nothing.* "That's Elvis singing. Don't you want to *do* something?" He smiled what he hoped was a submissive smile. Submissive wasn't his style, but for Julia? Anything.

Out of the corner of his eye, he saw Carlos shake his head, then leave the building. His attention returned to Julia.

"You still believe that garbage Candy fed you?" Her eyes glittered, turned predatory. "Fine. Maybe I do want to *do* something, Mr. Connally."

Before he had time to react to the danger, she'd pushed away from him. Without warning, she grasped both sides of his shirtfront and yanked. Obligingly, all the buttons popped off.

"Hey! That was a new genie shirt. You'll have to sew—"

Sewing didn't seem to be on her mind as she slid the shirt

141

off his shoulders, then lifted his medallion from his chest and kissed the spot where it had lain. Carefully, she replaced the medallion. Messages of hope arrowed to central control. Central control sent out appropriate directives.

She pursed her lips, then shook her head. "My, my, isn't that too bad. We'll just have to go to your place to get a new shirt. And while we're there, we can discuss . . . things."

What things? He had to know. "Sounds great." *Pathetic.* Even knowing her plans for Wonder World, knowing she didn't want him, he still wanted her. There, he'd admitted it. He wanted her.

Outside they passed a grinning Carlos. "Shut up," Dylan muttered. Carlos kept on grinning. And as Dylan closed the door to the legends, he could hear Elvis promising "Any Way You Want Me (That's How I Will Be)." Sometimes the King was downright eerie.

Dylan led Julia along one of the park's secluded paths. She made no comment about the brilliant flowers or tropical vegetation. *Silence. Curiouser and curiouser.* Maybe his home would pull her from her strange funk. She already knew he lived in the park, but she didn't know where.

When they finally emerged onto the banks of his private lake, he paused, waiting for her reaction.

Her eyes widened. "There's a pirate ship out there."

"That's my home." He couldn't help the pride in his voice. She'd probably think it was stupid, probably suggest he get something cheaper, like an authentic grass hut, but he'd always wanted to live on a pirate ship. Hey, it was *his* fantasy.

He wondered if she had any fantasies. *Yeah, right.* He'd bet she dreamed of a super sale at Wal-Mart.

"You live on a pirate ship?"

He wasn't prepared for the sparkle of excitement in her gaze. Maybe there was hope for her yet. "Come on board."

He guided her up the gangplank and onto the ship. "Welcome to my world, Julia."

She wandered the decks, exclaiming over everything. "Tell

me, Captain, do you make enemies walk the plank?'' Her question held something dark, intriguing.

"Only a select few. Okay, just one." He watched her disappear into his costume closet, and raised his voice so she could hear. "I found Raddock here in my cabin one day rooting through my things. Making him walk the plank didn't do any good, though. Slime floats."

While she was occupied in his closet, he went out and hurriedly pulled up the gangplank. He didn't want any unexpected visitors. When he got back, she was still in the closet. He'd about decided to see what was so fascinating when she came out.

His sharp intake of breath sent oxygen flooding into his system. He'd need it, because he didn't seem able to breathe.

A pirate she-devil stalked toward him, all feline grace and menace. She'd donned his black pirate pants, but on her they took on curves they'd never had before. She'd put on one of his white shirts, but hadn't buttoned it, only tied it at her waist.

His gaze riveted on the swell of her breasts exposed by the open vee of the shirt. He had only a vague impression of the red scarf tied around her head, gold earring in one ear, bare feet, and sword at her waist.

"Hey, Connally, I'm beginning to understand all this dress-up stuff. I can almost believe I'm a real pirate." She walked past him to peer out at the lake. "Why did you pull up the gangplank, and what're those women in grass skirts doing?"

"Damn." Striding over to stand beside her, he looked toward the bank. Sure enough, five women in authentic costume stood there. Even as he puzzled over why they weren't at the noon show where they belonged, they began the hula. But the music? He shook his head. He couldn't believe his ears. Elvis! The recorded strains of "It's Now or Never" drifted across the lake.

Who? What? He didn't want Elvis. Just Julia and him. No third parties allowed. Someone would pay for this.

"You play dirty, don't you, Connally?"

"What?" He wasn't prepared for her harsh question. "Look, I'm sorry. Believe me, I didn't have anything—"

"Save it for the fish. You thought you'd get me here, play Elvis, and I'd melt into your arms. Well, the worm has turned." She frowned. "God, you've got me talking in clichés."

"Listen to me, Julia, I—"

"I'm through listening. It's your turn to listen. Take off your clothes, Connally."

Chapter Four

Yes! I am pirate, hear me roar. Julia could buy into the fantasy. She'd be merciless, powerful. Today she'd make him listen to her ideas and prove she wasn't under some crazy hypnotic suggestion.

In this costume, she'd become Raine the Ruthless, scourge of the South Pacific. She'd bend him to her will. If she could keep her focus with Elvis singing and Dylan's body on display, then she could do anything. Topple empires, rule the world, get a thirty-percent discount from Larson's Fashion Jewelry. Okay, maybe not the jewelry.

"All my clothes, Julia?" He looked too hopeful.

"Not all. Definitely not all. I meant shirt. You have to change your shirt; then we can talk."

Dylan turned from her as he leisurely pulled off his shirt. Unblinking, Julia studied the smooth play of muscles across his tanned back, tried to deny the snap and tingle that spread like an electrical short crackling along her nerves until it reached her power source, then exploded in a shower of light and heat.

She breathed out on a deep sigh. *No.* There would be no snap, crackle, or pop so long as she was in control.

Elvis's voice rising and falling in the background pulled her from her ogling mode. *Stay grounded.* She had to make Dylan listen to her ideas or else Dad would withdraw his money. So what if Dad bailed out? What was the big deal? But it *was* a big deal. She'd think about why later.

Her feelings for Dylan? They couldn't be hypnotist-induced. They were too strong, too constant, too real, like the lush green of Alakai Swamp with its heat, its color, its texture. A primal force that steeped all the senses in its power.

But primal force or not, she had to prove she could resist Dylan. And the pirate outfit gave her the courage to do it.

"Mind change. Take off all your clothes. Today's Tuesday. My planner says: naked helpless victim at noon on Tuesday. That's you." She frowned. Dylan would never have *helpless* in his job description.

"Hey, you're really into the fantasy. Indulging your inner child, Julia?" She could hear the smile in his voice.

"No, my outer woman. You know, I thought I'd call myself Raine the Ruthless, but maybe I need something catchier. What do you think of Cutthroat Cathy, or maybe Dangerous Dixie? Hmm, Savage Sally has a certain panache."

"I prefer Sensuous Sally." Still with his back to her, Dylan took off his shoes.

"You're not clear on the concept. How about Evil Erline?"

"How about Erotic Erline?" He slid his silky genie pantaloons down over his lean hips.

Julia could almost hear the glide of cloth against his warm flesh. Then she was left with a panic-inducing view of blue briefs stretched over his to-die-for buns. "I . . . I think I'll stick with Raine the Ruthless," she ended weakly.

"And who am I, Julia?"

"You're . . . you." A symbol of her freedom from all restraints, of her willingness to spend her emotions wildly, impulsively, while still remaining in control where he was concerned. Female pirates through the centuries applauded enthusiastically. *God, that felt good.*

He reached for his briefs.

"Uh, stop. Halt. Maybe something should be left to my imagination."

He turned around.

So much for imagination. She glanced out the window before she'd be forced to pop her eyeballs back into her head. "Just checking on the hula. Interesting dance." She could do this. She just needed a moment to calm the mad pounding of her heart. "Tell me about its origin. Long and in detail."

"Julia, look at me."

She sensed his laughter. Pirate queens the world over howled their outrage. Captives did *not* laugh at their captors.

She looked at him—face, chest, stomach, briefs, legs, *briefs. Mistake* "Seems to be getting pretty crowded in there."

He glanced down. "Should I take them off?"

"No. Absolutely not. I'm not into embarrassing my captives." Her face felt like a five-alarmer.

"So." He lay down on the unmade bed, then folded his hands behind his head. "What *do* you usually do to your captives?"

"I . . . tie them up, then force them to listen to my money-saving ideas."

He grimaced. "You really know how to torture a guy. Tell you what. Tie me up and *try* to make me listen. Fair enough?"

Julia frowned. She was getting faint but definite danger signals here. "That doesn't seem very fair. I mean, you won't have any defense."

He smiled, a hungry shark smile.

She wouldn't think of this as sexual. *Are you crazy?* She'd think of this as simply a way to make him listen to her ideas.

What ideas? With him lying there like strawberry shortcake on a dessert tray, she couldn't dredge up one idea. Well, maybe *one* idea. Besides, *shortcake* didn't quite fit the description. *Hmm.* A cannoli? "Fine. How do I do this?"

He grinned. "Captain Bligh just turned over in his grave. Pirates are supposed to be bold, inventive. They don't ask their captives how to tie them up."

"Okay." She pulled off the scarf she'd tied around her head. "See me. Bold. Inventive. I need another scarf."

"In the trunk."

Opening the carved trunk at the foot of his four-poster bed, she yanked out a red scarf to match the one in her hand. She was color-coordinated in all things.

"Uh, stretch out your arms." Trying to ignore his glittering gaze, she tied his wrists to the bedposts, then moved a safe distance away. Futile. There was no safe distance.

"Going to leave my legs free?"

She shrugged. "Why not? What can you do with your legs?"

His smile turned wicked. "Sit on the bed beside me, and tell me your ideas." He looked hungry, just like the wolf standing in front of the third little piggy's door. But her resolve was brick-strong, and he could huff and puff all he wanted without making a dent in her determination. Huff and puff. His lips . . .

In the distance, she could hear Elvis launching into "It's Now or Never" for the fifth time.

Common sense told her to stay put, but that other part of her, the part that had stuck its defiant nose into the light the first time she saw Dylan and had grown increasingly vocal, urged her to accept his challenge. She'd prove once and for all that neither Elvis's voice nor Dylan's varied temptations could make her stray from the righteous path of saving money.

Raine the Ruthless didn't cringe. She used men, then threw the empty husks to the sharks. Her gaze drifted down his bare body to settle on the blue briefs. No empty husks there.

Shifting her attention to his expectant gaze, she moved confidently to the bed, then sat down on the very edge. No need to be overconfident. "Okay, let's talk cost cutting."

He settled his hips deeper into the white cotton sheets, and like a heat-seeking rocket, her gaze once again targeted the briefs. His movement had pulled the material low on his hips, and without the use of his hands, he couldn't pull them up.

Sure, she could pull them up for him. But why? She was trying to prove her power to resist him, and the greater the challenge . . . Fine, so she was a wimp. She didn't want to go anywhere near those briefs. She watched him bend one leg at the knee, stared in fascination at the play of muscle along his inner thigh, then quickly looked away.

His cabin. Purely male. Dark paneled walls, a rolltop desk, nothing extraordinary . . . except in his bed.

This was ridiculous. He was just a man. Raine the Ruthless wouldn't be turned into a mindless zombie at the sight of a man's body. A pirate queen would've sampled so many male bodies they'd all start to look the same.

She looked. No, not the same. All male bodies didn't make her lower regions moan and lick their lips.

While she was busy contemplating her lower regions, he moved his other leg until it rested against her hip, a burning distraction. She couldn't edge away without falling onto the floor. She wouldn't give him the satisfaction.

"Relax, Julia. Feel the heat, the rhythm of the island." He demonstrated by sliding his bare leg along her hip.

News flash, buster. I'm already feeling the heat. But she understood his game. Play Elvis, watch Julia's hormones kick into overdrive. Something small and vulnerable whimpered, then scuttled into hiding at the thought that he was still trying to use Elvis against her.

She drew in a deep breath. Fine, he wanted to play dirty; she could play dirty, too.

Scrambling completely onto the bed, she straddled his hips, then leaned over, her hair trailing across his broad chest. She watched the strands slide over his stomach, watched his stomach muscles ripple, felt the ache beginning low in her belly, and resisted the urge to sink onto him, to feel his heated flesh touching her everywhere. Did pirate queens go down with their ships?

No. Pirate queens didn't sink. "I thought we could start with all that expensive virtual-reality stuff you want. Reality is touch." She drew her index finger down the middle of his chest, over his flat stomach, then lingered at the spot where his briefs rode low on his hips.

She drew imaginary circles on his hair-roughened skin, then watched with satisfaction as goose bumps followed the path of her fingers. "Reality is taste." Her pirate-queen persona leaned farther over him and touched each hard nipple with the tip of her tongue, then gloried at his low, tortured moan. Julia would never have done that, but a pirate queen could do anything. "Can your expensive electronics duplicate reality?"

"Julia, I—"

She interrupted his hoarse plea. "I have some wonderful plans that are cheaper than virtual reality, but would have the same effect." She gently kneaded the inside of his thigh. His skin—hot, smooth satin over hard muscle. With each touch, heat pooled in the same area as her now-throbbing ache, urging her to move her hand higher, to push aside the briefs, to— She jerked her hand from his thigh. Quickly she drew the tattered remains of her determination around her. "When you're ready to listen." Had that strangled whisper come from her?

He grunted at her. Not a friendly grunt.

She paused. All this *reality* was making her breathe hard. "How about canceling your order for those exotic birds?" Gently she kissed the warm flesh at the base of his throat, sensed the hot rush of blood beneath her lips, felt him swallow hard.

"No!" His voice was husky, filled with something . . .

She forgot *something* as he raised his knee higher and pressed it between her legs. With a choked gasp, she fought the need to clench her thighs around any available part of him.

Ignore your thighs. They won't save money. But her thighs wouldn't be ignored. They sensed wet-and-wild times ahead, if they could just latch onto Dylan Connally.

In between the mental battle to clench or not to clench, she heard Elvis winding up for the . . . Darn, she'd lost count. *Remember Elvis, Remember the Alamo, remember something.* She'd also remember in her next incarnation as a pirate to tie legs.

"No?" She feathered kisses along his outstretched arm, admired the flexed muscles as he yanked at his bindings. And some small voice of truth yelled a warning to stop before . . . *Forget the voice.* She had Dylan right where she wanted him. Figuratively speaking, of course. "Birds have no sense of personal hygiene. What if one doo-doos on a customer's head?"

Was that a laugh? "Anyway, you can buy these realistic birds that flap their wings and make noise when the wind blows them. From far away, people won't know the difference."

"I'll think about the birds. Loosen my right wrist. I'm losing feeling in my fingers." He spoke in short gasps, as though he was having trouble pulling air into his lungs.

She understood. She was doing some heavy panting herself. Steadying her shaky hands, she leaned above him to reach his wrist. Too late she realized that he might not be able to reach her with his hands, but his teeth were a different matter.

Frozen above him, she felt the scrape of his teeth as he grasped the edge of her shirt and pulled it from her breast. Incapable of movement, she looked down into eyes hot with need as his lips closed around her nipple. His lids drifted shut as he suckled, and she moaned against the surge of desire. His lips, his tongue, his teeth teased her nipple, and she held her breath, letting the wave of hunger for him rock her.

But in the moment while she held her breath, she heard Elvis still droning on. *Remember Elvis. Remember what's at stake. To hell with birds. Time to move on.*

"Volcano Land. We have to talk about Volcano Land."

He released her nipple, probably surprised she could even speak. She surprised herself. With fingers she forced to remain steady, she pulled the shirt over her exposed breast.

Hard-hearted pirate queen, ha. Their bodies touching in any way reduced her to . . . No, that was wrong. She felt as though she'd weathered one of the drenching storms over Waialeale. Dylan's touch didn't *reduce* her; it made her feel more than herself, complete.

She drew in a deep, cleansing breath. "You plan to have people sitting in a theater to experience an eruption. It won't work. Pele needs to be touched, the power of the mountain felt." She leaned back, and with a fingertip that quivered, drew the nail of her index finger down the clearly delineated outline of his manhood straining against the material of his briefs.

His whole body shook, but she refused to meet his gaze. "You need to taste the fiery heart of Kauai." Leaning over, she ran the tip of her tongue along the same path her fingertip had taken. He tasted of Calvin Klein and sex. "So I suggest that we forget the IMAX experience and concentrate on creating a living, breathing volcano." *Breathing. Good idea.*

"Damn it to hell, woman, I can't take any more!" With a savage yank, he freed his wrists.

Uh-oh. Major eruption. But she didn't care. Not about Elvis, pirate queens, or saving money. She cared only about the angry man rising from the bed, his long hair spread in tangled glory over his shoulders, his eyes flashing a promise of delicious retribution.

He wrapped his arms around her, pushed her down to the bed, still warm from his body, and took her mouth in a searing kiss. This was no gentle touching of lips, but a hard, demanding kiss, hot and probing, telling her with his tongue, his raspy breathing, and the sweat-sheened slickness of his chest pressed against her that he wanted her. Now.

The sudden pounding at the cabin door would've awakened the dead, and Dylan promised himself a nice, leisurely murder if the pounding didn't stop.

"Hey, can we stop now? The girls can't hula any more. Marcy says her hips are locking up. Damn, why'd you pull up your gangplank? I had to wade out here. Got muck up to my knees."

"No, no!" Dylan buried his face in the curve of Julia's neck. He'd kill Gavin, then throw his body to the fake alligators.

"And if I have to play 'It's Now or Never' one more time I'm gonna puke."

Dylan felt Julia stiffen beneath him at the mention of Elvis. He sure did hope the song's title wasn't prophetic.

"Let me up, Dylan."

Exhaling on a puff of disappointment, Dylan moved off of her. He'd wanted to make love to her. To feel her heat, her want, her passion tangle with his. Without Elvis. It was long past lust. Lust didn't care what triggered the need. The fact that he cared so much said something. He wasn't quite sure what it said, but he intended to listen real hard from now on. Because no one had ever made him feel like Julia Raine did.

"You're low, Connally. You almost made me forget. I can't believe you still think you can turn me into a mindless sex machine by playing Elvis." She grew silent for a moment. "Okay, so it must seem like it worked to you, but it didn't."

"Huh?" The only part he'd heard was the part about making her forget. Making her forget was good, right?

"What did you think of my ideas?" She followed him around as he pulled on his jeans and a black T-shirt.

"What? You had ideas?" He ducked as she swung at him. "Do you want to change before I open the door?"

Casting him an angry glare, she disappeared into his costume closet. When she emerged, she was once again Julia Raine, cost-cutting dynamo. He sighed for the loss of his pirate queen.

He didn't try to explain to her. Explaining would take energy, and he was saving that to strangle whoever was responsible for "It's Now or Never."

Pulling open the door, he strode out of the cabin with Julia close behind him. "Were you responsible for this, Gavin?"

"Well, yes, but—"

"You're fired."

"Malia was the one who told me to do it."

"You're rehired." He scowled at the hapless Gavin. "And throw that tape away. Understand?"

Gavin gulped loudly. "Sure, boss."

Julia trotted to keep up with him as he slapped the gang-plank in place, then strode toward his office. "You didn't tell Malia to play Elvis?"

"No." Didn't she understand? He needed her to want *him,* Dylan Connally. Not because she was trying to make him agree with her ideas. He smiled. That had sure been a bust. He stopped smiling. Okay, once she got started he would've agreed to almost anything if only he could've touched her.

She suddenly stopped, then sat down on a large rock. "Wait up while I get these stones out of my shoes."

He squatted down beside her and reached for her foot. "Here, let me do that. Did you really mean what you said about Volcano Land back there?"

"Yes. You actually listened to one of my ideas?"

He smiled as he emptied the pebbles. Purposely, he slid his hand slowly down her ankle, then gently kneaded her foot before replacing the shoe. "Hey, I hear everything. Even the things you *don't* say." He took off her other shoe, then watched, fascinated, as she wiggled her toes. Boy, he had it bad when wiggling toes turned him on.

"I don't get it."

He looked up. "Think, Julia. Seems to me you threw the word *real* around a lot back there. You didn't like my idea for Volcano Land because it wouldn't be *real.* Sweetheart, your favorite word since you got here has been *fake.* A volcano reproduction would cost a lot more than my one-shot deal."

"Ohmigod. You're right." He felt her sudden tension all

the way to her little toe. "I'm morphing into a spendthrift. But I wasn't thinking about the expense; I was thinking about what would be best for the park."

"Bingo."

She leaned over, and her hair drifted around him like golden rainfall. He breathed in the fresh spring scent, longed to run each strand through his fingers, remembered the feel of it gliding across his body. Grew aroused at the memory. He dropped one hand between his legs to hide the obvious.

Her slow smile indicated she understood his problem perfectly. "Dad wants me to cut everything to the bone. That would be a crime. But if you'd listen to my ideas—okay, not *all* of them—you'd see there are places we could make the park better, but spend less."

Her smile turned tentative. "I have faith in Wonder World. I know you don't believe that, but I do. If Dad pulls his money, well . . ." She glanced away from his stare. "I have some trust-fund money I could invest."

"You'd do that?"

Biting her lip, she nodded.

Something warm and joyful flooded him, refused to believe this was just a business decision. "Knowing you offered is important, Julia, but I wouldn't take your money." *Won't take anything from you until I know . . . Is it Elvis or me?*

Moving her foot from his grasp, she ran her toes up the side of his leg, along the inside of his thigh, and under his protective hand. When she slid her toes slowly over his arousal, he gasped and knew his eyes must be glazing over.

"I don't know what you're doing to me, Connally. Or maybe it's the island. But somehow *real* is becoming important to me. Oh, and those birds I mentioned. Tacky, right?"

He was barely able to nod. "Tacky." He almost slumped to the ground when she removed her toes from between his legs.

"It's not me or the island, Julia. It's *you*." *Killer toes.* The woman had killer toes. "Tell me about your business."

She shrugged. "I don't know what Cheap Chic has to do with Wonder World, but I go out and find good-quality clothes, jewelry, stuff like that; then I buy them at bargain prices and resell to the public. They save and I make a profit. Simple."

"Julia, is this what you've always wanted to do? Does it make you happy every day of your life? Would life seem incomplete without it?" He didn't touch her as he replaced her shoe. Her answer was too important for distractions.

She frowned. "No. I mean, it's just a job. Dad taught me every way to save a buck, so it made sense to go into a business that would use what I knew. Why?"

He glanced away from her. "What *would* make you happy?"

You. Her automatic response shocked her all the way to her still-tingling toes.

Keep it light. "You know what would make me happy, Connally?" She smoothed a dark strand of hair from his face and felt the touch all the way to her heart. *Amazing.* Only a short while ago, the touch would've gone straight to her hormone happy hour without passing Go and without collecting two hundred dollars. "I'd like to stay at that big hotel I showed you. I'd like to get the biggest suite, order from room service, and . . ."

Dylan grinned. "Go on. You're doing great so far."

"And I'd like to sleep on black satin sheets." *With you.*

He whistled softly, then stood. "Black satin sheets?"

She smiled broadly. "Yes." Standing, she joined him as he continued toward his office. "You know, some people have to go to Weight Watchers? Me? I have to go to Wallet Watchers. I love things that are shiny and new." She frowned. "I've never told anyone that before. Dad would have a fit. Of course, I still recognize the value of a good bargain."

He cast her a glance she couldn't read. "Guess that leaves me out. I'm tarnished and cracked around the edges. I don't think you'd call me a good bargain.'' Then he smiled, put his arm around her waist, and pulled her close. ''But you know what? We have something in common. I like things shiny and new, too.''

Julia tried to think past the heat of his body pressed against her, the pressure of his arm around her waist. He'd just said something important, but she wasn't quite sure what it was. He'd almost sounded as though he cared what she thought of him.

She had no more time to think deep thoughts as they reached Dylan's office and he flung open the door.

''Okay, Malia, how much did Raddock pay you this time?''

Malia sat behind her desk, dressed as a ghost today. She cast Dylan an accusing glance. ''Hey, I promised I wouldn't talk to Raddock again, and I keep my promises, boss.'' She shifted in her seat, but didn't move from her desk. ''It's been tough, too. He calls every day, and he's getting pretty nasty. Says if you don't listen to him he'll make you listen.'' She glanced away. ''Oh, and I don't think I'll be a white ghost again. I hate white. How about a hot-pink ghost? A hot-pink ghost has style.''

Dylan advanced on Malia, and she paled to a shade almost matching her ghostly persona, but she still didn't move away from him. Julia sniffed. *Nail polish? Hmm.*

''Why did you send Gavin over to play Elvis, Malia? Think carefully, because your job is hanging by a toenail.''

Toenail. Of course. Julia walked around Malia's desk and peered under it. ''A nail dryer? You're drying your toenails with a nail dryer?''

''What?'' Dylan strode around the desk to get a look. ''I don't believe this. When did you get a nail dryer, Malia?''

Malia's defenses crumbled. ''I'm sorry, boss. Really sorry. I have this weakness, and when I realized I could have a nail dryer just by playing one song . . . Well, what harm could one little song do? Besides, I'm not responsible.'' She brightened. ''That's it. I have an obsession. I need a support group. Does your insurance cover therapy? A few sessions and I'll be as good as new.'' She glanced at Dylan, then looked quickly away. ''Don't make me give it back.''

Dylan leaned over Malia, every inch of his body radiating anger. ''Who, Malia? Who bribed you to do this?''

''I did.''

Julia watched Dylan swing his anger toward the person standing in the doorway.

She should've guessed. Heaving a sigh of angry resignation, Julia turned toward the door to confront her stepmother.

Resplendent in a flowing purple muumuu, Candy smiled in the face of his glare. ''Cosmic forces can no longer be denied.''

Chapter Five

"Cosmic forces. Right." Dylan glared at Candy.

Candy chose a seat on a gravestone near Malia's desk. "All great prophets are reviled in their own time."

"How could you, Candy!" Wow, there was a creative, insightful comment. But what else could she say? *Thanks, Candy for making someone I care about think I'm nothing more than a puppet, and that Elvis pulls the strings?* Or, *Thanks, Candy, for messing up something that was starting to feel very special?* The truth? Dylan already thought Elvis pulled her strings, and the special feeling was pretty one-sided.

Candy smiled serenely at her. "I dare everything, dear, when I'm convinced it's for the best. My last reading assured me it was now or never."

Julia winced. "Try never, Candy." Now that she had time to think, she realized Dylan would never trust that her feelings for him were real, any more than he'd trust her to help him with his park. Why should he?

Candy waved a dismissive hand in the air. "No problem.

Hypnotic suggestions can be erased just like that." She snapped her fingers. "We can go to Blue Hawaii and take care of it."

"I was not hypnotized!" Murder while under hypnotic suggestion. Sounded like a good defense to Julia.

"Hypnotized?" Dylan turned to Julia. "You were hypnotized?" He looked almost happy.

"No." Julia clenched her hands until her nails bit into her palms. *But are you sure?*

"Yes," Candy affirmed.

"Hey, my toenails are almost dry," Malia offered.

"Look, Julia, I can drive you to Blue Hawaii and get this guy to erase the suggestion." Dylan lightly stroked the side of her face, as though contact with him might change her mind.

"Great. Before, you thought I was just crazy, but now you realize my little *quirk* can be fixed." She fought the pressure of tears. "I'd think you'd want me to stay the way I am now—so easy, so manageable."

"Manageable? You?" His sarcasm didn't mask the hurt in his gaze. She almost wished she'd said no to Dad, stayed in her nice, safe life in New Jersey. Almost.

"You never trusted me, Dylan." Slowly she backed toward the door. She had to get out of here before the tears came. "You didn't trust me with Wonder World, and you didn't trust me enough to believe I could be reacting to *you,* not Elvis."

That was it. She was outa here. Turning, she walked from the office. Okay, so her legs were a little wobbly, her lips a little quivery, but all in all it was a dignified exit. She applauded herself. She could hear Dylan calling her name, but she kept walking. If he came after her, if he touched her, she'd either sock him or wrap her arms around him and never let go.

She stopped outside the Rock 'n' Roll Legends. Ignoring a CLOSED FOR REPAIRS sign, she slipped inside.

Silence—to think, to plan. She could get a flight home tomorrow; then she'd call Dad and tell him Dylan wanted no part of her plans. After he got through blustering and yelling, she'd tell him she intended to use her trust-fund money on the park, but that Dylan was to believe the money came from him.

Dad wouldn't be happy, but he'd do it. After all, for him it would be a win-win situation. Profit with no expense.

Moving across the dimly lit room to where Elvis stood, she sat down cross-legged in front of the figure and let the silence wrap around her.

"You messed things up royally, big guy." She stared up at Elvis. Elvis stared back. "Dylan will always wonder who turned me on, you or him. We both know that even if I were hypnotized, and I guess I'll always wonder about that, I couldn't be forced to do something I didn't want to do. But try telling that to Dylan."

She cocked her head and offered Elvis a half smile. "Know what? I never was too crazy about your music, except for that song, 'Can't Help Falling in Love.'" She softly hummed a few bars. "Too bad no one thought to play that song."

"What a surprise meeting you here, little lady."

Startled, Julia turned her head. *Oh, no.* Raddock. Just what she needed. "What're you doing here?"

"Oh, just had a little unfinished business to take care of." He glared up at Elvis. "Don't know what Connally sees in him. Should've replaced him with a cartoon character a long time ago."

"You shouldn't talk that way about the King." Now, why the heck was she defending Elvis?

"Too bad you didn't dump Connally. We could've made this place a real payin' operation." He rubbed his thumb and index fingers together, then offered her a sly glance. "Talked to your dad on the phone. He liked my ideas, but said he didn't need me because his daughter was takin' care of the situation. Huh! Is he gonna be pissed off when he finds out what's been goin' on here. I tried to tell him, but he wouldn't listen."

Julia stood. "Try minding your own business. You're not

161

getting Dylan's business. I'll make sure of that.'' For a moment her gaze shifted. She could've sworn she saw movement in the shadows at the back of the room.

A sound swung both of them to face Elvis. The King lifted his guitar into position, then belted out ''Jailhouse Rock.''

Run. She had to get out of here. What if she *was* hypnotized? Raddock? *Yech.* Kissing him would shrivel her lips. But this would be her chance to prove things one way or the other. The truth? She didn't want to know. She *wanted* to feel this need for Dylan, never wanted it to go away.

But was it fair to Dylan? No. And she cared too much to let him wonder. She'd stay. For Dylan.

Dylan froze in the process of striding from the shadows. *Damn!* He had to stop Elvis. He clenched his fists against the picture of Julia wrapping her arms around Raddock, kissing that slime the way she'd kissed him. The mental image made him want to gag, to kill Raddock. The force of his emotion rocked Dylan.

Without shifting his gaze from Julia, he fumbled behind him for the cutoff switch that would shut the King down.

His motion must've caught Julia's attention, because her gaze shifted to him.

He felt her warmth, her connection to him. But even across the width of the darkened room, he saw her fear. Not of Raddock, but of what Elvis's voice would do.

He also saw her courage.

Slowly, she shook her head, then mouthed, *Trust me.*

Trust her. He hadn't trusted anyone since he'd realized how his parents had manipulated his life. He'd trusted only himself for so long, but that was before Julia. She'd trusted him enough to offer her own money. What would he trust her with?

Love is trust. The simple truth stood beside him in the darkened room, warming him, suddenly making things so simple. He dropped his hand from the switch.

Raddock sidled closer to Julia. "You know, we could still make a great team, little lady."

Julia grimaced in distaste. "I don't think so. I think you should get out of here before Dylan finds you."

"Not before I do what I came to do." He pulled a baseball bat from behind him. "I'm gonna leave a little good-bye present for Connally. When I get through with Elvis, he'll never sing again." He raised the bat and stepped toward the King.

"No!" Julia moved in front of Elvis just as Raddock began his swing.

No! Dylan leaped from the shadows and raced toward Raddock, knowing he'd never reach him before he hit Julia. Despair pushed him onward. "You're dead, Raddock!" But he knew his shout couldn't prevent what was about to happen.

Suddenly a blur of motion stopped Dylan. He watched, dumbstruck, as Elvis raised his guitar high above his head and brought it crashing down on Raddock's head. The guitar shattered as Raddock slumped to the floor.

In a moment she was in Dylan's arms and he held her tightly, forcing aside mental pictures of what almost happened. Fiercely, he knew he'd trade his park and all his tomorrows to keep Julia safe. Forever.

She burrowed her head against his chest, and he could feel her tears soaking into his shirt.

"He wanted to destroy Elvis to get back at you." Dylan felt the vibration of her words against his chest, his heart. "And Elvis sacrificed his guitar to save me." Her sob came out on a hiccup, and he didn't even think about explaining that Elvis was only a mechanical figure.

Behind him he heard the door open and then Carlos's voice. "Is everything okay in here? I heard noises."

Still holding Julia tightly, he looked down at Raddock. "Raddock came looking for trouble. Call the police. Oh, and shut off the power to Elvis before you leave."

There was a brief silence behind him. "Elvis has been turned off all day, boss. He has been acting strangely, so I turned him off this morning until I could fix him.''

Dylan released Julia, and they both turned toward the power switch. *Off.* It had been off all the time.

Carlos shrugged. ''See? *Nada.*''

Dylan blinked. There had to be a logical explanation. He'd figure it out later, when he could think again. All he cared about now was getting Julia back to her motel room safely.

''Come on. The police will take care of Raddock.'' Putting his arm across her shoulder, he guided her to the door.

Carlos patted the King's arm. ''Do not worry, *amigo.* We will get you another guitar—gold, with your name on it.''

''Uh-huh,'' Elvis agreed softly.

Julia and Dylan walked to the motel in silence. But that was okay, because Dylan had a lot to think about. In that split second when he'd known he couldn't reach Julia in time, that he was too far away to keep her from harm, he'd realized he never wanted that to happen again.

He wanted her near him. Always. He now knew her response had been to him, not to Elvis. The knowledge made him want to climb to Waialeale's summit and shout his triumph. Okay, he knew her response didn't mean she loved him, but he could work with that. He'd make her love him even if he had to barter with his precious park. Whatever it took.

He shook his head at the irony. He'd trusted so little in his life, and now he was prepared to trust her with his life's work. Just call him all-or-nothing Connally. Fake monkeys? He winced. He'd even get fake monkeys if it would make her stay.

Sliding a sideways glance at her pensive expression, he had a sinking feeling it would take more than fake monkeys to keep her. Whatever it was, he'd do it.

When they reached her door, he grasped her hands in his, pulled her close, and gently kissed her forehead. What he really wanted to do was wrap his arms around her and kiss her senseless. She'd gone through too much today, though. He'd wait.

But if she thought she'd just catch a plane and taxi down the runway out of his life, she had another thought coming. Whatever it took. Even if he ended up with tire tracks across his forehead.

"Do you want me to stay with you?" *Say yes*. He tightened his grip on her hands.

She shook her head; then she smiled. "Oh, and I didn't feel a thing when Elvis sang. Not one darn thing."

He swallowed hard. *Thank God*. But as she closed the door quietly on his hopes, his dreams, he wondered if she was going to leave his love scattered all over Kauai.

Leaning against the closed door, she listened to his footsteps fade away, then walked across her cheap motel room. She was starting to hate the word *cheap*. Julia sat down in front of the mirror. Yes, that was her nose right in the middle of her face where it should be. She touched it to make sure. Eyes looked okay. She blinked. Yep, they still worked. Her mouth was a little quivery, but it was still her mouth. She touched the spot on her forehead where Dylan had kissed her. Funny, she could still feel the texture of his lips against her skin. Nothing wrong with her short-term memory.

If she looked the same as always, then what the heck had changed? Because she sure didn't *feel* the same.

When she'd glanced across that room and seen Dylan's expression as he reached for Elvis's cutoff switch, she'd known. She couldn't leave him. She couldn't fly back to New Jersey, to her shop, and pick up the pieces of her life.

That was what the old Julia would've done. Play safe, don't take chances. But a new and improved Julia was about to be born, one who'd fight for what she wanted.

She wanted Dylan. Her advantage? He wanted her, too. He might not love her, but he wanted her. She hadn't missed the heat in his gaze. Want was a start.

She was about to reach for the phone when Candy arrived. "Are you all right? Dylan told me what happened." She fluttered around Julia like an overwrought butterfly.

"I'm fine, Candy. There's—"

"I saw it in the cards, but I ignored the warning. They said someone would make a heartbreaking sacrifice. This is all my fault."

Candy in her breast-beating mode was like Julia's dad when he sensed money to be saved—hard to slow down and almost impossible to stop.

"Elvis."

"What?" Surprisingly, Candy's mea culpa cries ceased.

"Elvis whacked Raddock over the head to save me. The King sacrificed his guitar, and I intend to buy him a new one."

Candy, she of the tarot cards and midnight seances, opened her eyes wide and gazed at Julia with awed wonder. "I knew Elvis was your spirit guide. Wait till I tell your father."

Julia sighed. No use arguing. "I'd appreciate a few favors, Candy. Would you call Dad and tell him Dylan has great ideas, and if he won't support Wonder World, I will? He can use my trust money, but I don't want Dylan to know the money came from me." She opened drawers until she found the phone book. "Dad'll rant and rave, but not for long. He can keep collecting profits without investing a dime. That's Dad's kind of deal."

"Forget your trust fund. *I'll* speak to your father."

Uh-oh. Julia almost felt sorry for Dad.

Candy frowned. "You sound as though you won't be there to tell him yourself."

Julia opened the phone book, then started to scan addresses. "I'm staying here. I have some unfinished business to take care of." *Good.* There was the name she'd been looking for.

"Yes!" Candy floated around the room on a sea of purple. "It's Dylan. You're staying for Dylan. You love him. I knew it. Your astrological chart said this would happen."

Like a whirling purple top, she didn't look like she'd be winding down anytime soon.

While Candy was busy spinning and making happy noises,

Julia quickly wrote a note. "Would you make sure Dylan gets this?"

Candy abandoned the top routine in favor of the jumping-in-place exercise. "I am *so* excited. We'll do the wedding in purple." She suddenly stopped jumping. "You *do* like purple, don't you?" Her tone suggested that not liking purple indicated lack of oxygen to the brain.

Oh, boy. "Don't plan a wedding yet, and yes, I love purple."

Julia got up and headed for the door.

"Where're you going? We have things to talk about."

Julia glanced over her shoulder and grinned at Candy. "I'm going out to spend money. *Lots* of money. And you know what?" She flung open the door with a flourish. "I might not come back till it's all gone."

Wow. When Julia upgraded lodgings, she did it in a big way. Only Michael Jordan or a visiting head of state could afford a suite in this hotel. And this room? The seduction suite.

Dylan stood in the shadows cast by the flickering candle-light. Exotic flowers with their rich scent and dark, elegant furniture created a picture of sin and opulence. And in the center of the room was a carved four-poster bed with black satin sheets made for sex.

"One Night." Dylan thought of the song as he watched Julia step into the hotel room. A great concept, but not nearly enough.

Her red silk muumuu clung yet flowed, like a flaming ribbon winding down the side of a volcano, dangerous but sensuously beautiful. Her golden hair lay across one bare shoulder, and in his mind he brushed the silken strands back, then touched the hollow of her throat with his lips, felt her quickened pulse.

Damn. Even thinking about her aroused him, and his pirate pants didn't allow for growth patterns. He moved restlessly.

167

He saw the moment she realized he stood there—the widening of her eyes, the soft smile that touched her lips, the heat and sizzle that always connected them.

She glanced around the room, and he followed her gaze. Everything was muted with only candlelight. Except the bed. She turned back to him.

He smiled. "Only flame, black satin, and the night."

"And the night," she echoed.

She sniffed. "Vanilla? I didn't order vanilla candles, and I can't picture a ruthless pirate ordering them either." She sighed. "Candy read my note." It was a statement.

"You thought she wouldn't? She said to tell you the vanilla would help to calm you. Personally, calm is the last thing I want tonight."

"What *do* you want?" Her voice was soft, tentative.

I want tonight to be magical. Forever. "We'll discuss that later. Your note was very specific about what you wanted."

Silence stretched across the distance between them as Dylan unbuttoned his shirt, stripped it off, then dropped it on the floor. His feet were bare, and he slid his black pants over his hips, then kicked them aside.

He hoped his smile only teased and didn't look like the hungry grin of a wolf. "Been here, done this. Right?"

She looked as though she couldn't have spoken to yell *Fire.* He reached for his red briefs. Fire was a very real possibility. The tension, the anticipation filling the room needed only a spark. He slipped the briefs off, then straightened.

He started to reach for his medallion.

"No."

Her one word startled him. Afraid to move, to breathe, lest the thrumming need that stretched between them snap, he waited till she stood in front of him.

As in a dream, she lifted the medallion from his chest and closed her fingers tightly around it. She lifted her gaze to his, and he stifled a groan at the desire, the passion he saw there. Or was it merely a reflection of his own feelings?

"Leave it on. Cold metal against warm male. An incredible combination." Her sudden smile upped the heat index in the room by at least ten degrees.

She carefully laid the medallion back against his chest, and he shuddered as her fingers slid across his skin. Had she said cold metal? *Hah.* Right now it felt like a brand, a burning circle of fire seared into his flesh.

Shifting his gaze to ease the tension, he watched the flickering candlelight cast larger-than-life shadows on the wall. But that was all this was, too, a shadow of what he and Julia could have. A mating of light and dark, hard flesh and smooth skin.

Hard. He glanced down. If he got any harder, Pele would have an eruption to end all eruptions to celebrate. He looked up to find that her gaze had followed his down.

He felt her desire like an invisible net, holding him, drawing him nearer. "This is your fantasy, at least that's what your note said. What now?" His own need made his voice harsh.

She shook her head. "I don't know. Okay, I *do* know, but I'm not sure how . . ." Peeking up at him, she offered him a gamine grin. "Lord, I have the verbal skills of a gnat. Sorry for babbling."

Without comment, he stretched out on the black satin sheets. "Come here, Julia."

He watched her swallow hard, then fix her gaze on the darkened window with the intensity of a trapped moth. "I thought spending money would make this easy, free me. I had it all planned, but you were the wild card." Her gaze skimmed his body, then returned to the window. "You, the black satin. There's something about the way you look tonight . . ."

He grinned. "Elton John. No Elvis. We're making progress." He heard her muffled laughter, but she still stared at the window.

"You look like a million bucks tonight." Now he was the one babbling.

She finally met his gaze. "Close. Very close."

He sat up cross-legged on the bed and watched her glance

Nina Bangs

drop to his arousal. She licked her lower lip. His need to trace
her lips with his own tongue, to feel her lips part . . . He drew
in a deep breath to keep from dragging her onto the bed and
showing her what a real pirate would do.

Glancing down, she smoothed her hand across the muumuu.
"Paradise Fashions. Three hundred dollars. I could've bought
the material at Clancy's in Camden for seventy dollars and—"

"Julia?"

"Hmm?"

"It's gorgeous. Take it off."

Her eyes widened, and for a moment he thought she'd bolt
for the door. Then she smiled, a slow, sensual smile that had
his sex drive burning rubber to get off the starting line.

"I thought you'd never ask."

His hyperactive hormones held their collective breath as she
shimmied out of the dress, then shoved it aside with her foot.

A red bra. Well, almost a red bra. There wasn't too much
material to identify. He closed his lips tight to keep from panting, then dropped his hand between his legs. *Down, boy.*

She reached for the front clasp of the almost-bra, then
paused.

No, no. He swayed forward, as though the force of his will
could strip the wisp from her body.

"Island Lingerie. One hundred dollars. I could've gotten it
for thirty at Colman's." She unfastened it, then flung it away.

Her breasts—full, beautiful. He couldn't keep his gaze from
her pink nipples, couldn't help but remember their taste.

Without warning, she turned away from him. He almost
moaned. A thong. A red thong. He pressed his hand down on
the body part that was reacting wildly in an attempt to get a
peek. *No.* This was for his eyes only.

As she wiggled out of the thong, he followed the motion of
her magnificent bottom with awed wonder. He'd cup that bottom in his hands tonight, as he lifted her to meet his—

She glanced over her shoulder. "Intimately Yours. One
hundred fifty dollars. Can you believe it?"

The Hunka Hunka and the Penny-Pincher

"No. It's unbelievable." So smooth, so perfectly round.

When the silence grew too long, he finally dragged his gaze from her smooth, long legs, her wonderful bottom, her incredible breasts, to her face. For an instant he read uncertainty there; then she turned and walked to the bed.

He was afraid to speak, to breathe, for fear she'd dissolve into another dream. And he exhaled in relief as she sat down on the edge of the bed. Not too close, not too far. "You spent a lot of money. Was it worth it?"

Tenderness, and something deeper, moved in her gaze, then was gone. "Yes." She reached for his hand, which held a very excited body part in check. Gently, she pushed his hand aside. "At first I thought that spending the money would be the ultimate thrill. Then I thought the things I bought would do it. I was wrong. The money and the things were only important if they made you..." She shook her head. "Forget it."

Forget what? He couldn't think. "Don't look at me like that or this will be the shortest fantasy on record." He lifted the medallion from around his neck, then gazed into her eyes. Purposely, he let her see the hunger, the raw need he felt. The love. He hoped she recognized it.

Shifting his gaze, he slowly swung the medallion back and forth, watching it arc. "This hypnotism stuff gave me an idea. I thought you might be open to a few suggestions tonight." He looked at her.

The hint of mischief in her gaze dared him, excited him. "I'm an open person. I..."

Hot. He was so hot. *She* was so hot. He needed something cool before he went up in flame. He lowered the medallion to between his legs, then slid it along himself, back and forth, back and forth. *Ah.* He closed his eyes. *So good, so... hot.*

"Suggestions are great...." Her lips didn't seem to want to obey her. With each stroke of the medallion over his flesh, she could feel it between her own legs, and she clenched her thighs around the sensation.

She forced her gaze away, studied one of the candles intently before she exploded with need. For him, only him. "I think you're supposed to swing it in front of my eyes."

"Sorry, sweetheart. I'm too excited to swing. You ever see the commercial where the fresh pickle snaps and Brand X bends? Right now I'm fresh and ready to snap."

She was supposed to laugh, to relax, but she couldn't do either. Suddenly she felt the touch of metal against the side of her neck. She refused to look at him as the medallion slid down her neck to rest between her breasts. His knuckles scraped her skin and she shivered. She had no idea why she shivered, because the metal was still warm from his body, still held the scent of sex and desire.

"Look at me, Julia." His voice was a harsh whisper. Close, so close she felt his breath warm against the side of her neck, heard his rapid breathing, sensed his control slipping.

She looked at him. Even though the room was cool, a sheen of moisture made his torso glisten, delineating hard muscle and raw need.

"Relax, Julia. Tonight is a time for spending emotions."

As though in a trance, she allowed the touch of the medallion to follow her down as she lay back on the bed.

He leaned over her, his hair falling in a dark curtain to blot out the candles, the night, her doubts. Dylan was her love, and tonight she'd spend more than she had in a lifetime. She hoped it would be enough.

She shivered as he trailed the medallion over her stomach, between her parted legs. She resisted the urge to clench her thighs on it, feel the smooth metal ease her need to be touched, picture how he'd looked as he'd used it on his own flesh.

Slowly he lifted the medallion from her. Locking his gaze with hers, he kissed the metal where it had lain against her, then slipped it around his neck. "This is only the first thing we'll share, love. May the sharing never end." She saw the white flash of his smile. "We'll toast that later."

She hadn't the time or working brain cells to think about

what he'd said before he kissed her. At least it started out as his kiss, but her need was too great, her patience strung short. She took his lips as he took hers, opening her mouth to meet his thrust, to taste and store the memory.

When he broke the kiss to trail his lips down the side of her neck, between her breasts, she moaned and grasped his hair, guiding him to her breasts.

He heeded her silent plea, ringing her nipple with his tongue, then closing his lips over it and suckling as he teased her other nipple with his fingers.

She would spend it all tonight, experience all of him. As he trailed his tongue over her stomach, she ran her fingers down his strong back to those amazing buns. Later, she would hold them later. Reaching between their bodies she clasped his manhood, felt the size and texture of him, reveled in his groan, the spasm that shook him.

"Not too soon. I want . . ." What he wanted became evident as she loosened her grasp, and he moved down between her legs.

He touched her with his lips, his desire, and she cried out, lifting her hips, begging for his thrust, moaning when his tongue slid into her—moist, hot.

No more. She couldn't take any more without shattering into a million shards of pleasure-agony. "Now!" She had breath for only one word as he rose above her.

His thrust was power and light, and she rose to meet him. Grasping his hard buttocks, she pulled him deeper, until he touched her heart, her soul.

Above her cry of release, she heard his hoarse shout. And within those precious moments when there was no thought, only wondrous sensation, she felt her love in every part of her that touched him, a joyous, pulsing reality.

It was only when she was once again aware of the outside world that she heard the music. "Dylan, listen. Outside our window. It's Elvis."

"I can't help falling in love with you. My thoughts exactly.'' He wrapped his arms more tightly around her and nuzzled the base of her neck. ''*Aloha au ia oe*. I love you, Julia. Marry me. You can save me from myself, and I can show you how to spend your emotions. We balance each other.''

''Try to stop me from marrying you, Dylan Connally.'' She brushed his dark hair from his face. ''I love you so much that—''

''You'd pass up a half-price sale at Tiffany's to make love with me?'' His laughter was warm on her cheek.

''Hmm. Half-price, huh? At Tiffany's?''

''You'd pass it up, right?'' He circled her nipple with his fingertip.

''I'm thinking, I'm thinking.'' She yelped as he swatted her bare behind. ''Okay, I'd pass it up.''

''Good thing.'' He rolled away from her and sat up. ''I wonder where that music is coming from? It just hit me that we're ten stories up.'' Throwing on his robe, he walked onto the balcony.

She followed him. Outside, the night was magic. Far below, she could hear the crash of the surf, and a full moon made the water shimmer in shifting patterns of diamond sparkle and shadow.

Listening carefully, she heard the last notes of Elvis's song fading in the night. They came from everywhere and nowhere. ''I told Elvis that 'Can't Help Falling in Love' was my favorite song and that no one had played it for me.''

Dylan was still searching for the music's source. ''Darned if I know where it came from.'' He looked at her. ''You *told* him?''

''Yep. And I think he sang it just for us tonight.''

He didn't laugh at her as they stood with the warm Hawaiian night wrapping them in soft folds of happiness.

''Thanks,'' she whispered into the darkness, and she could almost believe she heard a faint *Uh-huh*.

Smiling up at Dylan, she wrapped her arms around his waist. ''We can go in now. Elvis has left the building.''

To Viola Ferrante
For always believing.

ANN LAWRENCE

HEAVEN SENT

Prologue

Fenway Park, Boston

The relentless August sun beat down on the pitcher's mound. Jack Ryan wiped the sweat from his brow. The searing air gusted in and out of his lungs. The fans fell silent. In left field, the Green Monster with its manual scoreboard, the last vestige of old-time baseball, told the story.

Boston Red Sox 1, New York Yankees 0.

Jack settled his Red Sox cap lower on his brow and imagined that the man who operated the scoreboard held his breath along with the crowd. Time stood still. No one moved.

Three balls and two strikes on the batter.

The catcher gave the signals, quick gestures between his thighs, each one shaken off. Jack knew he must choose his own last pitch.

A last, perfect pitch for a perfect game.

Behind him, in the outfield, a murmur rose in the bleachers. The sound grew, swelled, and pulsed around the park. "Wildman. Wiiiildmmmannnn,'' they chanted, over and over, the final syllable deteriorating each time to a Tarzan-like yell.

The name suited Jack's occasional pitching style. He swallowed against the sudden fear he might earn the nickname for all time—and be the rookie who threw away his perfect game on a wild pitch.

A rookie. A wild pitch. A possible perfect game for the record books.

His arm and shoulder stiffened. His back itched with sweat.

The park rocked to the sound of the chant. Jack took his place. His field of vision narrowed, tunnellike, to include only that perfect zone, that precise spot to place the pitch that could end a perfect game.

He lightly touched his Saint Christopher medal through his uniform. ''Oh, Lord, I promise I'll do anything you ask. Just let me finish pitching this perfect game.''

Chapter One

Boston, ten years later

Jack Ryan wound up for the pitch. He stood poised, the balled socks in his hand, then fired. "Fastball, high and inside," he said as the socks dropped into his suitcase, right on top of his sneakers. "Struck him out."

He plucked another pair of socks from his dresser drawer. The doorbell sounded. "Damn." He pitched the socks. With annoyance he watched them ricochet off the suitcase lid and land on the floor. "Double damn."

He took the stairs two at a time and jerked open his front door. "No," he said emphatically.

"Now, Jack, my boy, is that any way to greet an old friend?" Father Michael O'Malley shoved past Jack and strode into the living room of Jack's condo, which overlooked Boston Harbor. He went directly to the windows facing the USS *Constitution,* "Old Ironsides," where it sat at anchor, a monument to Boston's colonial history.

Jack remained in the doorway and frowned at the priest's back. How did one eject one's old parish priest from one's home? Father Mike, a rabid baseball fan, short and stout like a teapot, graying at the temples, rocked back and forth on his heels. Jack knew that stance—it spelled trouble.

"The answer is still no," he said, his voice too loud. "I have a date. An important date. In New York." He consulted his watch. "In four hours."

Father Mike shook his head and turned back to Jack. "I never tire of this view—it's lucky you are to see it each day. And I'm really sorry, you know I am, but when He calls"— the priest pointed at the ceiling—"we must do His bidding. You did promise, you know."

Yes. He had promised. Ten years ago.

Jack suddenly realized that today marked the tenth anniversary of his rash promise. He hadn't a—he wouldn't say prayer—chance of avoiding whatever Father Mike planned for him.

"If you hadn't decided to help me out that day, I wouldn't be in this predicament."

Father Mike shook his head. "Now, there's no taking back what's done. I merely did what came naturally. As did you."

Jack continued. "Oh, yeah, what did you tell me? You thought you'd say a little prayer for me. Something like this, if I remember correctly: 'Oh, Lord, please let this wild-pitching, Irish rookie complete his perfect game.' You probably started that Wildman thing, too." Jack flung the door open wide and gestured out. "Without your prayer's added boost, I'm sure I'd have thrown the pitch over the catcher's head, the batter would have walked, and I'd have never made it into the record books."

"Complaining, are you?" Father Mike abandoned the view. "Seems like life treats you pretty well. Plenty of free time— now you're retired—to write those interviews you like so much. A comfortable level of fame—not too much, not too little."

"I've served my penance for that rash prayer; I've done seven missions for Him—"

"Enough, son. You can't talk your way out of this."

"But, my date." He tried once more. How did anyone tell Him no? Especially with the evidence of His help to be found all around the condo? The enshrined last pitch from that perfect day? The cleats, the hats, the . . .

"Here." Father Mike closed the open door and held out a small slip of paper.

"If Heaven's so great, how come the inmates keep escaping?" Jack muttered, defeated. He took the paper and held it with as much trepidation as if he were still a pitcher and this slip might be a message sending him down to the minors. He swallowed. Who would he have to find this time? Some minor-league bozo who'd prattle on endlessly about what might have been until Jack sent him home?

Jack opened the folded paper and read the name. There must be some mistake. He looked up and searched the priest's face. "This is a joke."

Father Mike shook his head. "He's gone AWOL—not for the first time, either. He wants him back."

Jack made it to a leather recliner just before collapsing. He tipped his head back and burst into laughter. "Elvis? Elvis!"

"Yes. I have to say I was a mite surprised by this one myself." An amused grin took ten years off Father Mike's face.

"Obviously this is a mistake. What the heck do I know about music?" Jack gestured about the sparsely furnished condo. Mementos of his eight-year career as a major-league pitcher crowded the walls. Framed sketches of long-demolished stadiums and autographed photos vied for space with a tall glass stand. On the stand, as if frozen in midair, sat the ball—the perfect ball from the perfect game.

Father Mike shrugged and patted Jack on the shoulder. "We're never asked to give more than we're able to handle.

Just do what you usually do—find him, figure out what his problem is, and fix it.''

"You make it sound so easy," Jack said. "Last time I had to find a guy's missing daughter, reunite her with her mother, take them to—"

"You did it, didn't you?" Shoving his hands into his pockets, Father Mike sauntered around the room, admiring the memorabilia, whistling. "I'm not sorry about your date, though. She's not right for you. Probably some model with artificial breasts, for heaven's sake! You need a warm, natural woman. You should be married by now and raising a family."

Jack frowned. "We both know marriage is impossible for me. What sane woman wants a man who finds escapees from Heaven?"

Father Mike took the slip of paper from Jack's hand and, brandishing a lighter, set fire to the corner and dropped it into the cold hearth of Jack's fireplace. Both men watched the note turn to soft gray ash. "I know how you feel, Jack, but maybe you aren't giving womankind enough credit. I'm sure there must be a fine lady somewhere who—"

"Would drop everything, without a moment's notice, to run off to hunt down heavenly parolees? Not a chance."

Father Mike smiled. "Maybe it'll take some doing, finding that woman, but for now, forget the New York colleen and get cracking on this case. Elvis is always big news. You know how it'll be, wild rumors, sightings everywhere if word gets out . . . and it always does."

Jack raked his hands through his curly hair and blew out a long breath. "Cheryl will never understand, never," he muttered, mentally composing his excuses.

"Cheryl can replace you."

"Gee, that's what my manager kept saying to me," Jack said, breaking into a grin. He stood up and squared his shoulders.

"Face it," Father Mike said as he eased the door open,

"you've graduated to the big leagues, my boy, being asked to bring this one back."

"Very funny." Jack picked up a baseball and rolled it around in his palms. "What if I don't find him?"

"Oh," said Father Mike, "I think you'll be okay. Somehow I think this one is right up your alley."

After Father Mike left, Jack contemplated Boston Harbor for a few minutes. Where should he look? His other missions had been relatively easy—baseball-wise. He'd just "haunted" baseball hangouts, bars, and clubs until he'd tracked down his quarry. The hard part was solving the problems that drew them back to earth.

He went into his office and uncovered his computer, which he hadn't touched since his last mission for Father Mike. Between missions for the priest, Jack filled his time as a staff writer for *Sports World* magazine. He wrote on yellow legal-size pads with a number-two pencil. He hated technology of any kind.

On his blotter lay his latest piece, a profile of the hot new home-run hero. Sports was his expertise, not music.

With a sigh of resignation, he turned on the computer. "I suppose I'll have to go someplace like Memphis. Maybe I can detour past Baltimore and catch a game." He spent five minutes trying to remember his password, then accessed the Internet and started a search for the elusive escapee.

Three hours later, his back and neck stiff from sitting so long, Jack shut down his computer. He squared the piles of paper he'd printed out—lists of Elvis websites, lists of Elvis fan clubs, lists of Elvis sightings. He began to sift through the mass of information.

One name occurred over and over. One name joined each list. She hosted a website, was the current president of a fan club established in 1958, and twice headlined in the tabloids with Elvis sightings.

He looked at the clock over his computer—a plastic baseball with bats for hands. He'd start out tomorrow.

An itch started between his shoulder blades. The scent of the infield rose about him.

"Okay. Okay. Tonight. I'll start tonight," he said aloud.

And Jack knew where to start looking. Maybe Elvis had traded one heavenly home for another.

Paradise, Pennsylvania.

Chapter Two

Jack checked his dashboard clock—three A.M. He rubbed his eyes. Exhaustion was a place he'd passed about ten miles back. On either side of him, the land stretched dark as pitch beyond the small businesses and houses that sat immediately on the road. To stay awake he read billboards, both Biblical and for beer.

He swallowed a yawn. He needed a motel—any motel. Kinzers' Firehouse advertised a sauerkraut sale. He shuddered and drove on.

"Where the hell am I?" he asked aloud. As if in answer, a signpost loomed up before him.

BLUE BALL 15 MILES. INTERCOURSE 6 MILES. PARADISE 5 MILES.

"Great. What I'm feeling, what I'm missing, and the last place I want to be," he muttered.

A few miles later, up a low hill, on the left, he saw a pulsing light. It mesmerized him. Across from it, a southern plantation–style building proclaimed Paradise Elementary School.

He pulled into its horseshoe drive and faced the pulsing light. It was a neon sign.

THE STRIKE ZONE.

"This one's right up my alley, all right, Mike. I guess the joke's on me."

The bowling alley drew him like Cooperstown drew baseball fans. Without question or further thought, he coasted his car across the road and into the gravel lot. He got out and leaned against his car to stretch his cramped leg muscles. It was hot as Hades in Paradise—a thought he didn't want to dwell on. The need to go in was as strong as the smell of manure in the air.

A furtive sound rustled in the cornstalks off to the left. He peered into the dark. The hair on his nape itched. He imagined a ghostly monster leaping out at him. Something about the size of a mouse ran out instead. He took a deep breath.

Too much imagination, too much Stephen King. Too much quiet.

With great longing, he looked back at the dark stripe of road that rose over the hill and disappeared. New York and Boston seemed worlds away.

He locked his car and set the alarm. The bowling alley's door swung open with a gentle nudge, and he stepped into a small lobby area, lit only by the colored lights from a row of video arcade games. A peculiar smell, a blend of wood polish and cigarettes and . . . bowling stuff, wafted to him.

He walked into the dark main room filled with lanes. The orange and turquoise color scheme reminded him of his aunt Katherine's living room. A hand-lettered sign proclaimed tonight '50s Night, with nickel sodas and fifty-cent games.

Soft music floated around the room, coming from everywhere and nowhere. Far away, at the end of the two dozen or so lanes, a light gleamed on polished wood. The light did not draw him, but the vision poised at the head of the lane did.

She stood very still, a pink bowling ball pressed to her chest. He shook his head and rubbed his eyes, but the vision remained. Her black full skirt shifted like a bell as she paced forward. In a clunk and a whoosh, the bowling ball left her hand and ran down the lane. He watched it carom off the pins, scattering them. A strike.

He clapped.

She whirled about, one hand to her chest. His eyes went there. Soft—a pink, fuzzy-sweatered dream. He took in her long blond ponytail, her rhinestone eyeglass frames, and wanted to pinch himself. If not for the sign advertising '50s Night, he'd have thought he'd stepped back in time.

"We're closed." She came forward, stepping from the pool of light into the shadows. A large pink poodle with a glittery leash graced one side of her skirt. She reached out for a bowling ball and held it loosely at her side. He realized she held it like a weapon.

"I'm sorry to disturb you." Jack shoved his hands into the pockets of his khaki shorts and tried not to look like an evil despoiler of women. "I'm lost." It wasn't a complete lie. He was always lost when it came to pretty girls in poodle skirts.

She smiled. Her shoulders, rigid in her soft, clingy sweater set, relaxed. Carefully she placed the ball back on the rack. "Where are you supposed to be?"

Getting lucky. In New York. "Whatever motel is open."

"Oh, dear." She plucked off the ludicrous glasses suspended from a chain of pearls and dropped them to her chest.

Jack forced himself not to follow their journey. Instead he examined her face. Deep-set eyes, perfectly arched brows, smooth skin, and a stubborn chin. Her platinum blond ponytail with just the right touch of dark roots tantalized the hedonist in him.

I'm in lust, Jack thought.

"Oh, dear," she repeated. "I doubt there's a vacancy in town. Colleen Ryan and Steve Trader are getting married this weekend. Every room's probably taken. Are you here for the wedding?" She tipped her head to the side and looked up at him.

Jack had a firm policy about weddings—he never attended them. After all, he wasn't going to have one of his own. "Sorry. I don't know the happy couple." He shrugged. "Maybe I'll just head back toward Kinzers. I saw an intersection with gas stations and fast food—"

"I know!" she interrupted. "The Good and Plenty Bed-and-Breakfast! Mrs. Bickley might have a room open. She's not partial to wedding crowds." Then her face fell. "Unfortunately, she turns out the lights by ten. You'll be in big trouble if you try to wake her up now."

"Something deadly in my cappuccino?"

"More likely no ice cream with your shoofly pie."

They laughed together like old friends.

"I'm Jack Ryan, by the way—no relation to Colleen, the happy bride." He held out his hand.

Her small hand fit snugly into his. He wanted to reel her into his arms. Music, a familiar melody made for close dancing, played in the background. An Elvis tune, something slow and haunting about a whippoorwill—the kind of song that made women cry.

He shook her hand and quickly released it before he did something rash, before he forgot his mission. He must be really tired. This was not a sophisticated underwear model like Cheryl; this was a country girl.

"I'm Tuesday Evans."

"Tuesday?" He smiled. Somehow the name went with the garb.

She smiled back at him. Dimples. Deep ones.

"My mother saw this movie once, and ever after wished to be Tuesday Weld. Naming me after her was the next best thing. You're better off driving on, I think. Once you're out of Paradise, you'll find plenty of motels."

He couldn't leave Paradise. Not until he got a lead on Elvis, anyway. "Isn't there any place I can go around here? I'm almost too tired to drive."

"I might be able to fix you up at my place, if you're not too fussy."

Her place! He almost swallowed his tongue. He'd found Heaven in Paradise.

"Come on." She gestured him after her. Beneath the hem of her gently swaying skirt, her trim calves rose from a froth of lace-edged ankle socks and shoes with a number eight on the back. He imagined nibbling on her toes—at her place.

"Back off, buddy," he said to himself as he waited by the long Formica counter that ran across one side of the room. One end of the counter appeared to be a café with stools; the near end held an old-fashioned cash register.

She walked behind the business end and changed her shoes. When she rounded the counter again, she wore black-and-white saddle shoes. She flicked a switch. The room fell dark. The only light left, that of the video games near the entrance, pulsed red and cast a luscious gleam on her full lips.

"You're from Boston, aren't you?" she said, leading the way through the door and locking it behind him.

He gestured to the Massachusetts plates on his car that sat alone in the gravel lot. "Yes. I'm originally from South Boston. Where's your car?"

"Oh, I walked here. I'm just down the road. It's really a zoo at the Strike Zone on Fifties Night, so sometimes I help out."

He raised his key ring and pressed the button to unlock the car. The lights went on; the horn sounded. In a panic, he hit the other buttons on his remote. The trunk popped up. The horn continued to blare, shattering the still night. He pointed the remote at the car and frantically punched buttons with his thumb. Tuesday snatched the key ring from him. The doors opened. The car fell silent. The lights went off.

"I just bought it," he said lamely.

"No kidding." She shook her head, her hand extended, the remote offered. "Who'd you think would steal your car out here, in the middle of a cornfield? A cow?" Her eyes twinkled

189

with amusement. "I think it might be safer if we walk to my place." She examined him from head to toe in a manner that elevated his temperature. "Who knows, you might be a dangerous criminal." Her bantering tone told him she didn't view him as such.

Jack pulled his suitcase from the trunk, closed it firmly, and reset the alarm. "Trust me, I'm harmless." He donned his safest smile. "Lead on."

He felt energized. He could walk a country mile if Tuesday Evans led the way. Her scent, something light and floral, drifted to him as they walked along the shoulder of the road. "I can't believe how dark it is out here."

"That's because you're in Amish country. Many of the farms here don't have electricity, and farmers rise early. They've been in bed for hours."

The thought of being in bed reminded him of Cheryl's parting shot when he'd broken their date. "Strike three, Jack. You're out." The memory made him set his mouth in a grim line. This charity work for Heaven really cost a lot.

"We're in the middle of nowhere," he said.

"No, we're in Paradise."

They walked in a companionable silence for only a few blocks back in the direction he'd come from. "Here we are." She stopped at a white building. It bore a small sign: PARADISE CLASSIC CARS. The converted barn gleamed with fresh paint and glossy red trim.

So much for her place. She unlocked a garage door and hefted the door up in a lithe motion that demonstrated a supple athleticism. He loved a fit woman.

She disappeared for a moment. Light flooded the interior. A row of what used to be animal stalls of some sort stood to his right. Each held a car. He recognized a 1957 Chevrolet Bel-Air. His grandfather still drove one. A rusty Mustang filled another stall, and half-way out of one poked a long boat with fins—a 1960-something Cadillac. On the walls, large posters of cars from hot rods to old Thunderbirds rubbed shoulders with the obligatory modern insurance warnings.

He gave a low whistle. "This place is yours?"

She nodded and flicked on the lights. "There's an empty room upstairs. I used to rent it to my mechanic, but he's gone now—ran off with Miss Pennsylvania Dairymaid. Would you like to see it?"

He followed Tuesday up the stairs. He loved the lacy socks. Or maybe he loved the graceful legs, or the trim ankles. He pulled himself up short. Country girl, country girl, he reminded himself.

The hot, airless room contained a single bed made with military precision. It looked like heaven at that moment. "This will be fine." He plunked his case on the foot of the bed.

She drew the drapes and turned on the air conditioner. Its low hum filled the air. "Mrs. Bickley will be up at dawn. You can find her by driving straight along Lincoln Highway to Nirvana Street. She has the beautiful brick building on the corner. Just lock the door on your way out. Bathroom's through here." She opened a door to a closet-size bathroom complete with a stall shower.

For a moment, their business concluded, they stood awkwardly before each other. "So, what brings you to Paradise?" she asked, twisting her glasses about on the chain.

"I write freelance articles. I'm doing an Elvis piece."

She stiffened. Her eyes grew round. Green eyes. As green as the grass in Fenway's outfield. "Elvis?"

In an instant, the room's temperature plunged to subzero.

"Sure," Jack said, puzzled by her change in demeanor. "He's always a popular topic. I'm going to profile folks who actually claim Elvis is still alive. I'm looking for an Opal Dinkman. Maybe you can help me. Do you know her?"

"No. Now I have to go." Without an explanation or a good-bye, she darted from the room.

"Thank you, Miss Evans," he said, and hurried after her as she ran down the stairs.

She waved a negligent hand at him. Before he could say

another word, she raised the garage door and slipped under it. She brought it down behind her with a bang.

Jack retreated up the stairs. He stripped and slipped between the sheets. The air conditioner cranked a blast of cool air at him. It did nothing to dispel the smell of oil and hot metal from below. He punched the lumpy pillow and tried to banish the sight of Miss Tuesday Evans from his mind. The image of her, poised in a pool of light at the bowling alley, haunted him. But the frost of her departure cooled his ardor more than the overzealous air conditioner.

Chapter Three

Tuesday walked quickly along Lincoln Highway, the main street of Paradise. She forced herself to ignore her libidinous response to Jack Ryan's smile. When he'd appeared out of the darkness, she'd thought maybe the devil had come to claim her—with all that black hair it was an easy comparison—but the instant he'd spoken and smiled, she'd dropped her wariness. Foolishly, it seemed. She'd bedded the fox down with the hens. "Oh, Tuesday, when will you ever learn? Just because a guy's got a great smile doesn't mean he's harmless."

She hurried up the front walk of her mother's house. The modern ranch sat on the corner of Nirvana and Bliss, just two blocks off Lincoln Highway, and two blocks past the Good and Plenty Bed-and-Breakfast. The sign on the mailbox said DINKMAN.

She felt under a pot of pink geraniums for the spare key. She let herself into the house and quietly tiptoed into her mother's bedroom. The soft whistle of a light snore led her to her mother's bedside.

193

"Mom," she said softly. Her mother stirred.

"Tuesday? What's wrong?"

"Everything, Mom. He's back, isn't he? Why didn't you tell me!" She flipped on the bedside lamp.

Opal Dinkman pulled herself up to a sitting position and touched a hand to her crown of pink, plastic rollers. "Now Tuesday, don't take on so."

Tuesday paced, wringing her hands. "I can't stand it, Mom. You know what it'll be like. The reporters. The sly looks—"

"Now, dear. Would you ask me to lie?" Her mother rose from the bed and slipped a cotton robe over her pink shorty pajamas.

"Yes!" Tuesday cried. "Yes. Just for once. Lie."

"You know I could never do that."

Tuesday collapsed onto the bed and buried her face in her hands. When she looked up, she tried to sound less exasperated. "Where is he?"

"Why, where he usually is, I would imagine."

"No, he's not," Tuesday hissed. "I was just there. I was alone. I'd have seen him."

"Maybe he's in the back, fixing lane thirteen. You know Harold says its been giving us trouble lately."

Tuesday groaned.

"Relax, dear. You know he doesn't like to come out during the day. He promised to stay out of sight."

"Oh, marvelous. Promises from a dead guy." Tuesday scrubbed her hands over her face.

"What you need is a nice, cool drink." Her mother left the bedroom and hurried into the kitchen. She took a pitcher of pink lemonade from the refrigerator. When Tuesday joined her, she poured them each a glass. The air lay like a sultry blanket of heat in the kitchen. No breeze lifted the curtains at the open window.

Tuesday's sweater set, which had been comfortable in the air-conditioned bowling center, now prickled her skin. She used the glass to cool her brow. Maybe, just maybe, if she'd not been ensnared by the reporter's devilish smile, she'd have stepped more warily, sent him up the road to a motel as she'd first suggested. She was more than a little angry—with herself.

Tuesday placed a hand on her mother's and tried to reason with her. "Mom, you just don't understand—"

"Oh, yes, I do. I remember how the kids in school teased you when he visited a few years ago—"

"Mom, that was more than just a few years ago—"

Opal Dinkman prattled on. "Seems like only yesterday when you came home from school crying and swearing you'd push in Bobby Brewster's face if he didn't stop calling me 'Dotty Dinkman.' And the time after that, when your husband ran off."

"Yes, that's what I'm talking about. Not school, Mom. The last time—when Sam left."

"Your father and I, may he rest in peace, never liked Sam."

Tuesday rose and leaned against the counter. She crossed her arms over her chest in exasperation. Her mother perpetually rewrote history. "You liked him fine until he left. I didn't need an Elvis uproar then, and I don't need one now."

"Sam just didn't want a wife who made more money than he did."

There was more to Sam's defection, but now was not the time or the place to try to set her mother straight. In fact, Tuesday thought grimly, she would likely never be able to set her mother straight. It had gotten worse since her father's death three years ago. It was why Tuesday had moved back to Paradise. Her mother needed looking after.

"There's a reporter here. He'll probably be staying at the Good and Plenty. Please promise me you'll stay away from him and the Strike Zone. Promise me you'll deny any Elvis rumors."

"A reporter?" Opal's hand went to her curlers. "Is he young? Is he single?"

"Mom!" Tuesday gritted her teeth. "Who cares if he's as handsome as an Irish god? He's trouble."

"Irish, is he?" Opal rose and dug in a cupboard. "I have a wonderful recipe for soda bread somewhere."

"Mom, you will not be baking for him. I forbid you to speak to him!" Tuesday snatched a cookbook from her mother's hands.

"Now, Tuesday, that's no way to talk to your mother."

Tuesday whirled around. *He* stood in the doorway. She slapped the book on the counter and confronted the source of her agitation. "You stay out of this. And what are you doing here? Don't you have something better to do? Sing hymns? Seduce seraphim?"

Elvis laughed. Opal poured him a glass of lemonade. After a long swallow, he placed the glass on the table. "You sure do know how to make lemonade, Opal," he said in familiar honeyed tones. Although he was older and grayer than he was usually pictured, the sculpted lips and melancholy eyes remained the same.

Her mother beamed at Tuesday. "He promised he'd wear a hat."

A hat. Marvelous. Tuesday fisted her hands on her hips and stepped between Elvis and her mother. "Look. I don't care why you're here, but I won't have my mother harassed. She may not have the sense to keep quiet about your visits, but I do! Now help me out here," she pleaded.

"I wonder if this reporter would like to have lunch?" Opal poked around in the meat drawer of the refrigerator. "Some cold chicken would go nicely with the soda bread."

"There'll be no lunches, Opal," Elvis said. "Tuesday's right. We'll keep a low profile this time. I'm just here for a rest. Can't rest if everyone's hangin' about takin' pictures of my favorite fan club president and askin' nosy questions."

His unexpected support surprised Tuesday.

Her mother smiled. "If you say so. I'll try not to let the cat out of the bag. Now, are you hungry? I have bananas and peanut butter around somewhere. I could fry some bacon."

Tuesday left them haggling over the late-night menu. How

much could she trust Elvis to keep her mother in line? How miserable would her life become in the next few hours?

Her clunky saddle shoes echoed on the wooden porch. She swung her leg over the porch railing, dropped onto the lawn, and crossed to her own house. Her nineteenth-century Victorian monolith contrasted sharply with her mother's neat rancher. She flung open the door, muttering to herself. "Why don't sleazy tabloid reporters look like toads? Why aren't they ugly, fat, and sweaty?" She slammed the door.

She kicked off her shoes. She shed layers as she walked through the house, draping each piece on the mismatched furniture—stuff rejected by Sam in the divorce. In her bathroom, she stood before the sink and popped out her tinted contacts. Dragging the elastic band from her ponytail, she rubbed her sweaty neck. "Yes, a man's appearance should definitely match his job." She poured a glass of water and inspected her face. Faint lines edged her mouth. A deeper line dug a furrow between her brows. All put there by her mother and You-Know-Who.

"Well, Jack Ryan, you're never going to meet my mother. Not if I have anything to say about it. Never."

Chapter Four

Tuesday rose just before dawn. She painted her mother's mailbox pink with large yellow flowers before the clock struck six. She stood back, hands on hips, and surveyed her work. No more DINKMAN on that mailbox. Thank heaven her mother believed in unlisted phone numbers.

Now to mobilize the troops.

Harold Sauder worked the counter at the Strike Zone. He knew everything worth knowing about the bowling center—and Opal. *Everything.* He answered the phone on the first ring. In his gravelly voice, he agreed to her every request. She also trusted him to brief the part-time employees.

One last call and Mr. Sleazoid Reporter would never meet her mother.

She dialed the number of the Good and Plenty Bed-and-Breakfast. "Mrs. Bickley? This is Tuesday Evans. I hope you don't mind, but I recommended you to a man named Jack Ryan—" She listened for a moment. Her stomach fluttered, and not from hunger. "Arrived just now? Yes, I know he talks funny. He's from Boston. Eating breakfast, is he?"

I hope he gets heartburn to match the heartache he's going to create.

"Having seconds on your scrapple? Glad to hear it." She crossed her fingers—on both hands. "I have to warn you, though, as nice as he seems, I think he might be part of the group that wants to buy the Wohler farm and the Strike Zone and build an outlet mall." She said a silent prayer asking forgiveness for the lie. "That's right. Now, if you don't mind, could you avoid telling him where to find Mom? Uh-oh. You've already told him she owns the Strike Zone." She bit her lip. "Well, don't let him know where she lives."

Mrs. Bickley didn't need any more persuasion. She headed KOOP: Keep Outlets Out of Paradise. Just the mention of off-price shopping threw Sarah Bickley into a tizzy. Her lips were sealed.

At eight o'clock, Tuesday reported to the Paradise Clip and Curl. As her friend Ruth whipped a plastic robe about her, she asked, "What are you doing to me today?"

Ruth, well rounded and apple-cheeked, frowned at Tuesday's blond ponytail. Freckles dotted her nose. Her red hair framed her face in a cloud of wild curls. A blue streak added a certain panache to her elfin appearance. "Today I think we'll go a light brunette, as close as I can get to your natural color, if you don't mind. Maybe shoulder length. We'll comb most of it behind your ears, leave some loose in that careless look. How's that sound?"

"Just make it fast. I've got a mechanic coming for an interview. If he doesn't work out, I'll be fixing Mr. Hinkle's Mustang myself." She stifled an urge to rush her friend. For the first time, she regretted her promise that she'd be Ruth's portfolio model. It had sounded like such fun a few days ago—a new look every day. The request had come at a low-tide moment in her life. Until Ruth's call, Tuesday had had nothing more exciting going on than tuning up her '61 Caddy.

As much as she wanted to help Ruth get out of Paradise and into the world of Manhattan chic, Tuesday chafed at time spent away from Opal and the Zone. She needed to run interference for her mother. A shiver passed down her spine. How long did she have until Elvis fever overwhelmed her mother and she began to spill the beans to just one or two "special" friends; or worse, began posting revelations on her website?

"I wish my mother would give in and marry Harold," she said as Ruth magically converted her from Barbie blond to blah brown, as Sam had referred to her natural hair color.

"How many times has the poor guy proposed?" Ruth asked.

"At least nine. He's so patient. And without him and . . . and his expertise, the Strike Zone would fall apart." Tuesday bit her lip. She'd almost said without him and *Elvis*. An unpleasant thought intruded. Could it be that her mother kept turning Harold down because of Elvis's occasional visits? Did her mom harbor some secret hope that one day Elvis would return to Paradise and stay?

How could a slightly deceased boyfriend be better than a live one—even on the worst of days?

Tuesday fidgeted in her seat, tense, waiting for Ruth to finish. Two and a half hours later, and still one mechanic short, Tuesday pulled her white '61 Cadillac into the parking lot of the Strike Zone. She groaned. Jack Ryan's sleek German car sat in the same slot as the night before. She debated her two options: spend the rest of the day under a hot hunk of metal or run interference for her mother. The heat and humidity of the day pressed in on her like an overheated radiator.

Her quarry leaned on a stool in the cafe section of the Strike Zone, a small spiral-bound notebook in one hand, a cup of coffee in the other. Harold perched next to the reporter, chatting intently.

Tuesday hurried up to the two men. They looked far too cozy. "Don't you have work to do, Harold?"

Harold colored to the roots of his mane of white hair. He

tugged at his large, bushy mustache. His Adam's apple bobbed as he answered. "Sure, Tuesday, but I couldn't resist chatting with Jack here. I'm a real fan."

Tuesday would never have guessed Harold read tabloids. *Mechanics Illustrated* or *Sports World* maybe, but not supermarket rags.

She eyed the reporter. He wore khaki shorts with a navy blue golf shirt. The color darkened his eyes to a deep sapphire, eyes that examined her as if planning a story guaranteed to please the public and humiliate the subject.

"Please see to lane thirteen, Harold. The sweep's out of whack."

Harold nodded, hitched up his jeans, and hurried off in the direction of the lanes.

Jack tucked his notebook into his pocket and swiveled on his stool—the better to view the new Tuesday Evans. "I'm not sure I'd have recognized you," he said. "No ankle socks."

Instead she wore thin, strappy sandals and a crisp dress in blue linen. Her shoulder-length hair, the color of a well-aged pitcher's glove, skimmed her bare shoulders. The woman of the previous night, the one who took in strays and ruined a man's sleep, no longer existed. He mourned her loss. In her place stood a long, cool column of ice.

He blinked. Her eyes were brown, dark as iced tea. Funny, he could have sworn they were Fenway green just a few hours ago. Of course, a few hours ago he'd have sworn a heavenly power had forced him to stop at this bowling alley in the middle of nowhere.

"Did you have trouble finding the Good and Plenty?" She tapped his coffee mug. "I'm sure you could get a better breakfast there than here."

"Mrs. Bickley took good care of me. 'Lots of good food and plenty of it,' she said, and she wasn't lying. She also sent me here. Said Opal Dinkman owned these lanes. I thought you

201

didn't know her.'' He tried to keep the accusation from his voice, but failed.

She ignored his last statement. "Yes, Opal owns the lanes. She's a bit of a recluse. Doesn't come in often.''

"Maybe you can tell me where she lives. Mrs. Bickley said she didn't know.''

"I have no idea. Don't know her that well, either.'' She turned and walked away.

Jack frowned. Wherever did he get the idea she was an innocent country girl? She looked just like one of a thousand well-dressed businesswomen he saw on a daily basis exiting their air-conditioned cars to work in air-conditioned offices in Boston or New York.

A headache bloomed behind his eyes. He rubbed his temples. Not enough sleep and too much food. Real food—butter, bacon, sausage, eggs from running chickens, for heaven's sake! And what the heck was scrabble made out of?

The only good thing about this trip might be the food. The Good and Plenty, a culinary heaven, reminded him of home— without all the prying family members, of course.

He wrote *lunch* in his notebook next to the restaurant suggested by Mrs. Bickley, a restaurant famous for chicken pot pie. The only pot pie he'd eaten in his life came from the freezer department of the grocery store.

Jack tucked his notebook into the pocket of his shorts and followed Tuesday. When she detoured along a strip of polished wood separating lanes fifteen and sixteen, he took a seat at the score table for lane fourteen. Part of the wall at the end of the walkway turned out to be a swinging door. She held it open a few inches and spoke to someone in the shadows.

He contemplated the view. Her movements were elegant, graceful, authoritative. Very authoritative for someone who didn't know the owner very well. Harold Sauder sure jumped to do her bidding.

Ladies in shorts or skirts and purple T-shirts that proclaimed them to be the Bowling Babes of Paradise warmed up on lanes one to six. The sounds of clunking balls and well-oiled machinery filled the air. A teenager who manned the cash register announced, "Number four waiting for pins," over the PA.

Jack's previous missions had taught him a few things. One, he generally got what he wanted if he waited long enough. Two, folks loved to confide in reporters. Three, escapees usually had a compelling reason for going AWOL.

Whatever Elvis's reason, Jack needed to ferret it out and make it disappear. In the past, he'd used a modicum of charm and a generous helping of common sense to accomplish the task.

This mission made his stomach clench. Or was that his breakfast scrabble coming back to haunt him? Or maybe the baked oatmeal he'd consumed on top of everything else before culinary sanity asserted itself.

Indigestion or not, he felt as if the designated-hitter rule had been repealed and he'd been suddenly called on to bat. A man needed to know his strengths—and his weaknesses. Jack reasoned well with sports figures; he knew their habits. Musically, he knew only the theme song to the local sports talk-radio show.

His thoughts returned abruptly to Tuesday Evans. She turned gracefully and came back along the polished wooden walkway, eyes down. She gnawed her lower lip between her teeth. Did she bite her lovers? The thought hit him like a bean ball.

He loved a provocative woman.

She skirted the score tables. Her eyes narrowed as she noticed him. "You're still here?"

Provocative? Problematic. "I thought I'd hang out and see if Opal came by."

Tuesday searched for a reason to send him away.

With a burst of "Blue Suede Shoes" on the sound system, The Big *E* came through the door by lane thirty—far enough away to be just a mechanic in nondescript overalls, but moving ever closer. He wore a black-and-teal baseball cap with IN-TERCOURSE, PA stitched across the front.

That certainly wouldn't attract anyone's attention!

From the corner of her eye, she watched the source of her agitation stop at lane seventeen and start up the machine that oiled the lanes—close enough to curl her hair.

"How about a lesson while you wait?" Tuesday yanked a bowling ball from the ball return. She shoved it into Ryan's chest. As she hoped, he automatically grabbed the ball. She tugged him about until his back was to the pins—and Elvis. "It's pretty simple. Let me show you," she said.

She stifled an urge to giggle at the puzzled expression on Jack Ryan's face. The nearness of *him* demanded action, however.

"Put your fingers here." She guided his hand. A warmth spiked through her body at the contact. They stood inches apart. She felt the heat of his body.

Jack stared into Tuesday's face. Cold brown eyes? No. He thought instead of warm mulled cider. Her sweet scent beguiled him. His headache disappeared.

He studied her hands. Short nails, no polish. *No rings.* She snatched her hands away as if embarrassed by the intimacy of their contact. Might as well throw the ball; maybe she'd help him hold another.

With little grace, he dropped the ball to his side and turned toward the pins.

Elvis shifted over to lane sixteen. Tuesday felt the situation slip from her grip. She darted in front of Ryan and grabbed the ball just as it reached the apex of its swing. "This is the wrong weight for someone your size. Let me get you another."

She tugged on the ball. A flush rose on his cheeks as she twisted him about like a pretzel, the ball firmly attached to his hand. She pulled harder. He groaned.

They danced about at the head of the lane. The Bowling Babes giggled and pointed. She froze, her face hot. The ball rested between them, cupped in their palms. It was all that separated them. Nothing separated Ryan's line of vision from the man oiling lane sixteen.

In a wild moment of panic, Tuesday leaned forward and kissed him. Ryan's lips were smooth and warm. He smelled wonderful. Just like the coconut soap from the garage shower.

It took him less than a moment to respond. When he did, he made up for that lost nanosecond. A shock ran through her system. Two wall-mounted televisions showing a rehash of the previous day's Phillies game went white with static. Tuesday's brain went white with static, too. She leaned into him and sighed against his mouth.

Jack thought of hot summer nights and slow dances. Only the bowling ball prevented him from melding his whole body to hers. A thread of sound, a melody, floated in his head, a song of flowing rivers and warm autumn days. He slipped his free hand around her waist. She moved with him, gently swaying, responding, her kiss soft and sweet.

Tuesday broke the contact first. She kept her eyes down and murmured something unintelligible.

"What?" he said, his voice a frog's croak.

"Your hand. We should do something."

Her gaze met his. He saw a vulnerability there that did not match the sophisticated outer woman. "I guess so. I'd sure hate to wear this all day." He gave her a smile that he hoped reassured and yet told her how much her kiss had affected him, too.

"This way." She led him to an unmarked door. Once inside what turned out to be a small kitchen, she steered him to a deep sink. The ball clunked on the porcelain surface. Their hips touched as she poured liquid detergent over his fingers. Then she tortured him. She stroked the slick soap up and down and around his fingers. He closed his eyes. The image of her rubbing her hands elsewhere with just this amount of patience and gentleness stoked an unwanted fire. He jerked on the tap.

Cold water gushed over his hand and the ball. With a quick tug, he extricated his fingers.

Tuesday handed him a wad of paper towels, two flags of color on her cheeks. He dried his hands and then plucked the ball from the sink and shook the water out of the finger holes.

His voice sounded harsher than he'd intended when he thanked her. "Maybe a lesson isn't a good idea right now," he said. "I just want one thing—"

"Intercourse!"

"W-w-what?" Jack stuttered. Heat surged through him. He bobbled the ball, saved it at the last moment from falling on his toes.

"Intercourse. You want to go to Intercourse. A town near here. Opal sometimes volunteers at the Amish Heritage Center in Intercourse on Fridays." Her words tumbled out in a rush.

Jack covered his embarrassment by carefully drying the bowling ball. He offered it to her. "Really? Fascinating." Busy little recluse, he thought. "Maybe you could come along while I check it out."

Tuesday thought of at least ten reasons to refuse his invitation to Intercourse. Number one on the list was their kiss. It complicated an already complicated situation.

She'd never kissed a man she'd lied to before.

On the other hand, she could think of two super reasons to accompany him. One, Elvis. Two, Opal. "I'd love to."

She racked the ball and followed Jack Ryan to his car. He tossed his small notebook into a battered briefcase on the backseat. A larcenous thought occurred to her. Maybe she should peek at his notes. *No,* she chastised herself. *I've enough on my conscience without adding snooping.*

He pulled from the Strike Zone's lot, spitting stones. "Slow down!" she shouted.

Jack's heart leaped into his throat. He jammed on the brakes, fishtailing a bit before coming to a halt at the side of the road.

"A buggy," she said. She pointed to the top of the hill.

Over the rise came a horse towing a black-and-gray carriage that looked like a narrow box on wheels. As the horse and buggy passed, Jack caught a glimpse of a man with a full beard, no mustache, and a straw hat. He gave Jack a stern look.

"I didn't mean to shout, but you need to drive with care here. The Amish have a right to road space, too, and have less ability to maneuver."

"Thanks for the warning," he said. His blood thundered in his chest. His imagination painted a vivid vision of a ton of car colliding with half a ton of horseflesh. "You sure have a powerful set of lungs. I almost lost my scrabble back there," he said as he pulled out onto the road at a more sedate pace.

"It's scrapple, with two *P*s."

"Scrapple. I see. And what's scrapple?" He smiled at her. She looked wonderful in the sunlight. A thousand separate shades of brown glistened in her hair. It suited the honey tones of her skin as the blond could never do. She put on a pair of sunglasses. Designer glasses. The same make as the ones Cheryl wore—sophisticated Manhattan Cheryl.

"It's a pork product. My mother always says it's everything but the oink."

"I'm sorry I asked. How do I get it shipped to Boston?"

It took them only a few minutes to leave Paradise behind for Intercourse. The tiny town consisted of two main streets that came together in a vee, streets packed with summer visitors. It was more picturesque than Paradise, more planned, less homey. Tuesday directed him to a public parking lot behind a minuscule library.

After Tuesday had detoured into the fifth shop, Jack began to suspect their visit was less a means of meeting Opal than a way to avoid her. The oppressive heat brought back his headache. He felt as if Mrs. Bickley had flattened and fried him on her griddle along with the scrapple.

"I really can't carry all these packages," she said as they

stood outside a jam shop. "Can we go back to your car and unload?"

"Not necessary. I'll be happy to carry them for you." Jack grabbed her bags. Filled with jars of local apple butter and chowchow, whatever that was, they weighed a ton. "Now, the Heritage Center?"

"Let's just pop in here first," she said, and disappeared into another house converted into an antique shop. He crossed the wooden porch, determined to halt her shopping spree before he lost complete control. Father Mike expected swift results, not souvenirs.

Inside, the smell of old wood and cinnamon-scented candles filled the air. A pile of brochures on the Pennsylvania Amish country lay on a simple pine table. A quick glance through one on Intercourse sent his temper soaring. An ominous rumble of metal on wood made him look up. "No." He said it emphatically. "No."

"But—"

"No, no wagon wheels." The wheel, banded with rusty iron, stood a yard high.

"But this is a great example of an old Amish buggy wheel." She knelt by it and looked up at him from under her lashes. "Mrs. Bickley will love it." She smiled.

His insides flashed hot. *Sweet Lord!* "No wagon wheels in my new car."

Ten minutes later, they headed back toward the parking lot. Tuesday rolled the wheel along like a hoop. He cringed as he wedged the wheel against his leather backseat along with her shopping bags.

"That's your last purchase," he said in a growl.

She leaned into the car, giving him a great view of her long legs, and patted the wheel. "Spoilsport."

He hooked his arm through hers. "Speaking of sport, I think you've played your game long enough."

Thrill to the most sensual, adventure-filled Historical Romances on the market today...

FROM  LEISURE BOOKS

As a home subscriber to the Leisure Historical Romance Book Club, you'll enjoy the best in today's BRAND-NEW Historical Romance fiction. For over twenty-five years, Leisure Books has brought you the award-winning, high-quality authors you know and love to read. Each Leisure Historical Romance will sweep you away to a world of high adventure...and intimate romance. Discover for yourself all the passion and excitement millions of readers thrill to each and every month.

SAVE AT LEAST $5.00 EACH TIME YOU BUY!

Each month, the Leisure Historical Romance Book Club brings you four brand-new titles from Leisure Books, America's foremost publisher of Historical Romances. EACH PACKAGE WILL SAVE YOU AT LEAST $5.00 FROM THE BOOKSTORE PRICE! And you'll never miss a new title with our convenient home delivery service.

Here's how we do it. Each package will carry a 10-DAY EXAMINATION privilege. At the end of that time, if you decide to keep your books, simply pay the low invoice price of $16.96 ($19.98 CANADA), no shipping or handling charges added.* HOME DELIVERY IS ALWAYS FREE.* With today's top Historical Romance novels selling for $5.99 and higher, our price SAVES YOU AT LEAST $5.00 with each shipment.

AND YOUR FIRST FOUR-BOOK SHIPMENT IS TOTALLY FREE!

IT'S A BARGAIN YOU CAN'T BEAT! A Super $21.96 Value!

LEISURE BOOKS A Division of Dorchester Publishing Co., Inc.

GET YOUR 4 FREE* BOOKS NOW—
A $21.96 VALUE!

Mail the Free* Books
Certificate
Today!

---

4 FREE* BOOKS 🌹 A $21.96 VALUE

Free *Books Certificate*

YES! I want to subscribe to the Leisure Historical Romance Book Club. Please send me my 4 FREE* BOOKS. Then, each month I'll receive the four newest Leisure Historical Romance selections to preview for 10 days. If I decide to keep them, I will pay the Special Member's Only discounted price of just $4.24 each, a total of $16.96 ($19.98 in Canada). This is a SAVINGS OF AT LEAST $5.00 off the bookstore price. There are no shipping, handling, or other charges.* There is no minimum number of books I must buy and I may cancel the program at any time. In any case, the 4 FREE* BOOKS are mine to keep—A BIG $21.96 Value!

*In Canada, add $7.95 US shipping and handling per order for first shipment. For all subsequent shipments to Canada the cost of membership in the Book Club is $19.98 US plus $7.95 US shipping and handling per order. All payments must be made in US dollars.

Name _____

Address _____

City _____

State _____ *Zip* _____

Telephone _____

Signature _____

If under 18, Parent or Guardian must sign. Terms, prices and conditions subject to change. Subscription subject to acceptance. Leisure Books reserves the right to reject any order or cancel any subscription.

(Tear Here and Mail Your FREE Book Card Today!)*

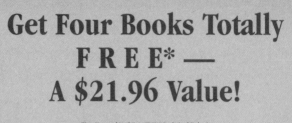

Get Four Books Totally
F R E E* —
A $21.96 Value!

(Tear Here and Mail Your FREE* Book Card Today!)

PLEASE RUSH
MY FOUR FREE*
BOOKS TO ME
RIGHT AWAY!

Leisure Historical Romance Book Club
P.O. Box 6613
Edison, NJ 08818-6613

Chapter Five

"Game?"

Damn, she looked innocent and sultry at the same time. Jack slipped on his sunglasses for a modicum of protection. "Yes, and I'm leadoff man now. Follow if you like." Madder than a batter called out on a bad call, he forged his way through the crowds. According to the brochure, the Heritage Center was on nearly the opposite side of town from the library's lot in which they'd parked. There was also a sizable parking lot directly behind the Heritage Center.

She drew alongside him after a block. He ignored her with a stubborn silence. At the Heritage Center it came as no surprise to learn that Opal wasn't on duty that day and wouldn't be for another week.

Sweat trickled down Jack's back. He should be in an air-conditioned hotel room in New York City. With little of the gentleman about him, he gripped Tuesday by the upper arm and led her to a gazebo on the corner. There he released her and dropped onto a narrow bench. Tuesday sat next to him.

The small bench meant their thighs almost touched. He felt her heat.

Lust was not going to get in the way of his job. He jumped to his feet and shoved his hands into his pockets. He adopted the same voice his father used to quell rebellion in the Ryan household.

"Explain this game—and I'm too hot to listen to a fairy tale."

Tuesday swallowed hard. He sure sounded cranky. She crossed her fingers on her left hand, out of his sight. "Opal said she really didn't want to meet you. She thinks you'll hound her over this Elvis thing, so she asked me to run interference."

"Now why would I hound her? It's just an interview."

"Do you see that man over there and those tourists? I'm sure they think it's just another photograph." Tuesday nodded and Jack looked where she directed. He saw an Amish buggy in front of a white clapboard building with a small sign saying HARNESS SHOP. A young man, dressed in black, stood with his back to a couple who tried to take his picture. Jack noted the stiff set of the young man's shoulders as he tied up his horse and then moved into the privacy of the doorway.

The laughing couple bulged from shorts and T-shirts that said, ATLANTIC CITY OR BUST. Another buggy approached, an open carriage much like a sulky used in harness racing. The Corvette of buggies, Jack thought. Then he frowned. The couple crowded close to the carriage and fired off more pictures. Jack felt indignant on the driver's behalf.

"I don't know how the Amish stand it—people gawking, pointing, trying to take their picture. Every day of every year. Why don't we leave them in peace?"

"Opal shouldn't have to go through that either. She may be a bit eccentric, but that shouldn't make her a tourist attraction. And that's what your article will do to her."

Jack sympathized with her concern. He heard it in her voice, saw it in the clench of her hands in her lap. How he wished to tell her he had no interest in Opal; he just wanted Elvis.

Still, he didn't want anyone pointing fingers at him, either. Seven missions had taught him never to directly ask for his quarry. To do so was to face ridicule and scorn. He could put her mind at ease in one respect.

"You can tell Opal I'll promise not to put her name in my article." Not a lie. There would be no article.

"What guarantee does she get that you're telling the truth?"

Jack made an sign on his chest. "Cross my heart. I won't name her in my article. It's all I have to offer."

Tuesday desperately wanted to believe him. She searched his face for some clue to his inner thoughts. He sounded and looked sincere. She found it hard to picture him writing stories about alien babies or encounters with dead entertainers, but that was what he did for a living. "I'm sorry. You might not name her, but there are sure to be facts in your article that will indicate her to those who live around here. Please, can't you write about something else?"

"My boss calls the shots, not me." That wasn't a lie, either.

Jack watched disappointment flicker across her face.

"I can't help you," she said softly.

"Then I'll find her another way. Let's go." Jack walked quickly back to the car. She kept pace with him all the way. They didn't exchange a single word. When they reached the car, he carefully punched the button that unlocked the door. He didn't want to look like a fool while acting out righteous indignation. There was no doubt in his mind that Opal was in Paradise, maybe even sharing shoofly pie with Elvis.

Father Mike would have a field day with this one. The great Jack Ryan led on by a country girl in city clothes. He felt like a rookie pitcher who'd let himself be distracted from the batter by the antics of a runner about to steal a base.

Chapter Six

The Strike Zone's cafe gave off the smell of frying hamburgers and French fries. Jack's stomach growled.

Tuesday tucked errant strands of hair behind her ears. "What are you going to do now?" she asked and bit her lip.

He flapped his notebook in her face. "I'm going to ask every person here if they know Opal."

"Go ahead. Ruin her peace of mind!" She stalked away along the lanes and through a door at the far end.

He watched her go. Never had he met a more determined woman.

He loved determination.

When this mission ended, he was coming back to Paradise. And not for bowling lessons.

"Mom?" Tuesday called softly, peering into the gloomy corridor at the rear of the lanes. Jack Ryan's pronouncement sent shivers down her spine. The Ladies' League, thanks to Harold, thought Jack was a prospector after outlet sites, but what about casual drop-ins?

"Mom," she whispered again. The sound of machinery scooping up pins and returning balls to bowlers echoed about her. Down one side of the corridor, rank after rank of circular openings housed the works of each lane. Opposite, tall metal shelves, stuffed with the parts necessary to keep the lanes in action, filled the space, floor to ceiling. "Mom?"

"You asked her to stay home, and that's where she is."

He came from the dark end of the corridor, his face shadowed by the ludicrous baseball cap. He stopped to wipe down one of the huge vertical wheels that spun the balls back to the bowler.

"Look. How can I convince you to go away?"

"*You* can't. I've business here. When it's done, I'll go."

Anger surged through her. "What business? Monkey business? You drop in every few years and wreak havoc in Mom's life. How's she supposed to be content in Paradise when you're gone? Don't you think you two are a bit old for this?"

"Nothin' improper's goin' on between your mother and me. She's been a loyal friend, runnin' my fan club hereabouts for forty years. She's unhappy. I'm here to help her."

"Help! How can you help her?" She gestured wildly to the busy lanes behind them. "If anyone even took half a moment to really look at you, we'd be on the front page of every paper in the nation. There's a reporter twenty feet away, right now!"

"Calm down. Lower your voice." Elvis ignored her as he pulled a jammed bowling pin from the back of lane eight.

Tuesday jerked the pin from his hand. She shoved it back into the chute that would send it to the pin turret. The air-conditioning did not reach to this narrow place. Sweat trickled down her brow. A hint of peanut butter filled the air. The hair on her arms crackled with static.

Dead he might be, but he sure looked fit and healthy—far more fit and healthy than on his last live tour. Heaven agreed with him. "I am calm. And why doesn't my dad ever visit?"

He shook his head and moved down the line of lanes. "Some folks don't have unfinished business. They've got everything they need there. As for those women recognizing me"—he shrugged—"they won't. People see what they want to see. Hear what they want to hear. Twist events to suit themselves."

"This reporter named Jack Ryan says he's hanging out here until he talks to Mom. You're very much on *his* mind. He'll see you, I know it."

He climbed onto the works of lane thirteen. He put a hand on the gearbox and looked down on her. "Whatever is to be, will be."

"Grrrrr." Tuesday charged back along the corridor, flung open the door, and stormed out. She felt suddenly damp and defeated, like a rumpled bedspread. What had possessed her to wear linen on such a humid day? Jack Ryan, that was what—or who.

Despite her aversion to Jack Ryan's profession, she did not want him to remember her as " '50s Barbie." The object of her concern strolled from customer to customer, chatting, laughing, oblivious to the agitation he raised in her.

Two men in pin-striped business suits strode into the café area. "Oh, no," Tuesday muttered. They placed identical black briefcases on the counter.

"Hello, Mrs. Evans."

"Mr. Stewart. Mr. Fletcher." She gave them a cold nod.

Jason Stewart and Ian Fletcher looked as out of place in the sweltering heat in their suits as Elvis did in his overalls.

"We've been looking for Mrs. Dinkman. No one seems to know why she hasn't come in today."

Tuesday stifled an urge to swear. "She gave you her answer last month. She doesn't want to sell."

Mr. Fletcher unsnapped his briefcase. He extracted a sheet of ivory paper. "Maybe she'll reconsider."

The number of zeroes on the page widened Tuesday's eyes

214

and tightened her stomach muscles. She folded the paper in half. Her hand shook. "I'll be sure to pass the information on." Until this one, all offers from these men and their company, Starcorp, had been vague. Suddenly, a shopping mall to replace the Strike Zone seemed an uncomfortable reality.

Fletcher usually did the talking, but she sensed that Mr. Stewart ran the show. He rose first. "Don't take too long, Mrs. Evans; the Wohlers are anxious to see our final plans."

The implication could not be clearer. The Wohlers were selling their farm. Opal would no longer have a bowling center at the edge of the Wohler's cornfields, but a bowling center in the middle of a concrete cash cow. The knot in her stomach rose to her throat.

She sank to the stool vacated by Mr. Stewart, dropped her head onto her hand, and sighed. She couldn't halt progress, but it hurt to watch it creep toward her. She'd grown up here, done her homework at the counter where she now sat.

The Strike Zone lacked the amenities of the newer and bigger bowling centers. Modernization, in the form of wide-screen televisions and computerized scoring, cost more than $150,000.

Fletcher put his hand on her shoulder. He licked his lips and darted a look at Stewart, then whispered, "Your mother can't afford the consequences of refusing."

"I beg your pardon?" She half rose from her seat. "Are you threatening her?"

"Good day, Mrs. Evans." Fletcher scurried out the door in Stewart's wake. She stared after them, Jack Ryan and Elvis forgotten. What consequences did he mean? Going broke? Or worse?

Another hand touched her shoulder. She looked up into Ryan's dark blue eyes. Concern knitted his brow. "What's wrong? What did that guy say to you?"

Ryan looked ready to defend her honor. *Impossible. Honor and sleaze in one container? Impossible.* "H-h-he didn't say anything."

"Bull—baloney. Your face is white. Your hands are shaking." He took hers into his warm ones. A strange sensation spread from the contact up along her arms to her throat. Her pulse fluttered and stuttered. In the background, from the speakers, a recording of Elvis crooned about leaving one's cares behind. "What did that guy say? Let me help you."

The urge to blurt it all out, Elvis included, rose along with her heartbeat. The feel of Ryan's kiss still lingered on her lips. He chafed her cold hands with his.

She had to defend herself from his seductive voice and touch; he made his living ridiculing people, exaggerating the truth. And because he did, she silently vowed to tell the truth for the rest of the day. "It's none of your business."

He dropped her hands as if they burned. Without a word he walked away. Somehow she felt lost, not triumphant.

"What's wrong, lovey?" Harold perched next to her.

She rubbed the backs of her hands. "Nothing I can't handle." Liar, she thought. She swiveled to face Harold. "Starcorp made another offer, high enough to tempt even the Wohlers to sell."

Harold placed his warm, callused hand on hers. "Don't fret. Opal's perfectly capable of making a sensible decision. Stop trying to save the world."

"I wish my dad had planned better." Her eyes teared up.

"Your dad loved cars, not bowling, just like you, honey. Take care of Paradise Cars like he wanted, and leave the bowling decisions to Opal." He patted her hand. She leaned over and gave him a hug.

"That young man sure can bowl." Harold jerked a thumb in the direction of lane twelve.

She frowned. Jack Ryan bowled like a professional. So much for lessons. Tuesday avoided Harold's amused gaze. "If you say so." She needed an antacid to combat the roiling pit called her stomach. How long before Ryan found someone who knew where her mom lived? "I hope he slips and sprains his back. I'll personally hook him up to the traction equipment. That should keep him out of Mom's hair.''

"He's a pretty impressive young man.''

"Yeah, well, I've learned not to trust a handsome man.'' *Or, I'm starting right now.* She cringed at how easily she'd let Jack Ryan invade their lives. "I'm going to check on Mom. Keep an eye on Mr. Muckraker.''

Harold chuckled. "He looks pretty harmless to me.''

Tuesday slowly rose to her feet. "You're forgetting he could make a laughingstock of Mom, not to mention You-Know-Who.'' She jerked her head in the direction of lane twelve. "I hope I never see him again.''

Harold was wrong. Harmless and Jack Ryan didn't belong in the same sentence. At the very least Ryan sent her blood pressure into the red zone. With her luck, she'd have a stroke. The humidity slapped Tuesday in the face as she left the Strike Zone.

Once in the parking lot, she yanked open the door to her car. The seats and steering wheel of the convertible were molten-metal hot, despite the fact that she'd parked in the shade. "I'm buying an air-conditioned car tomorrow. A real car. One made after the Vietnam War. One with air bags. Maybe even a CD player,'' she muttered as she drove to her mother's house.

She parked her car in the garage behind the house, just in case Mr. Relentless Reporter drove by.

The kitchen smelled of baking. The busy oven pushed the temperature in the room into the high nineties. Tuesday took a deep breath and tried to control her exasperation. Two loaves of soda bread sat cooling on the counter. Her mom was rolling Irish potatoes in cinnamon.

"Mom. I thought I told you that Jack Ryan is *not* coming to lunch.'' She looked at her watch. "Or dinner.''

"I know, dear,'' her mother said with a beatific smile. "But these recipes were so tempting, and I haven't made Irish potatoes in years. Have one.''

"No, thank you." Tuesday sat at the table and let the familiar sight of her mother busy at a recipe soothe her. "Fletcher and Stewart brought you another offer." She placed it on the table.

Opal glanced at it. "My, that's a big one. Sure would buy a good-size RV."

"Yes. It would. One for everyone in town, as well. Do you think you'll take their offer this time? It'll be hard for the Wohlers to refuse."

With a negligent wave of her hand and a scattering of cinnamon down her hot-pink shorts, Opal dismissed the idea. "I think the Wohlers are just as determined as I am to keep Starcorp's pesky outlet out of Paradise."

"If you took Starcorp's offer, you'd be set for the rest of your life."

"There's more to life than money. I'll get by," her mother said. Stubborn determination colored her words.

Tuesday knew the bowling center lost money. Even the popularity of '50s Night and bumper-bowling parties for children could not make up for the long hours when very few made use of the lanes. Folks did not come to the Amish country to bowl. "Look. I'm doing really well, I could set up—"

Opal slammed her hands palm-down on the table. "None of that! I'm perfectly able to take care of myself. If I want to sell the Strike Zone, I will.

"Now, how's that lovely young man doing? Has he asked you out yet? You probably should have stayed blond. Men prefer a blonde, you know." Opal touched her perfectly curled ash blond hair.

"Jack Ryan is not going to take me out. He's here to torment us. Now don't forget you promised to stay home and not answer the door."

"Sarah said he has a very healthy appetite and wonderful shoulders—"

"Mother! You and Mrs. Bickley should not be discussing—"

"We think he would be just perfect for you."

Tuesday flopped back into her chair and laughed out loud. "Oh, marvelous. Matchmaking—Paradise style." The laughter released some of her tension, brought her back to the sane, comfortable world of home.

Opal popped an Irish potato into her mouth and winked.

"I think you'd fix me up with the counter boy if he showed an interest."

"No, dear. I want you to be happy. I want you to find the man of your dreams. This is Paradise, after all. You might miss your little brokerage firm in Philadelphia, but you know your first love is cars. One day a man will walk into the garage and sweep you off your feet."

Tuesday had sold her share of the brokerage firm to her partner and come home to run Paradise Classic Cars, not because of her love of cars, but to protect her widowed mother—from herself. Tuesday realized her financial background condemned her to showing her mother the advantages of Starcorp's offer, like it or not. As for any man sweeping her off her feet . . .

"I'll think about the man of my dreams when the Starcorp issue is settled."

"And I think I'll see if Elvis needs anything." Opal rinsed her hands at the sink.

"No, Mom! Stay here, please, or visit Aunt Garnet."

Her mother stared at her. "I can't desert Elvis. He needs me."

"Needs you? Strange. He seems to think *you* need him. What could a dead guy find here?"

Her mother drew herself up to her total height of five foot two. "I did not raise you to be uncharitable. Elvis has given me—and the rest of the world, I might add—great pleasure. Why, he knows a song for every occasion from Christmas to weddings. All he's asking is a place to rest. How can I refuse?''

Tuesday gritted her teeth. "Rest? From what? Too many gigs on the Elysian fields?''

"That's enough. You'll never attract another husband with that attitude.''

Tuesday changed the subject. "Starcorp will be as persistent as Jack Ryan, but Starcorp knows your address. Great. There's a thought. Starcorp joining forces with Mr. Ryan.'' She shuddered.

"There's only one way to make sure Starcorp stays away from Mr. Ryan, dear. Keep him busy yourself.'' Opal started to lay neat rows of Irish potatoes in a box. She hummed a few bars of "Suspicious Minds.''

Tuesday plucked at her rumpled linen dress. Keeping Jack Ryan busy meant peacemaking. Flirting. She shot off her chair, through the door, and over the porch railing.

Thirty minutes later, showered and changed, wearing a fresh yellow sundress, Tuesday pulled her Cadillac into the driveway of the Strike Zone. Ryan's car was gone.

"Why can't the darn man stay put?'' she asked herself. She drove slowly along the highway, glancing left and right. She didn't have to look far. She pulled her car into a space in front of the Good and Plenty Bed-and-Breakfast. Jack Ryan sat in a wicker chair on the front porch with Mrs. Bickley, the buggy wheel propped at his side. He gestured and swung his arm in a circle. Mrs. Bickley giggled like a schoolgirl. *Disgusting.*

She walked up the front walk of the inn. Built in 1904, the beautifully proportioned brick house stood three stories high, with a side portico that once sheltered horse-drawn carriages.

"I was hoping I'd find you here,'' Tuesday said when Ryan turned his blue eyes—glacial blue eyes—in her direction. She'd better watch out or she'd need mittens to handle him. That thought made sweat break out on her palms.

"Just delivering your gift.'' He patted the wheel.

"Can't imagine why you bought me a buggy wheel," Mrs. Bickley said, her head cocked to the side.

Tuesday's mind fumbled through a list of possible lies, but Ryan interrupted her. "Mrs. Bickley's been telling me about KOOP. Seems Opal helped found the group," he said. His tone implied she might have told him herself.

Mrs. Bickley leaned forward in the rocker. She winked at Tuesday behind Ryan's back. "I told Jack, here, that Opal's probably hiding from those Starcorp vultures. He's not likely to find her until they're gone."

Good going, Mrs. B. Tuesday nodded. "Why didn't I think of that? I guess you can go back to Boston. Little chance of an interview now."

A long silence developed.

Ryan stood up, rolled his shoulders, and flexed his right arm. The fluid grace of the motion reminded her of an athlete warming up. She warmed up a few degrees herself. She looked away. Carrie, a high school student who helped with the cleaning at the bed-and-breakfast, came out onto the porch with a pitcher of lemonade. She also paused to admire Ryan's languid stretch.

The manner in which the girl simpered about as she served the reporter made Tuesday want to spank her. Was anyone immune to his charm? Was she?

He sampled the tall, cool drink and then turned his gaze on her. "That guy who upset you. Was he from Starcorp?"

Concern colored his voice, concern she didn't want or need. She just nodded and shrugged.

"Are you sure I can't help you?"

"Just go. Your presence muddies the water." The unexpected plea popped out tart and cold.

Mrs. Bickley cleared her throat.

Ryan finally broke the uncomfortable silence. "I don't see any reason to rush off. I need a vacation, and Mrs. Bickley said the Dutch Country Diner serves the best chicken pot pie in Lancaster County. Maybe you'd like to check it out with me this evening?''

Mrs. Bickley shoved in her two cents before Tuesday opened her mouth. ''Tuesday makes a better pot pie than any restaurant.''

Shush, Mrs. B! The last thing I need is Jack Ryan in my hot kitchen—right next door to Opal and her Irish potatoes.

''No, no. Let's go to the diner. I haven't cooked anything more complicated than a microwave meal in years.'' Keeping him busy might not be so difficult.

''Great.'' He bounded down the porch steps and held her car door open. As she slid into the driver's seat, he leaned in. If she turned her cheek, she'd be able to kiss him again. ''I'm disappointed,'' he said softly. His warm breath tickled the skin by her ear. ''I'm sure anything you cooked up would be intriguing.''

Chapter Seven

Jack, weighed down by two huge servings of chicken pot pie, took over the driving after dinner. They headed west out of Intercourse for Bird-in-Hand. "I'd like to see some of the countryside before it gets dark," he said, then peered up at the sky and added, "or it starts to rain."

Everywhere he looked, he saw contrasts. Cars and tour buses zipped along past horse-drawn buggies. He saw a microwave tower and a windmill, a satellite dish and a man hitching up a team of mules. Two young Amish women in bonnets and sunglasses walked by the side of the road. Road apples lay under an Amtrak bridge.

Tuesday pointed straight; he turned left. She jerked around to face him.

"Time to get back." He pointed up. The bank of clouds looked like a black mountain with a golden halo around it. Streaks of red radiated from the golden halo. Heaven's on fire, he thought.

Tuesday sat as tense as a batter with a full count. He needed to earn her trust. The thought ate at him. How could she trust a liar? Lie to her he had and would again if it served his purpose. In the past, the incongruity of a liar working for Heaven never failed to amuse him. Today it shamed him.

Jack pulled the car over to the shoulder by a covered bridge. He climbed out, leaned on the hood, and looked out at the winding stream. "Does this mighty river have a name?"

She rewarded him with a ghost of a smile. "Pequea Creek."

Across the road, crows filled a tree. Fields of corn and some other green plant stretched off in both directions. He relished the relief of the cool breezes that bathed his face as the storm built.

Tuesday got out of the car and put up the ragtop. Each stretch of her body pulled her dress close on her hips and legs.

He strolled through the bridge to the other side. When she came after him, he slipped his hand into his pocket and withdrew a small camera. She looked delicate and fragile as she emerged from the shadows.

Gusts of wind lifted the flowing yellow dress about her legs. Just as he snapped her picture, she hesitated in the opening. For a moment she looked ready to run. He turned and walked away a bit to take pictures of the bridge.

Tuesday suppressed a desire to push him off the bank into the creek. She pictured the headline over her picture: COUNTRY GIRL TALKS TO ELVIS. Her cheeks flashed hot. First she'd lied to the man; now she was going to steal his camera.

Jack sighed. Her eyes were glued to his hand. "What's that growing over there?" he asked to distract her.

"Tobacco." She crossed her arms. Her knuckles went white.

"No kidding. Cool." He shot several pictures of the field. "Who'd have thought there was tobacco in Pennsylvania?"

"Why don't I take a picture of you and the bridge?" she asked. Her hand covered his. Her skin appeared pale against his dark tan. If he gave her the camera, would she just toss it into the creek or would she play out some ludicrous drama that ended with the camera smashed?

He held it out. The pictures were unimportant. What she did next was not. "Do you really think Opal's hiding out from these Starcorp people?" He leaned on a fence post and watched the row of crows across the street as she backed up and focused on him.

If so, maybe that's why Elvis had come to Paradise. He wanted to help his number one fan. Maybe that explained all the other Elvis sightings, too. Maybe Elvis popped back to earth now and then to help out his special fans.

How on earth could Elvis help Opal this time? Jack knew heavenly escapees had no access to their wealth. Elvis couldn't tell Starcorp in person to get lost. No, Elvis had only his persuasive powers to help Opal withstand what was probably a frontal attack of the most lucrative kind. That had to be why Elvis was back. The situation had not changed his task.

Find Opal. Find Elvis. Solve Opal's problem, solve Elvis's problem.

He saw the indecision on Tuesday's face. The crows took off in a flurry of wings and cries behind her. She held her hair back and watched them go. The camera dangled from her fingers, against her leg. The wind sculpted her body with the soft yellow cloth. His blood hummed and heated. He waited.

Very slowly, she turned. Their eyes locked. She held out her hand, the camera on her palm. "Here," she said softly. He pocketed the camera.

He loved a woman who did the unexpected.

She leaned next to him and lifted her hair to let the rising wind bathe her neck. The pose tantalized him badly. The skin at her nape looked soft and smooth. He took a deep breath. "Does Opal want to sell the bowling alley?"

Grudgingly she gave him an answer. "I don't think Opal knows what she wants to do. The Strike Zone loses money, and she's not getting any younger. These giant shopping outlets are both a blessing and a trial. They bring tourists and their dollars into the area, but some small businesses have difficulty competing.

"There are two huge outlets just down Route Thirty. Why do we need one right in town? And Lincoln Highway's only two lanes. Starcorp's proposal stinks. It's dollars, not sense, and I don't mean c-e-n-t-s. It'll be a nightmare—right across from the elementary school. But most of the town think Opal and Mrs. Bickley started KOOP too late."

"Hmmm." Jack forced his attention from her neck, her throat, the gentle slope of her breast, and watched two children at a nearby farmhouse push each other on a swing. The boy wore identical black trousers and suspenders as a man who walked through the yard. The girl wore a colorful dress with an apron. "What would Mrs. Dinkman do with the money from the sale?"

"Retire. Buy an RV and tour the country. She's always wanted to see Grace—I mean the Grand Canyon." How could she make this man, who made his living off the prurient interests of others, understand? Why couldn't she take his camera? One toss and her picture would have drowned in the Pequea.

"Then maybe Starcorp's offer makes sense for her. What about the Wohlers?"

"Opal and Mrs. Bickley hope the Wohlers will buy into a living-history foundation. The Wohler farm, next door to the Strike Zone, dates from the eighteenth century. Because it had Amish owners until about twenty years ago, it's pretty much preserved. Imagine a place where children can see a working farm as it was in Colonial times, or a way for tourists to experience an Amish farm without intruding. . . ." She felt the heat rise on her cheeks. Jack Ryan must not see how important these ideas were to her and the other KOOP members. He might exploit them in a negative way.

A car came over the hill and passed, swirling dust. Jack walked back into the now-dark interior of the covered bridge. He waited until Tuesday joined him. He put a hand on one of the graceful supporting beams. "Either way, doesn't it mean the end of the Strike Zone?" he asked.

"Yes, but Opal would rather be the parking lot of a museum than the parking lot of an outlet."

Her yellow dress gleamed against the aging structural beams of the bridge. "Don't you have preservation groups here?" he asked.

She moved closer. "Sure. KOOP appealed to them all. Unfortunately, the Wohler farm's not located very advantageously—and they'd have to want to farm, or sell to folks who wanted to farm. The Wohlers want to lie on a beach in Florida."

"If Opal could work out a deal with an independent group willing to finance the living-history idea, would she feel more at ease?"

His face was an inscrutable shadow in the dark interior. Why should Jack Ryan care if Opal was at ease? He would splash her latest claims of an Elvis sighting all over his paper, ending ease in Paradise for months.

"I wouldn't know. I don't know Opal that well."

Jack moved close to where she stood. He examined her face. She had a bone structure that would make her lovely into old age—if her face didn't freeze into the lines of disapproval etched there now. He wanted to reach out and use his fingertips to soothe the furrow from between her brows. He wanted to solve all her problems. Maybe her concern for Opal stemmed from her passionate interest in KOOP.

He loved a passionate woman.

Very slowly, he smoothed a few strands of hair behind her ear. From there, it seemed natural to skim his fingertips down her throat. He searched her face for refusal and saw confusion instead.

She tasted as sweet as he remembered. This time no bowling ball prevented him from drawing her against him, from feeling the heat of her body through the thin dress. She felt nearly naked in his arms. His soul felt naked, too.

This time the kiss did not stay gentle or passive, nor was it one of startled acceptance. The kiss went wild, like a pitch hitting the dirt and bouncing erratically past the catcher, bringing in runners and stealing the game. He no longer cared who won; he wanted more. He pressed her against the bridge railing, accepted the arch of her body that fitted perfectly to his. She was soft where he was hard, curved where he needed curves.

He lightly bit her lips. She moaned into his mouth. Her hands kneaded his chest, then encircled his waist. Her throat arched, baring her soft skin, and he pressed his lips there, too, savored the heat of her, the throb of her pulse that surely matched his own. A kaleidoscope of colors and scents and emotions cascaded through him.

She ran her hands down his back and gripped his waist.

A sound—horses' hooves—clip-clopped against the road-bed. Her body went rigid in his arms. Two tiny headlights attached to a buggy illuminated them. She pushed him away.

He released her, his chest tight, breathing difficult. She darted past him and ran from the bridge. He stayed a moment to calm himself. Wide-eyed children hung out of the back of the buggy. One child crossed her eyes at him, her face barely visible in the gathering gloom. He smiled. He felt a little cross-eyed himself.

When he left the bridge, fat, cold drops of rain began to fall. They pelted his shoulders. The way he felt, he expected them to sizzle as they hit. He started the car, glancing over at Tuesday. She stared down at her hands folded tightly in her lap. This was not a "kiss once and leave" kind of girl.

He'd kissed many women with indifference, not because he did not enjoy the kissing, but because he knew the relationship was going nowhere before it began. Somehow kissing Tuesday was in a different league, one whose rules he didn't know. He was a bit afraid to step up to bat.

"Maybe we could get together tomorrow? We could finish this . . . discussion. You could introduce me to the restaurant with the second-best pot pie. Or maybe cook one up yourself.''

The huskiness of his voice made molasses of Tuesday's spine. Her mouth felt bruised, wonderful. Her body felt imprinted with the contours of his. Tuesday thought of Jack Ryan in her kitchen, maybe sweating over a hot stove with her— Opal next door.

Distance. I need distance.

I don't want to like you, Jack Ryan, she shouted in her head. *You'll hurt me. You'll hurt Mom.*

"Are you sure you'll be in town?" It came out cold. *How can I sound cold when my body and soul are on fire?*

His face went blank. His hands flexed a moment on the steering wheel. Without a word he started the car and turned it toward Paradise.

After a few miles he spoke. He sounded bored. "I'll be staying until I talk to Opal Dinkman. Then I'm out of here."

He would never talk to Opal if she could help it.

Chapter Eight

Mrs. Bickley met them on the porch. She flapped her apron at them. "Oh, Jack. Some nice man named Michael O'Malley called. Said it's important you call him back. And Tuesday, Ruth's trying to reach you, too. Sounds frantic."

"You first," Jack said as Tuesday preceded him into the cool interior of the Good and Plenty. "Frantic outweighs important."

She went to the registration desk to call Ruth. Maybe she'd just follow Jack Ryan upstairs to his room. That was one way to ensure he stayed indoors tonight.

What's wrong with you! Are you out of your mind? One minute you hate the guy, the next you want to tour his bedroom!

"Thank God I found you," Ruth said gasping. "The shop wants my portfolio tomorrow! If you can get over here first thing tomorrow morning, the photo shop will develop the last pictures by ten, and I can be in Manhattan for my two o'clock appointment. Please, Tuesday, please."

Tuesday turned her back to Jack Ryan, who leaned on the doorjamb. Despite his casual pose, he exuded an air of impatience. "Sure, I'll be over at, say, seven." She gently replaced the receiver. How could she keep an eye on Jack Ryan from the Clip and Curl?

He placed his hand on the phone and lifted a straight black brow. When she didn't move, he spoke. "I need to make a call."

Tuesday flapped her hands at him. "Go ahead. Help yourself."

"A private call."

To your editor, most likely. For more instructions on how to wreak havoc in Paradise.

"See you tomorrow," he said. "Where should I pick you up?"

"Paradise Classic Cars, but don't come by till ten, okay?"

As she left the Good and Plenty, Tuesday whispered to Mrs. Bickley, "Keep him in tonight."

Sarah patted her arm. "No problem. I'll just feed him and tell him stories of your childhood. He really seemed interested in that softball trophy you won."

"Oh, I'm sure he doesn't care about my pitching!" She automatically rubbed her elbow. "Maybe he'd like to hear about KOOP instead."

"Somehow I think his interests lie elsewhere."

Tuesday unlocked the garage door and stood in the cavernous bay area. Mr. Hinkle's Mustang sat there in silent accusation. Why couldn't she find a decent mechanic? There must be someone, somewhere, who loved and understood old cars.

The Mustang leaked oil. With a sigh of resignation, Tuesday opened a cupboard and pulled out a change of clothes, then climbed the stairs to the bedroom. The bed looked a little rumpled. She mitered the corners and smoothed the blanket.

She stepped out of her sundress and let it drop to the floor.

What was she going to do about Jack Ryan? Why didn't he just go away? Her eyes drifted to the bed.

A familiar noise in the garage brought her up short. She jerked on a T-shirt and stepped into overalls. Donning socks and sneakers, she crept cautiously down the stairs.

"Elvis?" she whispered. "Hello?"

The garage stood empty of all but shadows. On the workbench, "Suspicious Minds" blared at top volume from an unplugged radio.

"Stop it, Elvis. I get the point!" She turned off the taunting sound with a decisive snap. "Get a grip, Tuesday. It's just Elvis playing his usual tricks. Now fix Mr. Hinkle's leak. Maybe you'll be less jumpy after an hour under a hot car."

Jack had no success getting through to Father Mike. According to the priest's housekeeper, he was keeping vigil at the hospital—a vigil expected to last through the night.

A message from Father Mike spelled trouble with a capital *E*. Mike never bothered him on a mission. Now he'd have to wait for news until morning when Mike returned from the hospital. Not for the first time, Jack thought of hiring a secretary.

Then sanity returned. *Right.* Who on earth would believe a job like that? *Here, Miss, call Father Mike and find out what Heaven wants now.* He'd really be a candidate for the funny farm then.

Jack lay in the soft cocoon of the four-poster bed. The quilt at the foot of the bed, like almost everything else in the Good and Plenty, was original to the house. Mrs. Bickley's great-grandmother had furnished it with love in 1904. Luckily, great-granddaughter Sarah believed in central air and cable television.

The TV on the dresser was definitely out of tune with the decor. Speaking of tunes, he thought, as he tossed and turned, did everyone in town love Elvis? Some song about dreams coming true played softly from the guest room next door.

He had no time for dreams.

Questions whirled around in his head. Why had Tuesday lied to him? She probably lunched with Opal Dinkman twice a week. He imagined them on the phone, laughing over his discomfort. But could he really be angry when he'd been lying all along, too? And why? To protect himself.

He closed his eyes and contemplated Opal, Starcorp, and Tuesday's luscious legs. Tuesday's legs finally took over, along with Tuesday's soft lips and sweet taste, the feel of her against him, the eager way she'd returned his kisses until the buggy had broken it all up. What would have happened next?

He knew the answer to that. He'd have broken it up himself. He would have had to. He lived an impossible life with impossible demands. Only self-absorbed women like Cheryl tolerated his lapses of attention—at least for a while.

Tuesday Evans deserved more than a roll in the hay. She deserved commitment, marriage, kids.

He thrashed about, sweating, despite the air conditioner. Tuesday's face, her taste, the feel of her against him haunted his mind and body. He stopped fighting it. Instead he replayed every moment he'd held her in his arms.

Hurry, dawn. I need my oil changed and I know just the mechanic I want to handle the job. He fell asleep with a smile on his face.

Chapter Nine

Ruth worked her miracles. Tuesday went from brunette to raven's-wing black in moments. There was no time for the last color change; Tuesday wore a wig instead. She hated the wig, a short, auburn pixie look.

Ruth's husband, an optometrist, supplied the sample colored contacts. She liked the exotic look the violet lenses gave her. What an improvement over her natural hazel eyes.

Jack woke up slowly. He fought it, for Tuesday in a poodle skirt and nothing else bowled through his dreams.

After a cold shower, he threw on a pair of clean khaki shorts and a white polo shirt, then took the stairs two at a time. The tall grandfather clock at the foot of the stairs struck nine. He hadn't meant to sleep so late.

The smell from the kitchen—baking bread and fresh coffee—tantalized him. He forced himself to detour to the front desk and the phone first. Carrie bopped and swayed through the entry with a mop. Jack frowned. He really would have to get over his dislike of cellular phones and buy one. There wasn't always a private phone when he needed one. He dialed Father Mike's number. He loved Mrs. Bickley's old rotary phone, though.

"Hi, Mike. What's up?"

He listened to Father Mike for a moment. His blood ran cold. "By midnight tonight? Or he's stuck forever?"

He'd never been given a deadline before. Heaven had always been so casual, so laid-back.

"What's the problem? Why the sudden need for haste? I'm not sure I want to go to Heaven if it means deadlines and timetables."

Jack winced through Father Mike's tirade.

"Okay. Okay. Who are we to ask questions?" Jack's shoulder suddenly ached where he'd torn his rotator cuff, the tear that ended his pitching career two years before. "I'll try to speed things up. I'm looking for a woman named Opal Dinkman. I haven't found her yet." So much for his date with Tuesday. A wave of disappointment swamped him. He shook it off.

"While I'm working on this end, call Rick Myers and ask him if he's still into educational foundations. If he is, tell him to hop a helicopter for Paradise, PA—pronto."

Jack hung up. He sighed and raked his fingers through his hair.

"Excuse me, sir," Carrie said. He turned and forced a patient smile. "I couldn't help overhearing you say you can't find Opal Dinkman. I know where she lives."

"Really?" A surge of excitement swept through him. It was only nine-fifteen. Maybe he could find Opal, then Elvis, solve his problem, get him to leave, and still see Tuesday on time.

"Sure. She lives in a pink rancher on the corner of Nirvana and Bliss. Her name's on the mailbox."

Two minutes away!

The girl smiled. "I heard Sarah talking to Opal yesterday."

"Really?" He glanced toward the kitchen. Mrs. Bickley

knew Opal? Why lie about it? "What did they say?"

The girl moved closer, one arm hugging the newel post, and beckoned him near. In a whisper, eye to the kitchen, the girl said, "They're trying to fix you up with Opal's daughter."

"Really? Is she pretty?" He feigned interest.

The girl screwed up her face and thought for a moment. "I suppose. But she must be at least thirty."

"I'm thirty-two," he said with a smile.

Her face lit up. "Besides, you'd know if you thought she was pretty. You saw her. Of course, Tuesday might not be interested in you. Her ex-husband treated her poorly, you know."

"Tuesday?" A lump the size of a Rawlings baseball formed in his throat.

"Yeah, I know it's a stupid name. I mean who ever heard of naming your kid after a day of the week?"

"Yeah. Who ever heard of such a thing?" Disappointment drove any excitement right out of his system. Suddenly he didn't really care where Opal Dinkman lived or whether Elvis missed his heavenly deadline. "So what's this Tuesday like?"

"I don't really know her. Sarah can tell you, though. It was her idea that you and Tuesday would make a cute couple."

Jack turned in the direction of Mrs. Bickley and her baking bread. His appetite disappeared. "Do you happen to know where Tuesday lives?"

"Sure. Right next door to Opal—in a big, old Victorian."

"Of course," he muttered.

Jack ignored Mrs. Bickley's call as he stormed out of the Good and Plenty. Tuesday Dinkman Evans lied like a pro.

He drove the two short blocks to Opal's house. The pink rancher and Tuesday's Victorian stood out like the Mutt and Jeff of suburbia. The morning sun painted a bloodred stain on the pink of Opal's house.

She opened the door on the first ring of the doorbell.

"Mrs. Dinkman?"

"You must be Jack Ryan. I told Tuesday you'd find me. Said I wouldn't lie if you did."

Jack nodded his thanks as Opal invited him in. She led him to a room fitted out as an office. The latest in computer hardware stretched across a long, tidy desk. "I'm very busy, young man."

Opal Dinkman, a shorter, plumper version of her daughter, proved Jack's theory that Tuesday would be lovely even as she aged. He imagined that Opal turned heads at the senior center.

"I'm just updating my website—or rather, the fan club's website. Have to keep folks up on what's going on here in Paradise."

And just what is going on here in Paradise?

"Do you have many members in your fan club?" Jack watched Opal handle her computer like an expert.

"Oh, quite a few. We cover three counties, you know. I've organized several trips to Memphis for our members. I'm hoping to go along on the next one."

"Opal. I need your help." He sat on a folding chair.

"I'm sure you do. Tuesday's as prickly as a cactus since her divorce." Opal placed a hand on his knee. "Her Sam left her, you know." Then she silently mouthed, *For another woman.* She smoothed her blond waves. "Ever since Sam left, Tuesday's been stuck on this idea that I need someone to look after me." She arched a delicate brow. "Do I look like I need care?"

Jack grinned. "No, ma'am. You look able to look after yourself, but I didn't mean I need help with Tuesday."

"Of course not. You men never admit when you need help. Now, if you had an old car, you could ask her to look it over—"

"Opal." Jack used his sternest voice. He suspected that conversations with Opal rarely went from *A* to *B*. "We need to talk about Elvis." There. It was said.

"So Tuesday informs me. I promised not to." Opal pressed

her lips together and then pantomimed pulling a zipper closed.

Jack sighed. "Tuesday thinks I'm going to exploit you in some way." He crossed his finger over his chest. "I promise, that's not my intention."

"Well, your kind of magazine does tend to exaggerate. I would never admit it to Tuesday, but I do occasionally sneak a peek at a story or two. Did you write that lovely article on Princess Di's hairdresser's uncle who claims he saw her on the Eiffel Tower?" The entire time Opal talked she did magical things with her computer. Jack found his attention divided between the screen and her words. He made little sense of either.

"No. That's not my thing. I do—"

"No, of course not. But being Irish and all, I'll bet you did the one on that Celtic dancer who married his dog—"

"Opal! I'm not writing an article. I just used that as an excuse to find Elvis."

"Good heavens!" Opal's hands fell still. "Why ever would you want to find him if you're not writing an article?" She glanced away from him. "Oh, darn. I've lost my FTP connection."

"That's not all you've lost," Jack muttered. "Now, Opal. Where's Elvis?"

Opal stood up. The computer screen filled with bowling balls knocking over clusters of pins. "I designed that screen saver myself," she said. "Would you like a nice slice of soda bread?"

Jack dropped his head into his hands, defeated. He suspected Opal knew what she was doing—and she did it very well. "Sure," he said. "Got any milk?"

Tuesday cruised by her mother's house on the way to the garage. She saw Ryan's car parked out front. Who'd spilled the beans? she wondered. She felt numb. Her hands and feet tingled. She pictured the headlines, the articles, the reporters camped on the lawn—just like last time.

She pulled in front of Ryan's car and got out. "I'm going right in there and . . . and . . . and apologizing for all the lying." It hadn't stopped him for long and only made her feel crummy. "What about the kisses, Tuesday? How do you handle them?" In reality, after she apologized, she should thank Ryan for reawakening something precious.

"Talking to yourself, Mrs. Evans?"

She turned toward the voice. She never finished her greeting. Darkness swooped in and possessed her.

Jack gave up after four slices of soda bread, a cold glass of milk, and seven Irish potatoes. He promised Opal his mother's recipes for both. "This feels like the ninth inning, Opal, and the bases are loaded. Now where's Elvis hiding out?"

She shook her head, a secretive smile on her lips.

The only pitches Jack had left were wild ones. The game was as good as lost. Opal steadfastly refused to divulge Elvis's location. Only thirteen hours remained to work a miracle—find Elvis, solve his problems, and get him to return to Heaven.

"Thanks for breakfast." He stood up.

"You're welcome, young man. I'm really sorry Tuesday didn't stop by. I'm a bit worried about her. She promised, and she always keeps her promises." Opal bit her lip and peered out the kitchen window toward Tuesday's house.

"Maybe she saw my car. I don't think I'm her favorite person right now."

"If I know Tuesday, if she'd seen your car, she'd have barged in here like a knight to defend me." She wrung her hands.

Jack went to the front door. "I'll drive around to the Strike Zone and see—"

"I have a phone, Mr. Ryan. We'll just call."

"Don't bother," he said. Tuesday's convertible sat at the curb.

Opal jerked open the screen door and darted outside. Jack

239

followed her and stood at the curb, hands on his hips. "I know Paradise is . . . well, Paradise, but would Tuesday leave her purse in the car?"

"Never! Something's happened to her!"

Jack walked around the Cadillac. The sun glittered on something lying by the wheel. Keys. He picked them up. A plastic Phillies logo hung from the ring.

"They're Tuesday's!"

If Jack knew one thing about Tuesday, he knew she wasn't careless. The memory of Tuesday's face, pale as milk, a man's hand on her shoulder, came to him. "I saw a guy bothering her at the Strike Zone, pin-striped suit, overfed—"

"Mr. Fletcher. He keeps pestering me to sell the Zone. He was quite rude yesterday when I tore up his offer." She pawed Jack's arm. "Please help me."

Jack's stomach knotted up, but he spoke calmly. "Don't worry. I'll find her. Call Harold. Ask him to get a hold of a Father Michael O'Malley at Saint Rita's church in Boston—"

"Saint Rita! The patron saint of desperate causes!" Opal clapped her hands over her mouth.

Jack hugged Opal. "Tell Father Mike I desperately need Rick Myers to fly down here. And while he's at it, ask him to see if he can find anything useful on Starcorp."

"Do you think they've done something to Tuesday?" She twisted her hands in his shirt.

He gave her another squeeze. "We're probably worrying for nothing. Now get to Harold and tell him to make that call!"

Jack drove directly to Paradise Classic Cars. The door rolled up easily. "Tuesday," he called. His voice echoed about the cavernous space. A sudden cool breeze whipped about him; the hair on his nape lifted.

He climbed the stairs. One of her dresses lay in a puddle of buttercup yellow on the floor of the mechanic's room. Carefully he lifted the dress and pressed it to his face.

The scent of her lingered on the fabric.

He pictured her earnest face as she explained how uncomfortable Opal would be with adverse publicity. Tuesday, who merely wanted to protect her mother, had run afoul of who knew what. And didn't that fit with what he knew of her already? She took in strays, looked after people, championed underdog causes.

As a Red Sox pitcher he knew all about underdogs.

He draped the dress on the foot of the bed. Time to find her.

Chapter Ten

The man who carried Tuesday over his shoulder finally tired and dropped her onto something hard and sharp. She pulled the grain sack off her head and stared about in surprise. She'd been dumped into the rear of an Amish buggy missing its backseat.

She gathered her wits. Her stomach ached from bouncing against the man's shoulder. Before she could move or protest, the buggy lurched off. The driver glanced back at her.

"Fletcher!"

He ignored her. Carefully, mindful of her woozy stomach, she forced herself to her knees. The carriage rocked. Her head spun.

"What the hell are you doing?" she asked.

"Be quiet." He shoved her back with one hand. For a moment she lay on her side, stunned. Sweat trickled along her scalp.

The closed front doors of the buggy, constructed half of glass and half of wood, effectively prevented easy escape over the front seat. The soft leather sides and back, which were lined in fabric, could be rolled up, but Fletcher had them fastened down from the outside. It was a hot, steamy box on wheels.

Paradise slipped by in a fast trot. She tried again, this time with a pathetic voice designed to make her appear feeble. "Please, why are you doing this?" She raised a sniffle—not entirely a fake one.

Fletcher glanced over his shoulder and brandished a pipe wrench. If he hit her, he'd kill her. "Stewart said I'm finished if I don't get your mother to sign. You'll persuade her or else."

She crouched on her heels as the buggy rumbled over the covered bridge where Ryan had kissed her. She looked about for a weapon. Nothing. Only the seat fastenings broke the smooth expanse of floor.

She had no other weapon than her mouth. Maybe if she badgered Fletcher with questions he'd throw her out. "Where are we going? So what if you're fired? What's the worst that could happen? Unemployment?"

He gave her a pathetic look. "Humiliation then. I see, your pride would be hurt," she said smugly.

"Mary said if I lost one more job, she'd leave me."

"Ahhhh." Tuesday leaned forward and spoke loudly in his ear. He winced. "Your girl might not be worth all this trouble. Maybe I could talk to her. Make her see that Starcorp isn't such a hot job. I mean, they scare little old ladies." She hoped her mother wouldn't find out she'd referred to her as a little old lady. "Extreme pressure would just have upped KOOP's chances with the preservation board, you know."

"That board preserves land that folks want to farm. The Wohlers want out. Your mother's twenty thousand in debt! The board won't help her. Why don't you just sign our offer?"

Fletcher trembled. His voice quavered. This Mary must really be a terror. Tuesday scanned the road.

"Look, Fletcher. If we use our heads, talk to my mother and the Wohlers with the KOOP people—"

"No! Stewart wants the deal finalized today. He won't wait."

"And if Stewart fires you, your girl will leave you." She crossed her arms over the front seat and leaned her chin on them.

Fletcher handled the horse pretty well. He veered a bit too close to traffic, but otherwise did okay for a man whose hands shook and who jerked about in his seat. He drove around in circles along the side roads of Paradise.

"My husband left me, you know," she said. "I thought it was the end of the world. Funny thing, after a while I realized that he was all wrong for me."

"Mary's not wrong for me!" Hysteria crept into his voice. The wrench lay forgotten on the seat—a few inches from her hand. Tuesday pushed him closer to the edge.

"I really wanted Sam back, but he'd cheated on me. Now what made me want a man who cheated and lied? I finally understood that I wanted him back only because I was afraid to be alone. I was worried I'd never find someone else to love."

"We've been married for twelve years." The reins went slack in his hands. The horse wandered a bit. A wheel hit a stone, jolting the carriage and bringing Fletcher back to reality. He picked up the wrench and firmed his hold on the reins.

She continued, one eye on the wrench. "Once, I learned it was okay to be alone, that I could make it by myself, I was fine."

As she spoke, she touched her head. *If I'm so fine, why am I so dissatisfied with plain old me?* "I guess I needed to appreciate myself before I could see—"

"Stop it. Shut up."

Tuesday scanned the road ahead. She ordered herself to take action, to grab the reins, swerve the buggy into traffic. A car filled with children passed them. No swerving. No accidents.

"What are you going to do with me?"

"If you don't shut up, I'll lock you in the Wohlers' chicken coop. Then I'll call your mother. She'll sign to get you back."

"You can't put me in a chicken coop. Do you have any idea what that will smell like on a hot day like—"

"Shut up!"

Tuesday sat back. She decided to kick out the back panel at the next stop.

Sweat ran down her face. Thunder rumbled in the distance. The air held a quality of waiting. *Poor Fletcher.* A dark patch of sweat stained his shirt. "You'll get your contract from my mom, but your wife will still leave you. Maybe not today, but soon."

"Shut up!" he shouted again.

The light at the next corner turned red. Time to escape. Tuesday leaned forward, scanned the street, ready to act.

Fletcher slapped a straw hat on his head to make himself less conspicuous. They would be just another buggy on the street. Only an astute observer would wonder why the back and side windows were closed on such a stifling day.

The buggy slowed for the light. A familiar car rushed toward them: Jack Ryan's.

Jack drummed on the steering wheel while he sat at the light. A buggy waited opposite him, ready to turn. He'd have to follow it down the one-lane road. More time wasted. Movement in the buggy caught his eye. A woman leaned forward. Just for an instant, before the man shoved her back in a very un-Amish gesture, he saw her clearly. He knew that face, knew those large eyes despite the fact that they were framed by a dark cap or bonnet.

The horse and buggy turned the corner, then pulled off the road and headed down a barely perceptible dirt lane that paralleled a cornfield. The driver must be Fletcher. Why take Tuesday off in a buggy?

Jack quickly signaled and made a turn into the field. His

245

car bottomed out on the high-crowned path. He slammed on the brakes. His car shuddered to a stop. The buggy with its high carriage sped away in a cloud of dust. Jack reversed straight back across the intersection and into a church parking lot.

A buggy decked with paper wedding bells stood by the front steps. The sign on the rear read, GOOD LUCK, STEVE AND COLLEEN. The teenager in a tuxedo waiting to drive it away was definitely not Amish. Jack hoped the newlyweds liked German cars.

He parked behind the buggy and left the keys in the ignition.

"Follow that buggy!" Jack shouted.

The young man stared about, bewildered. "Which buggy?"

Jack swore. At least three carriages bowled along the road. "That one. There." He pointed across the field. The top of Tuesday's buggy could just be seen over the cornstalks.

The kid didn't budge. "You're nuts. This isn't a real buggy. It's a rental."

Jack jumped into the carriage and snatched the reins.

"Here." He shoved two twenties into the boy's hand when he tried to stop him. "Trust me. I know horses."

With raised hands, the boy stepped away. "Sure, bud. Help yourself."

The horse moved at a sedate walk no matter how much Jack slapped the reins and swore. What possessed him to say he knew horses? He knew they ate oats. He knew they wore iron shoes.

He slid sideways on the hard seat each time they hit a rut. A bottle of champagne and a basket of fruit toppled off the rear seat. Apples and oranges cascaded over his feet, but he kept his eye on his quarry. Once he reached the dirt path, the horse gained confidence and upped its pace to a swinging trot.

Sweat ran down Jack's face. Music played somewhere—like a station improperly tuned. It was "Hound Dog." It grated on his nerves. He glanced about for a radio, then realized the music came from nowhere earthly.

Thunder growled. His shirt stuck to his back. Acid rose in his throat. How in Heaven's name had Tuesday become so important in such a short time?

Her buggy veered off the rutted path into the high corn. It forged its own path, mowing down the thick rows of tall stalks—not the action of a sane driver.

Adrenaline pumped through Jack's system. What if Fletcher harmed her? His buggy bounced over the fallen corn. He swore a blue streak. Then Fletcher's buggy shuddered to a halt; the horse reared and heaved in its traces.

Fletcher jumped out with Tuesday, an arm locked about her neck. She fell to her knees. Fletcher hauled her up and ran into the rows of corn. Tuesday dragged her feet like an anchor.

"Good girl," Jack said. He snatched up an apple and abandoned his buggy in a leap. He stood by the horse, wound up, threw.

Fletcher yelped and fell. Just as Jack reached Tuesday where she knelt on the ground, Fletcher recovered and came at Jack, his head low, his shoulder leading. The wind rushed from Jack's lungs as Fletcher plowed him down. They rolled, kicked, and struggled in the corn. Fletcher's elbow caught his nose. In a spray of blood, Jack rammed his fist into Fletcher's ribs.

Tuesday watched the men, unsure how to stop the fight, not sure she should. Blood appeared on Jack's white shirt. She saw red.

Tuesday threw herself on Fletcher's back and wrapped her legs and arms around him. She screamed like a banshee in his ear and pulled his hair with all her strength.

Fletcher whipped around in a circle. Tuesday clung like a barnacle.

The world spun as Jack staggered to his feet. Blood dripped down his shirt. Then the world righted itself. He wasn't spinning; Fletcher and Tuesday were. He wanted to laugh, but worried he'd belittle Tuesday's efforts on his behalf. He snatched her off Fletcher, and the man crashed to the ground.

Despite the unfamiliar auburn cap of hair, he'd know her anywhere—know the feel of her against him.

For a moment she fought him; then she calmed. He let her slide slowly to the ground and set her aside. He hauled Fletcher to his feet. "Okay, Fletcher. The party's over. Go back to Philadelphia and prepare your lawyers. You'll be hearing from mine. We'll start with kidnapping."

Fletcher jerked from Jack's hold, but cowered away when Jack moved in his direction. "Mrs. Dinkman will sell. I'll win one way or the other," he said, panting. His brave words did not match his defeated stance. He wiped his bloody hands down his pants. He spit in the dirt. "I didn't kidnap her. She came willingly. Was all over me. Couldn't get enough."

"You creep," Tuesday cried. Jack grabbed her around the waist. She surged against his hold.

He clapped a hand over her mouth. "Get lost, Fletcher. Mrs. Dinkman will make her decision without pressure from you or any other Starcorp thug."

They watched Fletcher stagger, half-bent, back along the path blazed by the buggies. When he disappeared from sight, Jack became intensely aware of Tuesday pressed against his body. She wiggled her rear and tried to get free. A small moan escaped him. She fell still. He tightened his hold subtly, easing her closer.

His heart thudded hard in his chest. The sultry, humid air seemed heavy and hard to breathe. His blood thickened and pooled in his groin. They stood alone in a field of high corn, an angry dome of black clouds overhead, the world silent and as far off as another planet. The smell of the corn, lush and alive, entwined with her scent. He closed his eyes and kissed her hair—short auburn hair. The realization she was safe in his arms made everything else unimportant.

He spread his palms over her waist. She laid her head back on his shoulder, exposing her neck. He bent his head to kiss the smooth skin over the flutter of her pulse, but stopped. Bloody as he was, he should not be touching her—anywhere.

He cleared his throat and eased her away. She made a sound in her throat. One of disappointment, he hoped.

Then she rounded on him and stood there, eyes locked on his. They were violet today. He didn't care if they were chartreuse. He wanted to lay her down in the sheaves of fallen corn. He wanted to make love to her with the passion that heated the air. The rumbling thunder foretold what surely would come between them.

"Your nose!" She placed hot hands on his cheeks and peered up at him. "Do you think it's broken?"

"Damn, I hope not. At least it's stopped bleeding." He pulled his shirttail out of his shorts and scrubbed at his face.

"You're a mess," she said, and smoothed his hair from his forehead. "You'll have a shiner."

"I hope I don't scare Mrs. Bickley when I walk in the door." He lifted her hand and squeezed it gently. "Thank you for defending my honor."

She grinned. "And thank *you* for coming after me." She swallowed hard. "Poor Fletcher. If he doesn't seal this deal he's fired, and his wife will walk out. I almost feel sorry—" She yanked off her hair. "I can't think with this hot thing."

Jack just stared. The auburn pixie hairdo lay like a dead squirrel in the trampled corn. Her hair was as black as a New York Yankee's heart, cut blunt at her chin. Straight bangs touched her brows. She looked exotic and erotic. Cleopatra stood before him. He barely heard what she said.

". . . confession."

"What?" He shook his head. "Say that again."

"I have a confession to make. I know where Opal Dinkman is. She's my mother."

He loved an honest woman. "You're a credit to her. A real KOOP kind of warrior woman."

She laughed and ran into his arms. She fit like his favorite glove.

Jack led each horse around so they could leave the cornfield. They lingered a moment by Tuesday's buggy. He cleared his throat, suddenly at a loss for words. He had his own confession, but his might send her screaming.

She dragged her toe in the dirt like a child. "Would you like me to come with you to Mrs. Bickley's?" she said. "Maybe I could help you. . . ." Her voice trailed off.

They stared at each other. "Sure. I mean, I could use some first aid."

He stalled, hunting for the right words.

"Boy," she said as she untangled one buggy's reins, "you should play baseball; that was one heck of a throw."

He blinked. "I'll give it some thought."

"Where'd you get this buggy?" She plucked shreds of wedding bells off the ground.

"I think from Steve and Colleen."

An hour later they stood on the back porch of the Good and Plenty. Disheveled and bloody, Jack felt as if he were alone on a pitcher's mound again, deciding which pitch would save the game. He'd chosen wrong after the kiss on the bridge. Now her remark on the way he'd thrown the apple reminded him he had far more to tell her than he'd originally thought.

He should have opened up right there, in the cornfield. Told her everything. After all, he thought, if you're going to marry someone, you should have no lies between you.

Marry someone. He swallowed hard.

The sky opened. Sheets of rain ran from the roof, making a curtain enclosing them on the porch. She moved closer, out of the spray of drops.

He plucked his shirt from his chest. "I'll scare Mrs. Bickley half out of her mind like this."

"I don't think she's home." She read a small, neatly lettered card stuck in the door. "Back by three o'clock check-in."

She looked over her shoulder at him. A black wing of hair kissed her cheek.

He offered her an unspoken invitation. Her gaze met his,

then dropped. A flush appeared on her cheeks. He entwined his fingers in hers and drew her into the silent, cool house. He led her through his room, past the oh-so-soft four-poster bed.

In the bathroom, Tuesday looked away as Jack peeled off his shirt and dropped it on the floor. She picked it up and carefully folded it on a low bench. She avoided looking at him because the sight of his half-naked torso made her face flush. The memory of his body against hers sent a shower of glittering sparks from her breast to her stomach.

He washed off the blood, then inspected his nose in the mirror. Unbidden, she stepped forward and picked up the wet cloth. She slowly stroked it down his chest, past the Saint Christopher medal that hung around his neck, removing the streaks of blood that ran from his neck to his waist. She battled an urge to wrap her arms around him.

Her inspection brought his blood to a boil. Only the drumming of rain on the roof broke the silence. "Rain," he said.

"Yes. We need it. We're two inches below normal. . . ." They stood in awkward silence.

She moved behind him while he scrubbed his hands. When he straightened up, she locked eyes with him in the mirror. Very slowly she touched his shoulders. The sleek muscles of his back tensed when she pressed her lips to him. He smelled all male, his skin smooth, warm, tempting. She drew her fingertips down his spine.

He shifted, turned, and went into her arms. "I made a total mess of it on the bridge," he whispered against her hair. "I've wanted to apologize ever since. And I have a confession to make if we're going to be together."

A lump formed in her throat. *Together . . .*

The word made rubber out of her legs. He raised her hand and pressed his mouth to her palm. His lips felt hot, too hot. She cupped her hand about his jaw.

An urge, almost impossible to resist, made her move closer to soothe herself against his hard contours.

Jack encircled her waist with his arms. He heard music in

his head—the same music that had been playing in the bowling alley the first time he'd seen her. He swayed to the music, brought her close.

She seemed to hear the music, too. She hummed softly, mouth to his cheek, breath warm on his skin. With uncertainty, he brushed his lips against her hair. The scent of her, the feel of her soft curves against him aroused him, but not into a frenzy. He wanted to lay her down, savor her, learn her slowly, carefully this time, before he went home.

Home. Back to lonely nights and solitary meals. When he made his confession, it might end.

It. What a tiny word for such a huge feeling. He released her, turned away, and plucked a towel from the rack. He dried his face and chest without looking at her. While he hesitated, the clock was running out on Elvis.

"What's wrong?" Her eyes shone large and luminous in the dim light of the bedroom.

Jack pulled a clean shirt over his head before tugging her into his arms. He stroked her hair. "I have a confession to make, Tuesday. I wanted to meet your mother, but that's not why I'm here. I'm not writing an article like I said."

She stiffened in his arms. Her words came out muffled against his shirt. "Really? What are you doing here?"

He set her away from him. He prepared himself. Her eyes would widen. She'd take a step back. She'd mumble some excuse about having to go. He'd never see her again. The urge to lie, to find another way, one that would not paint him as insane, was almost impossible to resist. "I feel like a pitcher with three men on and—"

"You sure use an awful lot of baseball references."

He swallowed. "That's because I used to pitch. For the Boston Red Sox. I have another job. . . ."

"Wildman!" she whispered. "Jack Wildman Ryan."

"I'd like to forget that name, if you don't mind."

"No wonder Harold hung on your every word. He loves

baseball.'' Her smile disappeared. "So how'd you make the transition from baseball to sleazeball?"

Jack ground his teeth. "I write for *Sports World*. On sports figures. I do profiles of baseball personalities, an insider's look, so to speak." He crossed his arms on his chest.

"Not exposés on pregnant aliens?"

He shook his head.

"I jumped to a conclusion, didn't I?" She went up on tiptoe and nuzzled his neck.

"You're lovely when you jump. Jump anytime you like." His voice grew husky with emotion. Now the hard part. Now the important part of the truth. He savored the gentle touch of her hands. Despite the fact that his nose felt like a buggy horse had stomped it, he kissed her. This might be their last kiss. It lingered, drifted from her mouth to her throat. Her hands moved over him. A bolt of lust shot through him. He grabbed her wrists and stepped away from temptation.

"I'm not writing an article this time, though. I used it as an excuse. I'm looking for Elvis—the real Elvis. He's missing from Heaven."

Her face paled, but she didn't move. Too shocked to move, he supposed. "It's what I do when I'm not writing. I look for . . . I find escapees from Heaven. There's a time limit this time. Midnight tonight. I need to find him before midnight." He was babbling.

"Escapees from Heaven?" She stared at him, wide-eyed.

Jack knew he'd lost the game.

Tuesday grabbed his hand. "Then what the heck are we standing here for?"

She dragged him after her, through the house, out onto the porch, and into the torrent of rain.

Jack could barely speak. She shoved him in the direction of the passenger seat of his car. "I can get us there much quicker than you can."

The rain lashed the windshield as they sped through Paradise. "So how come you don't think I'm crazy?" he asked.

"Can't say you're crazy without saying I am, too."

He leaned over and put a hand on her shoulder. "What are you saying?"

"I'm saying Elvis has been a thorn in my side for twenty years. It's about time someone put him in his place." She blew her wet bangs off her forehead and gave him a smile with enough voltage to light Fenway Park. "I think you're just the man to do it."

Jack's world tipped askew. "You mean—"

"Yep. He's right here." She grinned, steered around a buggy, and pulled into the Strike Zone's parking lot. She jumped out of the car, then turned back and leaned in to him. He felt bolted to his seat. "Come on, Jack. I'm getting soaked."

Slowly, still in shock, he unfolded from the car. Tuesday practically danced into the Strike Zone, scattering raindrops. He followed at a more sedate pace. She opened the door by lane thirty. A long hallway opened onto the backs of the lanes. The sound of pins ricocheting and spinning, machinery turning, and balls dropping filled the small space. A man in overalls moved in the shadows.

"Elvis," Tuesday called over the noise. "Come meet someone special."

The man turned. A jolt ran through Jack's system, just as it always did when he found his quarry. Seeing a person—a dead person—in the flesh, walking, breathing, looking well and healthy, never ceased to punch him in the gut.

"I'll leave you two to get acquainted," Tuesday said, backing away.

Jack held out his hand. The man who shook it had a firm grip.

"Who're you?" The tones were *his,* the same ones that still tantalized generations of women.

He found his tongue. "I'm Jack Ryan. You probably don't know him, but Father Michael O'Malley sent me to find you. You need to go home."

They stood in silence; then Elvis shrugged. "You've delivered your message. Now I've got work to do." He turned away, but Jack knew he wasn't talking about the work on lane thirteen.

A moment of panic filled Jack. On his other seven missions, the targets had acquiesced without an argument. They'd all had good reasons for going AWOL, but all were just as happy to go home once their problems had been solved. They'd probably forgotten how annoying earth could be. Elvis didn't look as though he was going anywhere. Time for problem solving.

"You don't understand—" Jack started.

"No, sir, you don't understand. I'm not goin' anywhere."

"Oh, yes, you are. You've got a deadline."

Chapter Eleven

"Opal needs me here." Elvis wiped his hands on a rag. "She's supported me for forty years. The least I can do is stand by her while she makes a decision about the Strike Zone."

Jack could feel his face puffing up. Hot, steamy air filled the narrow corridor. "She has Tuesday."

Elvis climbed onto a tiny catwalk that ran between the works of lanes twelve and thirteen. "Tuesday just complicates it. Did you know she sold her stockbrokerage in Philadelphia to live near her mother? If Opal sells, she'd feel Tuesday had made the sacrifice for nothing. She's a good mother, is Opal."

Jack raked his fingers through his hair. *Tuesday, a stockbroker?* Mechanic, stockbroker, champion of the underdog— he looked forward to investigating every one of her personas.

"Look. I've called a friend of mine. He loves investments like this, and he thrives on making trouble for companies like Starcorp. When he gets to Paradise, he'll look this whole business over and help Opal make a sensible decision. You can go with a clear conscience.''

Elvis shook his head. He hauled a fat white pin out of a round metal turret. ''Can't get this to work. Every time I come visit, lane thirteen quits.''

Jack almost gave up. Who cared where Elvis spent eternity?

Suddenly the scent of dirt and grass, peanuts and hot dogs filled the corridor. ''Okay. Okay,'' he muttered under his breath. ''I'll try again.'' Aloud he said, ''What about a compromise? If Opal tells you to go, will you go?''

Elvis dropped the pin back into place. He studied Jack, then nodded. ''If Opal says she doesn't need me anymore, I'll do as you wish.''

Jack heaved a sigh of relief. Now if only Opal cooperated. ''You'd better put this on.'' He plucked a black-and-teal baseball cap from a hook on the back wall. Elvis settled it low on his brow.

When they entered the lanes, the bowlers played on, oblivious to who walked among them. Tuesday stood at the counter, worry etched on her face. Harold nodded, then continued to polish the score tables.

As they passed the televisions, static striped the screens. ''Blue Suede Shoes'' burst over the sound system. Elvis shrugged sheepishly. ''I really like that song,'' he said.

Great, Jack thought. *Party tricks.*

The glass doors burst open. Opal Dinkman ran into the Strike Zone. She stood poised in the entrance for a moment. Jack refrained from uttering any prayers he might later regret. She shrieked and ran straight toward him, then past him—past Elvis, too.

She flew into Harold Sauder's arms in a leap as graceful as her daughter's. ''Oh, Harold, darling! You have to meet the most charming man! He's buying the Wohler farm and the Strike Zone. He's going to make us into a museum!'' She kissed him on both cheeks. Tears ran down her face.

Behind Opal, and at a more decorous pace, strolled Jack's old friend, Rick Myers. He gave Jack a nod and followed Opal to where she hugged Harold. The men shook hands.

Jack sucked in his breath. Rick would see Elvis, would recognize him. He whipped around.

Elvis wasn't there.

On the floor where he'd stood lay the black-and-teal baseball cap.

Tuesday hurried to his side. She picked up the hat and brought it to him. "Do you think—"

"Don't think. I don't. I just pack my bag and move on." He put his arm around her and hauled her close.

They watched her mother. Harold's face turned cherry red as Opal alternated between kissing his cheeks and hugging the newcomer. Jack squeezed Tuesday's waist. "I think we've seen the last of Elvis."

Somewhere in the celebration that followed, Jack lost control of the situation. Opal insisted he sit with an ice pack on his nose; Rick insisted on outlining every boring detail of his contracts with the Wohlers and Opal. Somewhere along the line, he lost Tuesday, too.

With his hands deep in his pockets, and for the second time in two days, he walked to Paradise Classic Cars. The rain fell in a slow, steamy drizzle.

He lifted the well-oiled garage door and stepped inside. The hot, sultry air came with him. He looked around. Tuesday's tools lay in rows like soldiers. Music played. Not Elvis this time. Garth Brooks.

Her Cadillac sat in the last bay, top down, gleaming, shiny as new.

He'd know those ankles, those socks, anywhere. He reached down and grabbed the ankles that tantalized him.

"Gotcha," he said softly. With one pull she slid out, flat on her back, her legs straight up. She lay there, her ankles stiff in his hands. Soft hazel eyes stared up at him. Unsure.

She jerked her ankles from his hands and before he could prevent it, rolled aside and up to her feet.

"Why did you leave?" he asked, moving toward her.

She backed up. He crowded her against the car door.

The scent of her, soft, feminine, sent a jolt of desire through him. He pressed his hips to hers. Her eyes, wary hazel eyes, caught his. A soft sound escaped her throat, parting her lips. He wanted those lips. Craved them.

He bent his head to her throat, bared to him by her short black hair. He pressed his mouth to her, to the throb of her pulse under hot, delicate skin. With a groan he planted his hands on either side of her, caged her in.

"It won't work," she whispered. "You said it yourself. You just pack your bag and move on."

"I'm not going anywhere." He kissed her brow.

"You've known me only two days!"

He cupped her chin and tilted her face up to his, forced her to see him, really see him. "I've been looking for you for years."

"Oh, Jack. I don't know what to do."

"Didn't someone who will remain nameless sing something about fools rushing in? Let's be a couple of fools."

Her knees felt strangely weak. Slowly she turned her head to meet his lips.

A wild pounding rose in her chest. Wildman. The name throbbed along with her pulse as his warm mouth possessed her. Heavenly, paradise, the taste of him was warm, sensual, arousing. She felt the press of his hips, his chest, as he leaned closer, the sharp metal of the door handle against her buttocks. Then his hands lifted to her shoulders. He gripped them gently, kneading her as he tasted her.

She planted her hands on his chest and shoved. "We'll have to start over from scratch. I can't bear it if you think I usually lie—even if I did cross my fingers each time."

"I wasn't completely honest myself. At least we had good intentions."

Ann Lawrence

He lifted her hand and kissed her fingertips. "I have one more confession." Her back stiffened under his hand. "I don't take rejection very well. It makes me cranky."

"Reject you? Never. And Mrs. Bickley and Mom think you're perfect."

He stepped back and cupped her face in his hands. "I love you. You can send me to the minors for—"

She interrupted him. "I'm not the woman you think." Her hand went to her hair. "My hair's dull brown and these are my real eyes. Which Tuesday do you love?" A tremor sounded in her voice.

Very slowly he drew his thumbs across her soft cheeks. "I love all the Tuesdays. I love the Tuesday who takes in strays. I love the passionate Tuesday whose kiss sets me on fire. I love the determined one who defends her mother. Mostly I love the Tuesday that jumped on Fletcher's back. That one I want with me on my next mission. The others you can bring along. I'm sure I'll find a use for each and every one."

For a moment, only their desire and heated gaze joined them. She swallowed. He settled his hands on the hooks of her overalls. Very carefully he slid first one then the other open. Her breath escalated, her chest rising and falling rapidly. The bib of her overalls fell forward. His fingertips skimmed up the sides of her breasts. Tuesday went weak in the knees. As he lifted her T-shirt over her head, she closed her eyes and savored the heat of his hands.

He tumbled them both over the side and into the backseat of the Caddy. They landed in a welter of arms and legs.

"I love the determined Tuesday, the passionate Tuesday," he whispered against her breast.

Her skin flushed; her nipples tightened. She reached out and hooked her fingers into the waistband of his shorts. It was his turn to close his eyes. Her fingertips slid back and forth along the smooth skin of his belly, then tugged open the button. He gripped her wrist.

The sun burst from behind a cloud, arrowed through an

upper window, and showered them in spangles of gold. Jack pulled Tuesday up and astride his hips.

Sunlight striped her breasts. Sweat beaded his brow. Very slowly she took his golf shirt and did as he had, pulling the shirt up and over his head. She trapped his arms behind his head, locked her arms about his neck. The air turned steamy as her mouth found his again.

He tasted of her mother's Irish potatoes. She giggled, eliciting a groan from deep in his throat. She licked along his lips, nibbled the corner, stroked her tongue on his, savored the silk and rough texture of his mouth.

His hips arched between her thighs. An ache rose in her. She slid his zipper down, spread open his khaki shorts, then spread her hands across his abdomen. He was sweat-slicked, hard-muscled, rough-haired. Going onto her knees, she helped him out of his clothes. Each piece she tossed out over the trunk. Then she knelt at his feet.

"You're beautiful," she whispered. Her hands traveled up his thighs. He clamped his hands over hers, trapped them firmly on his legs.

"I love the Tuesday who says the unexpected." He leaned forward and captured her lips. He was not ready to have her touch him. Not yet. He felt as he did right as he released a pitch that was destined to go wild. He knew if she touched him he'd explode. Every nerve in his body throbbed. Sweat sprang up between the leather seats and his thighs.

She was lovely, kneeling at his feet, her overalls about her waist. He reached down and cupped the flare of her hips, drew her up and slid her clothes down to her ankles. When she went for her socks, he stayed her hand.

"I'm partial to them." She lifted an eyebrow. "Will you wear them at our wedding?"

"Yes. Oh, yes." She smiled and settled on the seat by his side, one leg bent beneath her. What a proposal. A Jack Ryan kind of proposal. A perfect one.

She planted her foot in his lap and wiggled her toes. He

groaned. Then she stopped playing games. "I love you, too, Jack Ryan."

The pitch was released, gone wild, floating out there, unable to be retrieved or caught. They met in a tangle of limbs and hands and feet. He elbowed her ribs; she bumped his sore nose. They meshed, joined. Where they touched, heat pulsed and blood throbbed. He maneuvered her astride him again, then bent his head into the cradle of her arms. Each touch of her seared his skin. Sweat rolled down his face, salted her throat, her breasts.

He slid his hands along her smooth hips, supported her as she arched back. He feasted on the view of her, joined to him, moving on him, her head back, her hands planted on his shoulders.

He groaned, gasped her name, and then with a shudder, fell still.

Every inch of Tuesday's body tingled from his touch. Her skin and emotions were raw from an overload of sensation. Sunlight streamed in the window, casting a golden halo about his black hair, shadowed his face, hooded his eyes.

"I feel like I've won the World Series single-handedly— only better," he said, and she sensed the smile in his words.

"I've never won much of anything, until now." Tears burned her eyes. "I feel as if I've won the blue ribbon at the fair, the ribbon for best of show." She cupped her arms about his neck and bent her head to him. "You're the best, Jack. Heaven-sent."

Two hours later, Jack's stomach growled. Tuesday pulled herself reluctantly from his arms and patted his rock-hard stomach. "You sound hungry."

"There's hungry and then there's hungry." With a laugh, she evaded his searching hand and clambered over the side of the car, flashing him a rear view that would be burned into his memory for the rest of his life.

He propped his forearms on the back of the front seat and watched her step into her clothes.

With her T-shirt half over her head, she suddenly whipped it off. "Oh, no," she wailed, the shirt dangling from her fingers. "We can't get married."

A pain as big as Fenway Park bloomed in his chest. He sat up straight. "What do you mean? You said yes."

"But I'm a Phillies fan!"

Epilogue

They no longer threw rice at Saint Rita's Church in South Boston. Instead they blew bubbles from tiny white bottles. These bottles were printed with two golden hearts—one that said *Harold and Opal* and one that said *Jack and Tuesday*.

The bright autumn sun glistened off the silky orbs that floated and danced about the two happy couples. Jack drew Tuesday into his arms at the foot of the church steps. He kissed her soundly and then hummed a bar or two of "Can't Help Falling in Love" for good luck. She smiled and nipped his lower lip, to the delight of the guests who crowded the steps and sidewalk.

One of Jack's former teammates from the Boston Red Sox called out from the crowd, "Pitch one in there, Jack."

He obliged by bending Tuesday over his arm and planting a long, heated kiss on her lips. The guests began to chant. "Wiiii-llld Maaannn. Wiiiilllld Maaannnn."

Jack swung Tuesday into his arms and spun her around. Her long white skirt swung out in a froth of satin and lace, tantalizing the crowd with a view of her lovely legs and lacy ankle socks.

Opal and Harold left the church at a more sedate pace. She wore a suit and hat that would have made a young Jackie Kennedy proud, and Harold wore his new blue suit. They linked arms and paused at the foot of the steps for a photograph.

While the crowd oohed and aahed at Jack's antics, Father Mike came to the couple's side. Jack set Tuesday down, and she kissed Father Mike's cheek. "Thank you for sending Jack to Paradise," she said. Tears welled in her eyes.

Father Mike smiled and patted her arm. "Don't thank me. *He* works in mysterious ways. Now, I've a bit of a gift of my own to give you." He held out a long envelope.

"Don't take it," Jack said, encircling Tuesday's waist and drawing her to his side in a protective gesture. A headache began to throb behind his eyes. A familiar touch of anxiety crept past the edges of his happiness. The sudden smell of an infield drifted by on the air, broke on his consciousness, just as the bubbles broke when they touched the earth.

Opal and Harold came near. "What wrong, my dear?" Opal asked him. "Is everything all right?"

"Now, Jack, have I ever steered you wrong?" Father Mike's broad, sheepish smile confirmed Jack's suspicions.

Everyone stared at the envelope in the priest's hand.

"Don't take it," Jack repeated.

Tuesday studied her new husband's face. With a knowledge some women took years to develop and others never did, she hugged him. She stood on tiptoe and kissed his cheek, close to his ear, and whispered, "You promised . . . and this time I'll help you. A team effort, so to speak."

Jack looked down at the smiling face of his new wife. His headache disappeared. He no longer needed to hide the other side of his life. No more lonely hotels or solitary meals. "I love you, Tuesday Ryan." He gave her a kiss—a long one, filled with the passion that shimmered so close to the surface whenever she was near.

He took the envelope.

"Ohhh, tickets to Hawaii," Opal gushed when he ripped it open. "What a lovely gift."

"For your honeymoon," Father Mike said. Friends and family surged close to see the bright blue folder. Tuesday flipped through the pages inside, tickets, hotel reservations on Maui, and a plain slip of paper with a name printed in block letters.

"Hawaii," Harold called out to those at the rear of the crowd. "Jack and Tuesday are going to Hawaii for their honeymoon."

"Haaawaiiii! Haaawaiiii!" children chanted as the guests gathered about the couples.

Tuesday wrapped her arms around Jack's neck, concealing the two of them behind her bouquet of flowers. She tucked the blue folder into the inside pocket of Jack's tuxedo. Her fingers lingered on his chest and felt his rapid heartbeat. She kissed him gently. "What was it Father Mike said? You've graduated to the big leagues?"

He pulled back, searched her soft hazel eyes. "Who?"

"Babe Ruth. He's surfing on Maui."

    This is for my family, who's eaten a lot of "scrapple" while
I write. I also want to thank Michael Brigidi for a fun peek
behind the scenes at Lans–Bowl (Any errors are mine.),
Fran Hand of The Olde Square Inn in Mount Joy for making
my stay in Amish country so comfortable, and Randy
Oestrich for showing me Boston. Finally, to Steve and
Colleen, happy future!

KATHLEEN NANCE

THE BEST-LAID PLANS

Chapter One

G. G. Johansson contemplated the red-and-white dive flag snapping in the Hawaiian breeze and gathered her courage to step into the dive shop.

"Elvis says you should go to Maui Pro Dives instead."

Slowly GG turned and stared at her twin sister. "Elvis sang, Pris; he didn't dive."

"The King's never wrong," Pris insisted, flipping a blond braid over her shoulder.

Whenever Priscilla claimed to be channeling for Elvis, she tended to be annoyingly persistent. According to her, the pop icon's words from beyond could not be ignored.

GG preferred to do just that, but she'd learned to let Pris have her say first. "What's wrong with this dive shop?"

Pris gave it a critical scan. "It's too clean."

The shop sparkled and shone; that was why GG had stopped. It was tidy, organized, and immaculate, just like her desk in the Detroit Med Center ER and her Grosse Pointe apartment.

"There's nothing wrong with clean."

"They should have better things to do than polish the tanks." Pris looked straight at her, a line creasing between her brows above her sunglasses. "I had a hunch; that's why I asked Elvis for advice."

Not for a second did GG believe that speaking to the deceased Elvis, or ESP, or any other psychic nonsense her mother and sister espoused, accounted for Pris's hunches. To GG's mind, they were reasoned deductions; Pris just processed subtle clues most people missed. Regardless of the source, however, Pris's hunches were irritatingly accurate. Still . . . GG glanced back at the store.

Pris gave a huff of irritation. "If you're going through with this idiotic scheme to learn to scuba dive, then you should at least trust me."

Her sister was a certified diver with over two hundred dives. Chances were she was right. With a final, regretful glance at the gleaming tanks, GG gave in. "Maui Pro Dives? Where's that?"

"Down that way. I've already talked to them."

They headed away from the shop, situated in the heart of the Maui town of Lahaina, and strolled to a less congested, less touristy section of the shore. The trade winds wrapped the skirt of GG's sundress about her legs and carried the scents of brine and sweet mango. Colorful hibiscus flowers danced in the breeze.

GG shifted her leather tote on her shoulder, feeling the weight of the multitude of dive books and guidebooks she carried. "You think my learning to dive is idiotic? Why? You dive."

"Why? Take your pick of reasons. I asked you to come to Maui for a restful vacation. While I'm at the convention, you're supposed to sit on the sand and do nothing but sip Mai-Tais and ogle beach boys."

"That's boring, not a vacation. C'mon, Pris. I'm grateful you insisted I come—honest, I am—but you know I have to be *doing* something. This fits perfectly into my five-year plan.''

"Five-year plan." Pris gave a snort of annoyance. "Five-year noose. Do you always have to achieve? Can't you ever just *relax?*''

GG shifted uncomfortably. Her drive for success contrasted with her sister's lack of ambitions and plans and was a fundamental difference between them smoothed only by the tacit agreement that neither one ever mentioned it.

How twins, raised by the same mother, identical in looks—if Pris would cut her hair to match GG's short shag—could be so different in personality was something she'd never learned in genetics class. One reason she wanted to learn to dive was to find a common element with Pris.

They passed the last of the gleaming white boats anchored in Lahaina's harbor. Waves from the glittering ocean lapped with happy abandon against the shore.

"Okay, I'm supposed to be lazy. Why else do you think this dive idea is lunacy?''

"Besides the fact that it's October and past the best of the dive season? How about the big one? You're afraid of the water.''

"I am not!''

"When's the last time you got in open water? You used to sail, ski, swim, until Gary's death—''

"I've been busy." GG's stomach churned, bobbing along the crest of memory that she refused to acknowledge. "Med school, internship, residency. I haven't had time. Besides, I swim. Every morning, from five to five-thirty, in the apartment pool.''

Pris looked skeptical. "That's confined water. It's different.''

"This is something I've always wanted to do. Remember, we talked about it years ago, and you got certified. I just haven't had time. It wasn't part of my five-year plan then.''

Pris shrugged. "Well, you've never failed at anything you've chosen to do. I guess you'll do okay."

Never failed? If Pris only knew.

A tiny sign on the door of a cement-block building caught GG's eye. MAUI PRO DIVES, it read in faded blue letters.

This did not look promising.

Inside, GG blinked from the sudden contrast between the bright Hawaiian sun and the dim interior, lit only by naked fluorescent tubes hanging from the ceiling. As she walked around, her sandals thudded dully on the concrete floor. No amenities, no polish in this barren shop.

Regulators and hoses for breathing were heaped on a scarred table next to tools and a gooseneck lamp. Obviously someone was overhauling the dive equipment. A portable radio, set to a classic-rock station, played low in the background.

Fins were stacked in one corner. Neoprene wet suits hung from hangers strung along a bare metal bar. Masks, snorkels, and buoyancy compensators—BCs for short, the vestlike devices for maintaining neutral buoyancy in water—hung from metal hooks on a Peg-Board.

GG looked over one of the BCs. From what she'd read recently, this was top quality. As was that brand of masks and the power fin. There wasn't a lot of selection for retail purchase here, but what was available was the best.

Okay, so the proprietors weren't exactly clamoring to entice the customers, but maybe she'd been a bit hasty in her judgment. She gave a delicate sniff. Too bad the place smelled like dried seaweed.

Pris shoved her hands into the pockets of her loose denim skirt. "This is the place for you, GG. I'm sure of it."

Good thing one of them was sure.

"No, Hal, I won't do it." A man's angry voice came from the back of the shop through the open double doors to the outside.

"C'mon, Ric," urged a second man, "with all the others on the rig, you're the only certified instructor."

"We're a commercial outfit, not recreational."

"We can do both."

"You know how I feel about—"

"Get over it," came the unsympathetic reply. "We could use the dough."

Through the open doors came two men wearing faded cut-offs, sandals, and white polo shirts with *Maui Pro Dives* on the pocket. The shorter one's sun-bleached hair and drooping mustache needed a good cut, GG noticed in passing, but she spared him only a glance, her gaze drawn to his taller companion.

An annoying quivering started in her stomach.

His close-cropped hair was dark. Sun and salt wouldn't dare lighten that unremitting midnight. His tan owed as much to DNA as to time spent on the water; she'd guess Hispanic or Mediterranean genes lurked in his genetic code.

He had the look of a physical man who spent a life outdoors and in the water—lean and solid muscles radiating power; loose, confident stride; faint crinkles around the eyes, a remnant of hours spent squinting into the sun.

Unbidden, GG's breath quickened. The quivering spread from her stomach to race up and down her arms then reach down deep and low inside her. It settled into a glow that warmed from the inside out. She clutched her tote more securely, smoothed her hair, and thought about last winter's ice storm.

"I'll do it, but damn it, Hal, you should have checked with me first." The dark-haired man, obviously unaware he had customers, grimaced. So he was the reluctant Ric.

Pris stepped forward and cleared her throat.

The two men looked up from their argument, startled.

Hal recovered first and gave Pris a professional smile. "May I help you?"

"Hal Dolinski?" At his nod, Pris smiled back. "I called about the dive-certification class."

GG noticed a tinge of red darken Ric's cheeks, and he

rubbed a hand across the back of his neck. Apparently the argument was about her lessons. Great, she'd be getting certified from Reluctant Ric, an unwilling instructor who had her gulping air just by walking in the door.

If she believed in omens, as Pris did, this was not an auspicious one.

If he believed in omens, as Hal did, this was not an auspicious one.

Ric Menendez rubbed the back of his neck. Letting the customer overhear him? He hadn't been that unprofessional even in his rookie days fresh out of the navy, but Hal's announcement had caught him off guard.

He focused on the blonde who'd spoken, a comfortable, earth-mother type with long braids and clunky sandals. With luck, she wouldn't realize what he'd been talking about.

"I'm Ric Menendez, ma'am, the instructor."

"Priscilla Johansson." She shook his hand in a firm grip and returned his smile.

"To become a certified diver, there's classroom work that has to be done first," he explained. "Depending upon how long your vacation is, and how much time you're willing to spend, you might not have time to finish."

"I'm the one getting certified," a cool feminine voice sliced through his pleasantries, "and I've finished the book work."

Ric dragged his gaze from earthy Priscilla to the other blonde. Damn, how had he missed seeing *her?*

Nothing about her spoke of quilts and home-baked bread. She was sleek, polished, expensive. She had high cheekbones, generous lips, and mermaid green eyes, all framed by nearly white blond hair that had been the stuff of adolescent fantasies in Puerto Rico, where he'd grown up.

Grace Kelly. She reminded him of Grace Kelly, one of Hitchcock's ice blondes, except her hair wasn't in a prim twist. It was cut almost mannishly short, but instead of masculinizing her, it gave her a feminine fragility. And there was definitely nothing manly about the curves and long legs beneath the dress.

The Grace Kelly blonde moved forward, beside Priscilla, and he peered closer, startled by the facial resemblance he now saw between the two. Sisters. Twins.

Grace returned his look with a cool calm that matched her voice and had the exact opposite effect on his hormones. She lifted her brows. "Is there a problem?"

Ric cursed himself for the lapse. He'd bet his next manta ray sighting *she* knew exactly what he'd been talking about. He cleared his throat. "Did you take the exam for the class work?"

"I have it here." She pulled a file folder from her smooth leather tote, then handed him a piece of paper from it.

One hundred percent. She hadn't missed a question, not even the obscure one about the *J* versus *K* tank valves.

Why wasn't he surprised?

"Very good." He gave her his professional smile.

She didn't smile back. "I expect to finish all my practice dives and my four certification dives while I'm on vacation. I'm willing to spend whatever time is necessary."

"We don't have any other people signed up for a class." He wasn't sure why he kept throwing out obstacles.

"I prefer it that way. I want only private instruction and private facilities."

Ric rubbed the back of his neck again. The commercial diving had been slow lately. Hal was right—they could use the money, but he hadn't taken on a class in two years. Not since Susan had left, not since that mess with the lawsuit. Too bad Hal preferred to spend his time with the engines and equipment and had never gotten instructor's credentials.

"I'm prepared to pay extra for the private time," she added.

"Only necessary during the final cert dives." He made a decision. "Okay, we're on."

"First I have a few questions, Mr. Menendez."

"Call me Ric."

"What are your qualifications as an instructor, Ric?"

Ric raised an eyebrow. The lady was careful. Not a bad trait for a diver. He leaned a hip against the worktable and crossed his arms.

"I've been diving for eighteen years, since I was thirteen. First rec—recreationally—then as a navy diver, then this for the last five years." He waved a hand around the store. "I've dived every beach, bottom, and surf condition in these waters. I'm PADI certified as a master divemaster, taught more people than any instructor on this stretch of the beach, and flunked divers I thought were too dangerous to be let under the water."

"When was your last class?"

How did the woman know which nerves to hit? "Two years ago," he drawled, hiding pain, and rubbed a hand along his chin. "Wouldn't want to spread myself too thin, you know."

Priscilla was talking to Hal, both of them with that goofy half-grin of first attraction flirting across their faces. She looked back at the cool blonde. "If you're going to do this, then this is the place. Trust me."

The Grace Kelly woman stared thoughtfully at him, then replaced the folder in her tote and pulled out a leather-bound book and a silver pen. She clicked the end of the pen. "When can we start?"

Apparently he'd passed the inspection. "No time better than this afternoon. One o'clock."

"Fine. One o'clock." She penned the time into the book she held. "I already have the gear I need."

"I'll need to see it first." Too many people borrowed some-body's old regulator that hadn't been checked in years or bought kid flippers instead of fins. He never took anyone in the water without proper working equipment. "There's also some paperwork to fill out, Miss—"

"Doctor. Dr. Johansson. Call me GG."

She looked more like a Grace than a Doc. And definitely not a GG.

Grace closed the book with a snap, clicked the pen closed,

carefully stowed both away, and then hitched her tote onto her shoulder. "I'll see you at one and fill out the paperwork then, while you check my equipment."

"Don't forget to wear a bathing suit, GG," he called after her as she left. A bikini, he added mentally.

Static crackled on the radio playing on the table. A guitar riff interrupted the drone of the morning news, and the clear, rich voice of Elvis filled the store.

"Follow that dream," Ric sang along absently. He had dreams, all right, but they didn't include cool, prim blondes with leather totes.

Even if the lady did have mermaid green eyes.

Chapter Two

As he'd thought, Grace had expensive taste. Her equipment was spanking new and all top quality. Ric looked over the array. She had a ton of it, too—everything that could possibly be recommended to a novice diver and then some. Apparently when the lady decided to do something, she put everything she had into it.

Was she like that with a man? Was she cool to the touch or a white flame?

Get your mind out of the sheets, Menendez. Grace is a client, and you're never going to find out.

"Breathe in lightly," he told her, forcing himself back to the task at hand. "The mask should stay in place without being held on by a strap."

She did as told. Her eyes were wide beneath the glass while Ric checked the seal of her mask, his fingers brushing the soft skin of her face. She gulped, and the mask dropped off. Ric jerked his hand back.

"It fits," she said hastily. "I tried it out in the pool at home."

"Not the same thing as being sixty feet deep, but it's okay. Pack up your gear while I go over the paperwork. You know how you're supposed to do it?"

"In reverse order of use. Fins first. Mask, weight belt and weights, BC, regulator."

"You got it." He glanced over her medical information and liability release, starting a file on her. "What's GG stand for?" he asked, pencil poised to fill in the blanks.

Dead silence. He looked up. She busily stuffed gear into two dive bags. "Hey, what do the initials stand for, Grace?"

She looked over sharply. "What did you call me?"

"Grace."

"The name's GG."

"You remind me of Grace Kelly."

"I take that as a compliment."

"It is. She was one of Hitchcock's classiest blondes. *Rear Window*—movies don't get any better than that."

GG smiled, the first genuine one he'd seen from her. "*To Catch a Thief* is my all-time favorite. Hitchcock had such a brilliant touch."

"Are you a Hitchcock buff?"

"You got it. He's the master. You, too?"

"Yeah. So what's GG stand for?"

"I just go by GG." She zipped the bags and stood. Her feet, encased in white mesh water shoes, were firmly planted and her hands rested on her hips. Did she have a bikini on beneath those blue nylon shorts and gray "Doc Fun Run" T-shirt?

"I need a name," he persisted, intrigued by her resistance.

"No, you don't. All anyone gets is GG."

"You have to tell *someone*."

"The only person I'll tell will be the one lying next to me on my honeymoon."

* * *

As soon as the words left her mouth, GG wished she hadn't said them. Ric Menendez didn't appear to be a man who'd resist a dare.

The light of challenge flared in his eyes, along with something else. Something just as primal for the male of the human species. Something that found an answering spark inside her.

He acted upon neither challenge nor attraction, though. "Guess I'll just have to call you Grace then."

Grace. In a way, she liked it, so she let his statement ride and picked up her daily planner and pen. "What's the schedule for my dives?"

Ric peered over her shoulder. "What is that book?"

"My daily planner. I take it everywhere; I'd be lost without it. See, it's got my weekly schedule, monthly outline, to-do lists, and back here"—she riffled through the pages—"my five-year plan."

"You know what you're going to do five years from now?"

"Well, I do write it in pencil, so I can make adjustments if I have to, but yes, I have firm plans for making chief of emergency medicine." *Among other things, like putting a ghost to rest.*

Ric's blunt finger moved down the detailed list. "That's quite a schedule."

"Don't you have one?"

"What with unpredictable weather patterns and new jobs arising and personnel changes, I can't even predict what I'll be doing two weeks from now. That's what makes diving fun."

"What a chaotic way to live."

"It's a free way to live, answerable only to myself and the jobs I accept."

"So what's your freedom-loving schedule for my dives?"

"We have to work that out as we go along."

GG closed her daily planner with a snap. "Irritating man," she muttered.

The Best-Laid Plans

Unfazed by her annoyance, Ric picked up his black mesh dive bag. "Let's go. My truck's outside."

She looked at her two bulging bags, then back at his single tote and made a face. "I've got too much stuff, don't I? No wonder that salesman was so pleased."

"Well, you'll be prepared for any disaster, including a few I've never encountered."

He reached for one of her bags, but GG waved him away. "I know the rule. You bring it; you carry it. Tomorrow I'll be leaving some of this in the hotel room." She hefted both bags and followed him outside.

He nodded, a hint of humor twitching his lips. "You probably don't need the knife during the pool work. Or the pony bottle of air. Or the night-dive lamp. Or the—"

GG burst out laughing, and Ric joined her while he stowed their gear in the back of the truck, along with the tanks of air fastened into specially designed holders.

Cripes, when had she last laughed like that? Maybe Pris was right; maybe she had been focused a little too much on work, but she intended to be an ER director and in the forefront of emergency medicine research, and that wasn't going to happen by chance or by allowing distractions.

"I confess," she said as she climbed into the truck, "I was a model Girl Scout."

He threw her another of those elemental glances that heated her, then put the truck into gear. "Good thing, because I was never a Boy Scout."

Other than his refusal to schedule all her dives, GG liked Ric's easy manner with her. She knew some men found her intimidating—her efficiency, her coolness, her brains—and that they joked behind her back about her mania for neatness in the chaotic ER. To tell the truth, she'd deliberately fostered the remote image, since it was the only way to hold ground in the male-dominated halls where she worked. The only way for her to keep focused on her goals and function within the disorderly tempest of an ER.

But the medical center was 4800 miles away in Michigan, and Ric didn't seem the least bit intimidated.

She was on vacation, the first in too many years. The first since Gary . . . She pulled her thoughts back. Could she retire the daily planner for a few days?

During the short drive toward the Kaanapali resort area, GG leaned against the truck door and eyed Ric.

Pris said she should ogle beach boys. Ric wasn't quite that laid-back, but he was relaxed and unfettered enough to spend days teaching a lone novice diver. And he sure was easy on the eyes.

A serious affair—that definitely wasn't part of the five-year plan, not with anyone—but a little vacation flirting, maybe that could be penciled in. It didn't have to go any farther than that—she'd be leaving soon—but it could be a harmless way to put a small hole in her self-woven cocoon.

Ric pulled up to the side of a smaller hotel on the beach and got out. GG followed.

"We'll be using the adults-only pool at the far end," he said, striding ahead of her. "It's deeper."

GG took one look at the pool area loaded with swimming tourists of all ages and halted. "No," she said.

"Just set your gear over by the wall and—"

"No," she repeated.

Ric finally realized he was talking to empty air and came back to her. "What do you mean, 'No'?"

"I said I wanted private facilities as well as private lessons. There're too many people here."

"You've got to do confined water first, and you won't find a pool any less crowded."

"I don't have to find one. You do." GG couldn't tolerate the idea of all these people watching her fumble around in the water, seeing her failures. Nobody saw her failures. Nobody saw her less than in control. Maybe it wasn't rational—okay, it wasn't rational; she'd had enough psychology training to recognize that—but it didn't change the fact that she refused to take her lessons where anyone could watch.

"You expect me to find a pool on Maui where there will be no chance of anyone else swimming?"

GG heard astonishment and frustration behind Ric's evenly spaced words. She lifted her chin and gave him her well-practiced haughty look. "Yes."

He closed in on her. GG looked up. She hadn't realized he was quite that much taller than she was. Or that his shoulders were quite that broad. There wasn't any fat on him either. He smelled nice, too, of suntan lotion and fresh sun.

The quivering at the pit of her stomach rose again.

"Ain't going to happen, Grace. This is the place we use."

"Then I shall take my business elsewhere."

His lips were nice, too. She'd bet he knew how to kiss—really kiss—a woman.

What would it be like if he kissed her? Dear God, she wanted him to kiss her.

Ric quieted, as if sensing her thoughts or noticing where her attention was fixed. The quivering anticipation and need in GG made her fingers and toes tingle. She looked up into his eyes. They were very, very dark brown.

"Bossy woman," he muttered. His head lowered a centimeter.

From a distant radio came a beautiful ballad, Elvis singing that he couldn't help falling in love.

Ric stopped, then straightened and hooked his thumbs into the belt loops of his cutoffs. "Okay, let's go."

GG thought he intended to return to the shop and bid her good riddance when he turned toward Lahaina. They drove past the gleaming resorts at Kaanapali Beach, the green of a Robert Trent golf course to their left. Dark clouds gathered at the tips of the ancient volcanic mountains at the center of the island and shaded them dark green with rain, but the beach area remained sunny. To her surprise they passed through Lahaina, then followed the shore until hotels turned to houses.

"Where are we going?" GG asked.

"To a pool."

He drove into the hills, at last pulling into the drive of an isolated bungalow nestled among banana palm fronds. He jerked the truck to a stop. "Pool's out back, with all the privacy you demand."

GG slung her bags over her shoulders and followed him.

The pool belonged to someone who enjoyed swimming, she decided. There was little grass, but lots of water. A waterfall sprang from the lava rock behind the pool and cascaded into one side of the shallow end. A natural cave formed where the pool sliced deeper into the slide of rock. An irregularly shaped addition to the usual deep end looked deep and broad enough for a good dive.

It was beautiful. It was isolated.

She was alone here with Ric.

The busy hotel pool took on a new appeal.

"The owner won't mind if we use it?" she asked.

"The owner's going to be in the pool with you."

"This is yours?" She followed him back to the truck to help with the air tanks.

"Bought it years ago, before prices on Maui skyrocketed. From the first time I saw Hawaii as a raw navy recruit, I always knew I wanted to settle here."

They laid the tanks beside the pool. "First thing," he said, "you've got to swim the length of the pool and back five times without stopping, then tread water for ten minutes."

GG nodded. Although strong swimming skills weren't needed to scuba, you did need to master the rudiments. She slipped off her shorts and shirt, then, hearing a soft, unintelligible sound from Ric, glanced over her shoulder.

"No bikini," she thought she heard him mutter.

GG faced the water, fingering the strap of her one-piece black suit. The natural setting, the blue of the water, the size of the pool, all made it appear more like open water than a man-made facility. She took a deep breath, her nerves suddenly fluttering.

It was a pool, not Lake Michigan, a pool. She closed her eyes and walked down the steps into the shallow end. The water was warm, bathed by the afternoon sun, but shaded by the rock and surrounding foliage. Water lapped across her while she slipped one arm through it, learning its silky touch, slowing her heart with deep breaths, opening to relaxation.

"Anytime, Grace."

Be brave as a hound dog, baby. Take that first stroke. A resonant drawl sounded inside her.

Her eyes popped open. Drawl? Ric didn't have a Southern accent. In fact, the voice sounded like—

No, it couldn't be. She thrust away that thought. "What did you say?" she asked Ric.

"I said, anytime."

She eyed him closely. He sprawled in a lounge chair at the side of the pool. He'd taken his shirt off, and she was momentarily distracted by a tiny tattoo on his shoulder. What was it? It was almost lost against the bronze of his skin.

GG shook her head, erasing the strange voice, then dove into the pool. She swam with easy strokes. As she sliced through the quiet water, where the only waves were the tiny wake made by her passage, her nervousness settled.

Her afraid of water? Not a chance.

Relaxed, his buoyancy trimmed, Ric hovered just above the bottom of the pool and slowly breathed the dry air in his tank. Floating beneath the water sometimes seemed more natural than walking on the ground. The tank at his back and regulator in his mouth had become a normal way to breathe.

He watched Grace practice her underwater skills. She took the regulator out of her mouth, then put it back in and purged the water. Good. Despite some initial fumbling with the unfamiliar gear and the awkwardness of it above water, she'd adapted well once they'd descended to the bottom of his pool. Like all new divers, she had a tendency to float up or sink down, her buoyancy under tenuous control, but other than that she'd performed each skill with intent attention and determination to master it. She was an apt pupil.

He'd never had a student who'd gotten it all so right from the first. Or one who'd been so annoyed when she made a mistake.

As her confidence grew, Ric felt tension that he hadn't acknowledged recede. The way she swam spoke of familiarity. She might not be a diver, but she'd been around water. He must have imagined her initial reluctance.

This was not going to be a disaster. Not like the last time he'd taken out recreational divers.

And he found he was growing partial to seeing a prim black suit instead of the more obvious bikini.

The shadows deepened along the pool, and his skin tightened with the cooling temperature. Colors faded, but there was still enough light to see the faint tightness around Grace's lips that told him she was starting to chill. Her movements had slowed and grown slightly jerky. It was getting late. They'd finish with clearing a partially flooded mask—that should take only a minute—and call it a day.

He tapped the front of her mask, reminding her of what came next, and she nodded in understanding.

Ric lifted the bottom of her mask and allowed water in it. Even in the best-fitting equipment, water in the mask was a common annoyance and divers needed to handle it routinely and automatically. Most neophytes scrunched their eyes closed or peered through tight lids. Despite the splash of water against her lashes, however, Grace stared straight ahead. The stream of bubbles from her exhalations grew.

He tapped her on the forehead, indicating she could clear out the water.

She didn't move. The strands of her blond hair formed a pale nimbus around her, eerie in the darkening waters.

He tapped again, then laid a hand on her shoulder. The stream of bubbles foamed around her, and a faint trembling coursed through her.

Damn! He'd kept her down too long. She didn't have the heat-conserving abilities he did. Cold could impair the judgment. Keeping a firm grip on her shoulder to give her a physical point of contact, he tapped her mask, then jerked his thumb up, the diver signal to surface.

A shudder traveled across her. She blinked, looked at him, and shook her head.

He jerked his thumb up.

She shook her head again, then tilted her head back and pressed the top of her mask until the water left her mask. Only then did she jerk her thumb up in agreement.

They surfaced.

Once out of the pool, Ric threw a towel at Grace. "Dry off and get warm." Briskly he dried himself off and shrugged on a T-shirt, then stalked over to her.

"Let's get one thing clear, Grace. Under that water, until you have your own personal PADI card, what I say goes. If I say surface, you surface."

"But I hadn't cleared my mask."

"You don't need a clear mask to surface. The important thing was, you were chilled and it was affecting your judgment. That means it's time to abort the dive. Most important, *I'd* decided to abort the dive."

"I wasn't—" She broke off and another shudder ran through her. "I *was* cold. That's what happened."

"Did you hear me? Don't ever question one of my calls again."

She lifted her chin, cool and haughty. "I know my limitations."

"But you don't know a diver's limitations. I've got eighteen years' experience on you. Trust that I have learned something in that time."

She said nothing, then after a moment gave a short nod to announce her capitulation. They collected their gear and loaded the truck in silence, then headed back to her hotel.

On the way, Ric berated himself for not pulling her out of

the pool earlier. Sure, it was a simple problem and easily remedied, but he should have noticed.

Just as he should have noticed the symptoms of nitrogen narcosis in that diver two years ago.

Two years ago, Susan, his fiancée, had asked him to help out a pal who was taking an advanced open-water class to depths of 120 feet, the limit for a recreational diver. Ric knew from the first that one pair of students was trouble. They were hotshots, so sure they knew it all that they refused to heed advice, an attitude that had no place underwater. Rather than keep them from diving, though, Susan's friend, the divemaster, had expected Ric to keep them in line. Ric's instincts had told him to abort, but he'd gone along because Susan asked.

Fascinated by the coral and fish, one of the hotshot pair forgot a cardinal rule of diving and ignored his buddy. Unfortunately, preoccupied with stopping the oblivious one from breaking fragile coral and sticking a hand into a moray eel hole, so had Ric.

Until the other half of the dangerous duo dropped another twenty feet, pulled his regulator out of his mouth, and slashed himself with the dive knife.

Nitrogen narcosis, that giddy feeling from too much nitrogen in the blood and a risk at greater depths, was insidious and could happen to even the most experienced diver, and the hotshot was far from experienced.

Ric had taken the nitrogen-intoxicated diver on an emergency ascent, and the guy had fought the whole way to the surface. He'd been a strong bruiser and had escaped Ric's grip once, with the result that the diver had surfaced too fast, gotten a case of the bends, and had to be airlifted to the nearest hyperbaric chamber.

Altogether a disaster. Especially afterward, when the guy had sued. Eventually Ric had been exonerated, but not before Susan had returned to the mainland, deciding her stint at slumming it with the dive instructor just wasn't part of her plans, and not before his business had almost folded.

The experience had reinforced his determination never to let pleasure or personal affairs affect business decisions. Not to follow someone else's plans.

Ric pulled up to Grace's hotel and jerked to a halt, but to his surprise she didn't get out right away. Instead she leaned against the truck door and smiled at him.

Her smile tempted him to forget all about keeping business separate from pleasure.

"I think this is going to work out just fine," she said. "You're an excellent teacher, Ric, and the facilities are perfect, and . . ." Her voice trailed off as her gaze darted to his mouth, then lingered. Her tongue touched her bottom lip.

Damn, he hadn't been imagining the subtle signals she'd been sending. The lady felt something, too.

That quickly, the resolve to keep his distance shifted to pure, unadulterated desire.

He slid closer. This was probably one bad idea, but in this fundamental need there were no strings attached, no expectations between them, and he couldn't resist the compelling, heady urge to taste her.

"Stop me if you aren't the least bit curious," he said, his voice lowering, "and we'll just forget this ever happened." He waited, but she merely gazed at him steadily. "Well?"

"Are you a good kisser?"

She was direct; he liked that in a woman. A rush, like bubbles from a free-flowing regulator, sped inside him, pricking him with heat where it popped and burst. She tilted closer, a tiny involuntary movement, but it was all he needed.

Ric pulled her to him, also liking the softness of her skin against his palms and the rub of firm muscles beneath her slick nylon shorts.

"You tell me," he murmured.

Chapter Three

He was a good kisser, GG realized in an instant, full of contrasts that drew a woman into deep waters. Firm lips and a gentle touch. Sweet, with a sprinkling of spice.

His mouth teased hers with a sensual invitation, and she accepted. At once he deepened the kiss, took it that extra step of intimacy. Her analytic brain shut off, and GG responded with a telltale groan and a touch of her tongue. Had she ever been swept into a whirlpool of need with such dizzying rapidity?

Slowly Ric pulled away from her, and she let him go.

"What's the verdict?" he asked, his voice ragged at the edges.

Good kisser? Beyond good. Try stunning or stupendous.

Lightly she touched his lips. "You've done this before."

"Once or twice. Do we take it any further?"

Yes, clamored every nerve and hormone.

No, these chaotic feelings weren't part of the five-year plan.

290

Needing to get herself back under control, GG shook her head. "I'm not looking to jump into bed."

At least, not tonight, added the rebellious hormones.

Ric raised his brows. "Did I ask you to?"

She flushed and ran a tremulous hand across her hair. Apparently she'd read a lot more into that kiss than he had.

Ric leaned back, his hand draped across the steering wheel. "What do you say we just start with dinner?" He said it as though he didn't care one way or the other.

Why should he care—they'd just met—though it was lowering to admit that after the way she'd responded to his kiss. Best just to get out of this with her remaining dignity—and her reawakening emotions—intact.

"Thank you, but no," she answered, calling on hours of practice at keeping her voice calm. One trick she'd perfected in the ER was blotting out all emotions except cool rationality, and now she used that to refocus.

Unfortunately that ability also seemed to be on vacation.

Nonetheless, she plowed ahead. "Pris is busy with her convention, but we planned to spend our evenings together."

He accepted the refusal good-naturedly. "Then I'll see you tomorrow morning."

When GG got to her room, however, Pris was nowhere to be seen. All that remained of her flighty sister was a note stating that she had borrowed fifty dollars and had gone with Hal to dinner and to watch an Elvis impersonator.

Her sister hated Elvis impersonators.

No Ric, and now no Pris. GG suppressed a tiny stab of disappointment and pulled out her briefcase. She could put the time to good use. Although Pris had commanded her not to bring work, she'd sneaked in some reports and journals. She'd call room service for dinner while she studied. Papers in hand, GG stretched out on a chaise situated outside on the lanai, the balcony.

Concentration proved elusive, as the persistent memory of

291

the kiss distracted her. GG touched her lips, certain she could still feel the imprint of Ric's touch, then jerked her hand away and muttered a distinctly unladylike curse.

The kiss wasn't a problem—the kiss had been very nice—but this fluttering response was. She was acting like a silly, lovestruck schoolgirl, while Ric had been casual about the whole thing. Why not? She supposed, for him, if one haole tourist wasn't willing, then the next one would be.

No, that was unfair. He'd responded to that kiss, too; that much she did know. And, as laid-back as he seemed, she didn't get the impression he was out trolling for tourists. Quite the opposite, actually.

Resolutely, she turned back to the article on resuscitative methods after cold exposure. It would complement the paper she was preparing that highlighted similar innovative rescue techniques she'd found successful.

In the distance she heard singing. Probably the Elvis impersonator, since he was singing "Rock-A-Hula Baby." The distant song chided her for wasting the tropical night, for working when she should be shaking her grass around.

The trade winds caressed her with a heady, sweet scent of ripe mango. That haunting memory of Ric's lips, their just-right pressure, returned and set her skin tingling.

GG dropped the papers and leaned her head back against the chaise. Generally her work had no trouble holding her attention, but tonight, she admitted, it was a lost cause.

What to do? she wondered, her thoughts drifting. Kiss Ric again? Maybe take things further? Pris was always telling her to loosen up. Well, why not now?

The next time, she'd be expecting the surge of desire. She'd handle it better.

Live a little, baby. Love a little, too. The drawl inside her mind interrupted her pleasant reverie.

GG shot to her feet. *Not again!* Why, in the name of all that was sane, had she started hearing Elvis's voice? It had to be the Elvis impersonator or Ric's voice that she'd transformed or some other, equally logical explanation.

She gripped the railing of the lanai.

She was not—repeat, *was not*—experiencing the nonsense that Pris and her mother believed in about channeling Elvis, about the King being as sweet and generous in the afterlife as he had been in real life. She was the sane one, the practical one, the one who planned for the future. She had to be.

It was stress. Simply stress. And fatigue. The diving had tired her out. Maybe she shouldn't be working. She should retire the papers along with the daily planner. Take a complete vacation. Have a vacation affair even.

Needing to drown out the distant singer along with the riotous emotions, she went back inside and flipped on the television. *Blue Hawaii,* one of her mother's favorites, was on.

How many times had her mother and Pris watched this, Pris listening to Mom's stories about the filming, while GG sat diligently at her desk studying?

As a young girl in Memphis, GG's mother had met Elvis before the King's army stint—when he was the hip-swinging rebel—and she'd been smitten. He'd been kindly tolerant of the young girl's crush. From then on, Mom had hung on the fringes of Elvis's life, treasuring each look or word, nabbing bit parts in his movies, haunting the fence at Graceland, and occasionally being invited inside. Except for her mother's brief marriage to an army sergeant in the '70s—Pris and GG being the only tangible results—Elvis had been Mom's life. She'd been outside Graceland, seven-year-old twins in hand, the day he'd died.

Six months later, she claimed Elvis spoke to her, and Pris had "inherited" the talent. When GG came home with hundreds on all her semester exams, her mother patted her on the shoulder with a vague murmur of pride. When Pris squeaked by with *C*s, she received undivided attention because Elvis spoke directly to her during the tests.

Mom hadn't been cruel or neglectful, just confused by her bright, ambitious daughter. And the teenage daughter had been excruciatingly aware that her mother and sister were considered "a little odd."

Early on, GG had accepted that she would never be like her mother or sister—content to live without ambition, expecting some spirit to solve their problems. She was going to make something of herself, be a success.

She had everything laid out in her five-year plan. Her first papers were being cited by other researchers in the field, and she was due for promotion to associate professor. She was on track, and could not allow distractions or deviations.

GG snapped off the TV and retrieved her journals. "Rock-A-Hula Baby" teased her. With an oath, she threw down the papers. It was a conspiracy. She had to get out of there.

I'm not looking to jump into bed.

Did I ask you to?

Hell, yes, he'd asked. *He'd* have jumped in a moment.

Ric's hands tightened around the truck steering wheel. Only Grace's cool response had knocked some sense into him.

He was her instructor, and he needed to keep his attention on the diving. The last thing he—and his business—needed was another messy lawsuit.

Besides, he'd learned from his ex-fiancée that Maui was a great place to visit, but a mainlander didn't have a second thought about going back when the reality no longer matched the fantasy.

His life was fine right now, and he didn't need a two-week affair, despite the fact that Grace tangled around him tighter than nylon filament.

For that reason alone, he knew to leave her be.

Damn, but he wanted to kiss her again. Kiss, and more.

Ric flipped on his cell phone to check in with his voice mail. While he was baby-sitting a neophyte diver, he still had a business to run. Two messages were potential jobs. Good. Competition was fierce, and Maui Pro Dives could use the work.

Although he had no desire to make his company the biggest, shiniest, or most visible, he wanted it to be known as the best, the place to come when you needed a difficult job done well and on time. He had good divers working for him, and he vowed to keep them working.

One call asked if he'd volunteer to teach a lifesaving class at the Y, while another asked for his help on an environmental cleanup campaign. He called back with positive responses to both. One call he deleted without answering—a woman he'd dated last month. She was nice, but he found he had no desire to date her again since he'd met Grace. The final one was from Hal.

"Hey, Ric. I'm at the hotel. GG isn't here, so Pris and I are assuming you guys decided to catch some dinner. We'll do the same, then go to the show down at the Maui Revue. Did you know her mother actually *met* Elvis? I can't wait to hear about it. See you later."

Sounded like Hal was moving fast; he hadn't even realized the two had made plans to meet.

Grace would be at loose ends for dinner.

Ric did an abrupt U-turn and headed back toward Kaanapali, his mental arguments against a cool blonde with mermaid green eyes no more solid than crumbling sand.

GG strolled from her hotel to the beachfront, but the busy hotel restaurants filled with vacationing couples held no appeal. Instead she wandered into a bar located at the water's edge. In addition to drinks, the sign said it served pupu platters and mahimahi burgers. Trust the Hawaiians to make even appetizers and fish sandwiches sound exotic.

Like many establishments in Hawaii, the bar was open-sided, so the sound of the surf competed with the juke box, and the touch of damp spray and breeze washed away the scents of alcohol and grease. She sat down at one of the tables on the fringes of the building and ordered a mahimahi burger and fries.

"You want a beer with that?" asked the bartender, who served as waiter.

"What have you got on tap?"

"She doesn't want a beer." Ric's voice sounded behind her.

GG pivoted in her seat to see Ric slap hands with the bartender.

"Hey, Dave. How's it hanging?"

"Aloha, Ric. You with the lady?"

"I'm the lucky man." Ric sat in a chair across from her. "She's diving tomorrow, confined-water skills, so no beer tonight."

"You got it. How about a virgin colada? Made with fresh coconut. And a beer for you?"

"Make it two virgins. I'm her instructor."

"You teaching her?" Dave whistled, then gave GG a frank stare. "What's your secret? Ric never takes—"

"Bring us a pupu platter, too," Ric interrupted.

Dave glanced between them. "Sure, bro."

"I haven't needed someone to order for me since I could speak," GG mildly told Ric when Dave left to place their orders.

"No alcohol when you're diving, not even the night before. It's part of the class rules."

"I read every paper you gave me, and that wasn't part of it."

"Sure it was. Right there between the lines." He grinned at her. "C'mon, Doc, you know I'm right."

GG laughed and admitted he was. She was well aware that the effects of alcohol lingered to the morning. After that disturbing incident in the pool, when the partially flooded mask had spooked her, and with her crazy reactions to this disturbing man beside her, she couldn't risk being less than one hundred percent in control.

"So, what are you doing here?" GG asked.

"Hal left a message that he'd gone out with Pris, and I knew you'd be alone. No pretty wahine should spend an evening in Hawaii solo, so I came back. I saw you walking and followed, figured I'd reiterate my dinner invitation.''

GG gave him a pointed look. ''What happened to the invitation part?''

''I figure the best way to get what I want is to do it and not bother with the asking.''

''And what do you want?''

He looked at her steadily. ''Tonight? Just dinner.''

For the second time that evening GG felt a stab of disappointment.

Dave set two frosty glasses filled with a milky liquid before them, then added a monkeywood platter heaped with egg rolls, marinated beef to heat over the minibrazier, shrimp toast, fresh pineapple slices, and the ubiquitous hibiscus decoration. ''I'll put the mahi burgers on now.''

The virgin colada was icy and sweet with coconut milk and pineapple juice, and the pupus—appetizers—were delicious.

''Why was Dave so surprised you were teaching me?'' GG asked when he left.

Spearing a slice of beef with a chopstick, Ric didn't answer at first. ''Our shop doesn't usually do recreational certs.''

''Why not?''

He shrugged. ''We prefer commercial dives.''

Somehow that didn't seem to be the whole story. ''Then why did you agree to take me?''

''Hal accepted because we could use the money, and I never renege on a deal.'' When he looked up and caught her studying him, he gave her an easy grin. ''Besides, I didn't have a five-year schedule telling me to do anything else.''

''Sounds like a tough way to run a business. No plans.''

''I said I didn't have a schedule, not that I didn't have plans. We need to be flexible, so as to meet job requirements when and where needed. It can be hectic, but that's what makes it fun. Our divers can be on a dive miles out or a hundred yards offshore. Often Hal or I have to be on-site, too. Sometimes we have downtime, though, and we take on whatever we can find.''

''Must be hard to juggle that with family demands.''

''Which is why I have none.''

''No family?''

''None here. My parents are still in Puerto Rico along with four sisters and one brother.'' He grinned at her. ''My youngest brother took the rebellious route, too, and left the family business.''

''And what is the family business?''

''Real estate—lots of it. One thing I did learn from my *padre,* if you're going to do something, be the best. We just disagree on what that best thing to do is.''

''You think diving is?''

''I loved diving from the first moment I almost drowned in the family swimming pool when my homemade air helmet failed. He thought I should marry the girl next door, the one who's father owns as much property as he does.''

GG was trained to see beneath lighthearted words to hidden pains. Ric's goals might be more formless and unstructured, but they were as important to him as hers were to her.

She smiled inside. She was also woman enough to hear the underlying masculine warning—*no ties wanted.*

''Do you still keep in contact with your family?'' she asked.

''Sure, E-mail, phone. We get together for weddings and christenings. But, day to day, I keep free of entanglements. Is Pris your only family?''

''My only sibling. Mom lives in Memphis. My father hasn't been around since he heard the words 'It's twins.' ''

''Sorry.''

GG shrugged. ''I never knew him, so in some ways I never missed him. We tried to get Mom to join us on this trip, but she's happiest at home, only blocks from Graceland.''

As the dinner progressed, GG was surprised to find herself relaxing and enjoying the conversation with Ric. She never thought of herself as good with people; that was one reason she'd chosen emergency medicine—people were in and out so quickly, their only concern was the crisis at hand. Small talk, social conventions like sending cards for birthdays, dinner parties—things that came naturally to Pris—were all foreign to her.

One of the reasons she'd loved Gary was because they had so many commonalities that she'd never felt socially awkward with him. He was shy; they always had school subjects to talk about; he had never demanded too much in bed. After Gary's death, she'd retreated further.

With Ric though, to her surprise, there was no awkwardness, beyond that constant hum of awareness thrumming between them. He laughed easily and had a wide range of interests. They argued about which was Hitchcock's best film, talked about sights she should see on Maui, debated the merits of the latest tax cut, and agreed that no dinner was complete unless it was finished with ice cream.

GG stirred her spoon through her papaya ice, a specialty of the house that they'd gotten for dessert.

She couldn't deny that all night she'd been conscious of the physical, elemental side of Ric. His fluid movements, the dark hairs sprinkling his arms, the well-honed physique all set an unfamiliar wildness stirring inside her. More than once she'd caught herself staring at his hands, wondering what they'd feel like touching her with desire instead of helping her don her bulky BC.

Some deep instinct told her Ric would demand much from, and give much to, a woman in bed.

He made her feel so . . . alive.

After finishing his helping of papaya ice, Ric leaned back in his chair.

He'd enjoyed the dinner, he realized. Grace had been shy at first, which surprised him because he'd thought of her as socially adept. She was also smart, with a wide range of interests and no hesitation about arguing, pleasantly but with cutting precision, when they disagreed.

While he watched, she scraped up the last of the ice, her spoon catching the final drops. Another thing he liked—she didn't pick at her food, but despite the healthy appetite she ate delicately, with an inborn grace.

Grace. He couldn't seem to get the name out of his thoughts. It fit her so much better than GG. She personified grace and prim boundaries and high expectations for the men in her life. All things he swore to stay away from in a woman.

Yet if she looked at him one more time with that soft desire, he knew all the oaths in the world wouldn't keep him from kissing her again.

She finished the final bite, then glanced at him. At his hands, at his lips. Her gentle smile played into his frank need.

Ric swore to himself. One look and she had him growing harder than a steel tank.

For a woman who looked so savvy and sounded so smart, she was an absolute baby about hiding her emotions. It was as though they were all too new to her, as if she didn't believe they existed and so saw no reason to conceal them.

If so, she was dead wrong.

To delay having to get up and reveal his condition, Ric asked, "What kind of doctor are you?"

She licked her spoon, then set it down. Entranced with the tiny motion of her tongue, Ric almost missed her answer.

"Emergency medicine. I specialize in research on resuscitation and trauma prevention after water submersions."

"English, please."

She laughed. "Drowning and near drowning. Predicting who will survive. What's the best way to revive someone, to treat them, and to prevent infections and long-term problems. I do a lot of community work, too, teaching safety and CPR, since the first ten minutes after a drowning are critical."

A memory pricked at Ric. *Predicting who will survive.* Detroit. Dr. Johansson. G. G. Johansson. "Wait a minute. Didn't you publish a paper about a year ago, urging doctors not to give up CPR too early on drowning victims?"

"Yes." She gave him a puzzled look. "You read it?"

He nodded, looking at her with admiration. "I try to keep up on information like that for my work. The navy doc showed it to me and I keep a copy in my files. As much water as there is around here, we could use more research like that."

"My work's mostly with cold freshwater."

"I suppose that's natural, living around the Great Lakes. Does your sister live in Michigan, too?"

Grace shook her head. "She's in Memphis with Mom, where I grew up."

"So how'd you end up in Detroit?"

"My fiancé planned to go to med school there, so I applied too. When I finished, Detroit Medical Center offered me a job, and I stayed."

My fiancé? Ric's stomach burned. "You've got a guy back home?"

She looked at him directly. "I wouldn't have let you kiss me if I did. He died our last year in med school."

"Sorry," Ric murmured, feeling like an absolute heel.

"That's all right. It was a while ago."

But the torch still flickered, which explained the virginal air about her.

He was an absolute fool for thinking of possibilities.

Ric pushed to his feet and threw some bills on the table. "We've got an early morning. Let's go."

Without a word Grace picked up two of the bills, handed them to him, and replaced them with two of her own. "I'm ready."

She was right; keep it business. Hired instructor and client.

Walking Grace back to her hotel, Ric struggled to remember that. He'd lived in Hawaii for years and thought he'd become inured to the romanticism the tourist commission gushed about. He'd never strolled along the beach with someone like

301

Grace, though, while moonlight painted a silvery streak across the dark waters tipped with foamy caps.

She took off her sandals to let the waves lap across her feet. Ric shoved his hands into his shorts pockets to keep from taking her into his arms.

For all the conversation at dinner, they were both content to walk in silence in the sultry night. Talk had made him aware that he liked her as a person. The silence, however, combined with the sensuousness of the islands—scents of brine, mango, and flowery frangipani, warm breezes, flickering torches in the background dancing a pattern of light on her face and shiny hair—made him aware of her in another, very primal sense.

The silence—and the awareness—continued as they crossed the garden of her hotel. Hands still shoved firmly in his pockets, Ric paused beside the steps leading to Grace's second-floor room.

"I'll pick you up at seven. We need to finish early because I've got some other things I need to do in the afternoon."

"Fine."

A moment's hesitation; then Ric gave in to temptation. The last time, he promised himself as he leaned over and kissed her cheek. It wasn't a very satisfactory kiss, despite the feel of her soft skin and the faint fragrance of gardenia from her, but it was all he could risk.

Grace turned and kissed him back, on the mouth. Too briefly, just long enough for the sweet taste of papaya to tantalize him; then she drew back. "Good night, Ric. Thanks for the evening." She turned and ran up the stairs.

Pris drew back from the balcony rail, a satisfied smile on her lips.

"You were right," she whispered. "With me gone, they spent the evening together."

She hadn't been at all reluctant when Elvis suggested she spend the evening with Hal, who hadn't even blinked when

302

she told him why. Even if this didn't work out for GG, at least it had brought Hal to her.

She's got a long way to go, came the Mississippi drawl to Pris. *This ain't finished, baby.*

"But it's a start."

GG was starting to live.

Chapter Four

After their third day of lessons, GG stacked the used air tanks by the fill station at Maui Pro Dives, then wandered into the shop to tell Ric good-bye.

He was on the phone in his office. "You need six divers to finish before December." He paused, then walked over to a large dry-erase calendar fastened to the wall. "Let me work with our schedule."

If the different-colored entries on the calendar were all jobs, Ric was busier than she'd realized.

Catching sight of her, he held up one finger, silently asking her to stay. When she nodded, he handed her a pink slip of paper from his desk, then turned away and wrote on the calendar with an orange marker. "We can have the men available after next week. Same contract." He paused again, listening, then laughed. "Hey, you know we don't work for that price. Do you want good or do you want cheap?" He laughed again at the answer. "Of course you'll be getting the boss on this one. I'm ready to get out the office."

Idly listening to Ric's easy camaraderie with his customer, GG glanced around the room. His office was as utilitarian as the rest of the shop, with a metal desk covered with neat stacks of papers, a cracked vinyl couch, and four metal filing cabinets. Dive gear littered every surface.

The only note of color was a brilliant painting—one of Robert Lyn Nelson's undersea renditions inhabited by a variety of colorful sea creatures—placed on the wall where Ric could see it from his desk. It was a distinctly Hawaiian touch, as was the softening breeze that wafted through the open window. She was going to miss that fresh, sweet air when she left.

GG sat on the windowsill and glanced at the pink paper Ric had given her. It was a message from Hal. *Pris called. Something came up at the convention. She'll meet you at the souvenir shop at five.*

Disappointed, GG carefully folded the note. Though she and Pris had gone about their separate activities in the mornings, the afternoons and evenings they'd spent together. They'd visited an exotic-flower garden and drove up to tranquil Iao Valley, where King Kamehameha I had conquered Maui and united the islands. Today they'd planned to tour Lahaina and the souvenir shops.

For GG, the true gem of those hours was not the sights they saw, but the time with her sister. Not since she'd left home for college had they spent so much time, and such easy time, together. Maybe it had been even longer, since their differences were obvious from the day they had started walking and talking.

Now she had an unscheduled afternoon. When had she last had one of those?

For once, instead of feeling compelled to find something to fill the time, GG leaned against the window frame and simply sat. Planted outside were a lipstick plant and a hibiscus bush, and GG admired the red, tubelike flower of a lipstick plant and the yellow hibiscus blossoms while listening to Ric.

After a few minutes of negotiation, Ric concluded, "Okay, we're on. I'll send the contracts for your signature. *Mahalo*." Smiling, he hung up the phone.

"Success?" she asked.

"Yes."

He'd gotten the terms he'd wanted all along. Despite Ric's laid-back persona, his casual air and dress, the man generally got exactly what he wanted, she realized.

"You keep busy," she commented, nodding toward the calendar.

"I like to keep my divers working. That's how you hold on to the best ones."

"It sounded like whoever you were talking to thought *you* were the best."

Ric shrugged. "I've got to be if I want to make Maui Pro Dives the best, and that's my plan. Not the flashiest, but the best. Steady and solid."

GG rested her head against the window. "Why don't you usually do individual lessons? I'd think they'd be lucrative."

"They aren't what I want to do." Looking steadily at her, he leaned one hip against the desk. "Last time I helped with a lesson was at my fiancée's request. I ended up in a messy lawsuit that cost me several jobs. Even though I wasn't at fault, it was hard to overcome the stigma. The business suffered. I'll never let personal considerations come before business again, and amateur divers come with a lot of expectations of what you should do for them."

"What happened to the fiancée?"

"She went back to the mainland before the trial. Knowing about the lawsuit, do you want to finish the lessons and cert dives?"

He was ambitious, working steadily with his eye on the goal. GG liked that. And, unless her feminine instincts had atrophied from disuse, he was attracted to her, too. Perfect. The situation was perfect. They were attracted to each other, but neither one had plans for any entanglements.

She gave him a slow smile. "You don't get off that easy."

Masculine satisfaction flared in his eyes. Reaching over her shoulder, he plucked a yellow hibiscus bloom, then tucked it behind her ear. "You look good in flowers," he murmured and touched her cheek. "Though they're nothing compared to the glow of your skin."

Tropical winds did little to cool the fire starting inside. For this one brief interlude, GG's well-laid plans dissolved under the pleasures of a single moment.

Before she could respond, Hal sauntered in. It took him no time to take in the intimate scene. He backed out, mumbling, "Sorry," but the moment was lost.

Yet there would be other moments during this crazy hiatus from her five-year plan, of that GG was sure. She was also sure she would treasure each one.

"How do I ask a man if he'd like a brief affair, Pris? Are there subtle hints I can drop?"

After mulling over that question, GG had not come up with a good plan—except to ask Pris later that afternoon. Her sister wasn't promiscuous, but she'd had more . . . variety in her life.

A pinch-lipped woman overheard the question and, with a sniff, abandoned the aisle where Pris and GG stood. GG flushed. Maybe the middle of a cavernous souvenir shop wasn't the best place to talk about this.

Pris was unfazed by the question or the locale. She dropped a souvenir shell key chain into her loaded shopping basket. "Men don't require subtlety in that area, GG. Only willingness. What exactly do you want?"

"A vacation fling."

"A short-term affair?" Pris sounded skeptical.

"Yes," GG answered firmly. "But I can't just come out with, 'Do you want to sleep with me?' "

"Why not? I do."

Although this trip had drawn her closer to her sister than they'd been since leaving the womb, obviously some of the differences between them were still very active.

"That's not my style, Pris."

"I hate to break this to you, but nothing's your style with men. Say, do you want that night-light you're holding?"

GG held out the shell she hadn't realized she'd picked up. "No, you can have it. But—"

"Thanks. Aren't you going to buy anything but a can of macadamia nuts?"

"Don't change the subject, Pris."

Pris sampled some coconut candy, then added a box to her selections. "Okay, you're not the type to announce, 'Hey, Ric, I'm ready.' " She arched her brows. "We are talking about Ric?"

"Of course."

"How do you feel about him?" Pris gave her an intent look.

"He's fun. Knows his dive stuff." A pale answer, she knew, but it was all she could admit. "I like him." *That* was a major understatement. Even in fins her toes curled when he touched her.

"Sexy, too," Pris said, flashing a knowing grin.

GG grinned back. "Oh, yeah."

"Good. Okay, tomorrow's Friday, your last day of confined water and my last day at the convention. You'll be too tired that night, so we'll have to go with Saturday. We'll ask them to go with us to a luau."

"Them?"

"Hal and Ric." A crooked grin lit her sister's face. "Actually, I already asked Hal. Planning a few unsubtle hints myself. I've been trying to figure out how to tell you. Am I glad you finally decided to live a little! Ask Ric to the luau."

"What if he refuses?"

Pris gave her an incredulous look. "I've seen how he looks

at you. He's just waiting for the willingness signal. We'll find you something sexy to wear. A sultry perfume. Ric will get the message. C'mon, let's go look for a dress.''

Pris dragged her over to a rack of muumuus.

"How's your convention going?" GG asked while she flipped through the dresses.

Her sister was a clerk in an ecological boutique; they carried clothing and items made from alternative and recyclable sources, like rubber from discarded tires, and previously owned, gently used clothing. A lot of GG's wardrobe came from things Pris sent her because they were too conservative for the boutique's clients' tastes. The convention was a trade show for possible new lines; Pris was sent because she was good at knowing what people wanted.

"Mixed bag." Pris picked out a bright pink dress, wrinkled her nose, and put it back. "There're some people doing interesting work with hemp, so I'm going to suggest we carry their clothing line. Others . . ." Pris shook her head and sighed. "They have no clue."

"Sounds a bit like an AMA convention," GG commented. "Maybe a blood-and-gore doc and a tree hugger do have things in common. Do you like this?" She held up a red-and-white flowered dress.

Pris shook her head. "Not you." She put her hands on her hips. "Yuck, these are all too missionary."

GG had to agree.

"Aha!" From a table stacked with cloth, Pris pulled out a large square of silk. "But this is perfect."

"Pris, it's a scarf."

"Too big. It's a pareu. Like a sarong."

GG fingered the fluid silk. It was beautiful. Navy blue and sea green swirled in a pattern that hinted of ocean and sky. Did she dare wear something like this? GG of Detroit never would, but Grace on vacation . . .

"How do you wear it?"

"Like this." Pris draped the fabric around GG and tied two ends over one shoulder. "Or this." She wrapped it around from the back, crossed the ends around GG's neck, and then tied them. Pris twirled her to look in a full-length mirror. "It's pretty versatile. Of course, it will look better without the shorts and T-shirt underneath. Better yet—with nothing underneath."

With nothing underneath. GG sucked in her breath. The silk flowed across her curves, highlighted her skin and hair, made her feel beautiful. The invitation was subtle—and unmistakable.

"Pris, you're a genius. You know, with your flair, you should be running that store."

The mirror reflected Pris's startled, contemplative look; then she shrugged. "That's not me."

"And this wasn't me, until your eye saw what I needed."

"I'll think about it." Pris adjusted the neckline. "So will you wear it?"

"I will. This dress will knock Ric's socks off."

"And, with luck, a few other items of clothing."

Friday was GG's last day of confined-water skills. So far, she'd had no trouble with the pool work and no repeat of the strange uneasiness she'd experienced with the flooded mask.

The voice of Elvis had also remained blessedly silent.

Ric was an excellent instructor: knowledgeable, business-like, and patient. He insisted she repeat each skill until she had it mastered.

Not that GG quit until she perfected anything, anyway.

Ric floated effortlessly beside her. "Only three more skills left. We'll go to the dive section of the pool. On the bottom, I want you first to demonstrate neutral buoyancy."

No problem. Divers balanced the weights around their waist with air in their lungs and BC in order to hover at a given depth. It was a skill requiring practice to fine-tune, but GG was confident she'd have no problem passing, having spent extra time on it.

"You did the partially flooded mask the first day," Ric continued. "This time I want you to completely flood it, wait until I tap you on the shoulder, then clear it. The final skill is buddy breathing. First, on the bottom, I'll come to you as though I'm out of air, and you let me have your spare. Then you come to me and we'll buddy breathe off the same regulator during our ascent. All set?"

GG nodded, ignoring the fluttering in her stomach. This was her final test. She was ready.

As she expected, the buoyancy test was a snap. In fact, floating, with the water cradling her, as close to weightless as possible on earth, relaxed her. She hadn't realized how tightly wound she'd been.

Sunlight played across the rocky walls and Ric's dark hair. His eyes, slightly enlarged from the mask and the water, crinkled in pleasure. She grinned back at him, a smile big enough to be seen around the regulator in her mouth.

He gave her the thumbs-up, then held up two fingers, indicating she'd passed and they were on to skill two. She settled slowly down to sit cross-legged at the bottom of the pool. Ric tapped her mask, telling her to flood it, and GG lifted the bottom, breaking the seal around her face.

Water rose to eye level. It splashed into her eyes.

It splashed into her eyes.

She didn't like water splashing in her eyes.

GG was so relaxed, so confident, that at first she didn't recognize the initial wave of panic. Nausea clutched her throat, and her eyes squeezed shut against the rising water. The stream of bubbles from her regulator gushed past her ear.

Tightening her lips around the mouthpiece, GG willed the link to her air to stay with her. In. Out. Control.

It wasn't working.

Stop flooding the mask, drawled an inner voice.

Elvis again? Oh, cripes, not now! I am not hearing the voice of the King, she insisted. *Go away.*

Can't do that, baby. You need me.

Strangely, the resonant voice had the effect of breaking through the panic. GG's fists dropped to her sides; her knuckles brushed against the bottom of the pool. She was in the pool.

Open your eyes, baby, drawled the voice.

Stop calling me baby. Now she was answering.

Open your eyes. Ric's there.

Ric would be in front of her, watching her. She'd gotten this far with her dream of diving; she wouldn't fail now.

That's right. Follow your dream. The voice faded.

Breathing got easier.

Ric laid a hand on her shoulder. His touch was warm in the cooling water, the calluses faintly rough against her skin.

The touch reassured, calmed, replaced the inner panic with a new fluttering, a good one. His hand tightened. Despite the water in her mask, GG opened her eyes. Ric was blurry, but solid. Real. An anchor.

His brows raised, and he made a circle of thumb and forefinger. *Are you okay?* the signal asked.

GG nodded. Her muscles loosened; her throat relaxed. She refocused on the business of diving.

Ric repeated the signal. *Are you okay?*

She needed to give back a signal, needed to be clear for him. GG returned the okay signal. After a moment, Ric tapped her mask, and she cleared it of the water.

He stared at her, then nodded and held two fingers side by side, indicating for her to follow him swimming. GG complied, her confidence returning. When Ric turned to her, took the regulator from his mouth, and slashed a hand across his throat, she was ready.

The out-of-air signal. Buddy breathing, the last of her tests.

Regulator assemblies usually had two separate mouthpiece-and-hose combinations connected to the air tank.

One for the diver, one, referred to as an octopus, as a spare, in case of regulator failure or to share with an out-of-air diver. GG pulled the octopus off the Velcro, anchoring it to her BC, and passed it to Ric. He nodded approvingly and took a breath from it.

Sharing air—she hadn't expected the intimacy of it. They swam along the bottom, Ric no farther than the four-foot hose allowed. He didn't quite touch her but was close enough that displaced water slid across her skin with each effortless stroke. Her gaze caught his. For one moment, one eternity, they floated: motionless, weightless, breathing as one, united.

Ric took one more long breath, then replaced his regulator in his mouth and held hers out to her. She attached it to its Velcro holder, avoiding his dark, intent eyes.

His hand reached out, as though to caress her cheek; then he closed his fingers. Water, a breath of warmth, whispered across her throat when his hand lowered. GG raised her eyes to his and nodded at his silent question.

Slowly he reached behind her. His eyes never leaving hers, he turned the valve on her air tank off. GG took a breath, a second deep one that came harder, then a third. No air.

Human instinct to breathe is strong and primal. GG controlled the instinctive gasping and swiped her hand across her throat to signal that she was out of air. Ric took the regulator from his mouth and held it to hers. Her lips tightened around the rubber where his lips had just been. With the press of a button, she purged out the water that collected with the transfer and took one deep, blessed breath, then a second.

After the second breath, she let Ric take the regulator from her so he could breathe. Slowly she exhaled small air bubbles, as instructed, until he returned the regulator. Two more breaths, then his turn.

The intimacy deepened. This hose was shorter, so they had to float face-to-face, legs tangling, his hairs rough against her smooth skin. Each rested a hand on the other's shoulder to keep within reach. Since losing the regulator was an unacceptable risk, the diver with the tank—in this case, Ric—kept it in hand at all times, establishing the rhythm of air for both.

He was, very literally, giving her the breath of life.

Just as he had breathed life into her sleeping heart.

GG closed her eyes briefly. No, hearts weren't a part of her agenda. This was only a pleasurable, but manageable, fling, an interlude in her five-year plan. A tiny walk on the wild side for a woman who had never pierced anything other than her earlobes.

Ric's hand on her shoulder tightened. He jerked one thumb up, the symbol to ascend to the surface. GG mimicked his gesture, indicating her readiness.

Just as he regulated their shared breath, Ric controlled their ascent. They circled slowly up, gazes locked, hands on each other's shoulders, one in movement. Ric gave her air; GG raised her arm to guide their safe path. The intimate contact grew closer when Ric's hand slipped from her shoulder to her shoulder blade, inching her closer until their bulky, vestlike BCs brushed.

GG's head broke through the water's surface to the warm Hawaiian air, and she gasped for breath. Ric dropped the shared regulator, cupped her cheek with his hand, then kissed her.

His lips were fresh, clean, faintly chlorinated. His strong hand was cherishing in its grip. GG urged him closer, but the BCs prevented their hugging, the skin-on-skin touch she craved. She tilted her head back.

With a clunk, the back of her head connected against her air tank, jerking her from the kiss.

Ric's hand cupped the back of her head, protecting her from the air tank. "You okay?"

"Fine," GG answered, wondering if she truly was.

"Congratulations," he said. "You passed."

* * *

By unspoken assent, as they had each day, they doffed BCs, fins, and weight belts and swam around Ric's pool, splashing under the waterfall or floating faceup to the sun. The tiny dolphin tattoo on Ric's shoulder fascinated GG. When he swam, it rippled, emphasizing how at home he was with the sea. Feminine tension coiled deep in her belly.

She watched Ric and devoured each memory. Sunlight glistening on the water droplets in his black hair. His lazy crawl. The rich sound of his frequent laughter.

Ric, lying on his back, paddled with a desultory grace. "What happened when you flooded your mask down there? You spewed bubbles like a shook-up bottle of champagne."

"I have this thing about getting my face splashed. It startled me when the water got in my eyes. That's all."

Ric swam over to her side. "You sure?"

"Of course I'm sure. I did everything else fine, didn't I?"

His gaze drifted to her lips. "More than fine."

GG flushed. "When can I do my cert dives? This weekend?"

Once she'd finished the confined-water training, the final step was to go into open water and demonstrate, on a series of four dives, that she had mastered all the necessary skills. Only then could she get her certification card.

Ric shook his head. "Diving is strenuous, especially for a rookie. Better to wait until Monday."

"I don't feel sore or tired." She'd come this far; she was anxious to finish it.

"You mean to tell me you haven't dropped dead asleep as soon as your head hits the pillow each night?"

Come to think of it, she had slept pretty hard.

And there was that luau.

He didn't wait for her agreement. "We'll schedule your dives for Monday and Tuesday. We'll get an early start, get to Molokini crater before the snorkel crowds get there."

"Sounds good."

They levered themselves out of the water, dried off, and

then rinsed off their scuba equipment. They'd loaded Ric's truck when GG paused and looked up at Ric. He was broad and strong in his T-shirt and cutoffs, the breeze ruffling his damp hair.

Do it. Ask him now, she urged herself. *Ask him to the luau. Ask him for more.*

"They say no visit to Hawaii is complete without a luau. Tomorrow night, would you like to go to one with me?" she asked in a rush.

"Hal said Pris asked him." He tilted his head. "Is this invitation just so you won't be a third wheel? Or so your sister doesn't feel bad about leaving you? I don't want to . . . misunderstand."

GG flushed, but met him squarely. "No. I want to go with you. I want you."

Satisfaction coursed through Ric. Grace wanted him as badly as he wanted her. The blood surged low inside him, at once making him hard and taut.

"I'd love to go to the luau with you."

She leaned forward. "I want you," she repeated softly.

"And I want you." Ric bent over and kissed her, his hand sliding beneath her T-shirt across the slick nylon of her suit.

He found his objective, the generous swells of her breasts, separated from his fingers only by a layer of thin fabric. He brushed cautiously across the tips, waiting to see if she would pull away.

She didn't. Her nipple tightened beneath his palm, and she wrapped one arm across the back of his neck, holding him close for the endless kiss. Her tongue found his even as she reached low to caress him.

Ric groaned with the touch. "Everything about you feels so damned good against me," he growled.

An insistent buzzing intruded, slicing through the desire.

"What's that?" she asked, her voice slow.

"What?" Ric groaned, but in frustration this time. "It's my cell phone." He lifted away from the kiss to check the number.

It was from one of the dive sites. "Sorry, I have to get this."

The call took only two minutes, but it was long enough to cut off any other pleasurable plans. A snafu at the dive site that had to be dealt with, and he'd made the choice long ago that to succeed on his terms, the business came first.

"I've got to go into the office," he told her, surprised by his regret at leaving her.

Grace took a shaky breath. "If there's anything a doctor can understand it's having to take a call. Can you still make the luau?"

"A typhoon wouldn't keep me from that." He ushered her into the truck, then rested his arm along the open door. "Afterward, Sunday morning, would you like to go to Haleakala, Grace?"

Haleakala was the huge, dormant volcano that dominated the east end of Maui.

"We'd have to get up very early," Ric continued, his finger tracing the curve of her ear, "to allow time enough to drive and see the sun rise over the crater's edge."

Ric knew Grace caught the implications from the way her skin got that delicate tint. What an intriguing mix she was. Bold one moment, shy the next. Competent, yet with an air of vulnerability with every emotion bared.

"Seeing Haleakala was part of my plan," she answered softly.

Her skin was soft beneath his callused fingers and still cool from the pool. Ric gave in to the drugging temptation and ran a thumb lightly across her lips, then followed with a short kiss. Too short, too sweet, but deliberately ended.

He wanted more. He wanted to feel more than the skin at her throat. He wanted to see every inch hidden by that prim black bathing suit and hear her heart pounding strong as the surf. He wanted to hold her while she convulsed with pleasure, and he wanted to be deep within her.

"Good," he answered, his voice husky.

He was probably crazy, he knew, wanting her to stay the

night. Yet he needed this time. They'd have a few days together; then she would leave, he knew that.

It was easier that way. Better for both of them. No false protestations of love or devotion. No strings or ties.

Whistling, he strolled to the driver's side.

Tomorrow night, for a short time, she would be his.

Chapter Five

"It goes on your toe," Pris said. "It's a toe ring."

"Are you sure?" GG fingered the glittering ring Pris had just tossed her, while they dressed for the luau.

"With the pareu, it's the perfect seductive touch."

GG slipped the ring on her toe, then held out her sandaled foot, studying it. She'd never worn anything like a toe ring, but she kind of liked the way it looked. "Is the emerald real?"

Pris shrugged. "I have no idea. Could be. The guy who gave it to me liked to flash the real stuff."

"What happened to the guy?" GG asked, still admiring the ring. Imagine, wearing emeralds on her toe.

"Wasn't meant to be; he didn't recycle. I tried to give the ring back when we broke up, but he refused to take it."

"Does Hal recycle?"

"Yeah, he does." A smile flitted across Pris's face.

"You like him."

"A lot." Pris added three more silver bracelets to the four on her arm. "We're two souls destined for each other. I knew it when I first heard his voice, and Elvis confirmed it.''

"You aren't worried about the speed of it?'' GG made sure the pareu was still knotted securely about her neck, then picked up her perfume.

"No, and Hal isn't either.''

Such surety in matters of the heart—even if it did come through the alleged matchmaking of the King—would be nice. Two souls destined for each other. Was that the way love was supposed to be? She hadn't felt that way about Gary.

She would not let herself feel that way about Ric.

GG spritzed on the perfume. Spirit voices, destined souls. Such nonsense wouldn't overtake her life. That was allowing fate to rule, and GG didn't like trusting fate. It gave up too much control.

Fate was unpleasant.

It was too unplanned.

Speaking of unplanned . . . GG cleared her throat. "Are you going to come back to the hotel tonight?''

Pris, slipping on her sandals, gave her a lopsided smile. "I sure hope not. Do you mind?''

GG shook her head while she rummaged through her tote. "I thought maybe you wouldn't, so I, ah, got you these. If you want them.'' She thrust a box in a paper bag into Pris's hands.

Pris peered into the bag, then made a face at her sister. "I know you think I'm flaky, but I do know about safe sex. Hey, wait, these are ribbed. And colored.'' She gave GG a mischievous grin. "Didn't know you had such an adventurous nature, sis.''

GG flushed. "It was all they had. I'm sorry, I know you know about . . . I just thought you might not think about it until later and—''

Pris gave her a hug. "I'm not mad. It's just kinda funny.'' She reached into a drawer and handed GG a matching box. "I was thinking the same thing about you.''

GG burst into laughter. "I'm an ER doctor, Pris. I see the results of forgetting every week."

"Yeah, but I didn't think you'd get the colored ones." Pris gave her an arch look. "You aren't coming back either, are you?"

"No. Yes. That is, nothing's been said. Specifically."

"You're saying it all with that dress." Pris grew serious. "Are you all right with this, GG?"

"Very all right." She should be scandalized contemplating what she hoped would be a torrid, albeit short, affair or she should be worried about stepping outside her five-year plan, but neither seemed important right now. Instead it felt as though this was the most right decision she'd ever made.

Now she just needed the man to be willing. From yesterday, she'd judge that wasn't a problem. She also needed Elvis to stay silent. More problematic.

As they collected their keys and purses, slipping a few of the contents of the boxes inside, Pris said offhandedly, "I've been thinking about what you said yesterday. About me running the store. The owner suggested I do more of the buying— that's why she sent me here—but I didn't think I could do it."

"Why not?"

"All those numbers; I'm not very good at math. You were always the smart one."

"I was the studious one," GG corrected, following her sister into the hall. "You're just as smart, Pris."

"I was too busy envying you to study." Pris shut the room door.

GG double-checked the lock. "You envied me?" During all those hours she'd spent craving the closeness her mother and sister shared, Pris had envied her?

"You were so assured, and I always knew, in the clutch, you'd be there for me. Knowing that made me braver."

"I have plenty of doubts." *I wasn't there for Gary, not*

321

when it mattered. GG pushed the fleeting thought away. "And I've always known, if I deep down needed you, you'd be there for me. You can do this if it's what you want."

"That's what Hal said. And Elvis." Pris punched the elevator button. "I'm thinking I'll take some business courses."

"That's a start." GG moistened her lips. "How does Elvis talk to you, Pris? I mean, does he only come when you ask or does he just start talking?"

"Some of both," Pris admitted.

"How do you know it's not just your imagination?"

"It feels different."

The elevator opened with a ding and they got in.

"But you're sure it's Elvis?" GG persisted.

"You mean you wouldn't recognize that gorgeous voice?"

"Yes, I did. I mean, I would."

Pris stared at her. "Is the King talking to you, GG?"

Fortunately the elevator was empty. "It can't be him. I don't believe in that kind of thing. Besides, why start now, after all these years?"

"Maybe you never stopped long enough to listen before."

"What do I do about it?"

"Keep listening. He's never steered me wrong."

"I mean, how do I get rid of it?"

"I don't know; I never wanted to." A fleeting smile crossed Pris's face. "I always wished I could talk to you about the voice, but I knew you wouldn't understand and would try to tell me how to fix it. You always were generous with advice."

GG winced.

"Hey, sometimes your advice is helpful," Pris offered. "Like when you visited the shop. We used one of your suggestions."

"Which one?"

"About displaying the merchandise. I ordered a plastic skeleton and used that."

A skeleton? She'd suggested using coat trees. "Not the one about advertising?"

Pris made a face just as the elevator door opened and they got out. "No. This twin-bonding thing we're doing here is great, but we don't agree on *that*. Success isn't always being at the top of the heap."

"I suppose that depends upon the heap you're climbing on."

"I suppose." The bracelets on Pris's arm clinked as she opened the door to the lobby. "You know, that's one of the things I like about Hal. His definition of the right heap is like mine."

Ric and Hal—dressed in leis, aloha shirts, and shorts—were waiting at the other side of the lobby. Since the men were engrossed in watching a football game on the barroom TV and hadn't noticed them yet, GG took a moment to drink in the sight.

Ric touched something deep inside her, and she hadn't felt that touch in such a long time. It wasn't just his looks—although he was easy on the eyes—but *him*. His humor, his drive, his patience, his easy confidence.

She took a deep breath. The plans were set. Time to start an affair.

"Are you ready?" The question, though soft, grabbed Ric's attention from the football game with no trouble. He turned to Grace and at once his blood surged, dropping low in his body. Yes, he was ready.

He'd thought prim was devastating? That was before he saw sexy. She was long legs and silk, a blush upon high cheeks, inviting mermaid green eyes. And she definitely wasn't wearing a bra beneath the silk. One tug of the knot holding up her slip of a dress and she'd be bare, her sweet curves his to hold.

Her gleaming blond hair was brushed behind her ears, revealing two simple gold dots, her only jewelry. They drew his attention to her bare neck, perfect for kissing or inhaling her gardenia essence.

She gave him a tentative smile, and Ric realized he'd been

staring. He cleared his throat, then took one of the leis from around his neck and slipped it over hers, kissing her, first on each cheek, then on the mouth, too briefly. "Aloha, Grace."

She buried her nose in the petals and drew in an appreciative breath. Her lids lowered as she cast him an inviting glance. "It's beautiful, Ric. Thank you."

He slipped an arm around her, resting his hand on her bare shoulder. She fit into the curve of his embrace as if she'd been designed for it. *Add warm and willowy to sexy.* Her gardenia perfume teased him again. Ric inhaled deeply, then slowly exhaled.

"Time to go," he reminded Pris and Hal, who were sharing a tender, but extended, kiss.

They walked the short distance to the luau, which was held on the beach. There they sat on mats next to low tables, watching the sunset painted before them and listening to the string band play Hawaiian love songs. Torchlight flickered across Grace's skin, giving her a glow enhanced by her smile.

"What's that?" She motioned to the fire pit. "Whatever's in it smells good."

"It's an *imu*," Ric explained. "An underground oven. They're roasting the pig in there."

GG's stomach rumbled and, laughing, she put her hand to it. "I hope it's about done. I'm hungry."

He loved her laugh. *Like*, he corrected; he *liked* her laugh.

Ric rested his hand over hers, lacing their fingers together against her flat stomach. "It will be soon. In the meantime"— he picked up a cleaned scallop shell containing a purplish paste—"when you're hungry is the best time to try poi. It's pounded taro root and nutritious, but the most complimentary comment about its taste is usually, 'not too bad.' But a luau isn't complete without it."

Grace glanced around. "Where's the spoon? Wait, there's no silverware."

"The best luau is all fingers. Even poi."

The look Grace gave him made him burst out laughing.

"Just scoop it up. Get a little messy." He held out the shell to her, his other hand still entwined with hers.

She didn't seem to mind it there.

Tentatively she scooped up the thick goo with two fingers and ate it. "Not too bad," she said.

Ric laughed and set the shell down.

"Kind of tasteless," she continued.

With a finger, he scooped up a few drops that had fallen to her chin and held it out to her. Slowly she licked off the poi, and the warmth from her tongue sent a lick of flame straight to his groin. His fingers tightened around hers.

"It's better with the taste of you," she added.

That lick of flame became a conflagration, and Ric knew no power on earth—except a no from the lady herself—could keep Grace out of his bed tonight.

Other than the tasteless poi, the luau was delicious. The roasted pig was so tender it fell apart without the services of a knife. There was fresh pineapple and coconut slices, lomi-lomi salmon, greens she didn't recognize, and a macadamia-nut cake for dessert. GG had just polished off the last of the crumbs when the mellow background music stopped and all but a few of the torches were extinguished. After a moment's silence in the deep tropical night, a pounding of drums rent the darkness.

Two male dancers, dressed in loincloths and feathers, leaped onto the sandy performance area. They twirled flaming torches in time to the driving drumbeat and their feet pounded against the sand. Behind them came a line of ti leaf–skirted female dancers, their hips moving faster than the torches.

There was no music beyond the sound of the drums, the pounding of the dancers' feet, and the swish of the skirts, yet GG found herself swaying with the insistent beat. Its exuberance and power and primitiveness cracked restraint and caution. She cupped her hand about Ric's neck and drew him down to her lips.

Although he let her control the kiss, he responded with satisfying eagerness. They were both breathing heavily when the kiss, and the song, ended.

Promises for the night sped between them, unspoken but understood. Content, the decision made, GG leaned against Ric and watched the rest of the show.

Fast-paced Tahitian dancers opened the show, which went on to demonstrate the native dances from the other Polynesian islands, ending with the graceful Hawaiian hula. As a finale, the emcee invited the audience to come up and learn the hula.

Pris leaped to her feet. "C'mon," she laughingly urged Hal. "Let's do it." Together they joined the other brave souls.

GG nestled against Ric, and he looked down at her, his eyes dark in the night. "Do you want to go up there, too?"

She took a look at the row of neophyte dancers, all taking their awkwardness in good humor, and shook her head. "Learn on a stage? Not in this lifetime."

"Didn't think so," he said. He held out his hand. GG took it, and Ric rose to his feet, pulling her up with him.

"Where are we going?"

"Just wait and see."

He led her by the hand around the luau to a rocky outcropping on the beach near the softly rolling waves. It was dark there, so dark she could barely make out Ric's outline. The light from the luau didn't reach this far, although the sound of the hula music carried to them in faint lilts. Clouds scudded overhead, and the breeze off the ocean set her silk waving.

GG felt, more than saw, Ric's hands settle at her hips. His solid fingers spanned her pelvic bones, resting gently, but with strength. He hummed along with the music and started her hips swaying back and forth to the tune.

"Just listen to the beat and move to it," he said, his voice low and resonant.

He stood close; she caught the faint scent of soap and suntan lotion from him. Heat, hotter than the balmy night, radiated from his grip, across her, bringing a flush to her cheeks. She thanked the darkness.

"Bend your knees a little. Now slide. Three steps left. Three steps right." The low commands came from the darkness, compelling in their isolation.

She swayed, and his hands guided her. She moved, and he moved with her. Their only touch, his hand at her hips, bound them more firmly than the strongest grip. Together they moved in the sensuous dance, slow, feet sliding across the damp sand, a cool counterpoint to the rapidly heating night.

"Very good," he murmured. "Now the magic comes in the hands. Let your hands tell your story."

"What story? What movements?" she whispered.

"You decide. Out here, there's no wrong motion, no wrong steps."

For a moment GG's mind went blank, incapable of thinking of what to do. She lifted her hands, trying to remember hulas she'd seen performed on TV or in the movies.

"Don't think," Ric whispered. "Simply dance."

Simply dance. Music moved inside of her, became part of her. The swaying flowed. Using instincts beyond sight, beyond logic, she reached out and touched Ric's cheek. Her hands caressed, sliding along his ear to stroke the thick strands of his hair.

With her touch, she told her story of want and need, and, as the last chord faded, she leaned over. With unerring instinct, she found his lips.

"Let's get out of here," he whispered, the edge of passion roughing his words. "Let me make love to you."

"Pris and Hal?"

"Will figure it out. Hal and I came separately."

"Let's go."

Ric didn't move at first. "I don't want to go back to your hotel room," he said. "I want you to come home with me. To spend the entire night."

Vacation flings were in hotel rooms. This was something more; she'd known that yesterday when he'd first hinted at it. For a moment GG hesitated; then she nodded. "All right."

Chapter Six

In all the days of her lessons, GG had never been inside Ric's house. They had always gone directly to the pool outside.

The furnishings were sparse, simple, functional. It was designed to be a house where the outside beauty, brought in through walls of glass windows and sliding doors, took precedence over anything man-made.

"I like your home," she told Ric. They had said little during the ride, and, although the need still simmered deep within, the urgency had abated.

"Thanks. Would you like a glass of wine?" He toed off his sandals and pulled his tucked-in aloha shirt out of his waistband.

GG shook her head, dizzy enough from the sight of him relaxing in the intimacy of his home.

He closed the gap between them and ran a hand through her hair to rest at her neck. One short, powerful kiss; then he lifted. "You're tense. You're thinking again, Grace."

Grace. A smile flickered across her face. She'd gotten used

to hearing him call her Grace, found she liked it. Would the list of things she liked about Ric ever stop?

His fingers made tiny circles against the muscles in her neck, and GG rested her cheek against his arm. Taking a deep breath, she plunged ahead. "Are you sure about this, Ric? You know I'll be leaving next weekend."

The circling touch stilled a moment, then resumed. "Isn't that supposed to be the guy's line?" he asked lightly, but she sensed her question touched him much more deeply. With the side of his other hand, he traced the edges of her hair. "I want you, Grace, and I think you want me, too."

She nodded in affirmation.

"Then let's just take it at that, okay?"

Her question wasn't intended to reassure him, GG realized, but herself. Yet only if Ric were reluctant could she find the strength to walk away from this night's siren call.

"Okay," she answered.

Ric gathered her close, and suddenly everything was so very right. All doubts, questions, plans disappeared, buried under desire and caring. She wrapped her arms about his neck and pressed against him, feeling the bulge of his arousal. Using the swaying motion he'd taught her earlier, she danced against him.

"I've been like that since you tasted the poi," he said. "And you ask if I'm sure?" He bent for another drugging kiss.

She stroked his dark hair, explored the smooth angle of his muscled shoulders, unbuttoned his shirt. He shrugged it off, and she ran her hands across his chest. The fine hairs teased her palms while the flowers of his lei brushed across her hand.

Ric slid his hands along her bare arms, then delved beneath the edges of the pareu. He tempted her with a light caress that sent waves of pleasure through her. Nudging the lei aside, he leaned over and, through the silk, took her breasts in his mouth, first one, then the other. The warm, lingering tug of his lips created a hunger that was inescapable.

"More," she whispered.

"As you command," he murmured, and undid the knot at her neck with one deft move, allowing the pareu to pool at her feet. When he gathered her into his arms again, GG sighed with the joy of the embrace. She raised her lips to share a kiss that left her aching and heavy.

Ric's long sigh stirred across her sensitive skin. "So cool on the outside, so fiery within. Do you know what you do to me?"

She gave a shaky laugh and pressed against him. "No hiding that."

Reaching down, his blunt fingers stroked her with an expert, claiming caress. When she arched against him, she felt his smile against her neck. "And what I do to you, there's no hiding that either, is there?"

"No."

"Come." He tugged gently on her hand and she followed, the haze of desire rendering her compliant. To her surprise he led her outside, instead of to the bedroom.

"No one can see us, Grace," he urged at her hesitation, "and I would like to see you dressed in moonlight."

A warm breeze, light as a whisper, brushed across them. Water flowing in the waterfall was the only music they needed. The sweet scents of Hawaii perfumed the air.

On the strip of grass near the pool, Ric unfolded a thick, double towel he'd gathered on his way out, then, without further comment, knelt before her and stripped down her panties, leaving her only the lei. GG braced her hands against his shoulders when he leaned forward and kissed her. The intimate kiss, the touch of his tongue, the fire that burned deep—she had no more solidity than gauze.

He broke from the kiss, then raised her foot and removed her sandals. The toe ring winked in the night. Ric circled it with his finger and grinned up at her. "You are full of surprises."

With a swift move he pushed to his feet, shedding his shorts in the same gesture.

He was well formed everywhere. GG soaked up the sight. Every inch of him was a pleasure to gaze upon. So masculine, yet he wasn't afraid to keep on the flower lei. Her insides tightened, then softened in anticipation.

"You are so beautiful, Grace." One finger stroked across her cheeks, her neck, her nipples, the juncture of her thighs. "So beautiful here and here." He touched her forehead, then the skin above her heart. "And I want you." Knitting his fingers with hers, he lowered himself to the towel, pulling her atop him.

One moment of sanity intruded. "I, uh, brought some protection. In my purse. I'd better—"

"So did I," he said, stopping her move away. He reached into his shorts pocket, then laid a handful of colorful foil packets on the grass. "Now kiss me, Grace. Touch me. Everywhere. Anywhere you want."

And she did. The freedom of being outside with only sky as a ceiling, the freedom to explore his body and respond as he explored hers was a heady elixir to GG. She touched, and when he caressed her deep and slow she ignited. She stroked his skin, his hair, kissed him in all the places she'd imagined. No plan, no regimens, only a burning desire for this night and this man.

When Ric attended to the foil packet, rolled her over and entered her in a swift, determined stroke, GG exploded. He stilled, holding her close and murmuring endearments until she peaked and started the soft downward slide. Resuming his strokes, he brought her back with him. In return, GG clutched and kissed and caressed until his breath tattered and his strokes raced. The plumeria flowers from their leis crushed between them, releasing a heady scent that swirled in the night breeze.

GG exploded again, and Ric gave a harsh groan of release with her. Together. One.

She floated down, as weightless as neutral buoyancy, Ric's

body warm and comforting above her. Only their silence spoke, more eloquently than words. He nuzzled at her neck, his breath slowing in concert with hers, and his arms tightened about her, as though he feared she would leave.

But GG was content in his arms.

Only some time later, as sleep stole across her, did she ask, "Should we go inside?"

She felt rather than saw him shake his head. "Let's stay here. We'll doze, swim, make love, get up early to go see a sunrise."

It sounded like a perfect plan.

As he said, they dozed and swam and made love; then they moved into the comfort of his bed to rest and make love again.

Darkness still ruled the hours when Ric propped himself on his elbow to gaze at Grace. Though shadows engulfed the bedroom, he could see her blond hair gleaming against his pillows. Lightly he touched the strands, taking care not to wake her yet.

He knew so much more about her now. The pink tint of her skin when his touch aroused her. The musky scent of her desire. The throaty laugh that tickled his insides.

Something about her wove around him, and the longer she stayed, the more enmeshed he became.

She wasn't going to stay. He gave her credit for her honesty from the beginning, though he hadn't liked the reminder tonight. It would be hard to watch her leave, he realized.

One week. They had one week left, and that was all he could risk. Anything more, anything longer, would tug at him, pull him from his work and his plans for the future.

One week. For one more week, in his arms he held paradise.

He leaned over her, and the floral oils on her skin, mixed with the scent uniquely hers, taunted and aroused him. His hand drifted to play with her breasts, to stroke their delicate undersides as he whispered to her, "Grace, it's time to get up if we're going to Haleakala."

Her eyes opened instantly, clear and without the confusion of sleep.

"Were you awake?" he asked, his lips kissing behind her ear, another soft, sensitive spot he'd discovered during the night.

"No. I learned to wake up fast during my on-call nights. When do we leave?"

"Half an hour. How much time do you need to get ready?"

She reached down and circled his arousal with nimble fingers. "No time at all," she whispered, and Ric was lost in a maelstrom of yearning desire.

A whistling wind stung GG as they picked their way from the Haleakala visitors' center to the massive crater's edge. She huddled deeper into the jacket Ric had lent her, inhaling the scent of him embedded in the clothing. At 10,023 feet above sea level, both oxygen and heat were scarce. Lava cinders crunched beneath their feet.

Then the crater of Haleakala stretched before GG like a dark Martian landscape. In awe, she stopped. Vast and desolate, it was beautiful to behold. Far, far below her spread the predawn charcoal of empty sea and sky. She was standing on the tip of the earth.

Wind whipped around her, and she shivered again. Ric wrapped his arms about her and nestled her against him, her back to his front, and instantly all chill vanished.

"Haleakala means House of the Sun," Ric said in a low voice, his body strong against hers. "Legend has it that the mother of the demigod Maui wanted the sun to shine longer to dry her tapa cloth. So Maui crept up to Haleakala one night and hid, perhaps right there." He pointed toward a small mound of lava. "When the sun poked its toe over the horizon—"

As if on cue, the first red streak of dawn washed across the crater.

"—Maui rose from his hiding place and lassoed the sun.

He let it go only after it promised to travel more slowly across the sky. And that is why Hawaii is blessed with sunshine.''

So slowly, keeping its promise to Maui, first with streaks of red and pink and yellow, then with flashes of brilliant light, the sun rose over Haleakala. The dark spread of the landscape turned from black to brown and red, pink and green, still vast and desolate, but now with a primitive, painted beauty.

Ric's arms around her tightened, and GG leaned against his strength and warmth, savoring the shared moment.

"Do you see those two distant smudges?" he asked, his breath soft against her neck.

"Yes. They look like mountains floating in the clouds."

"That's Mauna Loa and Mauna Kea, the volcanoes of the Big Island." Slowly he circled around until she faced the other direction. The sea and sky were lightening, turning from pewter to the blue skies of Hawaii.

"Over there, you can see the islands of Lanai, Molokai, and Kahoolawe. If you look close, you can see a crescent-shaped rock."

"I see it."

"That's Molokini, where you'll be doing your cert dives tomorrow."

Pricks of white foam topped the waves, barely visible in the brightening skies, and GG drew in a deep breath, feeling her stomach knot.

"We'll need another early start to beat the snorkelers," Ric continued, "so we'll have to go to bed early tonight."

The feathery words drew her from the sight of the waves, replacing nerves with a different excitement. Was it always to be so with this man?

Always? When had *always* entered this relationship?

The last of fragile dawn disappeared under the brilliance of the tropical sun. Crisp air carried sunshine to her skin, and inside her something fresh and new unfurled to the light.

Ric took in a deep breath; GG felt his chest move against her and his muscles tighten around her.

334

"I love it up here," he said quietly, "sharing this with you."

Love.

"I love—" Her voice faltered. *You?* "—mornings," she finished hastily.

I love you? I love you.

No, absolutely not! Impossible. Love was not part of the five-year plan. She was too busy for love.

But GG recognized a lie when she heard one, even if it was her own.

The dive boat, the only visible conveyance in the fresh-born morning, surfed over the waves to Molokini Crater. Ric sat on the bench beside Grace and leaned against one of the tanks lining the sides of the boat, each nestled in its own slot and bungeed to keep from tipping over. It was a perfect day.

He propped his bare feet on the gearbox in the middle and gave Dave a thumbs-up. Dave, the bartender who took every opportunity to get out on the water rather than stay behind the bar, opened the throttle in the exhilarating ride. While Ric and Grace did the cert dives, Hal and Pris, sitting across from them, would do their own dives, and Dave would mind the boat.

If today was perfect, yesterday had been a dream day. He and Grace had made love with a rare intensity and an exquisite sweetness. In between, they'd browsed through the art galleries at Lahaina, visited a museum, taken pictures at the block-wide banyan tree, and finished the day by sleeping in each other's arms, sated and tired. Grace had been quieter than usual. He supposed she'd worried about the open-water dives today, but he had no doubts about her skills.

Yes, yesterday was a dream, but today was perfect. Sun, sea spray, a dive ahead, Grace next to him. Contentment filled him.

He gave Grace a grin, and she returned a faint smile. He brushed her hair back. "Hey, you're not getting seasick, are you? Dramamine needs to be taken before you start feeling sick, if you're prone to it."

"I know that. I'm just . . ." She shrugged.

"Nervous?"

"Yeah."

"Don't worry; you'll do fine. Relax, Grace." He gestured to the tank, where she'd attached her BC and regulator, fins and mask laid neatly beside it. "You've got the equipment all assembled and in working order, and you know what to do."

"I had a good teacher," she said faintly.

"Well, there is that," he agreed with mock boasting, then picked up a plastic slate, designed to be written on underwater. "This is the checklist of things we have to cover. We'll be doing these on the first dive today. Get those over, and then we'll tour underwater for the remaining time on each dive."

She nodded in understanding, but didn't say anything. Ric looked at her closely and noticed she looked a little pale. He swore under his breath. He'd tried to assure that they got plenty of sleep last night, curbing the urge to love her once more, but maybe she was tired.

"If you're tired, Grace, we'll cancel the dive. We can always do it another day."

"No. I'm not tired. I just want to do this right. I want it to be finished." She gripped the edge of the seat to keep her place as the boat bounced over another wave.

Ah, the perfectionism was bothering her. "There won't be anyone else there, just you and me. And remember, I've already seen you trying to put that BC on in the water."

She laughed at that, and he saw her relax. Grace reached for her mask. "I need the antifog."

Ric let out a tight breath just as the boat slowed. They were entering the Molokini Crater Preserve. They anchored, the four-foot swells rocking them. Not the smoothest surf to enter in, but not that difficult, and once he and Grace got underwater, the waves wouldn't bother them. He glanced over the side of the boat. The bottom was visible, even though it was forty-five feet below, and he could see the swarming butterfly fish and fat snappers. He'd have to remember to show Grace the hiding hole for the moray eel when they finished the skills check.

Everything was perfect.

They already had their shorty wet suits on, so they put on weight belts, then helped each other into their BCs. Her fingers brushed against his neck, and he noticed they felt cold.

Buckles snapped, fins donned, mask in place, regulator in mouth. He turned on her air. She took a long breath, then nodded and turned his on. Predive check done.

He pulled the regulator from his mouth. "All set?"

"All set," she repeated faintly.

"I'll go on in first, swim over to the descent line, and wait for you on the surface there. We'll descend together. Let Dave help you to the side. Fins and a tank are awkward out of the water."

Regulator in mouth, breathing easily off the tank, mask in place, Ric padded to the side of the boat, noting that Hal and Pris were preparing to enter the water off the other side. Once positioned, it was a simple matter for the diver to take one giant stride and be free.

He stepped out, balanced in the air for one exhilarating moment, then dropped down into the ocean, the rush of bubbles and water a homecoming he never tired of. He put a puff of air into his BC, then swam with easy strokes to their rendezvous point, the rope connected to the anchor that they'd use as a guide for descending and ascending.

The swells lifted and lowered him, splashed against his mask, but he kept his eyes on Grace, balanced to enter.

What was keeping her? He took the regulator out of his mouth. "Just a giant stride out, Grace. Don't worry; Dave will help. You won't hit the side of the boat, and I'm right here."

He saw her stare at him, although she couldn't answer because of the regulator in her mouth. Beneath the mask's glass, her green eyes were wide. Her fingers—pressed against her mask to make sure it didn't fall off during entry—were white.

Something wasn't right.

Just as he was about to swim back in, possibly abort the dive, she stepped forward and disappeared into the water.

For one endless moment he held his breath until she popped to the surface; then he let it out in a rush, running a quick visual check on her. Everything was intact, regulator and mask in place, air in BC keeping her buoyant on the surface. She was fine.

She swam toward him, her movements jerky and uncoordinated.

Ric swore. She wasn't fine. Normally Grace was as smooth in the water as she was out of it.

With swift strokes, he ate up the distance between them, watching her movements become more ineffective, her face whiter. What the hell had happened? What had scared her?

A wave splashed across her face, and she stopped swimming. Frantically she pumped air into her BC, then tilted her head back. She pulled the regulator from her mouth and gulped the regular air.

More than fear, this was panic.

Chapter Seven

Ric gripped Grace's shoulder, prepared to duck if she started swinging. A panicked diver could lash out with fear-induced strength, and it would do neither of them any good if she decked him.

He had to get her calm before he could get her back on the boat and find out what the hell had happened.

"Grace, Grace," he crooned, pulling her focus off her fear, keeping his hand on her shoulder. "Put the regulator back in your mouth. It's the air you need." He held the regulator to her lips. "Look at me, GG. Breathe through the regulator," he commanded in his best navy voice.

To his relief, she did both. She pulled big breaths on the regulator, her eyes locked with his, while she rested a hand against his chest. Bit by bit he inched her to the boat, all the while talking to her, reminding her to keep breathing, soothing her. The panic receded and control returned to her eyes, but each time a swell splashed across her, he saw her flinch.

Fins off, up the dive ladder, remove the BC and tank. The

mechanics seemed to help until she sat, head bowed and hands folded, and shook, trembling so hard he almost heard her bones rattle. He wrapped a towel around her, tucking it under her chin.

Hal and Pris, in full gear and poised to step off, paused.

Pris pulled the regulator from her mouth. "Are you okay, GG?"

Grace gave a nod. "Yeah."

"You need help?" Hal asked quietly.

Ric shook his head. "No, thanks. It's under control."

"What happened?"

"I don't know. Something panicked her, so we aborted the dive."

Pris gave a sigh. "I told her this was a harebrained idea, but she convinced me it wasn't a problem anymore."

Ric's insides turned cold. "What wasn't a problem?"

"She's afraid of water."

Afraid of water? She didn't tell him she was afraid of water. What the hell was she thinking? That diving was just a holiday lark?

Ric's vision blurred from a rush of anger, at himself as much as at her. If he hadn't been so caught up in the taste and scent and feel of her, he'd have recognized the warning signs. Her unusual quietness, the incident with the flooded mask. The signals were there, but he'd attributed them to cold or, God help him, contentment.

Damn, but he knew better than to let personal concerns interfere with business.

Ruthlessly he shoved his anger aside for later. He jerked his head at Pris and Hal. "You two go ahead with your dive."

Pris hesitated; then they jumped over the side. Dave tactfully went to the front of the boat and sat with his back to them, reading a newspaper. Ric gripped the edges of Grace's towel.

This was a private matter now, between him and Grace.

* * *

The insistent pressure of Ric's hand penetrated GG's misery; she looked up. White lined his lips. His eyes were narrow and black. He was angry and rightly so.

She should have told him, but she'd planned so carefully for this moment that she'd been sure of success. All the planning, all the practice, should have given her the control she needed, making her fear of water a thing of the past.

Her nauseating panic had receded, leaving only the weary aftermath of an epinephrine surge. In truth, it had begun to recede in the water, with Ric's touch and Ric's voice reminding her that this time was different. But the cold of her miserable failure, her humiliating lack of control, still gripped her, unfazed by the warmth of the towel or the heat radiating from Ric's hand.

"You're afraid of water?" he asked. "Didn't you think this was something I should know?"

She had to get things back under control, back into tidy spaces, back into the plan. "I'm all right in confined water, like pools. It's just the open water . . ." She waved her hand around, encompassing the vast ocean, the area around Molokini Crater now filling up with dive boats. "The waves bother me."

"Because you don't like to get your face splashed."

So he'd remembered that comment. "Yes."

"Why?"

She shrugged and gazed out at the boat anchored nearby, the divers excitedly preparing for their entry. "I felt seasick."

"You told me you don't get seasick. Why, Grace?"

"Doesn't matter."

"It does if you're going to dive. That panic wasn't one from a sticky dive problem. It was something else. Tell me what the problem is; then we'll get back in the water and work on it."

"I'm not getting back in the water." Let all these people, let Ric, see her out of control again? Not in God's blue ocean.

He rose. "Yes, you are."

His measured words jerked her out of her misery. She stared at him, towering over her with military posture and feet spread to balance against the waves.

Her eyes narrowed. "What did you say?"

"You're getting back in the water, Grace."

"No."

"Yes, you are, if I have to throw you in myself."

She shot to her feet. "Why are you so damned persistent?"

"Hell if I know." Fists braced on hips, he leaned into her face. "You must have wanted to dive pretty badly to swallow the fear all this time."

"I wanted to have something Pris and I could do together."

"You could have gone to the movies. What is it, Grace? Why start? And why stop now?"

The brilliant sun highlighted him, and her eyes teared from the glow. "Because I had to!" she shouted. Once started, the words raced from her. "I failed him, and I want to step back in time and do it again, do it right, but I can't. He *died* and I can't make it right, not ever. But I can make sure I never fail anyone like that again." The energy drained from her, and GG dropped to the hard seat. "Except I can't do it," she whispered.

Ric sat beside her, his shoulder brushing hers. "Who's 'he'?"

"Gary. My fiancé."

"You told me he died."

"Yes." She twisted the end of the towel into a coil.

"How?"

"He drowned."

Ric laced his fingers through hers, resting their hands together on her thigh. "You gonna make me get this out of you two words at a time or you just gonna tell the story?"

She hadn't let herself remember for so long.

"The story?" he prompted.

GG stared at their entwined hands. Ric was solid, strong,

yet he'd held her with such tenderness and care. He deserved to know. And she needed to tell someone.

"Gary was big on water sports. We swam, sailed, skied together. He liked diving and wanted me to learn so we could have a dive honeymoon." She gave him an apologetic smile, then returned to looking at Ric's hand with hers. Her lover's hand. Her love's hand. His silent support gave her the strength to confront the past.

"I wanted to learn diving, but I was too busy with med school, something always came up, and then . . ."

"What happened?" Ric asked.

"Gary and I decided to celebrate the end of the semester by taking a long weekend away. We went up north, to Sleeping Bear Dunes near Traverse City. Some wrecks are there, about three hundred yards offshore. They aren't deep, only thirty feet of water, so I was going to snorkel while he dove." Absently, she ran a thumb along Ric's hand. "Afterward I told myself I should have insisted he stay on the surface with me, but it was too late."

"He dove without a buddy?"

"He said it would be okay; it was shallow and I'd be in sight the whole time. And it wouldn't be for long."

Ric gave a snort of disapproval, but said nothing.

"It was early May," she continued, "a fine day, sunny, but Lake Michigan is cold. We swam out from shore, and even with our wet suits the water chilled us. The wind picked up while we were out, making it choppy, too."

GG shivered, clutching Ric's hand. Cold. She could still feel the numbing cold. The Great Lakes were big, and the iciness of winter stayed with them long into summer.

"What went wrong?" Ric leaned against her, sharing his body heat.

"To this day I'm not sure exactly. I think he bumped his head on something. That, with the cold, made him uncoordinated, his judgment poor." She looked at the past instead of at Ric. "I saw he was in trouble, but I couldn't get down to

343

help. I tried and tried, but I couldn't make it down that deep."
She closed her eyes against the tears. "Because I didn't dive,
I couldn't reach him."

Ric kissed the top of her head. "It wasn't your fault."

His words barely penetrated. Only his support did.

"Eventually he managed to get up where I could reach him,
and I pulled him to the surface. He was unconscious. I gave
him artificial respiration, but it wasn't very effective in the
water with the waves bouncing us." The words rushed out of
her. "I didn't know what else to do. I didn't know what to
do. Take his equipment off or leave it on? I tried to give him
his regulator, but it wouldn't stay in, and I didn't know if there
was something else to use. I didn't know how to work *anything*. The waves kept pushing us apart, so I towed him into
shore. Three hundred yards."

And each inch had been a frigid nightmare, with the water
stealing every parcel of body heat even through her wet suit.

Worst, however, had been the waves: icy waves washing
over her, blinding her as they splashed in endless monotony
into her face. She shivered again. "The Great Lakes are cold,"
she said, faintly, "not like Hawaii. And the waves were endless."

Ric wrapped an arm around her and pulled her against his
strong body. She sighed and sagged against the comfort.

Yet still she remembered. Invading cold had mixed with the
splashing waves until fear, desperation, waves in her face, and
a frigid, numb body became her only reality. Her hands,
clutching Gary's BC, had frozen in position. She'd tried to
talk to him, to keep him clinging to life, but in the middle of
the water, her voice had died.

"Onshore, I did CPR, but it was too late. He'd taken in too
much water," she said faintly. "He drowned." He had died
while the splashing water obscured her sight. "In the
waves."

GG's eyes misted, obscuring her vision again, and she took
long, shuddering breaths to force it clear.

344

*   *   *

Her fine trembling built an ache inside Ric. No wonder she had panicked. He circled a hand across her back in an effort to soothe her. "You did everything you could. Even if you had been able to dive," he said softly, "you might not have been able to save him."

"I know that; I've told myself that for years, enough that I've come to believe it, but I want to make sure it doesn't happen again. So I want to dive." She gave a shaky laugh. "Sounds stupid, doesn't it, when I can't even let water splash my face?"

"Not at all." Not stupid at all. Time would have diminished the acute tragedy of the loss of life, but not the pervading sense of failure that had driven her all these years. Now she needed to eliminate those last vestiges of fear.

Diving was her key. She needed to face the open water, to feel the waves splashing against her, and to continue on.

"You need to get back in the water, Grace," he said gently. "You need to finish this."

"I know, but I don't know if I can."

"You will. You're the stubbornest—and the bravest— woman I know."

Grace raised from his embrace and looked over the side of the boat. "The waves are still there."

"They'll always be there."

"A lot of people, too."

"It's common at dive sites."

For a long moment she said nothing; then she looked at him. "Pris and Hal should be coming up soon. When we moor at the second dive site I want to go in. We'll let Hal and Pris go out first, then us. I want to finish this."

She wanted to finish this, but he wasn't the man to help her. Ric's anger at himself returned. He was trained at this, yet he'd missed the signals of panic. He'd failed her because he was too personally involved.

"Hal will go with you," he said.

She gaped at him. "Not you?"

Ric shook his head. "I should have seen this before we ever got this far. You need someone you can depend on."

"I trust *you.*"

"I missed the signals."

Her eyes narrowed. "What signals? A little heavy breathing? Hell, we've been doing that all weekend."

"You weren't talking today."

"I have lots of days where I don't talk much. Doesn't mean I'm going into a panic."

"Hal will go in with you. You like him, don't you?"

"That's neither here nor there. He's not a certified instructor."

"He'll get you over the panic. Dave here can do the cert dives."

"Leave me out of this," called Dave.

Grace leaned back and folded her arms. Her straight gaze bored into him. "No."

"No?"

"I go in with you, now, today, or not at all. You've already seen the humiliating sight of me in a panic, and I'm not going to show that to anyone else. Every time I've been on the edge, you've pulled me back. It's you or no one."

She lifted that stubborn chin in the air, and Ric gave an audible curse. She was just bullheaded enough to stick by her word. And, like horseback riding, the sooner one got back on the horse, the better.

This was his Grace. Funny, stubborn, beautiful, exciting Grace. She was more important than any of his minor fears over personal involvement.

"All right. Next dive site, we're in."

As she had observed to Ric forty-five minutes earlier, the waves were still there. GG poised at the side of the boat, the tips of her fins over the edge, the dive ladder bobbing below her, Ric holding on to the side of it.

"Giant stride," urged Dave, who was helping her keep her balance by bracing her tank.

GG closed her eyes and tried to will herself to step forward. She couldn't do it.

She opened her eyes and stared at Ric. She wanted to be there with him. A wave splashed against his face.

She couldn't do it.

Step forward, baby. You've got a mountain to climb.

Oh, cripes. Just what she needed, the drawling voice in her head.

Go climb your mountain, baby.

It's not a mountain, it's water.

A conversation. She was having a conversation with Elvis! Along with the panic, she was going schizophrenic.

You know what I mean. Get in the water, GG.

I don't think I can.

You never backed away from a challenge in your life.

In some strange way, the insane conversation settled her, took her attention from her fear.

Tell you what. If I do this, will you promise never to speak to me again?

Never, I swear by a pair of blue suede shoes. You do this, you won't need me again.

GG took a step forward and plunged into the water.

Water and bubbles rushed around her, pulling at her, until her buoyancy popped her back to the surface. She took a deep breath from the regulator, then looked for Ric.

He was there at her side, one hand on her shoulder. The waves bounced her around, and GG could hear her respirations grow shallow and rapid.

Breathe slow, breathe long, she commanded herself, keeping her eyes locked with Ric's. He nodded in approval at the measure of control, then jerked his head to the side, indicating for them to move away from the boat. She could sense Pris and Hal hovering above, watching from the boat, but she kept her focus on Ric, his steady strokes and the even trail of bub-

347

bles from his regulator. He kept one hand on her shoulder, keeping them anchored together, chasing away the fringes of panic.

A short distance, and he stopped. Instead of giving the descend signal, however, he hung on the surface, letting the waves wash over them.

GG glanced around. Waves, everywhere, waves. They swelled and splashed across her. She'd gotten this far; she'd done the entrance. She scowled at Ric. Why didn't they just go down and get below all this?

Ric tapped her mask and pointed first to her eyes, then to his own. He wanted eye contact? She'd give him eye contact. She gave the thumbs-down descend signal. Ric shook his head. She glared at him. His cheeks hinted at the smile behind the regulator.

Water splashed into her face. She flinched and swallowed hard. Her gaze lost his.

He caressed her cheek and brought her attention back. His hand never left her shoulder. His stroke trailed from her cheek to her neck.

Another wave broke across her, and GG blinked, torn between the waves and Ric.

Ric was more important. He traced the line of her jaw, and this time she didn't have to remind herself to take a deep breath. His blunt fingers combed through her hair, tucking it behind her ear. As he replaced bad memories with pleasurable sensations, the motion of the waves underwent a metamorphosis from frightening to intriguing to thrilling.

How long they floated there, GG couldn't be sure. Not long, she supposed, until Ric drifted from her touch, still close, but letting her sway alone to the motion of the waves. They splashed against her, speckling her mask, tickling her ears, but the sick panic stayed banished.

GG looked down and was surprised to see lemon yellow tangs swimming between coral forty-five feet beneath her. A black-striped humuhumunukunukuapuaa, the state fish of Hawaii, darted up and checked her toes in case they represented a morsel of food. They didn't, and he swam away with a swish of his fin.

Suddenly she wanted to be down there among the fish, the coral, and the other divers. The waves were a nuisance only, something to be breached on her descent. She swam over to Ric and took the regulator from her mouth. His eyes narrowed, and his hand gripped her shoulder.

"I'm fine," she said, knowing he was wondering if she'd lost control again. "More than fine."

His hand at her shoulder was solid, strong. Ric had touched her with that hand—erotically, tenderly, teasingly, intimately— and he'd touched her in other ways, too. Yesterday she'd run from her newly discovered love, trying to pigeonhole it, fit it into a plan, shove it away, panicked by the wildness of it.

Today? Somehow the only thing that mattered was that she loved him. Failures and messiness—well, they were just a part of living, and she was tired of being only half-alive.

"I love you, Ric Menendez," she said, and kissed his cheek.

GG laughed at his startled look behind the mask. She returned her regulator, gave the signal for descent, then exhaled to begin the slow drift downward. After a moment Ric followed her.

This portion of the five-year plan—where she became a certified diver—had taken a few twists from the expected, but sometimes the detours were the best plan of all.

Chapter Eight

I love you, Ric Menendez. Four days later, as he stood inside the airport and watched Grace check in at the gate, Ric still brooded over her casual words.

She had passed the remaining certification dives with no trouble, and they had spent the rest of the time being together. They had gone diving, sometimes alone, sometimes with Hal and Pris, once on one of the big dive boats out of Lahaina, but mostly they had laughed, shared small moments, made love. She'd had plenty of time, but she'd never said those five words again.

He shoved his hands in his pockets. Her words were spoken in gratitude, out of relief for his help in getting her over her panic. If they'd meant anything beyond that, she would have made sure that she said them again. Grace was like that, precise and not prone to misunderstanding.

Nothing beyond gratefulness; there was no other conclusion. The idea rankled, but that was his problem, not hers.

He took in Hal and Pris's passionate good-bye. Pris was

coming back, planning to do some buying, maybe opening a branch of the store here on Maui. There was talk of marriage. But his gaze could not stay away from Grace.

Grace had had her vacation, and now she was leaving. Hell, the woman had even made arrangements for the airport shuttle. He wouldn't have had this final good-bye if he hadn't insisted on driving her to the airport.

She was leaving, as they had known she would from the beginning.

He didn't want her to go.

Watching her prepare to leave was like slashing his air hose. Something very vital to life was escaping, and he didn't know how to hold it.

Ric's hands fisted in his pockets as Grace came toward him, looking cool and beautiful in a turquoise shirt brighter than the Hawaii waters at their finest. Her leather tote hung from her shoulder, and he supposed she had that daily planner thing in it so she could adjust the five-year plan on the way back. Cross off one vacation.

"Thank you, Ric, for everything." Her voice was steady, modulated, cool.

Ric's teeth ground together.

"I'm very grateful," she continued, and held out her hand.

"To hell with a handshake." Ric tugged her outstretched hand and gathered her into his arms, knowing it would be the last time. He kissed her long and deep, knowing it would have to sustain him. If he was going home hot and needy, so was she. She clutched his shoulders, her fingers digging deep, and kissed him back. He held her close, the feel of her branded forever against his chest and thighs.

The insistent call for first boarding broke them apart.

She glared at him. "I told you I loved you. Didn't you think that called for a response?"

She loved him. My God, he'd been such an idiot. She hadn't said anything because *he* hadn't!

He braced his arms on her shoulders and rested his forehead

against hers. "I love you, too, G. G. Johansson.

She punched him in the arm. "You stubborn oaf, why didn't you say something earlier?

"I thought it was gratitude."

"Gratitude?" Her voice rose, bringing the glance of other travelers. "You thought I slept with you out of sheer gratitude?"

"No." He shoved his hands through his hair.

Grace fisted her hands on her hips. "You were afraid to tell me you love me."

"I told myself I was being realistic. These two weeks weren't real."

"They sure felt real to me."

"Well, you were the one insisting you were here only for two weeks. I *was* afraid," he admitted. "Afraid of how much I care for you. Afraid of how important you are to me. It took that cool good-bye to beat into me how much more I wanted from you. I love you, Grace, and I want to marry you."

"Yes," she answered simply.

He gathered her back into his embrace. "How soon can you move back here?"

She pushed against his chest and gave him a wary look. "Move back?"

"Yeah. Will you have much trouble getting licensed here?"

"No." She shook her head. "I thought you meant you were moving to Detroit. There's lots of diving opportunities there."

"Move to Detroit?" he asked incredulously.

"I've made associate professor in record time," Grace said. "My work is being cited by other researchers. I'm making progress in treating submersions, and I have patients and colleagues who depend on me. I've got plans, and I can't just erase them to move here."

Ric stepped away from her. "Neither can I. I've got a business to run, divers who depend on me, a partner. I've got my reputation established, and that took a hell of a lot of work.

I'm proving I can make it on my own terms.''

They stared at each other for one long moment, neither moving, love battering at the barrier of four thousand miles. Only the call for final boarding broke the stubborn silence.

Grace closed her eyes, then opened them and looked at him squarely. "Good-bye, Ric." She pivoted and marched through the gateway, never looking back, her sister at her side. Pris gave a final wave, and in a few moments the gateway door closed.

Hal came to his side, and together they watched the huge jet taxi away, watched until it roared down the runway and became a mere speck in the blue skies. Watched until it disappeared.

"You know," Hal said, "sometimes you can be real dense."

Ric only stared at the empty sky.

GG stared with blind eyes out the airplane window. Only when the green foliage and blue waters of paradise disappeared behind the clouds did she look away. She leaned her head back against the seat.

Hey, voice in my head. I don't know if you're truly Elvis or a figment of my imagination, but how about a little advice? Tell me I did the right thing.

Her thoughts stayed silent. She'd told the voice to go away, and it had.

Just like Ric. The difference was, she already missed Ric. Missed him so badly she could barely breathe. She'd known such joy with Ric. Would she ever feel that again?

"Wanna talk?" Pris asked.

GG shook her head. Talking wasn't going to help. With a sigh she opened her leather tote and pulled out her daily planner. She flipped to the back, to the penciled five-year plan.

For a long time she stared at it. Thinking. Adjusting.

Hadn't this week taught her anything about plans and schedules and taking chances? Hadn't it shown her what it was to love and to live?

GG picked up her pencil and, with a smile, began erasing.

It took three days before Ric admitted Hal was right. He missed Grace with an ache that wasn't going away. More than that, he loved her. Once he accepted that simple, profound fact, everything else faded in importance.

Grace was special. She didn't cling, yet she was strangely vulnerable, too, in ways that tugged his deepest emotions. He wanted to protect, to cherish, to love her. She was fun, determined, ambitious, a match for him. Could he ask her to sacrifice her career when he wasn't willing to do the same?

There was plenty of work in the Great Lakes, as she'd said.

Over the next week he stared at the phone, even went so far as to dial her number numerous times. Each time he listened to her voice on the answering machine, then hung up without leaving a message.

How could he say "I love you" to an answering machine? No, this had to be done in person.

It was cold and slushy and gray in Detroit when Ric stepped out of the terminal. Cars crept and slid along the iced streets. Ric shivered and lifted his collar against the frigid evening wind. Other than a few posts in the navy, he'd lived his life in the tropics. Watching a car's wheels spin as it sought traction, he decided against a rental car to Grace's apartment and hailed a taxi.

The drive seemed endless, through clogged, slick highways and city roads, but a thousand maybes and doubts kept him company during the ride. Maybe she'd given up on him. Maybe, once home, she realized she'd been seduced by the tropics, not him. None of it made a difference. He had to see her.

At last the taxi pulled to a stop.

"Here you are." The grinning taxi driver leaned over the

back of the seat. The harrowing ride hadn't seemed to affect his good humor one iota.

"Thanks." Ric hefted his duffel out of the taxi and paid the driver. He watched, bemused, as the man spun out of the parking lot; then he turned to Grace's building.

Night had fallen since his arrival, but he couldn't see lights from what he guessed was her apartment. His heart, still racing from the breakneck drive, thumped harder. As he rang her doorbell, the fleeting worries—perhaps she was at the ER, perhaps he should have called first, perhaps she'd close the door in his face—returned.

All disappeared when Grace opened the door. Her eyes widened, and without a word she stepped back to let him into the candlelit apartment.

Ric spared no glance for the rooms around him; only Grace held his attention. She was so beautiful, dressed in casual sweats with a picture of a young Elvis on the shirt.

"Gift from Pris?" he asked, pointing to the shirt.

"My mother."

He ached to hold her, but he had something to say first. Ric dropped the duffel onto the floor with a thud. "I love you, G. G. Johansson. I'll live with you wherever you want."

A grin big as Diamond Head split her face, and she leaped forward. Ric caught her in his arms and wrapped himself around her, never to let go. He kissed her blindly, fervently. "*Dios,* I missed you," he whispered against her lips. "I was such an idiot at the airport."

"Yes, you were." She stroked her fingers through his hair. "But so was I. I love you, too, Ric."

He loved the feel of her stroking his head. "I was wrong to expect you to move. I've been talking to some people I know in outfits here about working for them."

"Great Lakes diving's different from the tropics."

He shrugged. "I did some similar work in the navy. As long as I've got you and water, I'm fine."

"You'd do that for me?"

He looked directly at her. "I've already done it."

"Well, that could be a problem." She drew him farther into her living room, then tugged him to sit beside her on a couch. "I've been talking to the administration of a different ER. They offered me a job, and I couldn't turn it down."

Rubbing his hand across the back of his neck, Ric sat back, confused. "You're moving?" She had said she wouldn't.

A shining smile brightened her face. "It's a small hospital, but I've made a few adjustments in the five-year plan." She picked up a piece of paper and handed it to him. "The ER's in Wailuku."

"On Maui?"

"Yup." She nodded at the paper he held. "I've already started taking care of item one."

Ric looked down. It was labeled *Five-Year Plan,* but surprisingly had only four items. He read them aloud. " 'One, move to Hawaii. Two, expand research for saltwater immersions. Three, get married. Four, start a family.' " Slowly he smiled. "So you're planning to move to Hawaii and I'm planning to come here? How do you think we should resolve this?"

She went over to the window and opened it. Sleet blasted in on a gust of frigid air. "Outside your window is a waterfall and hibiscus blooms. I don't think it's much of a stretch to figure out where we should go."

Ric gathered her into his arms and nuzzled her neck. She shivered, a very satisfying response.

"Only thing," he said, his voice low with need, "you've mixed up number two and number three. I'm not waiting until you publish your next paper to make you mine."

She pressed against him. "I'm open to changes in the plan," she murmured. "How about we start practicing on number four?"

"Sounds like a good plan to me," he answered with a laugh.

*   *   *

They spent their honeymoon on a small island off Belize, where they had no plans and no expectations but to walk to the dive boat, show up for dinner, and make love in the thatch-roofed hut that served as their cabin.

After one particularly creative interlude, GG relaxed in her husband's arms, sated and content. The tropical breeze rustling through the grass cooled and soothed them. Their only light was a full moon shining between the fronds. She traced Ric's brows and nose.

"I am so glad Pris insisted I go to Maui Pro Dives for my lessons."

"How did she pick us?"

"One of Pris's hunches."

"That reminds me." With an easy but unstoppable move, he rolled over, carrying her beneath him. "You said you'd tell your husband on your honeymoon what GG stood for. So I'm asking, Grace, what's the big secret?"

"Not a big secret, I just don't like it." She squirmed against him, trying to get away from the question, but escape proved impossible. His weight was balanced on his elbows and knees, but she was effectively pinned into immobility.

All her movements succeeded in doing was exciting him. "Again?" she teased, kissing him, doing a slow hula beneath him.

"Whatever you say," he answered with a smile, trailing his lips down her neck. With lazy, languid movements, he kissed her, nibbled her, excited her, but he refused the final step.

"What's GG stand for?" he murmured.

Ric at his most easygoing could also be Ric at his most stubborn.

"Beast," she protested mildly.

"C'mon, Grace."

She liked the nickname he'd chosen. "I'll tell you only if you promise to keep calling me Grace."

"Deal."

"You know my mother was, is, a big Elvis fan?"

"I gathered that from the Elvis impersonator we had as a wedding singer."

"Well, she wanted names for us that reflected that. Pris got Priscilla, for his wife, and Minnie, for his grandmother."

"Priscilla Minnie?"

"Actually, it's Minnie Mae Priscilla. Mom wasn't too great with the naming concept. Anyway, his mother's name was Gladys."

"Gladys? Your first name is Gladys?"

"You can see why I shortened it."

"Definitely. Where'd the other *G* come from?"

"Graceland," she muttered.

"Graceland? His estate? You're named Gladys Graceland?"

She nodded.

Ric gave a whoop of laughter, and she punched him on the arm. "It wasn't funny growing up." Somehow, telling it to Ric, it didn't seem too bad anymore.

"No, I don't imagine it was." The laughter died, and tenderly he traced the strands of her hair. "But you are definitely a Grace. My Grace."

"I like that," she whispered, and drew him into an embrace that held him as surely as he held her heart.

Grace Johansson Menendez had one plan, to love this man, and it was one that would last her the rest of her life.

*For Grady, my technical consultant and personal hero.
I'll buddy breathe with you any day.*

The CAT'S MEOW

Victoria Alexander, Nina Coombs, Coral Smith Saxe & Colleen Shannon

"To persons of good character, free feline to stable home"

The ad seems perfect for what Gisella Lowell, an eccentric Bostonian gypsy, intends. While the newspaper ad offers only the possible adoption of four adorable cats, Gisella's plans are a whisker more complex: four individual tales of magic and romance. As the October nights grow chill and the winds begin to howl, four couples will cuddle before their hearths, protected from the things that go bump in the night. And by Halloween, each will realize that they have been rewarded with the most fulfilling gift of all: a warm, affectionate feline. And, of course, true love.

___52279-9 $5.99 US/$6.99 CAN

Anne Avery, Phoebe Conn, Sandra Hill, & Dara Joy

WHERE DREAMS COME TRUE...

Do you ever awaken from a dream so delicious you can't bear for it to end? Do you ever gaze into the eyes of a lover and wish he could see your secret desires? Do you ever read the words of a stranger and feel your heart and soul respond? Then come to a place created especially for you by four of the most sensuous romance authors writing today—a place where you can explore your wildest fantasies and fulfill your deepest longings....

_4052-2 $5.99 US/$6.99 CAN

Swept Away

Marilyn Campbell,
Thea Devine,
Connie Mason

Whether you're on a secluded Caribbean island or right in your own backyard, these sensual stories will transport you to the greatest vacation spot of all, where passion burns hotter than the summer sun. Let today's bestselling writers bring this fantasy to life as they prove that romance can blossom anywhere—often where you least expect it.

___4415-3 $5.50 US/$6.50 CAN

Dorchester Publishing Co., Inc.
P.O. Box 6640
Wayne, PA 19087-8640

Please add $1.75 for shipping and handling for the first book and $.50 for each book thereafter. NY, NYC, and PA residents, please add appropriate sales tax. No cash, stamps, or C.O.D.s. All orders shipped within 6 weeks via postal service book rate. Canadian orders require $2.00 extra postage and must be paid in U.S. dollars through a U.S. banking facility.

Name_____
Address_____
City_____State_____Zip_____
I have enclosed $_____ in payment for the checked book(s).
Payment <u>must</u> accompany all orders. ❑ Please send a free catalog.
CHECK OUT OUR WEBSITE! www.dorchesterpub.com

Spirit's Song

MADELINE BAKER

She is a runaway wife, with a hefty reward posted for her return. And he is the best darn tracker in the territory. For the half-breed bounty hunter, it is an easy choice. His was a hard life, with little to show for it except his horse, his Colt, and his scars. The pampered, brown-eyed beauty will go back to her rich husband in San Francisco, and he will be ten thousand dollars richer. But somewhere along the trail out of the Black Hills everything changes. Now, he will give his life to protect her, to hold her forever in his embrace. Now the moonlight poetry of their loving reflects the fiery vision of the Sun Dance: She must be his spirit's song.

___4476-5 $5.99 US/$6.99 CAN

Dorchester Publishing Co., Inc.
P.O. Box 6640
Wayne, PA 19087-8640

Please add $1.75 for shipping and handling for the first book and $.50 for each book thereafter. NY, NYC, and PA residents, please add appropriate sales tax. No cash, stamps, or C.O.D.s. All orders shipped within 6 weeks via postal service book rate. Canadian orders require $2.00 extra postage and must be paid in U.S. dollars through a U.S. banking facility.

Name_____
Address_____
City_____ State_____ Zip_____
I have enclosed $_____ in payment for the checked book(s).
Payment <u>must</u> accompany all orders. ❏ Please send a free catalog.
        CHECK OUT OUR WEBSITE! www.dorchesterpub.com

By the Author of More Than 10 Million Books in Print!

Madeline Baker

Headstrong Elizabeth Johnson is a woman who knows her own mind. Not for her an arranged marriage with a fancy lawyer from the East. Defying her parents, she set her sights on the handsome young sheriff of Twin Rivers. But when Dusty's virile half-brother rides into town, Beth takes one look into the stormy black eyes of the Apache warrior and understands that this time she must follow her heart. But with her father forbidding him to call, Dusty engaged to another, and her erstwhile fiance due to arrive from the East, she wonders just how many weddings it will take before they can all live happily ever after....

_4069-7 $5.99 US/$6.99 CAN

MIRIAM RAFTERY

Taylor James's wrinkled Shar-Pei, Apollo, is always getting into trouble. But the young beauty never expects her mischievous puppy to lead her on the romantic adventure of a lifetime—from a dusty old Victorian attic to the strong arms of Nathaniel Stuart and his turn-of-the-century charm. One minute Taylor and Apollo are in modern-day San Francisco, and the next thing Taylor knows, a shift in the earth's crust, a wrinkle in time, and the lovely historian finds herself facing the terror of California's most infamous earthquake—and a love so monumental it threatens to shake the foundations of her world.

_52084-2 $4.99 US/$6.99 CAN